Nimr

THE

EMERALD

TRUTH

Melanie Davies

THE EMERALD TRUTH

THE NIMRA WORLD
BOOK TWO

MELANIE DAVIES

DEDICATIONS

To those who are fighting their own demons.
I see you.
I hear you.
I'm here for you.

NIMRA

THE ARABELLA SEA

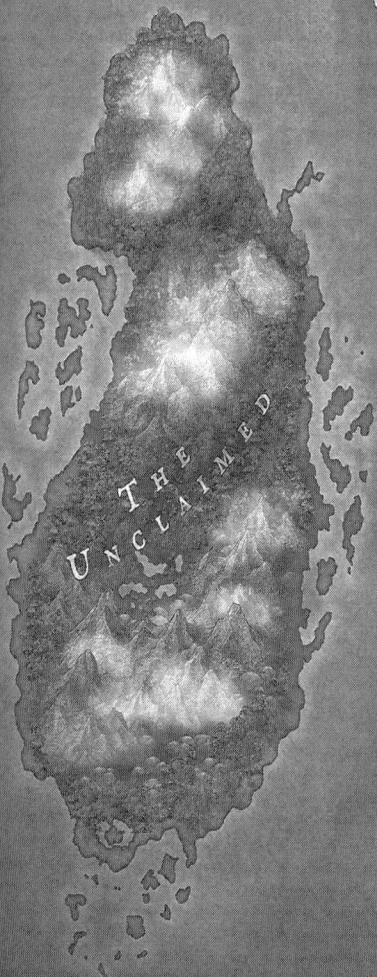

THE UNCLAIMED

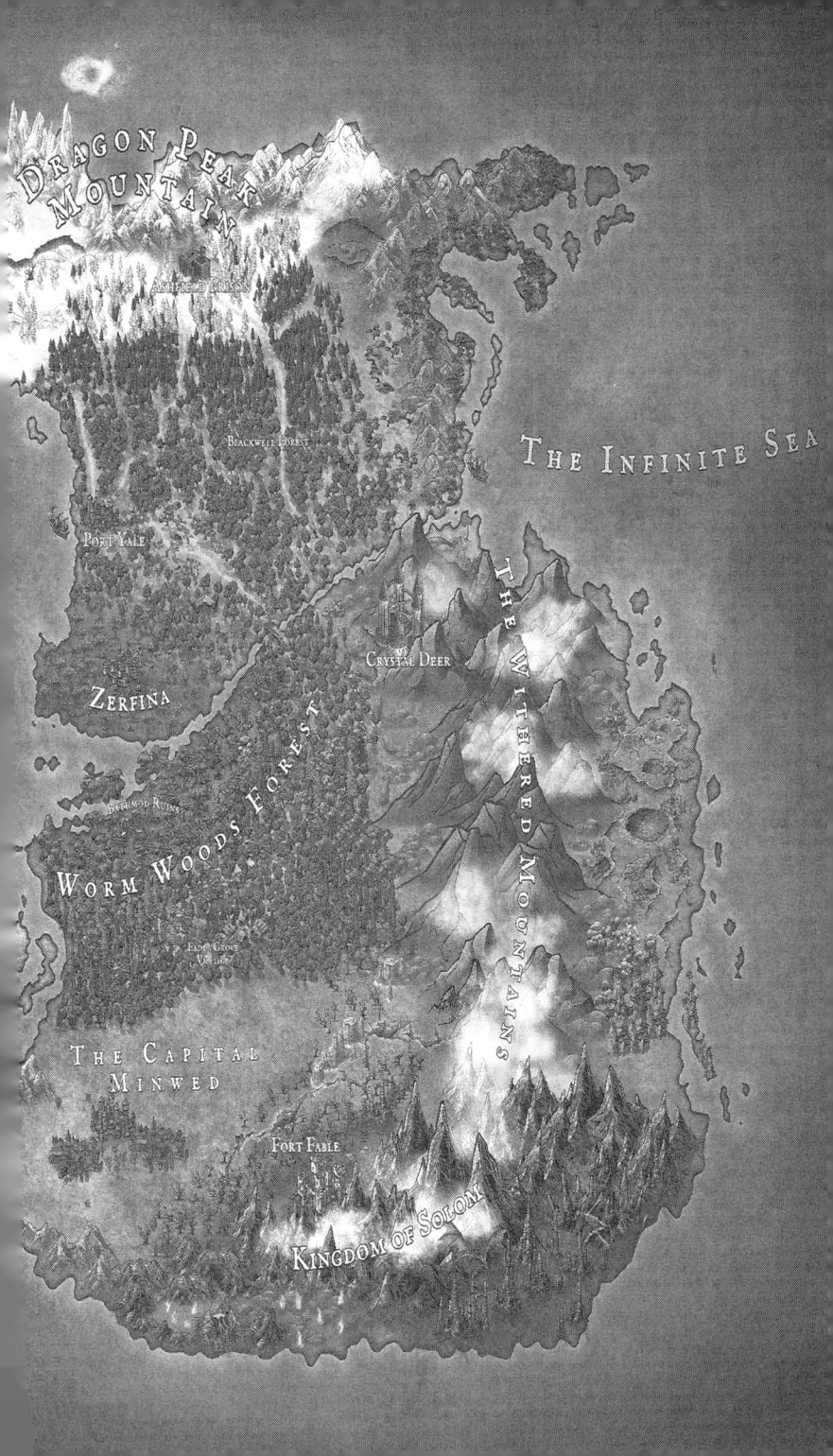

PRONUNCIATIONS

Names
>**Giselle -** Jis - Ell
>**Ayla** - Eye – Lah
>**Xandious** - Zay - And - I - Dus
>**Enelya** – En – Ell - Ya
>**Seniya** – Sen – ee - yar
>**Nefret** - Ne-fret
>**Fenella** - Fen – Ella
>**Aithne** – Are - Nee – ah
>**Elmery** - El – Mer – Rie
>**Alary –** Al – Lar – Rie
>**Leena –** Leen - Na

Realms
>Minwed
>Zerfina
>Crystal Deer
>Port Yale
>Kingdom of Solom
>Blackwell Forest

Worm Wood Forest

Dragon Peek Mountain

The Withered Mountains

Ashford Prison

Fort Fable

Bay of Maroon

Deity Temple

The Infinite Sea

The Arabella Sea

The Unclaimed

I

XANDIOUS

Silence, finally.

Giselle stopped screaming, shouting, and kicking every step of the way as we arrived back in Minwed under the cover of darkness. *Pathetic.* I didn't raise a daughter to cry over the death of others, it was weak, and she should have known better.

My fingers crackled as the shadows began to take hold. Every thought and movement, I was one with them. Sitting down on my throne in a once bright throne room, now shrouded in darkness and despair. Old blood stains covered part of the stone floor where many traitors met their deaths with my sword.

Leaning my weight onto my right and resting my chin on my hand, I began to contemplate what my next steps were going to be. Of course, I couldn't just execute Giselle in secret, many wanted blood for the death of Queen Enelya, and I would happily give it to them, in time.

First, I had to get the rebels off my back, and it would be too simple to just capture and kill them all. I needed to do it the correct way, and in a way that didn't mean I would end up with more earache from the other lords.

"I'm sorry to disturb you, your Majesty."

A voice appeared through the doors of the throne room, almost a whimper. I had become used to everyone walking on eggshells around me, it was delightful to know how fearful everyone had become, and I enjoyed the power I held. A footman stood there, bowed low to the ground, waiting for me to permit him to come in and speak to me. I didn't care for his name, the way he looked, or who he was. He was beneath me, and I enjoyed watching him tremble as he glanced up for a second, before almost shrinking more to the ground. He took a few steps into the room.

"The Princess has awoken. Shall I send for her to be brought here?"

"Tell me," I paused, looking at him, "When did you become in charge?"

Already anger was boiling inside me. A sinister smile fell to my lips as my eyes felt hot with rage. I could see him shaking as he fell to his knees. Keeping his head down and unaware of me rising from my seat, unsure of what to do with himself, I appeared with great speed in front of him. Grabbing him by his hair, I yanked him upward and onto his feet, holding him off the ground, I saw the tears begin to form in his eyes. *Fear.* And I relished every second.

"I – I – My – My apologies – your - your magnificent." His lips trembled as I tightened my grip. "I did not mean to offend."

Dropping him to the ground, satisfied he knew he would never make the same mistake again, I turned away, my cloak of darkness falling behind me as I took a few steps toward my throne. The stench of terror washed over me like liquid gold, filling me. Flicking my fingers out as green sparks formed, they flew towards the footman and flung him into the throne room doors with a loud bang and as he fell to the floor, I could feel his life start to slip away.

"Send for the Princess."

I ordered, taking my seat again and watching as the guard's lifted the body and headed out of the room, leaving me to my peace once again.

~

I DIDN'T HAVE to wait long for Giselle to arrive, which I was glad as I hated waiting. She was brought to me by Kara, still chained by the neck. It proved to be a good way of keeping Giselle under control. She looked a mess and not at all pleasing, I was ashamed to have her around me. She was no longer a daughter of mine.

"What do you wish for me to do with her, your Majesty?"

Kara, is such a little spitfire and one of my loyalist soldiers. She had become a close adviser to me and although she disappointed me when she failed to get Giselle before Shadow, I was happy with the substitute of Ayla, she would prove useful to my plans in the end, and I looked forward to seeing how far I was able to push and control her.

"Kara, my dear. You are to leave Giselle with me."

"But your Majesty, you said -"

"I suggest you don't finish that sentence. You know what will happen if you question me."

Kara looked at me with the same fire in her eyes I had seen many times before. Giselle kept herself low to the ground and it angered me slightly, she wasn't fighting, and this would not do. I wanted to see that spirit inside her so I could take it. Coming toward me, Kara held out the end of the chain to Giselle's restraints, then bowed before turning to leave the room. With a wave of my hand, the rest of the guard's left the room and it was now just Giselle and me. *Alone.*

"You caused me a lot of trouble, dear child of mine. Many lives were lost because of you. Tell me, did you really think you would be able to hide from me forever?"

She was silent and with a yank of the chain, I brought her to fall, her hands bracing herself as she landed on the stone steps in front of me.

"How dare you ignore your King!" I shouted pulling the chain once more and bringing her closer to me.

"You are no King of mine."

Her words of venom flung at me, just as vile as her mother. I would make her pay for her words and her actions, she would beg me for death, and I would not give it to her.

"I suggest you learn your place if you hope to survive Giselle, dear."

Another yank, I brought her to kneel by my feet. Using my free hand, I lifted her head, pinching her chin tightly, I heard the small whimper escape her lips as she tried to divert her eyes from me. I wished at that moment I could hear her thoughts as I felt her fear increase.

"You will learn to behave and do as you are told. And I may let your little friends live."

"I'd rather die than deal with you."

Spitting at me, I felt the darkness grow and I pulled her up to her feet using the same hand on her chin and her outcry brought me pleasure. She would beg for mercy once I was done with her and then I'll allow Kara to have her way.

"Oh, you will wish for death, but I will not give it to you. I will not release you to deaths door until you are completely under my control. Just like your friend Ayla."

4

Her eyes flew up to me as I sensed the realisation of my words and then she narrowed them, lifting her hands she tried to pull my grasp from her. All I could do was laugh at her failed attempt. There was no strength left in her to fight and I knew at that moment she realised no one was coming to save her. Her beloved soldier, dead and the rest of her followers were now too afraid of me. I let go of her chin and she fell to her knees, within seconds she tried to get away, forgetting I had the chain and as she reached the bottom of the steps, I pulled her back. Her back landed on the steps and another cry of pain echoed throughout the hall. *A beautiful sound.*

"Guards!" I shouted.

The door swung open, guards returned, bowing lower to the ground.

"Take the Princess back to her room. Send for a few ladies to help get her prepared for her return."

And with that, one of the guards came and took the chain from my hands and they left the room, Giselle being carried out.

I was going to enjoy my daughter being home.

2

GISELLE

I felt my world grow smaller as the walls closed in on me, air so tight in my chest I felt as if I was going to explode and gasp for breath. The cuff around my neck tightening as I tried to stick my fingers underneath it, pulling it away, my skin raw and blistering as the steel rubbed. My back already bruising from the brute force after landing onto the throne stairs.

So much of my home had changed, Xandious had torn down the bright lights, the beautiful tapestries were ripped and destroyed, and the rooms felt cold and dark, unwelcoming. A prison.

I had cried out all my tears as soon as I was thrown into the back of the carriage, away from Shadow's body as he bled out from his wound. The fire being doused out so no one would know to find us, and I knew deep down the rest of my men were already destroyed. I hoped someone from the group before us or after we left the camp saw the smoke and alerted the others, however as it had now been a week, I was losing hope. I knew I had to try and keep my spirits up and remind myself that at least Mason, Captain Smith, Mabon and perhaps even Quiver would come to my aid now that Shadow was gone.

Shadow was gone.

The tightness in my chest began to grow again as the tears started to form. I felt empty inside. Betrayed by my closest friend who I had deemed a sister, who I had agreed to come out of hiding for, to save and now she was on the side of my mother's murderer. I couldn't face her and yet at the same time I desperately wanted to wrap my hands around her neck and squeeze the life out of her.

I didn't want to live in a world where Shadow didn't exist, my fear had come true that I would lose him, and I could feel all the regret well up inside me. I had so many things left to say to him, to feel for him, to be with him and he was taken from me before I could even tell him how I truly felt. Was it love? I couldn't be certain, but I knew it was something strong and it had become unbearable that I couldn't feel his arms around me anymore.

Wrapping my arms around me as I sobbed on the icy stone floor of my old bedroom. A memory of what use to be, the room now made of rags, cobwebs and blackness. I shook from not just the cold but from anxiety. My worse fear was being lived and I had no idea how I was going to get out of this.

I felt soft warm hands touch my arms, without realising someone had entered my room and a jolt of surprise ran through my body. Falling backwards, I looked at a pair of gentle, welcoming, old blue eyes and realised then it was one of my mother's ladies' maids, her name I sadly couldn't recall but she opened her arms out wide to me and brought me into a hug and as I sobbed the rest of my broken heart out, she placed a reassuring hand on my head soothing me.

"Guard, please can you remove the Princesses chains."

Her voice was calm and relaxed, as if she had done this before.

"Has the King granted permission?" Asked the Guard.

"I am to tend to the Princess, that includes her wounds. Remove the cuff or I will send for the King myself."

The maid released me and seconds later, the Guard removed the cuff, and I felt the air fill up my lungs, the tightness easing. She waved the Guard away then and it was now just the two of us. Examining the rawness of my neck. Her eyes, although showed some concern, she just shook her head and held out her hands to me.

"A Princess should not be on the floor. Up you get, let's get a bath drawn for you and tend to your wounds. A hot bath will make the world of difference."

If only she knew a warm bath would not make the world right in any sense, I was grateful for her kindness and comforting words. The bath stung for the first few minutes, the burning sensation of my skin as the heat warmed the coldness out of me. Although not as grand as a bath would be for a 'princess', I couldn't have thanked her more for what she was doing for me in that moment. She put on a funny smelling paste onto my neck to soothe the sting and although I almost heaved over at the smell, it worked to ease the burn. Soon enough, I was dressed in warmer clothes and my stinking clothes thrown into a basket, I had not seen my armour since Kara stripped it off me when we arrived at the castle, and I was unsure if I was ever going to retrieve it, the same went for my weapons.

"I've sent for some food to be brought up, I'm sure you haven't eaten properly in the last few days, so I wanted to make sure you'd eat now, with me."

"Why are you helping me?" I asked, taking a seat down at the dressing table while she braided my hair.

"I am duty bound to help you, your Highness."

"I don't think my mother would be too impressed your taking orders from her killer."

"There are many of us here in the castle who know the truth and we will help you as best as we are able too, without causing a stir or creating problems for the King. My family's safety depends on me with keeping this job and the King happy."

Did she mean her and many of the other servants knew I hadn't murdered my mother? Or had the news of my return and the story Mason cooked up reached even the ears within these walls?

She placed the hair brush down and then went over to poke at the fire she had lit while I bathed, and I was happy for the extra warmth. Now I could see my bedroom more clearly, the curtains covering my balcony doors were half open and torn at the bottom, my four-poster bed had cobwebs in the corners of the beams, and I was sure the bedding that was on there, was the bedding I had on the day I escaped. My veil, for my wedding day was hanging on the door of my wardrobe and a lump formed in my throat as I fought back tears as it was my mothers.

"I will have a few maids come in while you eat to change your bed and get a heating pan ready to warm it up."

The maid gestured for me to sit in one of the old burgundy chairs in front of the fire as she wiped down a small table just next to it. As the bedroom door knocked, I felt my body tense as fear grew inside of me, I didn't want to know who it was and thankfully, it was just a footman who handed a tray to the maid and a jug of what appeared to be water to her and then left quickly. Placing the tray down onto the table, I saw a few scraps of salted meat, some vegetables, pastries and then a bowl of sliced fruit. Although I didn't have any appetite in me, I didn't know when I would be able to eat next. Swallowing every bit caused me to feel nauseous and it took me a while to finish even off a slice of fruit. The maid watched every mouthful as she drank from her cup.

"Do you have any idea how long I will be locked in this room, under guard?"

"I'm not sure your Highness. I am to be your lady in waiting however, so any news I will be sure to tell you. Once you finish this food, you must try and get some sleep and I will be back here in the morning to prepare you to receive the King."

"He is not welcome here." I said, anger burning in my eyes.

"I understand but please heed this warning, he is not the same man you once knew. A darkness has taken him and quite frankly we all live in fear of him. You should be careful what you say and do while you are here."

"He sits on a throne that doesn't belong to him!" I snapped.

"Please Princess, if the Guard's hear you, we will both be in danger."

I took a deep breath, realising my outbursts could cause her harm, her family harm and any other serviceman, and I didn't want anyone to be punished for my actions or words. I took a sip of my drink and contemplated everything that had happened. I had yet to cross paths with Ayla and I was hoping she was hiding or was stuck in a dungeon somewhere rotting away. I wanted so desperately to understand why she had betrayed me, telling me it was to keep me safe, but she knew the truth, she knew my father was an evil man and so it didn't make any sense to me what she did. Did I want to even understand? I wasn't too sure, my emotions were running so high, the moment of Shadow's death replaying in my mind every time I let it wander or closed my eyes. The only two closest people in my life now resided in the Netherworld and I would never see them again.

"Your highness, I do apologise but I must take my leave, I will be back early in the morning."

The maid rose from her seat and then curtsied, she then took my hand and squeezed it gently, looking at me with sad eyes. She lowered herself then and went close to my ear, whispering into it "Long live Queen Giselle."

My head fell back in surprise as she rose and left the room quickly, I hadn't even been called Queen by any of the men, I was still the Princess but to hear a servant of my father's household say it, gave me a small glimmer of hope that maybe I was going to get through this and would find allies within.

∾

A MEADOW FILLED with beautiful spring flowers surrounded my feet as I walked bare foot towards a large stone table. Odd how it was placed in a field, encircled by trees as tall as mountains, the sun shined brightly down, and I could feel the warmth of its rays. I could stay here forever if I were able too, but I knew it would only last for a few more minutes until the sunlight faded and the darkness began to fall.

As I took a few more steps towards the table, feeling the sense of dread overwhelm me and right on cue Shadow's body appeared, he looked so peaceful as if he were sleeping. Placing my hand on his cheek, I felt a few tears escape as they trailed down my cheeks. Feeling the tear fall and as it went to land onto my foot, it was no longer a tear but a drop of blood and soon enough, Shadow's blood was dripping from the table.

"You should have saved me."

A voice came from behind me and as I turned around quickly to see who stood there, I found no one. Turning back Shadow was now sat up staring at me, his hand quickly wrapped around my neck tightening.

"It's your fault I am dead. I should never have helped you; you should be the one bleeding out, facing the Netherworld."

This was new, this hadn't happened before and I gasped for air, pulling effortlessly on Shadow's hand to release me, begging him to let go and he just tightened his grip.

"You deserve death."

I could feel my mind begin to slip away, my body going limp and finally as he let go of me, I fell to the floor and then suddenly I was sat up in bed, the room still dark. It was just a dream, *just a dream* I told myself as I rubbed at my eyes and then felt around to my neck, still sore from the cuff but the paste the maid had used the last three nights had helped ease the bruising and the pain.

Three nights so far, I had been locked up in here, by myself and the only company I had was the hour or two when the maid visited me. Sometimes she'd send one of the other maids during the day to bring me some food and to check and see if I needed anything, but the others were too afraid to stay or speak to me other than what they were asked to say.

It was lonely and I the only real thing that gave me any comfort was the fact I could still go onto my balcony, although to high up to climb down, I did think maybe I could escape using some sort of bedsheet rope. To my disdain, Xandious had stationed guard's underneath and near so I wouldn't have been able to escape even if I tried. I knew deep down I had to find that fire I had inside me, that same fire I had before all this began. I couldn't allow Xandious to win at breaking me but the heart wrenching feeling of being lost and Shadow's death was excruciating. My demons louder than ever, telling me to give up and just give in. Give in to the pain and the suffering, if I wasn't here anymore, then I wouldn't have to deal with the heartbreak and the loss, I'd be free.

Looking across the plains of Minwed, the night sky beautifully lit with starlight and the hum in the air of the night crawlers, the late-night Tavern dwellers who had yet to head on home to their families. How my heart ached to be down there with them, to be drinking with friends, spending time filling my heart with love and laughter but alas that night would never come while I was stuck within these walls.

A wind chilled the air and goosepimples spread across my exposed arms, I had forgotten I was in a nightgown when I threw open the balcony doors and rushed out here for a gasp of fresh air, to rid myself of the nightmare.

Wrapping my arms around myself, I could feel the shivers as they reached down to my toes and knew if I didn't get back inside, I'd catch a chill. Going back into my room, I saw the fire had blown out and as I looked around the fireplace to find any matches, I found nothing, not even the poker left to poke the fire. They didn't want me to have anything that I could perhaps use as a weapon or even to try and set the room ablaze. With a huff I pulled off my blanket from my bed and wrapped myself up into it, knowing sleep was not going to arrive anytime soon, I just sat in the armchair, alone with my thoughts.

3
AYLA

ooking back at myself in the large mirror, I didn't recognise who I was anymore. I was not the same Ayla from the woods, no longer the person who would fight to the death for her friends and yet I felt awful for saving Giselle's life, clearly not in the way she would have liked but nevertheless, she was safe. Confined to her rooms but safe and that infuriating Shadow now out of the picture. We would be fine; we would get past this mishap and our friendship would repair itself in time.

The maids around me were fluffing up the layers upon layers of my burgundy dress, it was too fine for me, but the King had insisted I dressed more elegantly while I dined with him. A strange request as I was sure the King entertained guests far greater than I but for some reason I continued to be summoned, grateful for the fact I hadn't been sent down to the dungeons once we arrived at the capital.

Traitor. That inner voice speaking up as I carried on gazing at myself. *Betrayer.* My head ached from the voice as it grew louder and louder, shouting at me.

"Shut up!" I shouted back and to the confusion of the maids they quickly stepped away from me. I ignored them and moved away from the mirror, leaving my room to head down to dinner, accompanied by a guard as always. *Back-stabber.* My heart raced with the accusations, I wasn't what the voice said I was, no, I was keeping Giselle protected. If she had continued down the path of war, she would have died, and I would have lost her forever.

Stopping at the great hall doors, the guards either side opened them for me without even a glance, most likely use to me appearing around this time by now. Stepping into the room, I saw Kara standing closely behind Xandious as he drank deeply from a goblet. My body shuttered at the sight of them both, and I had to push myself to not relive those moments back with Lord Terrell, I was thankful I wasn't there anymore suffering underneath him or being tormented and tortured.

"Good evening, your Majesty." I curtsied and he just waved a hand for me to sit beside him, as if we had a routine now.

Kara eyed me with her dark sinister eyes and a small smile crept across her face, I had no idea why she was smiling, and I quickly dropped my eyes, unsure if I even wanted to know what she was thinking.

"Ayla," Xandious addressed me, the darkness oozing from his voice. "My daughter, she doesn't wish to leave her rooms to join us for dinner this evening. Kara had suggested she go and fetch her, but I believe it might be a nice idea for you to go get her, don't you think?"

"I will do as I am commanded Majesty, but won't Kara be better? I don't think Giselle would want to see me after everything."

"Well, unfortunately it isn't for you to think or discuss.

Go and get my daughter and bring her here at once, she is to join us for dinner."

My body shook at his sudden raised voice, and I knew I had to do as I was told otherwise, I would be punished for it and I couldn't handle any of that again, not in this lifetime or any other. Standing up from the table, I bowed and headed back out, down the many corridors and towards Giselle's rooms. She was in the east wing of the castle, kept away hidden from the world, the corridors were dark, damp and uninviting. I didn't want to think of what horrors were here during the time she was away, when the fires broke out or when the fighting started.

I wondered as I stood in front of Giselle's doors if I should knock first, perhaps she didn't want to be disturbed, maybe she had ignored the King's request as an act of defiance but now as I stood here, I knew I couldn't go back empty handed otherwise it would be my neck on the line.

She doesn't want to see the face of a traitor.

I shook my head a little to rid myself of the voice that was tugging at my mind and watched as the guard posted at the door looked at me oddly, I must have looked bat shit crazy, and I knew in many ways I was, or at least I felt it when I allowed the voice to win.

You are worthless, you should have died in that room. Your friend would be safe if it wasn't for you.

"She is safe." I whispered. "Open the door by order of the King."

The guard nodded slightly before opening one of the double doors to Giselle's room and when I entered a hard chill filled the space, the fire was unlit, not even a candle was a flame. Looking at the guard, I felt a small amount of anger appear at the disgrace my friend was getting.

"Light the fire for the Princess, she will die a death in this cold."

Bowing, the guard headed over to light the fire and once the room was lit, I could now see Giselle sat on the armchair huddled under a blanket and what appeared to be sound asleep. Inching closer towards her, I reached out to touch her shoulder and then suddenly she flung the blanket off herself, took hold of the guard's sword, pulling it from its scabbard she swung it up and pointed it directly at my chest. Using her other hand, she grabbed the guard's dagger and held that up towards him. Now she was standing in the middle of both of us, both of us unprepared and unsure of how we were going to get out of this unharmed and without the King finding out.

"It's not you I wish to harm." She said looking at the guard, flipping the dagger around and handing it back to him, he took it without question and then she turned her gaze back to me.

Her eyes were dark, ready and filled with rage as she took a step towards me, the guard still standing there and honestly, it looked as if he didn't even care what was happening and sure enough, he just bowed and left the room, leaving me with Giselle while she pointed the deadly blade at me. Shutting the door behind him, I looked at Giselle eyes wide as I tried to think of what my next move should be, this dress restricting most of my movements.

"How dare you come here, how dare you think I won't kill you where you stand."

"Elle, please."

"Don't you dare call me that!" She stepped forward and now the sword was beginning to stick more into my chest. I could feel the light pressure she was putting behind it and I waited to see if she would put any more on.

"Princess," I paused, looking at her.

She had become shallow in the face and had already begun to start losing weight from her two weeks of staying here. Although she had food being sent to her and a maid to tend to her, she had obviously not been eating or looking after herself correctly. Awful as it was, it gave me the disadvantage to disarm her if I wished but for some reason, I didn't want to.

"Princess, I don't wish to anger you or to cause you distress. I have come here to bring you down for dinner, you can't live off scraps and you need to eat something more filling."

"Why should I go anywhere with you, I know what side you are on."

"I am on your side."

She laughed a sinister laugh at my response, and it shuddered me to the bone.

"My side, that's funny. Where were you when I was bring captured against my will? Where were you when Shadow was being," She paused, and I could see her swallow the lump in her throat. "Murdered. – You are no friend of mine; you only care about yourself. Now get the fuck out before I slice you in two."

My inner voice again tried to break out of its tiny cage, that demon inside of me screaming at me, agreeing with every word that Giselle uttered. It wasn't the truth, I didn't know Shadow was going to be killed, although I felt some glee out of his death, I could see how it was torturing Giselle and I hated the pain it was causing her. She was everything to me and I didn't want to lose that, but I could see in her eyes she wasn't going to back down.

"Giselle please, the King will kill me if you don't come down with me."

"Good. I hope he does." She inched forward and lifted the sword to rest under my chin. "I said, get out."

I would just have to face the King without Giselle and fear swept through my body at the thought of it, he was going to punish me for my failure, and I didn't even want to think about it. Backing away slowly, I felt the door hit my back and as I fidgeted for the handle, I flew out backwards, Giselle still following me closely before she shut the door behind me. Looking at the guard who was just leaning against another door frame opposite, he didn't straighten and was clearly unbothered by the entire situation. I didn't know if I should include him in my telling to the King or leave him out of it, I would decide once I made that descent back to the hall.

When I eventually arrived back, my hands were warm and yet my body felt a chill, the feeling of dread washing over me. Walking towards the table, I stopped at the head closest to the door and watched as Kara smiled that same menacing grin, she had given me so many times before, the King had not looked up from his dessert and already I could see the darkness around him growing, his anger growing.

"And where is my daughter?"

"She will not come, your Majesty." I said taking a low curtsy, waiting for the shouting to begin.

"That's a pity." He took a sip of his drink and then rose from the table before striding towards me.

"You tried your best, I'm sure."

I felt it before I heard it and at almost lighting speed, his hand collied with my face and threw me a few inches across the floor. The wind was knocked out of me as I hit the side of a pillar and I winced at the pain, crying out. My injuries hadn't fully healed from the torture and now that same fear and lost fell over my eyes. The King took a few larger steps towards me and then kneeled, lifting my head up, I fought back the tears as he grinned at me.

"You will make a fine bride." he paused, looking at me with dark eyes. "For your sake, you best bare me a son or your head will decorate the main gates."

He dropped my face and then headed back to the table to finish off his food and all I could feel was sickness and grief. His bride?

4

QUIVER

My body took to the woodland as if it were second nature. No, it was second nature. My mind and body were one with the earth, connected straight to the deity Guinevere and each footstep I took, each passing touch of the forest brought me closer to her, to honing on the strength she had blessed my people and I felt a charge of energy surge through my body as I took a leap across a large stream, crossing it with ease and landing on the other side.

I had been with Queen Leena just short of a day and already I was missing being out in the open space, away from the eyes of court, the gossip of the younger she-elves as they begged for news of the world, of Princess Giselle and that of Lord Shadowbane, a legend in folk tale and stories, many were still to this day shocked to know of his existence.

Taking off into the woods, I prepared myself for my next leap, feeling the wind beneath me as I landed almost perfectly on a stone, standing up straight the wind wrapped itself around me and my senses picked up a familiar scent, Alary, one of my foot soldiers and right-hand man, had managed to track and find me deep within the woodland that surrounded my sacred home, the home of the Earth Elven clan, my people. Hidden deep under the Withered Mountains, veiled behind spells and protection runes.

"My Lord. The Queen wishes to speak with you."

It was all Alary had to say for me to shift my focus and leave the earth behind. Queen Leena was my everything, swearing a Sapphire Oath to her when I was very young, I had vowed to never question anything she said or did, to always be her devoted servant and more if she asked for it. But, since my return, I had been questioning her choices a lot lately.

Heading back towards the woodland city, it brought me great joy to see each Elves life being filled with prosperity and bliss. Although many of them had not seen past the cloak and ventured into the real world, they were at peace and wanted nothing else than the life they led. The Queen's castle wasn't grand such as the ones in Minwed and nor was it surrounded by groups of protectors, it was a large stone-built home on top of a hill within the city, the greenery of the earth protecting it from any danger.

Peace, a silly notion on the other side of The Withered Mountains but all Queen Leena hoped for was peace, so our people could eventually, and safety step out from the shadows and see Nimra in all its glory, and she believed Princess Giselle would be able to do that.

Stepping into what was normally used as the council rooms, Queen Leena was sitting patiently at her usual spot, she was the most beautiful creature I had ever landed eyes on. Her dark skin glittered in the sunlight as it fell from the window. As I stepped further in and bowed, her Emerald eyes flew up at me and a smile hit her delicate face.

"Ah, there you are." Her voice enchanting. "You didn't have to rush back; I know how much you long for freedom."

"It is never freedom from you, I just hate being locked away." I came up and headed towards her as she got up from her seat. Taking my hands into hers, she gave me that soft understanding smile she always did.

"Well, I wouldn't be surprised if my little brother did try to run away from me sometimes."

"I am only a few minutes or two, younger than you."

"And you never let me forget it." She gave me a wink before sitting back down and I took the seat to the right of her.

Leena was my older twin sister, although not identical, it did help when it came to hiding my identity. When our parents both died, sometime shortly after our three hundred birthdays', Leena ascended to the throne and although some would have liked for me to have been King instead, those thoughts were soon forgotten when they realised how wonderful of a Queen she was. Since her reign began, we had been safer than ever before.

"Come, sit, join me for a drink."

She gestured to the seat opposite hers and one of her maids poured us both a drink, she looked like she had something on her mind. I took my seat and patiently waited for whatever news she had to tell me.

"I have gotten word that something has happened to the Princess and her company." She paused and my eyes shot up looking at her with worry.

Although my time with Giselle had been short, I had grown fond of her, she had closely become a friend. I felt a tightness in my chest as I looked at Leena's expression change from concern to dire worry.

"What happened?"

"The King, he set upon them. I do not know the full story, but I do believe the Princess has been captured."

"What of Lord Shadowbane? The girl, Ayla?"

She took a sip of her drink and in that moment, I could feel the heat from my anger rising, I wanted to desperately throw it out of her hand and demand answers, but we were in watch of the guard's and Alary, I would not raise my voice or hand. Keeping them firmly on my lap, I took a breath, slowing down my heartrate and gaining back my composure.

"I don't know about an Ayla but Lord Shadowbane, he is in our infirmary. My scout found him."

I got to my feet immediately and started to leave before Leena grabbed my arm, looking down at her the same concern appeared on her face as it did earlier and I sat back down, realising one I had not been dismissed and two she clearly had more to tell me.

"Alex, he is in a bad way. I don't know if he will survive the rest of the night. I have sent for a mage to come and tend to him, you may go and see him, but I doubt it will do much good. He is nearer Aithne's door."

"If he dies in our care, Giselle may never forgive us. We must do everything in our power to save him and then we must save her."

She leaned back, letting go of me.

"We must not interfere with the world of men, I know you care for the Princess but if she is with the King we cannot go and rescue her, that would risk the exposure of our people, they will not be safe and will be hunted down and killed for their blood."

"Then you're a coward!" I spat my words out with hatred and could sense the room suddenly change.

"Giselle will bring peace to the entire world. We must interfere or we will continue to live in fear and hide away like the dark creatures that Aithne continues to unleash on the world."

Taking to my feet, I didn't want to listen to any more excuses my sister was surely to come up with. Before she could be object to me leaving, I left the room and started my walk towards the infirmary, Alary closely behind me. I was unsure if he was there for me or did, she send him after me to keep an eye and to keep me out of trouble.

Either way, I didn't care.

5

GISELLE

A yla was right, I hadn't eaten properly in days, and I had to keep my strength up to get out of here. I wasn't going to give up, the guards sword I had stolen from was stationed outside my bedroom door and I thought for a moment or two after kicking Ayla out that I could make a break for it, maybe the guard would look the other way but then hearing heavier footsteps walk the corridors I knew it wouldn't have been the ideal situation or time to try and flee. I had to make sure the timing was perfect.

Sitting down on the edge of my bed I felt the world on my shoulders, I was losing time and felt as if I were starting to lose my mind. The only things that were keeping me sane were the words of Shadow, his oath, and his belief in me. Quiver's message or whatever it was from Seniya kept ringing in the back of my mind, urging me to figure out the puzzle and to try and put the pieces together.

Beware the maiden with eyes of the moon for when the maiden of the sun and the maiden of the moon collide, chaos will ensnare.

It was stupid and useless; I had no idea who she meant or

any of it for that matter. Sighing, I fell backwards and laid there for a minute or two, uttering curse words under my breath, waiting for the day to end so I could just go to bed and be done with the day. The guard's sword hidden under my mattress, and I hoped no one would find it, that or the guard wouldn't tell someone what happened.

A few faint knocks fell on my door and at first, I thought it was my imagination and then another knock, louder this time and I thought for a second while lying there, should I answer? Why were they knocking? I was a prisoner and surely anyone could just wander in and do as they saw fit.

"Princess?"

A voice, almost a whisper appeared as the door opened slowly and I was quick to stand, to prepare for potentially the next argument or stand-off I was going to have. The guard, he straightened up as soon as he seen me standing there, eyeing him with confusion and I wondered why he felt the need to even come in here, he had been stationed at my door since I was locked in here and yet this was the first time, I had even heard him speak.

"I apologise for disturbing you." He said with a bow. "I won't bother you for long."

"It's not like I am doing anything." I said crossing my arms.

"I overheard her lady earlier saying you hadn't eaten much since your return, and I wanted to offer you something."

He turned quickly and headed back out into the hallway and then came back in with two trays. Placing them down on my dressing table, he took the lids off and underneath one revealed bunches of grapes, a pile of apples, bananas and oranges and on the other tray was a large fresh loaf of bread, some cheese, ham and butter. Again confusion, what in

Goddess name was he doing? And why was he doing anything that could perceived as kind towards me?

"What are you doing?" I asked him, cutting the silence.

"Eh – Princess." He paused and then took a step towards me, closing the distance. "You are the rightful heir to the Throne and Judith, your eh, lady in waiting. She told me to keep an eye on you when she couldn't attend you and although I cannot help you with dressing and such, I can help keep your strength up."

I eyed him up and down then, taking in his size and appearance. Short but not too short, taller than me with thick blonde curly hair. He had a young boy way about him and yet the wrinkles around his pale grey eyes made me think he was older than me. He lowered his head and averted his gaze from me when he saw I was watching. Looking down I saw he had replaced his sword with another, and it made me realise he never planned on telling the King or the head of the guards I had his original one.

"I stand with Judith when she says many of us are on your side and we only wish to help you."

"You can help me by getting me the hell out of here."

"I wish I could, but the King has every exit watched, every gate has doubled the number of guards and I'm afraid even the city people are too scared to venture out as they will fear being arrested and accused of helping the rebels. No one is safe here."

I sighed, uncrossing my arms and taking the seat back by the fireplace, gesturing for him to join me in the other seat, I had a feeling he would know about my comrades, the rebels and what they had done since my capture. He did not sit, remaining standing with his hand on the hilt of his sword, he was nervous, and it worried me a little.

"Can you tell me anything about the rebels?"

"Only that they have stopped, for now. Perhaps waiting to see how they can rescue you."

"Are you able to send word to my captain or them?"

"I am afraid if I do that, they will find my letter and I will be executed for treason and I cannot leave my younger sister, she relies on my wage to help her with her children."

"I understand but I must find a way to get a message out. No one would expect a guard to help me, you are too loyal to the King. I can't ask Judith as she will surely be searched whereas a guard, you won't be even looked at. Please."

"I am sorry your Highness, but I cannot risk it. Perhaps I can help you another way."

I looked at the fire as my mind ran a million miles an hour with different things that could perhaps help, and nothing popped up other than the message idea. Again, a sigh as I felt my stomach rumble from hunger and the guard heard it to. He quickly went to fetch one of the trays and handed it to me, urging me to eat something and I settled on an orange, easy enough and I would try and eat more later, once he had left.

"I cannot think of anything other than a message."

"Maybe, your Highness and please shoot me down if I am speaking out of place. Do as the King orders,"

I pulled a disgusted face and was ready to abject when he continued.

"I know this isn't an ideal situation but there might be the possibility of being allowed out of this room, to wander the castle and the grounds, I am your guard and to escort you anywhere you go so you would be safe and free to go as you pleased, provided we didn't get caught and then maybe we can plan your escape. Whenever that will be, I will be here and when no one is looking, we get you out of here."

"You have already thought this through then haven't you."

"No, your Highness, Judith, myself and some of the others, we know you can't stay here as you will surely meet your death and although we cannot help you ourselves, we might be able to buy you time, but you must be the one who does all the work."

"And I'm guessing if I am caught, I did it all on my own without any help."

Part of me believed he was on my side, wanting to assist me in any way he can and the same went for any of the others and yet the other half of me knew, they would happily throw me under the carriage if it kept their family alive and they weren't caught. It felt strange coming from an army filled with loyal solders to people who didn't really want to risk much.

"We will help you as much as we can, now I am due to finish my shift and I believe the next guard will be on his way soon. When I leave, I will be locking the door behind me, is there anything else you require?"

"No, thank you, you've done enough."

He bowed again and was out the door before I could even protest. Now I was left with more questions than I thought possible, a plan was brewing and if I were to suck it up and go to the dinners with Xandious and suffer through it, maybe I would be granted more freedom, to see the castle for what it was now, to learn how many guards were at what door and to try and get out of here, back to my men. I owed it to Shadow to at least try.

6

QUIVER

>───≫◈◇◈◇◈◇◈◇◈≪───

Alary was quick on my heel as I moved quicker through the woodland pathways towards the infirmary and although it annoyed me how he could keep track, I was impressed and reminded of why I selected him to my next in command. Gorgeous man with beautiful chocolate brown eyes and a smile to boot, he could stop hearts just by the flutter of his eyelashes, but he was leathful with a blade, and you never wanted to be on the receiving end of it.

"You know she will make you pay for your outburst." He said jokingly as I slowed my pace for him to join me at my side.

"She can carry on; she might be the Queen but I'm still her brother and she made me a promise."

"A promise?"

"Yes, a very important one."

We took a few more pathways, passing a few huts on our way, Elves bowing as I walked past them, I wasn't just their general but their Prince and next in line to the throne if Leena didn't have a child, which didn't look like anytime soon. She had many suitors from the other Elven clans that were hidden around Nimra such as the Prince of ice and air Elves in Dragon Peak Mountain, but she again was leaving the poor elf standing and waiting for her to response.

"Whatever happens Alary," I paused turning on my heel and looking at him sternly. "We cannot allow Lord Shadow to die, he and the Princess are the ones who will change our fate and bring the Elves out from hiding."

"But the Queen forbids us to interfere."

"No, she forbids the army to interfere, but I am not the army, and neither are you, if you still wish to join me."

He gave me a nod of acceptance and I patted him on the shoulder before heading into the door of the infirmary. Most of the beds were empty thankfully, the nurses were tending to a few minor wounds from some of the folk who tended to the crops. They all stopped dead in their tracks as they spotted me and were quickly to jump to their feet to bow and greet me. Waving my hand, one of the nurses put down a tray filled with bandages and then wiped her hands clean on her apron.

"Your Highness, how may I serve you?" She asked with a soft spoken and kind voice.

"I am looking for Lord Shadow, I believe he was brought in earlier today or sometime last night."

"Oh, yes, he's right this way. There is a mage with him currently, he arrived just moments ago."

Before we even entered the small room off the main part of the infirmary, I knew which mage she meant and was grateful for the familiar face.

"Mabon, lovely to see you. I thought you would have stayed with the others."

"Soon as I heard what had happened, I was summered back by Queen Leena, he is on the brink of deaths door."

"Can you bring him back?"

"It will be a great task, but I am sure with your help, we can get him to come back."

"My help? How did you even know I'd be here?"

Mabon gave me a look as if I were stupid and I closed my eyes sighing, of course he knew I'd be here. The man secretly knew everything, and I wish I knew how.

"Come, place your hands on him."

He gestured to me as where to place my hands and then he went to the head of the bed and put his hands on Shadow's head.

"You as well Alary, put your hands on Lord Shadow's feet."

With us all now in position, my hands resting on one of his arms, the same nurse joined us, and she came to stand opposite me, becoming the fourth person in the room, creating some form shape, ready to Mabon's spell no doubt. Watching him closely, he took a deep breath and then the room fell silent, the only noise were the faint sounds of Shadow's laboured breathing. I had seen Mabon use his magic before, but this wasn't a simple spell, already I could sense he was about to awaken a greater power within himself.

"I need you to all call upon the Goddess Guinevere, we must keep his Lordship from Aithne's gates and he must come back to our light."

A simple nod was all it took and then Mabon began uttering something in the language of the mages, it was a language that even the smartest elf had trouble learning, unless you were blessed with the skills of magic, it took many a centaury or two to learn just the basic tongue.

"You shall let him pass." Mabon spoke quietly as darkness began to fall around us. "He does not belong to you!"

He shouted again and the bed began to shake, the nurse almost breaking contact before I shot up to look at her.

"It's ok, keep your eyes on me, think of our Goddess, she will protect us."

The darkness grew around Mabon as the warmth in the room was sucked out, Shadow's breathing becoming more and more shallow, and I could see the sweat beginning to drip off Mabon's face. Closing my eyes, I centred myself, calling upon the world and its gifts, the power of the Elves and that of the Goddess.

"You will not take him!!" Mabon's voice grew loud, and a rumble could be felt throughout the entire room and no doubt the entire city itself.

The darkness began to sliver away and as it did Shadow's breathing slowed down and took to a normal rhythm. I hadn't realised that I had been holding my breath until I took a deep sigh and Shadow slowly opened his eyes.

7

SHADOW

I heard it before I felt it, the slash so deep my body fell into shock as I fell to my knees and then onto my front, the air stolen from my lungs as the shock started to set in. Giselle's screams filled the air as the world began to go dark and my mind filled with the brightest light I had ever seen. I was dying.

Such beautiful light, it filled me with warmth and joy, the pain was disappearing, and the world was growing quiet. It was this moment, the moment they tell soldiers what death feels like, what happens when you cross into the Netherworld and go through the gates to Aithne's world. I could stay here, if I wanted to and the feeling of calm was almost enough to keep me rooted here, away from the pain and loss.

"Shadow."

Her voice, a soft whisper flew softly through the air around me as I stood there, looking at the wide-open white space, the light on the other side drawing me closer, beckoning me to come. Which way should I go? Back to her, towards her voice or towards the welcoming light?

A step forward towards the light, it was begging me to

come near, but the pull back to Giselle was still there, screaming at me to turn away and to come back, she still needed me.

"You shall let him pass."

A stronger voice this time, shouting across the white plains and then a blackness fell, and the warmth was sucked away. I could feel a trembling beneath my feet as the place became so dark, I couldn't even see my own hand in front of my face.

"No... He is mine."

Fear filled my chest as I looked around trying to find the source of the sinister voice, not much good my sight did to help but I could still hear very well, and I listened to my surroundings.

"His soul belongs to me."

The voice again, this time closer and almost next to me. I took a stance ready to fight as no one was going to take me, I didn't belong to anyone, and I was going to put up a fight with whatever it was trying to claim me.

"You will not take him!!"

The voice shouted and the plain shook fiercely, unable to keep my balance I fell as something wrapped around my legs, pulling me towards it, the sinister voice was trying to take me. I had nothing to cling to and could only turn and twist, trying to get out of its grasp. And then as if by magic, I felt two sets of arms touch my shoulders and begin to pull me back, lifting me up out of the darkness and as they did, the pain started again, unimaginable pain and loss.

◞◞

MY EYES TOOK a while to adjust to the new light, the fussiness and blurs of shapes and colours as they came into focus, I had no idea where I was or if I was even still alive. Was this the Netherworld? Or something else entirely?

"Good, you're awake."

The same voice that shouted was beside me, my vision still not clearing quick enough to see the shape of a person.

"I thought for a moment she was going to take you. Thankfully you held on, and Quiver help greatly."

Quiver? She? What was happening and where in Goddesses name was I? Finally, my eyes fixed, and I could see Mabon standing there watching me closely, his eyes intense, he looked red in the face and sweat was dripping from his forehead. Quiver was beside him but without a look of wonder or even appeared to see I was awake at all. Nothing made sense and the pain in my stomach was still there, burning and screaming at me.

"Giselle."

My throat hurt from dryness and within seconds a cup of water appeared at my lips and a nurse was helping lift my head and urging me to drink. It hurt and I cursed the Goddess for such pain, but I was luckily alive. Well sort of.

"What happened?"

"You were stabbed, my Lord." Mabon's voice was a little harsh and he appeared to be angry. "The King I believe. The Elves found you while they were out scotting, I am unsure on the full details." Mabon looked at Quiver who still hadn't spoken up until this point. "The Prince can help you fill in the gaps."

"Prince?"

Confusion fell over me as I looked at Quiver more closely this time, he was dressed in what appeared as royal attire. I was growing tired of the confusion and anger was starting to appear, I needed to know what happened and what had happened to Giselle, my Giselle.

"What has happened to Giselle?" I demanded.

"The King has her Shadow. Queen Leena's men found you a few days ago and if it wasn't for Mabon, you would have been dead. Now, you can have a day to rest and heal a bit more but then we are heading back to the Governors strong hold. We need to get the Princess back, whatever it takes."

I tried to lift myself up more as I was still lying on my back and as much as it pained me to move, I managed to sit up a little, with the aid of Mabon and the nurse placed another pillow behind my back.

"Your Highness, if the Queen finds out."

Another voice, a male I hadn't even noticed was in the room with us, he came into view and looked at Quiver with a look I only knew too well, worried but also wondering.

"The Queen can punish me after we've got the Princess back safely." Quiver gave the male a side eye and then turned his attention back to me. "Shadow, we've already lost a week and the longer we take the further we are away from Giselle. I don't doubt she's in grave danger."

"Well, what are we waiting for? Mabon, is there any healing spell you can cast so this whole process goes quicker?"

"I can brew you a tea to help ease the pain and may help but your body went through a traumatic experience, it will need time to heal. Your mind especially. I will see what I can do."

Mabon quickly left us there in silence, Quiver still looking at me with a stern face and his companion looking at him with the same look. You could have cut the tension with a knife, and I wasn't about ready to ask what had gone on between the two of them as it was clearly something.

"Your Highness, I will go and prepare some previsions,

shall I get everything ready for us to ride out in the morning?"

Quiver nodded in response and the male left seconds later, now it was just the two of us and I didn't like it. I was still unsure of Quiver after our first few meetings together, he seemed very secretive and I hated the way I caught him looking at Giselle, like she was a spit pig on display at a banquet. He sat down and sighed, rubbing his face with his hands, he then leaned back in his chair and brought his feet up to rest on the side of my bed.

"Prince then?" I had to ask as the silence in the room was annoying me. "Does Giselle know?"

"I am not too pleased Mabon gave away my identity so easily. But yes, Queen Leena is my sister, and I am the heir to the Withered Mountain Elves and no, Giselle is unaware of who I am really."

He rolled his eyes as if it were a chore to be important to his people and it annoyed me even more.

"So, when you came to us you were spying on us."

"No, not spying as such. I had to report to Queen Leena my findings, believing we would be coming to aid but once I left and returned home, I found that she wishes to stay out of this war and keep us hidden in the woods."

"And you don't agree with that?"

"No, we have been hiding long enough and I believe Giselle will be the one who saves us and brings my people, all the Elves out from the shadows and into the light. She will unite us all."

"So that is why you want to help get her back?"

"My people deserve peace outside these walls and to see the world for themselves."

Leaving him to his thoughts, I winced as I shifted myself a little, taking the cup of water and drinking it slowly, my throat now soothing thankfully. Quiver didn't move from his seat for the next hour, carefully watching me but staying silent, as if he was planning his next move and before long Mabon returned with a foul-smelling liquid.

Almost throwing it back up as I downed the drink in one gulp as instructed, I felt it work almost instantly, the pain in my stomach dulling and becoming more of a numbing sensation and the exhaustion on my body was disappearing. I was already feeling the effects of the healing and grateful to Mabon for being there in my time of need.

"I will send someone to fetch you something to wear and we shall prepare to head off at first light." Quiver said before turning on his heel and heading out the door. "Oh," He poked his head back round the corner. "Your sword, it will be with Alary by the way, the scouts managed to find it in the remains of the village. It will be sharpened before we leave."

Grateful for whoever found me and brought me here, I made a note to find them before we left as I owed them a debt and hopefully, I could pay it someday. Now left in the infirmary room to myself, I found my mind wandering back to the white plains, the darkness, and the voice of Giselle.

The pull to her was so strong, I could feel it yanking at my heart and tightening in my chest. I needed her in my arms, safe and away from any danger. And hopefully that would be sooner rather than later.

8

GISELLE

The world was growing darker with each passing day, and I found it difficult to find the light. Although I hated every second of it, I agreed with the guard who still hadn't given me his name that perhaps a dinner or two here and there would be a good idea as it would allow me some freedom from these four walls, and I'd be able to plan my escape better. Xandious took great pleasure in seeing my discomfort most days as did Kara. Ayla had remained quiet for the most part and I was thankful as I knew I couldn't have been able to keep my composure if she spoke to me.

I had been fetched for this evening's dinner and Judith dressed me in a simple plan and royal blue gown, colours to dull me and make me not an easy target, it kept me from drawing any attention to myself. A few of Xandious nobles had joined us this evening and when I arrived, I overheard them discussing my men, Governor Mason and the rest of the rebels.

"Giselle." Xandious spoke up as he watched me walk in, at the slowest and quietest pace I could master. "We were just discussing your friends; how do you suppose we punish them for breaking the law?"

I scoffed and ignored him, while he and his friends laughed before they went back to continue their discussion, clearly enjoying the anguish they gave me. If only they knew I was adding them to a list in my head, a list of people I would kill first. Taking my usual seat at the halfway point of the table, Ayla sat opposite me and kept her eyes low, desperately trying to not make eye contact with me. Good, she was second on my list, after Xandious.

"Your Highness, how are you finding your return to the castle?"

A familiar voice startled me as a man came up to sit beside me, it was one of the nobles from my camp, one who had sworn loyalty to me. I could feel my heart begin to race as anger bour right through me and if we weren't in company, I could have jabbed my dinner knife into his throat. He looked at me with an intense look and I watched his eyeline move from me and then onto Xandious and then back to me.

"It's fine, thank you." I responded and took a sip of my drink.

Looking at Xandious, I watched him look at me and then went back to talk with his men. The noble now inching closer to me in his seat and under the table, I felt his hand and then something was placed on my lap very discreetly. A note.

"It is lovely to have you here with us, it was getting rather boring with you on your travels."

He was filling in the conversation and I no sooner caught on to what he was doing he was playing the role of a noble, I just wasn't sure which side he was on, mine or my fathers.

Opening the note once I spotted Ayla get up and leave the table to go stand with some other ladies.

"You are not alone here. I am still your ever loyal servant. I will do everything I can to help you."

Shock and dismay filled my lungs, I didn't know if I should even trust him, despite his words, no one was their true self here and I was starting to learn that everyone wore a mask, including Xandious. With a nod, the lord left his seat and headed towards one of the footmen who was standing with a tray of pasties before he sent him towards me, shaking my head at the idea of food, I just continued to drink my wine slowly, I knew I could have easily drowned my sorrows and I would have been happy to if I didn't have to keep my wits about me.

While I sat in silence just keeping my head down and occasionally looking around the room, remembering my advantage points. It felt strange that I was trying to escape my childhood home, but this wasn't home anymore, this was my prison. Soon enough a few more footmen came in with trays of food to feed the thousands and they placed them all around the dinner table, lifting the trays up to show a display of all different kinds of food. Fish, fresh meat, fruit, vegetables and mountain piles of bread. It disgusted me as I knew so many were already starving in the city and dying from hunger.

"Giselle, I wish you would smile a bit more." Xandious said as he had one of the footmen take a leg of lamb off the table and place it on the plate in front of him. All the lords, ladies, Ayla and Kara had joined for dinner, and now all their eyes were on me waiting for my response.

"Well, maybe I don't feel like smiling in this hell hole."

I knew my response would get a reaction from the ladies but it's what Xandious wanted, he didn't want me to just sit back and stay quiet, that wasn't something he enjoyed, and I knew if I continued down this path of winning him over to save my life and escape, I needed to play him at his own game.

"What would make you smile then Princess?" asked one of the Lords.

"Perhaps, if his majesty would give me more freedom, maybe to walk freely in the gardens I'd have reason to smile."

There, I played my card and did it in front of his peers, knowing he wouldn't show his true colours in front of the ladies, or at least I hoped he wouldn't.

"Is that all?" He asked with a mocking smile, "By all means, go and wander in that place but you will be always escorted. Something may happen to you should an intruder break in and we wouldn't want that now, would we?"

Although I would have loved to have thrown my drink across the room, made a distraction and run in that moment, I could feel the tension fill the air as Xandious tried to catch my bluff.

"Yes, thank you."

It was all I could master up to this point already. I just wanted out of this place. I let my mind wander then as everyone went back to talking amongst themselves to images of Shadow, lying peacefully next to me in the meadow, with the flowers in bloom. I missed every part of him, his scent, his laugh, his smile, and the constant little arguments we would have over who was in-charge and I would give anything to just have those moments again, even if it were for just a second.

My fingers touched the bottom of my lips, tracing his last kiss. Just a small, gentle kiss while we stood in Bathmod Ruins, before all of this and now I was alone again. I could feel a pair of eyes on me and as I looked up to see who it was, Ayla dropped her gaze, turning her head to look in a different direction. I hated how my mind and heart would argue with me at the fate I wished to give Ayla, my mind telling me to take my sword and run her through and then my heart reminding me, she was my closest friend and ally. She did what she thought was best, to protect me, no matter how stupid and idiotic it was. However, she wasn't Ayla anymore, I needed to remind myself of that.

I was thankful once everyone had finished their food and were making their way into the drawing room, whereas I waited and watched Xandious. I dared leave before he said anything, I wanted to see if he would go against his statement now that we were alone.

"You can walk the grounds but Giselle, if you even try to escape, I will punish you for it, in the worst way imaginable."

"Nothing you can do will ever break me."

"Oh, is that a challenge?" He leaned back on his chair and then placed both his legs on the table, "We shall see, in time, you will break and bend to my will."

"Go right ahead and try." I leaned towards him with a taunting smile, "You don't scare me, you're just a man with a large ego who needs knocking down a couple of pegs."

He laughed a loud and obnoxious laugh and clapped his hands together in a joyous motion before standing up and leaning his weight onto the table, looking dead at me.

"Your mother thought the same and look where that got her."

I felt my blood boil at the mention of my mother, and I knew he was just trying to rattle me. He was doing a good job at it.

"Now I suggest you leave before I put you in the grave with her rotting corpse."

He was such an asshole; I knew I could think of a worse word to describe him, but his words had shocked me to my core. This man who I used to see doting on my mother while I grew up, it made no sense to me how they were meant to be great loves and he just snuffed out her light as easily as one, two, three. Downing the remainder of my wine, I got up to take my leave from the room, happy to get out of there while he was silent.

The walk back to my room was cold, none of the heating lamps were lit and neither were the fires, Xandious clearly uninterested in keeping any of his 'guests' warm or at least not in the other wings of the castle. My guard trailing behind me, and we were silent of course, we were always quiet until we reached my room and only then would he utter a single word to me.

However, tonight I was feeling rather sick, dizzy and unable to keep my balance. Confusion as I stumbled and almost fell into a sideboard that lined part of the corridors. If I had to take a guess as to what was going on, I was drunk and yet that made no sense as I only had one glass of wine the entire dinner and it had taken me an hour or so just to drink that.

"Are you ok?" My guard spoke as I almost fell over my own two feet.

Coming up behind me, he wrapped an arm around my waist and hoisted me up onto my feet and then lifted me off the floor, carrying me the rest of the way. Once we had gotten to my bedroom door, I was ready to vomit up everything, the room was spinning and I couldn't see straight, he set me down in one of the armchairs and then quickly fetched a cup of water. I couldn't throw up in front of him and so I swallowed down any bile that was waiting to greet me.

"Should I call for the doctor?"

"No, just help me to bed and leave me please."

"Are you sure that's wise, maybe you should rest here. I can stay if you'd like."

"No thank you, just leave me alone."

I hadn't meant to come across as cold or nasty, but I was already fed up of this day and just wanted to lie down and rest and as soon as he left, I would be able to throw my guts up and go to sleep. With a huff he left, and I was so grateful when he locked the door behind him, I had gotten used to just being by myself and until I got out of here, that's how it was going to be.

Pushing myself up from the chair, I slowly made my way to the screen on the other side of the room where the chamber pot lived and although I hated the idea of being sick in something as disgusting as that, it was my only option. Well, it was that or throw up over the balcony onto one of the guard's heads.

"Just put one foot in front of the other."

I thought as I braced myself, using any bit of furniture I could use as leverage. Something must have been put into my drink, but I couldn't recall when I was looking at it or holding the glass, maybe it was when Xandious and I were speaking about the gardens? But who would want to drug me? Or at least who would be stupid enough to do it in front of everyone. Maybe Kara, she loved a good knocking out agent. I had to throw it up before the final effects took hold, whatever they were.

Finally reaching the screen, I almost knocked it over as I leaned my weight up against it. Once the contents of my stomach were finally gone, I laid down on the cold floor, waiting for the room to stop moving and closed my eyes, a headache appearing, and tears already formed in my eyes.

"Now you can't just lie there looking all helpless, you've got stuff to do."

Pushing myself up startled, I looked around the room looking for that voice. That voice that had haunted my dreams of late, Shadow. I spotted him, he was standing on the balcony, his silver hair bouncing off the moonlight. It didn't take a single second for me to clear the bedroom and join him, my heart ached for his touch, for his smell, for every part of him and when I finally reached him to wrap my arms around him, I ran straight through his form and caught myself at the balcony railings. Sadness welled up inside me as it was just a dream, just like it had been previously. Wrapping my arms around myself as I began to sob, the cold night air stinging my face.

"I miss you." My voice broke as I looked at him longingly. "I don't know how much more I can take."

"Well, that's not the Princess I know, one who is determined and ready to do anything."

He came up beside me and I could swear I felt his warmth radiating from his skin, we both looked out into the open space of the city, the wind almost ice cold as the snow was starting to fall. Winter had arrived.

"I don't know what I'm meant to do."

"Giselle, you grew up here, you know every single passageway and corridor. You know the secret entrances and exits. You're not using your head properly."

"How can I? When they decide to drug me, starve me or worse. I know what you're saying is true, but I don't have the strength."

I sighed as I heard myself say it out load, I didn't have the strength. I knew I had to get out of this prison but where was I going to run to? The person I wanted was long gone now and as much as I wanted a reason to fight, to go on, I didn't have one anymore.

"I know it's tough, but you must leave as soon as possible. Your safety is all I care about."

"But you're not even here anymore."

"I am always here…" He paused and turned to face me, "In here." He pointed to my heart and smiled his sweet, beautiful smile and I wished I could kiss him there under the falling snow and moonlight, forgetting all of this and just be together.

"Tomorrow, look for your exits, use this guard as bait if you must but you need to escape. No more waiting around."

His voice was assertive, and I knew he was right, I had waited long enough. I had to get out of here, one way or another. After breakfast arrived, I would pack a few provisions and use a pillowcase to store things. I knew I wasn't going to be able to get out with the sword I had concealed but perhaps I could trade it with the guard for one of his daggers, maybe. A plan was forming in my mind and as I turned back to look at the city, I felt his warmth disappear.

He was gone.

9

SHADOW

Q uiver wasted no time in getting us out of his homeland, equipped with horses and supplies to last us the journey and I thought I was a fast rider, but nothing compared me to him and his right-hand man, the speed they took and the way they rode their horses was incredible. I watched in awe as I tried to keep up with them and several times I fell back, to which they slowed and demanded I catch up. I felt awful for my horse and could only imagine how they were feeling and yet he didn't stumble or slow.

As we came to the edge of The Withered Mountains border and the end of the concealment spell of the Elvish world, it was as if a force flew over us as we rode onto the land on the other side. Magic was truly amazing and although I had only dabbled in some of it myself, I knew it resided in my bones and in my blood, untapped and left dormant.

"We shall rest near the creek up ahead for a short while, give the horses a drink and then we can continue." Quiver spoke just like a commander, and it was strange how I hadn't noticed before, he obviously played his mask very well.

"Where are we heading?" I asked as we slowed our pace and arrived at the creek.

"Lord Reid's manor, Alary and my scouts have told me that's where the Governor and the rest of the men went shortly after they were attacked and ambushed by Xandious's men."

"What? When did that happen? How long was I out?"

"About the same time, you were attacked, my Lord and when the Princess was taken. We believe there is a spy amongst your nobles, and he sent word to the King about where the armies were headed." Alary's words brought alarm to me and uncertainty.

"Any idea who this spy is?"

"None sorry, the Governor may know." Quiver sat down on the grass and took out his bottle to drink whatever liquid was in there. "Or he doesn't, and you guys clearly have a problem."

I sat down next to Quiver while Alary tended to the horses, taking them to the creek where they grazed and drank their fill. I had no idea how long we would sit here, I didn't expect long. Left to my thoughts for a moment or two, I tried to think who would have sold us out but no names sprung to mind, I highly doubted it was one of the nobles who offered up mostly all of their army or funded the cause, it may have been one who had something to gain by telling the King about our plans. I hoped I would find out who it was so I could ring their neck.

"How long do you think it will take us to get to Reid's home?"

"About a few hours, we will have this stop and then just

keep going. These horses are a special breed, they are used to long tireless journeys and will be fine."

It was as if he had read my mind, but I was grateful for the reassurance, I knew during this journey I would come to know Quiver a lot more and perhaps see what Giselle had seen in him those few short days they spent together.

"How come you never told any of us you were actually a Prince?" I asked as he handed me his bottle, drinking the sweet tasting liquid and although I had no idea what it was, it cured my thirst and hunger instantly.

"I don't like showing off my title, it's just a title. It doesn't make me who I am."

"Giselle, I'm sure would agree with you on that."

"I hate my sister for not sending more men with me and I have to resort to leaving this way, almost under the cover of darkness, like a common thief."

"The Queen might be annoyed but she will understand why." Alary finally came and joined us, sitting opposite us both as he pulled at some pieces of grass. "You're her blood and she knows not to argue with you once you've set your mind on something."

"I think this time, she might argue with me and throw a fit."

"Once we rescue Giselle, all will sort itself out." I spoke.

"Yes, well the sooner the better."

Quiver no sooner jumped to his feet and then gave me a hand to lift me up, my wound aching slightly and I wondered how long the potion Mabon had given me would work, it had mentioned that the pain would be a dwell ache and there until the wound was healed normally. Almost as fast as lighting, we were back on our horses and heading through a forest just north-east of the Minwed border. I was surprised to see not many of Xandious's soldiers patrolling, perhaps he felt there was no need now that he had Giselle. It angered me deeply to know I couldn't see her, touch her. The last day or so while I was back had shown me that I needed her next to me, her sarcastic comments, her beautiful smile and kind heart. I needed her. I hated thinking about how she must be feeling, knowing I might be dead and how lost she must be feeling, I needed to get back to her as soon as I was able.

We rode until the sun disappeared over the horizon and the moon greeted us with her beauty, the air around us was cold and quiet, most of the woodland animals already gone into hibernation and the others hiding away in their homes to stay away from the frost. Lord Reid's home was past Minwed and near the shores of the Arabella Sea, Reid had his own shipping dock which he used personally and was the only one to have access to it. During Queen Iris and Queen Enelya's reign he was looked after and rewarded handsomely for his loyalty. Many believed the reason he kept his shipping dock well-guarded was because he had access to the creatures of the sea, the mermaids and sirens and they blessed him with their magic of youth and knowledge.

Once we arrived at the manor, my legs felt as if they were about to fall off and I almost fell from my horse when Captain Smith and his men appeared in the courtyard, all of which were shocked to see me, just as I was shocked to see them all still alive.

"Where is Mason?" I demanded as I got my second wind of strength, not waiting around for an escort, I headed straight into the manor closely followed by Quiver, Alary and the Captain.

Finding the dining room was easy enough as I heard the voices from the room echo throughout the building. Mason and Reid shot to their feet when they spotted me walk through the archway, the same shocked face as the captain.

"My Lord Shadow, you're alive?" Reid said as Mason looked speechless.

"No thanks to you, you useless old goats." Quiver pulled up a chair at the table and huffed as he sat down, resting his feet on the table, "You're lucky my lot found him when they did, otherwise he wouldn't have been able to come back."

"But how? The village, we heard, was burnt to the ground, the Princess captured, and you killed."

"Mabon. He was able to bring me back but not much can be said about you hiding out here. What are you even doing to help get Giselle back?"

"It's not as simple as walking through the front door Shadow, a lot has happened since you were attacked, our army has been depleted greatly, we were lucky to get out when we did." Mason finally spoke up, his face looked tired, and he appeared to have aged a few years since we last saw one another.

"There was a spy, a noble, he got word to the King about the armies moving." Alary joined me at my side and I watched as Mason's face dropped and then anger appeared.

"Before you ask, we have no idea which lord that might have been but Mason, if it's true then we can't let anyone know our next moves, not until we figure out and capture the spy."

"Kill him more like." Quiver slammed a glass of wine down on the table and I swore I saw a flash of red in his eyes. Elves didn't show their anger very much, especially those of the woods and so this came as a surprise to me.

"We will have to gather our most trusted men to help me retrieve Giselle, she cannot be left in Minwed at the hands of the King, he will kill her." My concern was growing more and more with each passing second, she needed to be in my arms. "Captain, I want you and your men to join me on this rescue mission."

"I'd be happy to my Lord, however many of my men were lost in the attack and if we left now, it would be a suicide mission. The King will be expecting us to make a full assault. We need to think wisely on our next moves."

Taking a seat down at the table, we fell silent and unsure of what to suggest or do. This was going to take a lot of thought and planning secretly, especially now that we knew there was a spy but had no idea who that spy was.

"I will have my footman prepare some rooms for you all, you must be exhausted from your travels. Perhaps after a good night's sleep, we can discuss plans and what to do in the morning."

Lord Reid spoke some sense and I felt the tiredness and ache of my bones down to my core, I needed rest and a bath. Thankful for the suggestion, we headed off to our rooms once they were prepared and as soon as my head hit the pillow, I was out like a light.

10

GISELLE

This was it. My time was today, in the next hour and already I could feel my nerves building, wondering if I was going to be able to pull it off. I hadn't mentioned to the guard anything as quite frankly it would be easier if he didn't know anything. I was going to take Shadow's advice and use him as bait, this was going to be interesting.

During the night, I stayed awake, planning, plotting and reminding myself of where the secret passageways were, many of the doors hidden behind screens in main corridors, behind tapestries and places you'd never think to look. The servant quarters would be the first place I'd head to as soon as I saw a chance as one of the doors to the sewers were down there, somewhere.

Shadow and I had used the door once or twice during our adventures of sneaking out the castle and going into the market to see how everyone lived as I was only used to the large walls that separated us and them.

Being summoned for breakfast was just the normal routine now and yet this morning it felt different, the air didn't feel right, and this made me more nervous. As I reached the dining room doors, they swung open and out marched Lord Terrell, his red face was a picture when he saw me standing there, stopping dead in his tracks.

"Your Highness." He dropped to a bow before barging passed me and down the hallway.

"That Lord has been a pain in my ass since the very start." Xandious was already in a foul mood when I reached my seat, "Jenkins, he is not permitted in the castle until the masquerade and after that I want him to disappear. I don't want to see that small round face of his ever again."

Avoiding any drinks placed on the table, just in case my wits were taken from me, I just picked at a bowl of fresh fruit and a slice of bread with butter on. When no one was looking, I would pick up a few of the pasties and pocket them in my skirt.

"Good morning, dear," His voice always sent chills down my spine, "Did you sleep well?" Xandious winked at me as he took a sip of whatever liquid was in his goblet.

"Very well, thank you." A sweet smile appeared on my face as I kept the act up of the Princess.

"Your Highness," A voice from across the table brought my attention and it was towards a young girl, one of the noble ladies from yesterday. "May you be ever so kind to join me on a walk of the grounds this morning?" She smiled and then looked at Xandious, "If that is ok with his Majesty of course?"

"I see no issues. It will do Giselle some good to go outside."

"That sounds lovely, Lady - I'm sorry, I don't know your name."

"Lady Ivy, Your Highness."

Lady Ivy had a petite look about her, her jawline was sharp but her facial features soft, plain. She brushed a few strands of her brown locks of hair behind her ear and I watched as she smiled back at Xandious. A devious face, I already knew I couldn't trust her.

Shortly after breakfast and Xandious shooed everyone out of the room, I noticed Ayla hadn't joined for breakfast which was odd as she had been there every single time. Part of me wanted to know where she was and if she was ok but the other half, the one with the grudge, wished for her ill will.

Lady Ivy linked her arm in with mine as we headed to the gardens, strange how she wanted us to go for a walk considering how fast the snow was falling. I hadn't counted on the snow while thinking of my escape, it would mean I need to find myself a warm cloak. I knew I wouldn't be able to escape with a horse and on foot, I would die from the cold if I didn't try to dress at least warm.

"We should wrap up; it will be cold out there." I said as we headed towards the doors.

Two ladies were waiting there, one I knew, Judith. She held in her hands a fur lined coat with a white as snow edging and placed it over my shoulder and then tied a knot at the front. I felt the warmth instantly and knew this would be the cloak I'd keep.

"Judith, can you please take my cloak after our walk back to my rooms please, it would be useful while I stay on the balcony during the colder evenings." I looked at her hoping she would understand my meaning and just nodded before curtsying and leaving me to deal with Lady Ivy and her ideal chit-chat. She linked her arm into mine again as we wandered out through the doors and stepped out onto the freshly fallen snow.

"It is lovely to see you have returned, Your Highness, especially with all the fighting going on outside the city."

This was something my mother and I would do every year, on the first day of winter, we would walk the grounds. She would insist on not wearing a cloak as she loved the cold fresh air on her skin, she always looked so beautiful, enchanting when she would twirl in the snow.

"His Majesty was inconsolable when he wasn't able to find you, he would speak of nothing else but bringing you home safely," She paused and looked at me with a sly smile, "If it wasn't for me, he would have gone mad with grief. You really shouldn't have left when you did."

"Excuse me," I pulled away from her and she tried to keep her grip on me. "I don't know who you think you are, but you most certainly won't speak to me like that."

"Oh, forgive me, I am His Majesty's mistress."

"You mean his whore."

She was taken aback by how plainly my words were and her eyes glazed over in a darkness, the same darkness as Xandious. Of course, she was going to be an asshole as well, they all were. My first impressions were right.

"I was there for your father when you weren't."

"Oh, woopty fucking do darling," I had no idea where my attitude was coming from but perhaps it was just from all the prepped-up anger I hadn't been allowed to spill, "You keep his bed warm; I do not care and neither do I have the time to think on it. Just know this, you ever speak to me like that again," I paused, coming up close to her face and I felt her lean back slightly, "I will cut you down right where you stand. I might be my mother's daughter but you're forgetting, I am also my fathers, and I don't have the patience to be kind."

She fell silent and the glaze disappeared from her eyes, and she took two steps back, I could see in the corner of my eye my guard smiling a little as was his companion, my escort while I walked. This girl may have annoyed me but she gave me a brilliant idea for my escape and I knew now how to distract Xandious while I left and it was standing right in front of me.

"When the King hears of what you just called me, you will be sorry."

Those were her last words before she turned on her heel in a huff and stormed back to the doors, while I enjoyed the smell of fresh air and felt the chill on my skin. It was worth it.

～

I HAD MANAGED to wander the corridors for the next hour or so while my guard kept a close eye on me, still unaware of my plan and it was going to stay that way. Turning down one of the west wing hallways, I neared the door to my mother's dressing rooms and stopped. I hadn't even realised I was coming this way until I saw the beautiful white doors with gold edging appear around the corner. They were still clean and untouched by the dust and cobwebs that littered the hall. Someone had been tending to this part of the castle still.

Turning the golden doorknob in my hand, I felt the tension rush up my fingers and then down my spine. It had been nearly two years since I entered here and I was worried about what I would find, pushing the door open, it creaked, and I had to use some strength to fully get it open as the hinges had already rusted.

"I wouldn't go in there, Your Highness."

Ignoring the guard, I took the first few steps in and the room was dull and smelt of dust. I didn't know where to look first and had to remind myself of where the curtain string was to let in some light. There wasn't much light as the sun was hiding behind the snow clouds but enough light to see the room was still the same way as I remembered.

Xandious obviously hadn't been in here, no one had and although it saddened me that everyone had just left my mother's things to rot, it made me a little happy as it meant everything was where she had placed it.

The guard stood at the doorway keeping an eye out and refused to step in while I ran my fingers across the fabrics of her beautiful dresses and saw as the dust flicked in the air gently. Going over to her dressing table, I saw one of her tiara's were still placed neatly there, as well as her hairbrush and hand mirror. I would always steal the mirror as a child and hide it from her.

Opening the clasp, I saw the mirror was broken across the middle and then caught a glimpse of myself. I really had begun to lose weight, my face thinning and my eyes had dark circles around them, my glow was disappearing.

Placing the mirror back down, I turned to continue looking around and spotted one of her scarfs, it was thrown on the large navy-blue chaise lounge chair near one of the windows. Picking it up I held it to my face and breathed in her scent and instantly tears welled in my eyes.

Nothing had faded, it was her and my heart tugged and tightened in my chest, I missed her with every breathe and hated not having her at my side. Placing the scarf around my neck, I wasn't going to leave it here and would take it with me no matter what.

Sighing and looking around the room again, I had to leave, closing the curtains again to keep everything protected from the light and then shutting the door behind me, my guard looked at me with sorrow in his eyes.

"Are you alright?"

"I will be fine, thank you."

Holding my head up high, I took the scarf off my neck and then stuffed it down the front of my dress so no one noticed it and headed back to my rooms, to prepare, as soon as nightfall hit and dinner was served, I would make my escape. Using Lady Ivy and the guard to my advantage, I hoped and prayed this plan wouldn't fail. It couldn't fail.

≈

THE PLAN WAS READY, I was ready. Finally, I had gathered my courage and the strength I needed to get out of this place and find my way back to my people, to those I could trust. I knew if I stayed one more day, I wouldn't be able to control myself and head towards Ayla to finish off the job Kara clearly started.

With a deep breath, I changed into my now ragged clothes, throwing the damned dress I had been made to wear these past few days and threw it on the floor, standing on it as I threw on my trousers, thankfully they weren't that destroyed and would still help keep me warm on my journey. Swinging the cloak around me and tying it, I took my guards sword and looked at myself in the dusty smudged dressing table mirror and could see how much I had already changed.

"Guard!" I shouted and heard the door unlock as he stepped in. He looked me up and down and then nodded, clearly understanding what was about to happen. "Give me your dagger."

"Are you mad?"

"No, quite sane actually but if I go wandering the grounds with this," I lifted the sword up to show up, "I will be stopped so have your sword back and I will have your dagger instead."

"You will need more than a dagger to get out of here and

at least something else to survive out there in the wilderness. I will take it, but I will put it outside the garden gates, near the large oak tree when the guard's change shifts. No one will know it's there but you and I."

"That's fine. Now you must leave me, head back to the dining hall and distract the King and his court, explain to them I have a stomach bug and have gone to bed for the night, tell him Lady Ivy must slipped something in my drink during breakfast. That will keep him occupied."

"Now I know you have gone mad. The King knows his mistress isn't that stupid and won't believe me. You must be joking if this is your plan? You should wait a few more days, in case he suspects anything."

I sighed and took a step forward, looking up at him a little, the fire of anger burning inside me. I had lost my patience and had just about enough of being told what to do and ordered around. Squaring my shoulders, I felt the heat on the back of my neck rise while I tried to keep my anger from spouting out and losing it.

"Look, he doesn't have to believe you, I don't care what you tell him. Just keep him busy and away from investigating my room. Understand? As for his mistress, she could swan dive off the castle tower, and I wouldn't be concerned. Just buy me the time I need to get out towards the river."

"I don't know your Highness," He turned away and I could see him shake his head and pause before turning back towards me, "If you're caught, it will be my head."

"Simple, blame the changing of guard shifts, I don't know."

I knew I should have been concerned about his safety and I knew in another time or place, I would have put his life before mine however, that was not about to happen. I knew if I stayed here any longer, I would be killed, either in front of everyone or in my sleep, it was going to happen at some point, and I wasn't going to just sit around and let it happen. I was taking charge and getting out of here.

"Look, just do this for me and when this is all over, I will give you a reward, titles, land, I don't know! But you just need to do this. That's an order soldier."

He stood straight once my order was commanded and it was almost as if a switch went off in his head and he bowed and took his dagger out from its sheath, untied it and then held it out to me. Taking it, I gave him his sword in exchange and he again nodded, bowed and headed towards the door, leaving me to the rest of my plan.

"I will get the sword placed by the oak before I go and speak to the King. Please wait here for ten minutes before leaving, you will then have fifteen minutes to get out of here and to the river, collecting the sword on your way."

He left me then and I tied the dagger to my leg, waiting patiently but ten minutes was just to long for me to stand there and pray he hadn't been caught or worse. I flew to the door and opened it slowly, peering out into the corridor, I found it to be empty and dark, not a soul insight, even the ghosts weren't wandering around.

Stepping out and closing the door quietly behind me, I took to a quick pace but kept to the shadows as best as I could, avoiding any light that may have exposed me to any passer-by. Luckily and strangely no one was around, even the servants weren't off sorting out a room or two, I was hoping deep down they were just busy sorting out dinner for Xandious and the court.

Taking a sharp left, down a corridor and then another right, I came to my mother's dressing room. It had occurred to me while I was in there that perhaps, the servant's doorway hadn't been closed off and left untouched, just like her room had been. With almost all my fingers and toes crossed, I pushed open the door just a little so I could squeeze in through the gap and shut the door behind me.

Without any light, I had to feel my way around the room and almost bumped into one of armchairs that decorated the room. Finally, I felt my way to the dressing table and then towards the rails upon rails of cloaks and jackets mother kept, until finally I felt a space in-between them.

Pushing against the wall, I was pushed back, something heavy was behind the door. Shoving my body into it, I managed to budge it a bit more and within a few more shoves and pushes, I fell through the door as it opened, and a large crash happened on the other side. Whatever was blocking the way, I had managed to knock over and as the noise echoed throughout the servant's hallway, I felt my heart stop and fear escape me.

Waiting a few seconds as I laid on to the ground afraid to move and luckily, silence. No one was around to hear the noise and thankfully not come rushing to find out what it was. Pushing myself off, I brushed off the dust and looked around to see if I could recognise anything.

I had absolutely no idea where I was as everything appeared to have changed, the servant's hallway was littered with old furniture, many covered with white sheets and the thing I had managed to knock over was an old bookcase that housed serval books and upon inspection I realised the books were the ones my mother would read to me while growing up.

Knowing if I stayed here any longer, I would risk being seen, I headed towards the left, stepping over the bookcase and sticking close to the wall. Thankfully the hallway had some light, not much but enough for me to almost make out where I was going. Still no soul to be found wandering the corridors and I was starting to feel a little more on edge now, had I been wrong and naive to decide to escape tonight?

Feeling the goosebumps appear on the back of my neck as I turned a corner and the lights were now getting brighter, signifying that I was getting closer to where the servants were and my breathe caught in my chest. Voices. I stopped dead in my tracks, leaning against the wall, hiding beside a cabinet as two maids walked down the corridor in front of me chatting amongst themselves, holding freshly pressed bedsheets and laughing to themselves.

"Did you see how angry the King went when that guard arrived?" Said one of them.

"I thought he was going to pop a blood vessel, surely the Princess should be allowed to rest if she's not well."

"Jared, one of the guards told me that she's being held here against her will and has to do as she's told."

The maids passed me, and I was thankful they were gossiping too much to notice me as they walked on by. I let out a sigh as they went into a room just off the corridor and soon the silence reappeared and my heartbeat thumping loudly in my ears was all I could hear.

Quicker now, I headed down the corridor from where they came and more voices appeared, this time louder and appeared to be angry. My eyes widened as I saw shadows of bodies appear in front of me and without thinking, I opened one of the side room doors and rushed in, closing the door behind me, I listened closely as the rumble of feet went rushing by.

Turning around, I was greeted by four sets of eyes. Guards. They were all sat around a table playing cards and it took them a while to realise who had slipped into their room. One of them stood up from his chair looking at me stunned as did the other three.

"Your Highness?" The first one spoke and then cleared a few steps in front of him towards me, none of them in their uniform. Obviously off duty. "I don't think you're meant to be here."

He took another step forward and without thinking, I pulled the dagger from its sheath and held it up in front of me. He sniggered and then looked back at his friends laughing and then looked back at me, his face turned threatening, and my heart dropped, I knew if I made a run for it now, they would shout for the others and I would be caught, my escape plan failing already.

"I suggest you take a step back, before I,"

"Before you what? Stick that little thing in him." Exclaimed one of the other men as he laughed and took a swig of his drink. I hadn't noticed there were a few, if not several bottles littered around the table and the room.

"Tell you what boys, bet I could stick it in before she does." The one in the front looked at me with a hunger in his eyes, a hunger I had seen many times before.

"I'd like to see you try."

They laughed altogether and I could feel my body swell with angry as my grip tightened on the dagger, I had to get out of this room but knew if I darted out, they would shout and everyone else would come running.

The first one tried to close the distance between us and rested his chin on the edge of my dagger sniggering and I had to resist the urge to swing it across his throat and instead without even thinking fully, my foot went up and landed in-between his legs and almost in slow motion, I watched his eyes well up with tears as he gasped for air and cupped himself and fell to the floor.

That was it then, the other three were rushing towards me and I had to think fast, the room wasn't very large and if I tried to leave now, it would sound an alarm. Swinging the dagger, I threw it towards one of the guards and it landed deep in his chest, between his breasts and within seconds he was on the floor.

One of the guards came up behind me and tried to grip me, the same way Shadow had tried during training and my foot met his foot and then an elbow to the stomach and as he leaned down, I upper cut him into the nose and heard the crack as the bone broke.

The one who had been drinking came at me with his sword and I narrowly escaped, leaning back he pierced his friend and I pushed them both over, heading to the guard on the floor with my dagger protruding from his chest.

Pulling the dagger out was a little harder than I thought and as I yanked it out, the first guard was back on his feet and aiming for me with fists ready. He managed to get a swing to my face before I could dodge, and I could already taste the metallic taste of my blood as I spat it out.

He helped his friend up and now it was two against one and I was backing into the table, almost knocking it over. Grabbing a hold of one of the bottles of ale, I smashed it against the wood and held up the shattered top to use as another weapon.

"You think that will save you Princess."

"It only has to get me out of here," I smiled as they took a step towards me, unarmed.

As the first one lunged for me with his friend, I swung the bottle out and sliced the first one across his arm and he gripped my arm and threw me back, knocking me into the table fully. Almost losing my balance, I heard a sword sing as it was pulled out of its scabbard, that was going to be mine by the end of this.

Kicking myself for deciding to have the dagger instead

and although it had helped take one guard down, I now had two remaining and the only reason the one wasn't standing in front of me was because of a stroke of luck.

Another dodge and quick on my feet, I was back towards the door and both guards were either side of me, I had to pick which one to take out first and as I aimed for the one with the sword, I felt a sharp pain land in my thigh. Looking towards it I saw a shard of glass poking outwards.

"Shit," I thought.

Swinging the dagger back, I threw it towards the other guard catching him in the shoulder and then felt another blow, this time across my side as the sword sliced me, thankfully not a major wound but still hurt like hell.

"Fuck!"

Now I was fighting for my life, using the last bit of strength I had, I grabbed the sword with my bare hands and pulled it towards me, the sword cutting more into my side. Bringing the guard closer and his eyes widened, although my hand stung and I knew I had cut deep, I ignored the pain and brought my head forward, head-butting the guard with my own and as he stumbled back, he let go of his end of the sword and fell.

Swinging the sword through the air I sliced clean through the guard's neck and his head thudded to the floor. The last guard looked at me with shock and horror in his eyes before falling to his knees.

"Please no," He begged as his eyes welled up and although I didn't want to bring his life to an end, I knew if I left him here, he would go running and I would be captured.

"I have to, I'm sorry."

Another swing and the sword met his neck and as I pulled away, he grabbed his wound as the blood poured out and within seconds fell flat on his face, dead. Almost falling myself, I dropped the sword, and my head became dizzy, unsure and ringing in my ears appeared. I had to get out of this room, I had to get to the oak tree and to the river, to escape.

Holding myself up using the wall and opening the door, I stumbled out, the light in the corridor looked fuzzy and I couldn't quite focus on it. Taking a few steps out, I used the wall to guide me and I was now unsure where I was going but I just kept putting one foot in front of the other, aiming for the back door. The door I knew would lead me out into the grounds, the servant entrance and where I would be able to escape and find my freedom.

No one stopped me, no voices were heard and as I walked through another corridor and towards the door, I pushed it open, and the freezing air took me by surprise. My cloak, I must had lost it during the fight, shaking my head at the realisation that I couldn't go back and get it, I stepped out anyway and although it was unbelievably cold, I had to keep going.

The gate to the larger gardens was in view as the moon rose high in the sky, night had fallen, and I was grateful for the cover of darkness. The ringing in my ears now ever growing and the sting in my thigh painful, the shard of glass still poking out. I held onto my side, the wound appearing to feel deeper with every breath and as I made it to the gate, I leaned against it coughing, the pain unbearable. I was going to make it, my guard would find me when he got here and would help, he would get me to the river and out of reach.

But he never came and soon enough my eyes went dark, hitting the ground hard, I felt my mind drift away and as my eyes slowly closed, I saw many sets of boots running towards me and then it went dark.

II

SHADOW

L ying in bed was the last thing I wanted to do the morning after Quiver and I arrived and so I was up at the crack of dawn, much to the dislike of Lord Reid's household staff who clearly weren't used to having early riser guests. Throwing on a black shirt, trousers, and shoes, I took to wandering the grounds. The snow had started to fall heavily during the night, and we were lucky to arrive when we did.

Nimra always looked magical during the winter months, although it was incredibly cold and I should have been wearing a jacket, I enjoyed the cold against my skin. Taking out Winterthorn from its scabbard, I felt the weight fall into my hands and run up my arms, the sword that had been made for me felt perfect in my grasp. Swinging in through the air, it sang against the wind and the power felt marvellous, it had only been a week or so since I held it, but it felt like months.

Training was the only thing I found that would help clear my mind, quieting out the voices. How did I not guess Nefret's words of warning were about Ayla. Frustration and annoyance fuelled my blade as it swung and span, the steel and I one. I needed to get my hands on Ayla and desperately wanted to run my blade through Xandious if he had harmed Giselle in any shape or form. I didn't realise how much I missed having her around until we were apart. We had been joined at the hip once we embarked on this journey and now, I felt lost.

At the start I had become so torn as to what to do. When I found her the first time in Crystal Deer, I had thought to capture her there and then, after months of searching and following dead ends, I was ready to head home and face the wrath of Xandious and then there she was, sitting at a fountain in one of the city squares, drinking with Ayla and chatting to some other peasants and I just couldn't do it.

She looked peaceful, happy even and so I stuck around, waiting and watching until I thought it was the right time we should meet again. It was funny to me how even if she had a disguising spell of magic hiding away her identity, I knew it was her. I'd know her even if she shaved all her hair off, I knew her heart.

The sun started to rise as I slowed down my rhythm of Winterthrone, enjoying the movement and feel, wishing to savour it as best as I could.

My wound's echo hurt still and yet it was no longer visible, the pain almost phantom like and if you hadn't witnessed the injury, you would never have known it to be there. Stopping, I rested my sword against a tree and sat down on a low wall that surrounded a flower bed.

"You're up early," Mason's voice broke the silence as he joined me outside, "Restless I take it."

"You should have gone after him," Deep down I was furious they hadn't gone after Xandious to save Giselle.

"Shadow, we lost nearly half our men trying to get to her. Of course, we went after him to save the Princess," He sat down beside me, "Do you honestly think we wouldn't have risked everything to save her?"

"You should have died fighting."

"Yes, well what good would that have done? We were unsuccessful and had to retreat, to gather our numbers. We will get her back my lad, don't worry about that."

He placed a reassuring hand on my shoulder, and I shrugged it off. Standing up, I sighed deeply and stretched my hands above my head, hearing the pops in my shoulder and back, clearing any tension from my body.

"I'm lucky to be alive Mason. If it wasn't for Quiver's men and Mabon's powers, I'd be with Aithne now and Giselle would be lost to us all."

Turning around, I picked up Winterthorn and placed her back in its scabbard and took the rubber band on my wrist to tie my hair up in a low pony. Mason looked worse than me and I needed cleaning up. His face had lost a bit of weight and he didn't appear to be as chunky as the last time I saw him, he looked just as lost as I felt.

"We should head back in; the others will be waking soon, and we need to discuss the plan on how to get Giselle back."

"We will do everything we possibly can."

We needed to desperately get Giselle back safely without endangering her life or the civilians of Minwed. My heart raced and mind filled with anguish at the moment she was grabbed and how even if Giselle protested, I couldn't wait to get my hands on Ayla for her betrayal and would gladly end her life as quickly as she blinked away Giselle's.

Now sitting from across the table in Lord Reid's dining hall many papers and maps were in piles on the wood and spilling onto the stone floor. Mason and Reid talked back and forth, trying to come up with a plan that they believed would be the easiest and safest way to get Giselle back. She was our beacon, and we couldn't allow Xandious to keep her, she would surely die if we didn't rescue her.

"We need to just attack the Capital." Mason's voice grew louder as he tried to contain some of his anger.

Our original plan had failed badly after Elder Grove and after thinking it over, it was surprising how we weren't caught before we arrived in the village.

"We can't just attack Mason; we need to think logically about this. The Princess wouldn't want us to bring harm to any of the cities people while trying to get her back."

The last few hours, I had learnt more about Lord Reid and how he was once an advisor to her Majesties Queen Iris and then Queen Enelya. He knew what a war would bring to Nimra, and he knew how if we just dove headfirst in, millions would be lost. He was right, we had to think and plan logically, Giselle wouldn't be too happy if many died to save her life.

"There is another way."

Quiver, who had been sat next to me silently listening to the entire argument pipped in, finally. I would have forgotten he was here as he hadn't said much since we arrived.

"I have gotten word there will be a masquerade ball held at the castle, Xandious plans to celebrate the Princesses return and has invited many of the nobles who are still on his side to join him."

"You mean to just show the world she isn't dead or will it be an audience to Giselle's death." My voice was filled with sorrow and worry.

"And how are we supposed to get in?" Asked Mason.

"Easy, we walk through the front door."

All three of us looked at Quiver confused and unsure if he had lost his mind as walking through the front door wasn't going to happen, we would be killed on sight.

"What I mean is, we find the names of a few lords who are attending, lock them away so they can't attend and using some of Mabon's magic, we will get in. And since it's a masked ball, no one will question it anyways."

"If it were that easy Quiver, we would already be looking for the lords to impersonate." Mason sat down with a huff and flicked his fingers at one of his ushers who came rushing over with a glass of wine. Mason appeared a lot more stressed since my return, I knew it was due to the other lords worries resting on his shoulders.

"Well – Eh – Some might already be tied up and locked away in the stables."

Mason spat his drink out and then looked at Quiver as he shot him that dazzling smile Giselle had told me about. Elves, they were always full of tricks and one step ahead of everyone in any sort of game. I couldn't help but chuckle even if it hurt my stitches.

"How in goddesses name have you captured some of the nobles?" I turned and looked at him, confused.

"It was easy. Elves don't need much sleep and Alary and I decided it would be a good idea if we didn't get you lot involved," Quiver looked so unbothered, as if he had done this before, "We caught them just west of the border of Minwed, obviously heading to the capital."

"And when is this mask supposed to happen?" Asked Reid as he took his seat beside Mason.

It occurred to me then, Mason and Reid were now traitors to the King, as were the other lords who had joined our forces. They weren't invited to the mask, and it did make me wonder how on earth Quiver found out about it.

"In about three days' time." Quiver turned to look at me, his smile almost turning diabolical. "We will only have one chance at it. We would need to be in and out as soon as we get hold of her Majesty."

"That's all well and good Quiver but we would need a distraction, to get the King away from the Princess."

Reid was right, we would need something that would pull all eyes away from Giselle to get her out of the castle, undetected, and hopefully we would not be chased or captured in the process. Mason rubbed his temples and then took a large gulp of his drink, he looked just as worried as I felt, this would have to take careful planning and we would need to be cautious about who were told the plan.

"What about the lord's household? Surely, they will have noticed they're missing." I asked watching as Quiver got up to help himself to a drink.

"Distraction wise, I'm sure we can think of something when we get there and assess the situation. And as for the lord's servants, already got that covered to, Mabon has put them into some sort of sleeping curse. He will wake them up when we are ready and on our way to the mask."

"Seem's like you have all this under control Quiver." Mason's tone was condescending and questioning. "When did you come up with all of this? And how did you find out about the mask?"

"Queen Leena has many spies hiding within the city walls, that's all I can tell you." He took a sip of his drink and then turned to face the three of us again.

"All I can say is, this is our only shot to get Princess Giselle back. I have sent someone from my own personal team to get into Minwed under a disguise, he will be keeping an eye on things and shall send word if anything changes. You must trust me on this."

He then looked at me, his Emerald eyes staring at me as if they bore into my very being.

"Lord Shadow, you know I would never do anything to put the Princesses life at risk. I hope one day for her to help reunite my people with the rest of the world. She is our light out of all this darkness and I will do everything in my power to help you to bring her back safely."

12

GISELLE

Constricted and unable to move, I awoke to a feeling of a hard surface underneath me. Attempting to lift my arms up was a failure and infuriated me as soon as I realised what had happened, I hadn't escaped and clearly, I was now tied to something, a bed perhaps? This meant I wasn't going to be able to move or escape anytime soon.

My eyes welled up with tears as I tried to comprehend what had happened, how long had I been asleep? Was it only moments ago or longer?

The light in the room stung my eyes as I looked around trying to figure out where I was. My breathe appeared in clouds as the cold air clung to its warmth, the sound of slow dripping and what sounded like rats running across the floor. The dungeons. I was in a cell, turning my head slightly I saw the large steel bars, the cage that kept me in.

"For fuck's sake!" I said out loud, unable to hold my composer.

"Oh, good you're awake," That voice and my blood began to boil, "The King was worried for a moment you might have lost to much blood."

Ayla. She appeared behind the bars, dressed in what almost looked like one of my mother's gowns, a dark maroon dress with gold trimming. I noticed as it glittered in the light, a small silver tiara was placed on her head, decorated with beautiful diamonds. One of my tiaras.

"You've been asleep for an entire day. The doctors managed to stitch you and put you back together, some fight you got into. Are you ok?"

"Ayla, I mean this in the nicest way possible but seriously, would you just fuck off."

I was in no mood to be proper and the anger inside me was already reaching a point of screaming. I wanted out of these restraints and although I should have been a bit nicer to her, so she would come in and undo them, I had no ounce of it left in me, she was the reason I was stuck in this mess.

"Oh Giselle, please don't be so harsh. I am here to help you. I was the one who found you out by the back gate, if it weren't for me, you would have died."

"If it weren't for you, I wouldn't be stuck in this mess at all." I turned away, unable to look at her anymore.

"Guard, can you let me in there please so I may help her Highness," The guard was quick to unlock the bar door and as she walked in, I heard him remove his sword from its scabbard, clearly ready and waiting for me to cause a scene.

"I'd like her cuffs unlocked please, I'm sure she needs to move around, the doctor said it will be good for her to try and get back on her feet by today."

"But my lady, it won't be safe. You saw what she did to those other men."

"Yes well, it's his Majesty's orders that she healed and feeling better. I'm sure her Highness has a perfectly good explanation as to what happened back in that room, but we are not the ones who can pass judgement. Now please, unlock them."

His heavy footsteps walked across the stoned floor and the jingle of his keys came as he unlocked one of my foot chuffs and then the other. I didn't move a single inch, although I would have liked to had beat them both to the ground and escaped, I was I no fit state to do that. The wound from my side stinging as I breathed in and out, my hands were wrapped in cloth and stained a little from the old blood.

"And her hands please."

I could feel the hesitation and tension coming from the guard as I looked at him intensively. He was afraid of me. He unlocked the hand chains and as I lifted my right hand up, he flinched but all I did was rub my wrist, they were both tender and sore.

"You may leave us now," Ayla no longer sounded like the Ayla I knew, she appeared to be proper and just like a lady of the court, "I will be fine, just stand outside the door and if anything should happen, well then you may come in and sort it out."

The guard nodded and left us both. Lifting myself up off the bed was a struggle and Ayla stepped forward, almost to help me and I shot her a deathly look, she wouldn't dare touch me. No strength or not, I'd end her life whatever way I was able to.

"His Majesty wishes for you to be up and ready by tomorrow evening. He has decided to host a ball, a masquerade and you are his special guest."

"And why should I do anything for him?"

"Giselle, please," She sat down on the edge of my bed, and I shifted closer to the wall, to get away from her.

"This will be a good thing; it will help repair your relationship. He allowed you to freely walk the grounds and thankfully he believed me when I told him you must have been attacked by those men. There are many who wish to harm you, even within these walls. He only wishes to protect you."

She placed a hand on my ankle, and I had to fight every instinct not to kick her in the face there and then.

"Please, I know you're angry with me, but I did all this to protect you, to save you from fighting on a battlefield and dying. You are what matters to me, you are everything to me."

I narrowed my eyes at her, ready to sprout out more anger and abuse. She was an idiot and it infuriated me to no end how stupid she had become. Where was the Ayla who taught me how to shoot an arrow six feet across a plain and hit its target? Where was the Ayla who enjoyed starting bar fights and causing havoc everywhere she went? This wasn't her anymore, the Ayla I knew would never be so stupid to believe the lies of a man.

"Ayla, you are an idiot," I shot her a look of anger, and she removed her hand from my ankle, "If you think for one single second my father wants to repair my relationship with him, then you are more than an idiot. Have you forgotten who he is? What he did to my mother? What he wants to do to the people? He doesn't care about me, or you or anyone else for that matter. It is all about him and always has been."

She shook her head as if my words went in one ear and straight out the other. Was she so far gone into madness that she couldn't see pass the delusions and deceit?

"You're angry, I get that, I was to, but Xandious isn't as bad as you say he is."

"Xandious? Oh, you're on a first name basis now, are you?" I shook my head and leaned in towards her, "You listen to me now Ayla, Xandious made everyone believe he loved my mother and heck at one point he may have even believed it himself, but that didn't stop him from striking her down and taking the power he has always dreamt of. He will do the same to anyone else that gets in his way, that includes you."

She stood up then and started to walk away from me, which I was glad about as I finally felt I could breathe again. She turned to look at me, her hands firmly placed in front of her as they clasped together, and I noticed then the large diamond ring placed on her ring finger.

"You married him?" My breath caught with disbelief and more anger and if it wasn't for the fact I could barely stand, I would have thrown myself off the bed and on top of her, punching the life out from behind her eyes.

"No, not yet. The King asked me yesterday to become his bride and I accepted."

"You're more of an idiot than I thought. Your delusional."

"Say what you will and believe whatever you wish. The ball will be in celebration of our engagement, and he expects you to be there. I will send for a doctor to come and check on your wounds and then you are to rest until you are ready to be received."

I rolled my eyes at her and watched as she walked out the door, the guard quickly shutting it behind her and locking it. I could hear the ringing in my ears again as my rage grew. This was unbelievable, how did we even get here? How had he won Ayla over so easily? Was it magic perhaps? Yes, that must be it, magic is the only explanation for all this nonsense. She would never marry a man, especially since she appeared to only keep the company of females. No, it is magic. It just must be.

"It's all going to work out, you will see." She said as she left me to my thoughts.

∽

ONCE THE DOCTOR arrived and examined me, he appeared to be pleased that my body was healing fast but gave me an elixir that helped speed up the healing and reduce my exhaustion. The liquid tasted awful, and I almost threw it all back up, he admitted one of Xandious's magics made it and although I wanted to shout and proclaim my upset of their capture and torture, I felt it was best to keep quiet.

My emotions were starting to get the better of me and I had to keep reminding myself to stay calm, I was still my mother's daughter, and she would not be pleased with my lack of composer or the fact swearing had almost become second nature to me. But then again, I don't think she would have been happy to know her daughter had killed people blindly, even if it was for the sake of one's life.

Night fell and the only light sources throughout the dungeons were a few gas lamps dotted around the place. Dinner arrived of the form of a glass of water, a slice of bread, cheese and an apple, clearly a dinner that wasn't filling but enough to keep a person alive. I ate the apple first and it tasted soft and bitter, as if it had been left out to rot but as my stomach growled and protested, I needed to eat some-thing and most certainly wasn't going to eat the cheese that had green mould spores.

"I will take that if you're not going to."

My neighbour, I had known there was someone there earlier when I watched the guard give them a tray of food, but we hadn't shared any words up until now. I slid my hand through the joining bars and gave them the slice of bread and cheese and a dirty bruised hand took them.

"What happened to you?"

I asked as their face came into the light a little, exposing more cuts and bruises. My neighbour was a woman. Her long brown hair looked matted and dirty, and her lips appeared chapped and dry, my heart sank at the sight of her, she must have been locked in these cells for a long time.

"Your father is what happened to me," She snapped as she took a bite of bread, "You are what happened to me Princess."

"I'm sorry, have we met?"

"No, but if you and yours weren't in my Inn that night, I would have been left and safe and yet here I am and have been for months now, locked away in this prison, unable to escape and used as a weapon by your father."

"Again, I have no idea what you're talking about?"

"My name is Lady Adela and you, Princess; you came to my Inn searching for Lord Shadow."

My mind clicked into place as I realised this was Lady Adela, Shadow had told me about her back at the tavern after the party and as I thought back to that night, the night Ayla and I arrived in Port Yale and entered The Fisherman and Fox Inn. Shadow had been there, and we just followed his trail, I had no idea that we were going to be ambushed and I didn't know this Lady Adela was the one who owned the Inn.

"Shadow was staying in one of my rooms and when you and he were together doing goddess knows what, I was captured and then Lord Terrell's men ransacked the place, killed my staff and I had assumed they killed you and your girlfriend as well, clearly not as I saw her earlier," She paused finishing off the bread and then taking a bite out of the cheese, whole.

"If I had known how much trouble you would have caused me, I would have killed you myself."

"Ok, Lady Adela, I have no idea why you are blaming me for any of your misfortunes, I had no idea that any of that was going to happen, and I most certainly didn't know anyone had been killed other than Lord Terrell's men." I stood up from my bed and went to the middle bars to see if I could get a better look of her.

"And as far as anyone was concerned, the men were there to capture Ayla, not you or me. We were obviously just surprises. If Shadow knew his friend were in danger, he would have done everything he could to rescue you. We had no idea."

She got up from her bed and met me halfway, I could see her clearly now and she was just as Shadow described, beautiful beyond belief and a warmth fell under my skin as she looked at me with her hazel eyes.

"What are you?" I said out-load and she shot me a look of anger.

"Something your father wishes to use against others."

"He's not my father – not anymore."

"Even if you say he isn't, he still is, and you most certainly are his daughter."

Her words were harsh and filled with anger. I wondered how long she had been down here, and I felt regret as Shadow, and I didn't even think about her after the inn incident.

"I am sorry you are hurting, but you will find I am nothing like him." I paused and slid down the bars adjoining our cells, she turned away from me, "How long have you been here Adela?"

"Too long, time isn't something I keep track of."

"May I ask, what are you? Please."

"I am a creature long forgotten, something that was created right at the start when the world began," She paused and looked at me, that same warmth filled me up and it sparked a moment of what felt like pure happiness and then she dropped her eyes, "I am what the stories call a Siren."

I stared at her with disbelief, Sirens were the things of the past. Something the Goddesses Fenella and Nefret created. The story went that a siren was part mermaid and bird and they were able to shape-shift into humans, beautiful young women who would lure sailors and men to their deaths. Unlike mermaids who also ate the flesh of humans and took made killing as a sport.

"How old are you?" My eyes widened as she came towards the cell bars, the energy from her almost vibrating.

"Old enough, I was there the day this world was created. How beautiful it was," She looked away as if her mind took her elsewhere, "When Fenella and Nefret brought me to Guinevere I was young new and unsure on the world. I was surrounded by my sisters and we each were given a piece of the ocean, a place to call our homes and for many centuries we were left alone until man came and destroyed us," She wiped away a tear from her eyes and then sat down on the floor.

"My sister Rina was the first to go, she was the youngest of us all and very naive. She believed the man she loved cared about her and well we know how the story ends with betrayal and heartbreak. She went to Guinevere to end her life and when she refused, Rina flew into a rage and Guinevere wiped her from existence."

"I'm sorry," It was all I could say as I listened in awe.

"After that, my sisters and I hunted down the man responsible and well, you can guess the rest."

"Is that when the stories of your kind began? Luring men to their deaths. How do you do that?"

"I cannot speak for my other sisters, but I use a form of mind control. Once I lock onto you, it's very hard for you to resist me."

I bit the bottom of my lip as I thought about the warm feeling, she had already given me and wondered if that was part of her powers.

"Is that what you did with Shadow? Locked in on him."

"I have never used my powers of Lord Shadow and even if I tried, they would never work, that man is something else entirely."

Confusion and wonder entered my mind as I held onto her words, I knew Shadow had dabbled in magic and I knew he had incredible skills but that was all, he kept himself well guarded and although he had shared a few secrets with me, his childhood before me was off limits and I never pried.

"What is he? If he not human? Like me." It slipped out before I had a chance to think, my thoughts repeating outloud.

"Partly but it is not my business to tell. He would have to tell you himself."

My heart thumped in my chest as my eyes began to well up into tears, she had no idea he was gone, and it broke my heart as I now had to tell her about her friend's death.

"He's gone Adela. He died saving me, Xandious ran him through with his sword."

Tears escaped my eyes and I watched as the words hit her and whereas I thought she would be upset, she broke into a loud roar of laughter and for a few seconds I was angry, why was this so funny? It made no sense and once she calmed down, she looked at me intensively.

"You honestly think a sword can kill Shadowbane. Oh, my dear, there really is so much you don't know. Has he even told you about who his mother is?"

"No, I only know him to have lived with his aunt Countess Elizabeth. He came to her when he was a young boy."

"Ah did he now, hmmm" Her eyes looked as if she were teasing me as if she knew a secret and she wanted to tell me, "Shadow's mother is Guinevere."

My eyes widened as the knowledge hit me hard in the chest. His mother was who? My mind raced with all the possibilities, the stories he had hidden inside him, how had he come to being and the dots started to connect. It's how he was able to see through my spells, how he was very strong and why he didn't seem at all surprised to see Quiver and discover he was an elf.

"Is he a God?"

"No, a Demi-God I believe, I think that's what he was told. He was born a very long time ago, but his apperance is slow changing. He may appear around twenty-five to you and me now, but I believe he is a lot older than that."

"How old?" I couldn't believe any of what I was hearing, "I have watched him grow, I have watched him age though."

"I am not one hundred precent on how it works. For the first few years I think he appears to age, he would age the same as you as a child but once he came of age, maternity, it would slow and now I believe it isn't even at a snail pace."

"So that means I will die before he even looks fifty years old - If he is still alive."

"Oh Princess, I have no doubts he is still alive and most likely doing everything he can to get to you."

She gave me much food for thought and we sat there for a few more hours discussing folk tales, the legends of the Sirens and Shadow's adventures. Even things I never thought possible, and, in those hours, I felt my heart lighten, the pain of Shadow's death disappearing a little. I felt hope and certainty that perhaps Adela was right, perhaps a sword hadn't kill him.

13

QUIVER

———≋———

Although we had a just a few short days to prepare, I took advantage of the spare time to practice my swordsmanship and get to know Shadow a little bit better. Our first meeting didn't go as well as I had hoped, and it was still interesting to me that many of my kind believed him too not be real.

When the fighting had started to break out in many of the villages and cities around Nimra, Mason had called for his wife and stepdaughter to join us at the manor. It was the best place to be during the fighting as it was surrounded by a rather large wall and had never been taken in the history of Lord Reid's family.

I found Lady Alison to be quite interesting and although she appeared to keep herself guarded, it gave me a distraction, a challenge of some sorts to break down her walls and truly get to know her. Sitting out in the gardens, I found her wrapped in a fur lined cloak and she was sketching something on a piece of paper, the snow was falling slowly and barely noticeable.

I watched her from a distance so not to disturb her. She

had the deepest red hair I had ever seen, almost as if fire had painted her locks itself. Observing her as she moved the pencil up and down, she would glance up just for a few seconds to look at the scene in front of her and then back down to her paper. I had no idea she drew but then it made sense, most ladies of her wealth very rarely did anything other than writing, reading, drawing and perhaps sewing, or at least that's what I had been told and read in books about the other races.

Stepping forward my foot stepped on a twig and the crack almost sent Lady Alison flying backwards from her seat in surprise and before she fell, I was there at her side, catching her and lifting her back up. Her face flew into a shade of pink and her eyes widened in surprise as she realised it was me who had caught her.

"My Lord Quiver,"

"Are you alright? I'm sorry for startling you."

"Oh, that's ok I should be going in now, I have been out here for quite some time, and I believe my fingers are going a little numb."

Looking down at her hands, the tips had almost drained of colour and I quickly took them into my own hands, cupping them around and then as magic coursed through my veins, I watched my hands glow a little red and Lady Alison watched closely and as her hands began to warm up slowly, her shoulders relaxed.

"Can all Elves do magic?"

"Mostly yes, however Elves are gifted with other talents and those who don't use or have very little magic concentrate on their other gifts. Such as crafting, weapons making, tending to the grounds and things like that." I had no idea why I was rumbling so much, there was just something about Lady Alison that intrigued me.

"I hope once all this is over and we are on the winning side, you and the rest of your race can come out of the shadows and share with us those wonderful gifts."

"Perhaps one day, for now you are just stuck with my company."

"Oh – I like your company if it helps."

She smiled a beautiful soft smile and I watched her closely, her blue eyes almost appeared to flash a little green as the winter sunlight touched them. I realised then I was still holding her hands and although part of me didn't want to let go; I did out of respect and in case anyone had been watching us. She looked disappointed when her hands fell to her lap. Leaning down, I picked up her drawing off the floor as well as her pencil and examined the drawing now that I was able to see it.

"You are quite the artist."

"Oh no, that's just something simple."

"If this is simple, I would love to see your more complex sketches."

The drawing was filled with contrast and shadows as she had drawn the hill's rising in the northwest, far beyond The Arabella Sea. There were a few boats on the sea in the distance and the sky she drew must have represented her feelings, it was dark and filled with sorrow. I handed it back to her and then stood from the stoned wall we had been sat on, ready to take my leave.

"When do you and his Lordship travel?"

"Tomorrow, if we are to arrive on time for the ball."

"Will you return?"

"My Lady, I am not sure when that will be. If we can save her Highness, this might be the first place the King looks, and we need to keep her safe."

I had been thinking since my conversation with Shadow

in the dining hall about where we would go after the rescue mission. Really any of the cities were out of bounds and as we weren't one-hundred percent sure that there wasn't a spy amongst us, it wouldn't be safe to bring her back to Lord Reid's manor.

"Why don't you take her back to your home?"

I looked at her puzzled as she looked up at me under her long eyelashes and my breathe caught a little, she was beautiful.

"You know, you did mention it is covered and hidden by spells, perhaps the King wouldn't even think to look there. Especially since it doesn't exist."

Not only was she beautiful but she was also smart.

"That actually doesn't sound like a bad idea, thank you my Lady for your council."

"Please, call me Alison. I wish for us to become friends and calling me Lady all the time doesn't make me feel as if we can become that."

"Alison, yes, of course we can – we are friends."

I sat back down next to her, and she smiled sweetly.

"You can call me Alex or just Quiver if you wish."

"Alexander, why do they call you Quiver? Surely that isn't your last name?"

"Would you be surprised if I told you yes it was." She looked at me confused and then shocked as the words settled into her mind.

"Many Elves don't have last names and so we are given them once our first skill is found, mine happened to be archery as you can guess and so I was blessed with the name Quiver."

"Yes, indeed that does make sense and what a wonderful way to signify the start of your journey in this life."

"I am starting to think Alison, you are wiser than you make everyone believe."

She laughed a little under her breath before responding and although I meant it as a compliment, her reaction made me feel as if she didn't believe me.

"Mother has always taught me that men do not wish for a wise wife and so I keep that part hidden – Yet, with you, it comes out easily."

"Well, don't keep it hidden from me. I like a wise lady and a wise wife doesn't sound all that bad, you just need to find a man who respects that you aren't just beauty but also brain."

She blushed at my words, and I sensed she hadn't really been given any compliments about her true self, other than what was shown on the outside. Smiling, I placed a hand on her cheek, and I felt her lean a little into it.

"Don't ever silence your true voice to please others."

Her eyes went glassy as she smiled a little and one single tear escaped from her eye. Whipping it with my thumb, I then traced her lips with it, without realising what I was even doing and began to lean in a little more towards her and then something clicked in my mind, and I pulled back quickly, dropping my hand and then standing up.

"My apologises, that was very forward of me Lady Alison. I will escort you back to the house as the snow is falling faster, it would appear."

She looked at me almost disappointedly before nodded and pulled her cloak tighter around herself and then taking my hand, I linked her arm into mine and walked her back to the house, in silence.

Once we were inside, I bowed, and she took her leave of me. Regret started to appear within me but pushing it aside I shook my head. I came here to do a job and rescue a Princess, not get distracted in the process.

∼

"Heard you offended Lady Alison this morning?" Shadow asked at breakfast while we sat in Lord Reid's study.

"If offending a lady by not kissing her is wrong, then call me a sinner." I snapped taking a bagel from the table and cutting it in half to spread cream cheese across it.

"You didn't kiss her and she's annoyed? Well, I can't blame the lady. I'd be the same."

"Oh well in that case, pucker up." I winked at Shadow as he choked back a laugh and continued to eat his food.

We had been sat going over the plans for the last hour or so before Reid's household staff brought us any food and it was mainly the protest of Mason that they did. Complaining he was wasting away, and I had to hold back my tongue to tell him he could do with losing a few pounds.

"You leave tomorrow morning then, yes?" Mason asked while sipping at his cup of herbal tea, claiming it calmed his nerves.

"Early hours of the morning. We should leave before sunrise as to make sure no one see's us leaving."

Shadow was right as usual as we needed to be sure we weren't followed or spotted when we left the manor.

"Ah yes, good plan. We still haven't found out any more information on who could perhaps be our spy, but we shall."

"How are the other nobles doing at rounding up more men? I know you all lost shire numbers after the King attacked us." Asked Shadow.

"Not good I'm afraid. Lord Reid however has a few

favours he can call in with the sailors and that might help us a little."

I didn't know very much about Lord Reid, other than he was old on the inside but appeared still in his late fifties. I had overheard a few of Mason's maid's talking about a witch who blessed Reid with the gift of youth but that may have just been a silly rumour. And yet, it wouldn't surprise me as magic could do many things, you couldn't be made immortal however the aging process can be slowed down with a few elixirs.

"Lord Quiver, will your companion be joining you?"

Alary had joined us shortly after Mason had sat down with us, I had given him a special job to do and to prepare something for our journey. When he arrived, he had given me a nod of confirmation and then joined us for breakfast.

"I will not be leaving my Lord's side throughout this trip."

Alary answered looking over his cup of tea at Mason. He had already expressed his dislike for the Governor, and I couldn't blame him, the man did seem overbearing and demanding, believing he was incharge of this whole movement while the Princess was away and yet, it was Lord Shadow she had given the second-in-command title and so he was the one calling the shots.

"Do you think Giselle might have been harmed in anyway?" Shadow turned to me with a slight hint of worry in his eyes and then composed himself quickly.

"If the King knows what is good for him, she would most likely be locked away in a room somewhere as he doesn't want another rebel uprising again."

"Well, there will still be one, but we must replenish our supplies and prepare ourselves better. We can't make the same mistakes we have already made."

We fell silent then as we each finished our food and once Mason took his leave, as did his footman and we were in the room alone, Alary appeared to relax a bit more.

"My Lord's, I have acquired us the supplies we need for the trip as well as our attire for the evening. One of your scouts," He directed his eyeline towards me, "He will meet us at the gates with everything else we need."

"Thank you Alary. We will meet at the side gate before sunrise, and we will ride all morning if we must."

"Lake Gloverose, you said we will stop at. Isn't that near The Withered Mountains?" Shadow looked at me confused and I realised I hadn't caught him up with the plan after we received the Princess. Alary already knew as we were able to communicate through our minds, a handy trick to have during a fight and when we didn't want anyone know our plans.

"Yes, it is the safest place for us to be before we head into Minwed. It's a few hours ride to the capital."

Leaving to head to my room after many hours in the study, I was grateful for the peace and quiet. The room in which Lord Reid had graciously given me, was one that overlooked the Arabella Sea and although I was more of a woodsman myself, hearing the crashing of the waves in the distance did sooth my soul.

Wandering out onto the small Juliet balcony brought my mind some comforts as I thought about my sister and how annoyed she must have been to find out I had left without her permission. Although Leena and I were siblings, I knew she would make me pay for disobeying her orders and heading to rescue Giselle. I hadn't heard the door of my room knock or when someone came in so lost in my own mind.

"Alexander?"

Her voice was gentle and sweet and unknowing to even me, I felt my eyes widen a little as she came into view. Lady Alison, she was wearing a beautiful black gown with white lace trimming around the sleeves and her red hair was down in loose curls. I turned to look at her and got the impression she had something on her mind she wished to say and yet her body language appeared reserved, she was afraid.

"Twice in one day – To what do I owe this pleasure?"

"I'm sorry to disturb you, I know you must have many things to do." She paused biting her bottom lip and all I could think about in that moment was biting it for her. "I wanted to ask you something, well request it actually." A blush flashed across her cheeks, and I looked at her wondering. "You see, I eh," She stopped again and dropped her head.

"You may request anything my Lady." I said with my charming smile as I placed a strand of hair back behind my ear. "What is it you wish?"

"I wanted to know, this morning, when we were in the garden. Were you going to eh – kiss me?"

My eyes widened a little as the small shock entered my body but quickly, I returned to my normal stoic and looked at her as she kept her eyes from me, looking out towards the sea and I could sense she didn't want to know the answer.

"Yes, to put it plainly. Yes, I felt that urge." I turned away from her and went to lean over the balcony as she joined me at my side. "However, it isn't proper for me to do anything like that. I would first need your permission and I respect you too much to force a kiss on you when you don't wish to be kissed."

"Who said I don't want to be kissed?" She looked at me with a hint of sadness in her eyes but also determination.

"All girls wish to be kissed Lord Quiver, even the ones

who deny it." She turned away from me as I caught her eye line. "Would you? – Kiss me if I asked for you to?"

"I thought you wished to be friends."

"I am not asking for a lover Alex; I am simply asking would you kiss me should I ask for you to do so?"

"If you asked and the moment was right then yes, I would."

I turned to my side and looked at her as she kept her eyes on the horizon, the wind was chilly and blew through my jacket and I could see Alison wrap her arms around herself, to keep the chill at bay.

Taking her by the hand, I led her back into my bedroom and sat her down in the armchair that was placed in front of the fire. It had been lit this morning and needed some tending to, throwing on another log, I used the poker to get it to catch and sure enough the fire came back to life and began to fill its warmth through the room.

"Why are you concerned about kissing anyhow? Surely, you've had plenty of suitors who have wanted to be at your side."

Sitting down in the chair opposite, I watched as her face dropped while she looked at the dancing flames. She began fidgeting with the trimmings on her sleeve and I could see she was thinking of an answer or perhaps holding back one.

"Ladies like me aren't permitted to have stolen kisses from gentleman, even the ones we are being shown off to. It is only when we are engaged are we allowed to share such things."

"So, you've never been kissed?"

"No Alex, I have never been kissed."

"Oh, I get it now," I leant back into my chair and settled on the conversation at hand, she wasn't just talking about being kissed by anyone, she was talking about having her first kiss.

She appeared to become very nervous and almost aware of the room around her, although it was still the afternoon, the sun had already begun to settle and so the only light source in the room was the golden glow of the fire. I stood from my chair and took hold of her fidgeting hands and lifted her out of hers.

She still wouldn't meet my eye line and I couldn't blame her for that. I tucked a bit of her hair behind her ear and then lifted her chin to look at me and for me to look at her.

Those beautiful blue eyes like the pools of the ocean themselves were staring back at me, under her long black eyelashes. Her cheeks were red with blush, and she licked her lips a little.

"If you wish for your first kiss to be with me, you only have to say the words."

She held back a little and I could feel how nervous she was. Swallowing down her words, I placed my other hand that had just been dangling at my side now on the base of her back, drawing her in a little closer but not to close and not to tightly, I wanted her to feel safe enough to say no if she wished.

"You're a wonderful man." She dropped her gaze and I smiled. "If I let you kiss me, would that be it?"

"It would be it if you wished for it to be. I will not and never will ask for anything more than what you want to give."

"Hmm – Then," She looked back up at me with glassy eyes, "Yes, you may kiss me."

It was as if she said the magic words and although we had only begun to get to know one another, I found myself attracted and thinking of her back at Mason's house, all those weeks ago and although it was often talked about as a wrongdoing, mixing with humans, I did not care in the slightest.

She was the most beautiful woman I had ever laid my eyes on, even more so than Leena and Giselle put together and here she was, this amazing creature standing in front of me asking, waiting for me to be her first kiss.

"Are you sure your mother won't be angry with you?"

"Alex, we may die soon, we may live, we do not know what the world has in store for us but right now, right here, I know I would like to share this moment with you. And I hope you wish to do the same."

Nodding slightly, I pulled her in even closer to me and now she was only a breathes touch away from me. Leaning down towards her a little as I was a bit taller than her, I felt her body lift a little onto her toes and I wrapped my other hand to the back of her neck and helped pull her up.

Our lips were almost touching, and I could feel her heartbeat loudly against my own chest, she was holding her breath as was I. I had shared many first kisses, first times and been many first loves to others but this felt different. And with a crackle of the fire, I brought my lips down to hers. At first gently and then as she wrapped her hands around my neck and pulled me a little bit closer to her, the kiss deepened into wanting and desire.

As if this was the last thing either of us were ever going to do with our lives. My tongue parted her lips as it began to dance with hers, creating more passion and craving for each other and although I felt I could go further and we would be lost in each other, she had simply asked for a kiss. Breaking away and then being pulled back into another one made me chuckle against her lips and I felt her smile.

"If we do not stop now, I'm afraid you won't be just having a first kiss tonight."

I pulled away again and this time she let me go, both of us breathless but appearing to be happy with our choice. She slumped back into her chair, and I went to the small side table that had a decanter on filled with whiskey, pouring some into two glasses, I gave her one and then took my seat again, downing my glass in one gulp.

"If everyones first kiss is like that, well then call me greedy." She joked, taking a sip of her drink.

"Ah ha, yes, sometimes they can be very overwhelming."

"Was that, ok?" She asked leaning forward and appearing to become worried.

"Wonderful, I hope we can perhaps do it again."

"We can." She looked down to the floor and a smile appeared across her lips, "I mean, we can do it all right now."

"Alison, please don't say things you may regret in the morning."

"This might be your last night here, with us and I don't want to be filled with regrets of the what if's and why didn't I's." She looked at me with the same determined eyes as before.

"Maybe we can discuss this after dinner. For now, enjoy the moment and afterward we've got some food in our bellies and such, you might change your mind."

She finished her drink and nodded at me, clearly a little annoyed by my answer and stood up to leave. Grabbing her gently by the wrist, I pulled her back and stood up myself. Her eyes were glassy again, as if she were ready to cry and that was the last thing I wanted to do.

"Please don't be upset with me."

"It's fine, if you don't think of me that way, it's fine, I'd rather not face the embarrassment of being rejected."

"Alison, I have not rejected you. I am only thinking what could perhaps become a huge mistake for you." I dropped my hand and she headed towards the door, before stopping and turning back to me.

"My Lord Quiver, you have no business to decide what is best or right for me. It is only I who get to make those choices but if you wish to not take me up on my offer, then again that is fine."

"I do not wish for you to dangle yourself in front of me and then be angry with me when I decline. I am declining out of respect and care for you. If you were to understand that and see I do want you," I paused biting back my words.

"I am much older than you and I have been where you are standing right now. That first time should be with someone you love and care for, not because it might perhaps be the end of the world tomorrow."

She snuffed and appeared to be holding back tears. I didn't wish to hurt her or cause her any harm and as much as it pained me to see her upset, I knew I was saying the correct words. Yes, I would have loved to undo the strings of her corset and feel her bare skin against my own and hear her call out my name through pleasure.

However, out of respect for her and knowing if she went down that path with me, she would never be truly fulfilled, and her name and life would be ruined by some form of scandal.

"Please Alison, I care for you a great deal."

"Not enough to love me though is it."

"Love is a strong word and should only be used when that true feeling is there screaming out at you. What you feel for me is no more than lust."

Harsh words and they were hard to swallow but I needed her to understand that if I left tomorrow and should never return, she would face the consequences and I couldn't leave her in the mess, alone.

"Thank you for the drink my Lord, I will be taking my leave now," She curtsied to me and then turned to open the door, "Good day to you."

Slamming the door behind her, I fell back into my chair and rubbed my hand over my face. Women were beyond frustrating and no matter how chivalrous you were, you were still in the wrong.

14

SHADOW

L eaving at first light was the first major point of our
plan, the second point was making sure no one spotted
us as we rode out. During dinner it appeared to be a little
tense, Quiver and Alison sat on opposite sides of the table
and clearly, she wasn't over this morning's rejection. I
wasn't the only one who spotted it and Mason tried to ask
Alison if she was alright and yet she would only answer with
short blunt words before excusing herself.

Part of me did think I should go and check on her before
I retired for the night as Giselle would have if she were here,
however it wasn't correct for a gentleman to visit a lady's
chambers and so I continued towards my room, passing
Alison's along the way.

Quiver was sat in the small drawing room area of my
room. It was one of the largest in the manor and Reid had
insisted I had it. Quiver was just sitting there his face
appearing unnerved and thinking deeply. Pouring myself and
him a glass of whiskey, I handed it to him before taking a
seat opposite, waiting for him to clear the silence.

"How do you do it?" He suddenly asked me, I looked at him puzzled and waited for him to finish the question. "How do you not go mad with passion while you are around her Highness? How do you keep yourself at bay and not from tearing the clothes off her and ravishing her where she stands?"

I laughed a little and took a sip of my drink before looking at my glass as I swirled the liquid around, wondering how I was to answer that.

"What Giselle and I have, it isn't just blind passion, or at least that's what I'd like to think."

"So even given the chance, you wouldn't do what you desired?"

"Oh, I would. Given the chance and we have come close to it once before. But if there's anything I have learnt these last few days without being near her is that, as soon as I get her back, I am never letting her leave my side again," I paused having a sip of my drink and letting my mind wander a little at images of Giselle. "I didn't realise how important she had become until she was no longer with me."

"Hmm, you have more self-control than me it seems."

He lowered his gaze and began to look deep into the slow burning fire of the fireplace, barely touching his drink.

"My self-control will be less when I do see Giselle again." I smiled a coy smile as flashes of her skin appeared in my mind, shaking my head a little as to remove them, I shifted my weight a little in my chair, so not to give any signs of my thoughts away, changing the subject quickly.

"Is this about Lady Alison?"

He looked at me with the corner of his eye and then took a large gulp of his drink.

"I take that as a yes then."

"She is insuperable."

"Well, yes, she's a woman, they have a talent for causing us confusion, angry and lustful thoughts."

"She offered herself to me and I stupidly said no, thinking about what her life would be if her family found out. I was a coward."

"Ah, so that's what this is about. Surely you can just explain that to her and all will be well."

"I'm afraid she won't see me, and I doubt I will see her again, at least not for a long time."

"Well, you never know what may happen Quiv, she may even see us out when we leave."

He rolled his eyes at me and then finished his drink before standing to take his leave. Bidding me a goodnight, I was left to my own thoughts, and they turned to Giselle, just like they did every night. And my mind wandered back to that night in the Tavern, where I had her sat on my lap and I was ready to burst and then to the morning after where I woke up to her in my arms.

Life didn't seem so scary and complicated then, yes, we still had the impending battle ahead, but I didn't see what happened at Elder Grove coming. Ayla had ruined everything and now I had to fight my way almost back into Minwed to get my lady back. Sighing, I finished my drink and then went to fill it with another, and then another and soon enough I was five glasses down and feeling the slight buzz.

Knowing I needed to try and get some form of sleep, I stayed in the armchair deciding that would be my bed for the night, even if there was a large four poster bed just across the room, I didn't want to sleep in one until I had Giselle back.

My eyes closed and I felt myself drift off into a black

abyss, the same place I found myself each time I shut my eyes. A place that would fade to black until I opened my eyes again.

This time however, my dream felt a little different, as if there were another present within my mind, waiting and watching me. The black mist swirling beneath my feet with each step I took, until the abyss began to light up and at the far end was a spotlight shining down and under it a large willow tree stood. It was beautiful and underneath it stood a large creature. As the creature came into view, I saw the long silver hair reflect off the spotlight and noticed the large staff with a deer skull placed on the top.

"Visiting my dreams now are we Guinevere."

"Shadowbane, I bring you a message."

"So, no hello and how have you been? Oh, I don't know dead."

She stood from under the tree and her form towered over me, her entire presence was enough for anyone to tremble in fear. Guinevere was the most powerful of the deities and one even I wouldn't wish to anger.

"You were lucky I sent your friends the powers they needed to pull you out from the Netherworld before Aithne got her claws in you."

"That's very kind of you."

Her confession took me back a little, she never intervened with any humans especially those who were at death's gates. Looking at her she appeared to be wearier then last we spoke.

"What was your message?"

"The girl Ayla, you must destroy her."

"Destroy her? After what she did to Giselle, I will do more than destroy her. But why is it you want me to?

Normally you guys don't worry yourselves with that of us humans."

She turned away from me and began walking back to the tree and I automatically followed. Although she was my mother by blood, I knew only of the old stories Countess Elizabeth would share with me, she wasn't really my mother, Elizabeth was as she had taken me under her wing and yet, I always felt a pull in my heart to know more of Guinevere.

"I cannot explain to you why, but things are already being set in motion. I can only give you this."

She tapped her staff onto the floor and a dagger suddenly appeared in her free hand. She handed it to me, and I examined it carefully, it was beautiful. The hilt was incrusted with Emeralds, all shades and sizes, they glittered in the spotlight as I turned it.

"Keep that safe and with you at all times, it will aid you in your fight again the darkness."

"But how do I,"

I looked up and Guinevere had vanished, frustrated I held the dagger up and then as if a click went off in my brain, my eyes opened, and I felt groggy and as if I hadn't got any rest. Looking out towards the window, I could see the faint change of colour in the sky, the sun was starting to greet us, and I darted off my feet.

Quickly changing my shirt, strapping Winterthorn to my side and placing on my chest and shoulder armour, I went to leave the room, checking I had everything and there on the bed was the dagger. I hadn't noticed it while I was preparing, and I wondered when it appeared there. It was in its sheath already, tying the leather string around my belt tightly so it didn't move, I left the room to join Quiver and Alary out by the stables.

The snow was already hitting the ground and the chill in the air made me wrap my fur lined cloak around myself tighter. Quiver stood outside the stables smoking a pipe and looked as if he was contemplating life as it went by. I guessed Alary was inside finishing prepping the horses or perhaps he hadn't joined us just yet.

"Did you manage to get any sleep?" I asked Quiver as I took the pipe from his hand and took in a deep breath of tobacco smoke.

"A couple of hours, maybe three."

I passed the pipe back to him and he breathed in the tobacco himself before dousing out the pipe and placing it into a pouch on his belt. Alary appeared out the stable door once he heard us talking and took my bag of provisions off me to tie to my horse's saddle. We waited then for just a few minutes before he guided the horse's out to greet us. The sun was slowly rising in the east as there was a light orange tint to the sky, but the snow didn't appear to be slowing down.

"We best leave before the snow gets worse, it's about a day's ride to the lake."

"Well lucky for us, we still have our horses so speed shouldn't be an issue."

Alary climbed onto his horse first and I followed suit, however Quiver still stood there clearly still thinking about something and although we needed to leave, I didn't think it fair to rush him.

"Lady Alison will understand, and you will see her again." I tried to give him some comfort and hopped I was correct in my assumption of where his mind was.

Watching as he just shook his head and then quickly mounted his horse, we were finally off. The snow had slowed, and it started to rain, great, that would make the journey more difficult due to the deep mud we would no doubt encounter. Reaching the main gates of the manor, Quiver turned his horse slightly and appeared to be looking back at the house.

There was a light on in one of the bedrooms and a figure stood there watching, perhaps it was Lord Reid or Mason, maybe even Alison. Whoever it was, it made Quiver stop for a second or two before he turned back towards us and raced off in front.

It took several hours for us to cross the outskirts of Minwed undetected, thankful for Mabon's magic once again. Although I would have enjoyed bumping into the King's men and having a few rounds with my sword, it was good to go undercover.

The sun was almost high up in the sky once we reached Lake Gloverose. The lake sat at the border between Minwed and The Withered Mountains, acting as a divider and if you were to travel south down its shores, you would enter the Kingdom of Solom and no one even ventured there for it was filled with great evil, dragons and the legends of Aithne and her demons.

"When shall we head towards the capital?" I asked, dismounting my horse and then tied her reins onto a tree branch.

"You will be staying here," Quiver uttered as he took out his bottle and drank something. "You will blow our cover if you are recognised."

"Hang on, you really think I will stay here while you go and get Giselle. I don't bloody think so."

"It's not a choice, it's an order."

"And since when do you think I take orders from you?"

"Since I out rank you."

I tightened my hands into fists as I tried to hold back my furious rage. I took a step forward and closed in on Quiver, as an Elf we were even height, but I was still a lot stronger and I knew if I wanted to, I could knock him on his ass. Just as I got close enough to him, a sword appeared under my chin and looking towards its bearing, Alary was standing there.

"I suggested you calm down my Lord, otherwise I won't hesitate."

"It's quite alright, Alary." Quiver said using two fingers he moved the sword as Alary lowered it.

"I will be coming with you to get Giselle."

"You understand if you come with us and are spotted, you will put the whole mission into jeopardy, and we may lose her forever. I understand you want to keep her safe, but you will only put her in danger." He paused and took a step back, "And we must not let Xandious know you are alive."

I took a deep breath to settle my emotions and my fingers unclutched, rolling my neck. I heard the pop as it clicked and then looked at Quiver as he turned away and walked to the edge of the lake.

"I am not happy about this Alex," I rarely used his name, but I felt it was needed this time, "What if you fail and I am none the wiser?"

"There are plans ready for that and Alary has been instructed to get the Princess out anyway necessary, even if that means leaving me. She is our priority, and I will do everything in my power to get her out of those walls and back to you," He turned to me and placed a hand on my shoulder, "You have my word on that. However, as I don't think you will be able to help yourself and follow us -"

He stopped and as I looked at him confused, he lifted his hand up and then blew an orange powder towards me.

Instantly I could feel myself sway and as I felt my legs give way, I met the ground with a thud. Dazed with my eyes heavy and ready to close, I saw the shapes of Quiver and Alary climb onto their horses, and they ran off into the distance, leaving me in this state, unable to move and slowly my eyes closed.

15

GISELLE

The day of the ball had arrived, and I was not excited in the slightest, being moved from my cell that morning and leaving Lady Adela was the last thing I wanted to do. She had confided in me many more secrets of the world, the creation of our world and it's creatures, things I didn't even know existed. I asked her many times what my father had been using her for and she just said for interrogation of prisoners, and she wouldn't go into more detail than that. Clearly upset by his actions and requirements.

Judith had brought with her a beautiful royal purple gown with her, along with two other lady maids and I tried to hold back tears as it reminded me of the dress I wore to the gathering at Governor Mason's home, where Shadow and I danced the night away.

Putting my hair up into a high bun and detailing it with sparkling flowers and jewels, she placed some rouge on my cheeks and a light pink colour on my lips, expressing the need to only bring out my best features. I wasn't in the mood to engage with any of it.

She herself looked a little disappointed I hadn't made my

escape. Forcing me to drink a cup of herbal tea that was infused with some form of magic spell to heal the remainder of my wounds, she expressed I needed to be fit and ready to dance as it would be required of me.

"Judith, will there be many at this party this evening?" I asked, trying to make some form of conversation while the maids dressed me.

"The King has invited all the nobles, the court, and their families. I believe he has an announcement of some sorts and wishes for everyone to hear."

"Hmm, will Lord Reid be there?"

"No, your Highness, I don't think so."

She fell silent then as she went to pulling the strings of my corset tight and then the ladies draped the dress over me and tied it up at the back. Placing a crown on top of my head, dressing my neck with diamonds and tear drop earrings, I was to play the part of the dear sweet Princess it would seem. Lastly, she tied a purple mask onto my eyes, the ribbon neatly done at the back, I was ready.

Finally dressed and ready to go, the maids left us, and Judith stayed to accompany me to the hall, along with an armed guard escort. I was on longer allowed to roam the halls alone, many feared me and so they should be.

The room although still dark and gloomy, it was lit with candles and gas lamps, the chandeliers cleaned and on display, just like they use to be. The hall had blues, blacks, red and royal purple drapes around the marble pilers and across the floor were what appeared to be black and blue rose petals.

Xandious darkness loomed over him as he sat at his throne, Ayla next to him drinking from a glass. She wore a slender black dress that hugged her body, her arms decorated with jewels as they ran up to meet the high neckline of her dress, a black mask to match her dress. She looked just as dark as Xandious appeared. A perfect pair it would appear they made.

"Announcing her royal Highness, Princess Giselle."

My announcement came and may bowed as I walked past the nobles and headed towards my seat, the throne to the right of Xandious. Bowing as I reached the few steps and then heading up to my seat, I was offered a drink and took it gracefully, grateful for the liquid as it touched and burnt my throat a little.

The orchestra began to play again, a dreary tune and although beautiful, it filled me with dread. Couples dressed in all dark shades, not one lady in pink or any light colours danced with their partners, this would be Xandious court now.

Everyone wore their masks so elegantly and kept their identity hidden. Once the music slowed and grew quiet, Xandious shot a look at his announcer, and he stamped a staff to the floor and the room fell silent.

"I have an announcement I'd like to make."

Here it comes and already I could feel my heart start to beat faster in my chest and ringing in my ears. I wanted to fly at Ayla in that moment, knowing what he was about to say.

"A few hours ago, before this evening's ball. Lady Ayla and I were wed, and I would like you all to now address her as her Royal Majesty Queen Ayla."

I also spat out my drink as I felt the waves of shock roll through my body, she had told me they were going to announce their engagement, not their wedding. I wanted to hurt her even more now than ever. A footman appeared from the side holing a cushion and on top of it was my mother's own crown and I could feel my blood begin to boil.

"It is my wish that my dear Giselle will grant us her blessing by placing the crown on to Ayla's head, allowing her to become our new Queen."

All eyes fell on me, and I wanted to scream and shove Xandious sword into his own gut, but I had to play it off, I couldn't cause a scene now as I would have been very much outnumbered. Gathering up my courage, I smiled towards Xandious and then stood up from my seat.

"It would be my honour."

Taking the crown off the cushion, I turned towards Ayla who appeared to be a little confused and scared as I took a step towards her. Marrying Xandious was one thing but wearing my mother's crown was something else entirely and I would make her pay for it eventually. Placing it on top of her head almost too roughly, Ayla winced a little in pain and then I stood out of the way as Xandious took her hand and showed her off to the crowd, who cheered and clapped.

Taking another glass of wine, I gulped it down in one and then had another, it was going to be a long night and I had to think of a way to escape somehow. Sitting Ayla back down, Xandious turned to everyone and raised his hand, quietening the crowd once more.

"Lady Ivy, where are you?" He beckoned and out she appeared from the crowd, curtsying low to the ground. "Is it true you sent Princess Giselle on a little errand two days ago which resulted her in being attacked and almost mortally wounded?"

She looked up at him shocked and then towards me, unable to speak and clearly confused by what Xandious said, even I was confused.

"No your majesty, I have no idea what you are talking about."

"Are you calling his majesty a liar?" Shouted Ayla.

"I have evidence you sent my daughter word that I needed to see her in the gardens. Where she was later attacked by some men and stabbed, where she almost bled to death. It was lucky the Queen found her in time. And you are very lucky your head is still attached to your head."

Xandious looked at me, playing the part of the doting father and I looked away from his gaze, disgusted by the sight of him.

"However, it would depend on your answer and if I will allow you to keep your head." He paused and took a step down towards her, before looking back at me with a sly smile and then back towards Lady Ivy.

"But as I don't think its right to kill a lady and as you have been a friend to me in the past. Lady Ivy, I hereby banish you from my court. Should you ever return, you will face the crimes against my daughter, either by my hand or hers. Do you understand?"

Xandious decreed as Lady Ivy looked onwards and appeared to be holding back her tears, I knew it was all for show, he didn't care that any harm had come to me, and I did feel slightly bad for her to face the full extent of blame for my attempted escape. My guard must have really built up quite a story for even Xandious to believe his word.

"Yes, your Majesty, thank you for your mercy."

As she curtsied again, a few guards came to her side and began escorting her out from the hall and Xandious took his seat again.

"If you ever try to escape again Giselle, your head will be displayed at the gates."

He said under his breathe while taking a drink. As Lady Ivy was escorted from the hall, the orchestra began to play again, and many couples started to dance.

I ignored his empty threats and allowed my mind to

wandered to that night at Governor Mason's party, where Shadow and I glided across the dance floor and at the time I hadn't come to realised how important he would become to me, how I wished he were here with me, to save me and rid me of these dark feelings.

"Your Majesty," A nobleman appeared at the foot of the small staircase and bowed low to the ground as he greeted us, "Your Highness, may I be allowed this dance?" The nobleman smiled a beautiful, dazzling smile and I swore I had seen it before, my stomach tightening as Xandious looked him up and down.

"Lord?"

"Matthew's, your Majesty. From Ashfield village."

"Ah, near the prison. Tell me, how is it up there? I have been intending to visit." Xandious knew how to behave in the company of guests, although many still feared him, he kept on his mask of pretence.

"As good as it is to be expected, Majesty. The prison is full, and everyone is paying for their crimes as we speak."

"Good, glad to hear it. Now, I believe you asked my daughter for a dance, well I grant you permission, she's been looking very sour since she arrived, and I hope a dance can cheer up her spirits."

I rolled my eyes at his attempt to come across as concerned and stood up from my seat and took Lord Matthew's hand happily. Happy to be aware from Xandious and my traitorous friend. We headed to the floor space where many were already moving into a waltz and as without any guidance, he placed a hand on my lower back and then another in my hand, leading us into a step to the right, back, left and forwards and then a small spin.

"Are you okay?"

I looked at him confused as to why a stranger would ask

me if I was fine. Have we met before? Perhaps he had been joining us for the dinners the past week? Maybe.

"Mabon's magic must be strong if you can't even recognise me."

That smile again and as I looked at him closely, his brown eyes flashed an Emerald green and I had to stop myself from shouting as I realised who it was.

"Quiver." I said low so no one heard. "How? What?"

"Do you think we would just leave you here?"

"Is it just you or?"

"My companion Alary, he is over there by the buffet talking to some ladies. We came as two lords, undercover, so no one would be able to suspect us."

He spun me again and we joined the other couples as they went into a large circle as the music picked up a little tempo and then slowed down again.

"We need to get you out of here."

"How are you going to do that, everyone is watching me, and the exits are blocked."

"Trust the process, we have a plan. Just be ready to make your escape when I give the signal. Now head back to your seat and wait."

He swung me out into a last spin and then dipped me as I spun backwards, wrapping his arm around my waist and held me tightly before bringing me back up and then kissing me gently on the hand. The music quietened to signal to all couples to change and or leave the floor.

Quiver disappeared into the crowd of guests, and I walked back to my seat slowly, Ayla eyeing me as I took my seat, Xandious had also disappeared and had I cared enough, I would have asked someone where he had gone.

"You dance beautifully Elle."

"It's Giselle to you."

I spoke coldly, taking a glass of wine from the footman standing beside me. Ayla fell silent once again and I eyed the crowd, looking to see if I could spot Quiver. He was nowhere to be seen and then a lady with a harp and a man with a large cello arrived onto the dance space, they were both dressed elegantly in beautiful shades of purples and pinks, as if they were flowers ready to bloom. The room fell silent and Xandious joined us once again, he looked flustered in the face and annoyed at something.

Good, I thought as the piano from the orchestra started playing, not even a whisper could be heard in the room. And then, the lady with the harp began plucking at her strings. It was a soft, gentle melody, as if you were watching the rain fall on a summer's day and then her partner joined in with the same soft tone as he played his instrument.

It was the most beautiful sound I had ever heard, tender. Just like a person's first kiss but also very sad and it made me think of Shadow once again, his image playing in my mind.

The night we laid upon that bed, talking endlessly through the night about life and our adventures and as the tune grew a little more intense but keeping that same softness, a flash of his death suddenly appeared in my mind, and I felt a tightness in my chest and my breath came in rapid motions. I wanted to run away, to flee from this memory and yet I was rooted to my spot, unable to think of anything else other than the agony I felt in that moment.

The song fell to its last few notes and a clap echoed throughout the hall, bringing me to concentrate on what was happening there and not something that was now in the past and unable for me to change.

The musicians took their bows and then removed their instruments from the space, and they were replaced then by two men, one being Quiver in his disguise and the other his companion I guessed. They carried a tall rectangle box with them, tall enough to fit a person as well as many other objects, a tall black hat and something that looked like a wand.

"Ladies and gentlemen!" Shouted Quiver as he and his companion took a bow.

"Behold! What wanders to be believed! I will dazzle you all with spells that you can't even begin to imagine," Quiver looked up at me with a smile and I was unsure as to what his plan was.

"Now, watch as I pull a white rabbit from my hat!"

His companion handed over the tall black hat with a wave of Quivers hand's and as he shouted a few words which sounded made up, he put his hand into the hat and then suddenly pulled out a fluffy white rabbit. To which the audience were astounded and a few clapped, some mumbled words of disbelief and others didn't seem all that bothered.

"Here you go my lady," Quiver handed the rabbit over to a lady who watched with her eyes filled with wonder and she cuddled the rabbit into her arms, happy and pleased with her surprised gift.

"Next, I will ask our King if he will be ever so kind as to help me for my next trick."

All eyes turned towards Xandious and even I wondered a little to see if he would in fact join in and to my surprise, he seemed to be thinking the whole thing over.

"What is it you'd have me do?" He asked, his voice giving away a little sign of annoyance.

"Please, pick a card," Quiver rushed up the stairs towards us and handed Xandious a pack of cards.

"Any card and you may only show it to yourself and your ladies. And then place it back into the deck."

Xandious pulled a card from the deck and showed Ayla first, then himself and then me. A Queen of Hearts, how ironic I thought. He slipped the card back into the pack and Quiver shuffled them at such lighting speed, even I was amazed, and then he began to pull out a card.

"Is this your card, your Majesty?" He asked, showing up as the Joker of Spades and Xandious shook his head. "Hmmm, very strange. Is this your card?"

He then pulled out a Nine of Clubs, again Xandious shook his head and the mumbling started amongst the crowd. Sensing the crowd's displeasure, I wondered how Quiver was going to finish this trick and turning on his heel, he headed back to his companion who then handed him the wand and he waved it around, a clockwise circle and then a flick into the air.

"Lady Ayla, if you would be ever so kind as to lift up your right foot and show it to the crowd."

Confused, she did as she was asked and lifted her foot and attached to the bottom of the sole was a card.

"Now, can you show the card to his Majesty and tell me is that your card?"

"Oh, my Goddess, your Majesty, it is your card!" Ayla exclaimed as she showed it to him and Xandious just nodded in reply and smiled a fake smile.

"Yes, that is my card. Why Lord Matthew, you are full of surprises aren't you. Whatever will you do to top your last trick."

I knew the accusation behind Xandious's words and the calculating tone within them. He was wondering how Quiver could complete such tricks and if he was in fact magical? I was glad of his annoyance because if Xandious knew there was an elf within the walls, there was no telling what would happen next.

"Now, for my last trick. I need a volunteer," He scanned the room and then laid his eyes upon me, this was the signal. "Your Highness, if you please."

As I went to get up, Xandious put his hand on me and stopped me in my tracks. I shot him a look of disgust and he tried to cover his own expression with that of concern.

"Your Majesty, her Highness is perfectly safe, please, it will only take a moment of her time."

Quiver bowed and his words seemed to have worked Xandious over and he let go of me and I was free. Walking down to meet Quiver at the end of the stairs I took his hand and he guided me towards the large rectangle box and his companion opened it up behind me while we faced the crowd.

"Now I hope you don't mind but for a few short moments our Princess will step into this box, and I will make her disappear. But don't worry! She won't be gone for too long, at least not as long last time." He shot me a wink and his dazzling smile before spinning me around and helping me step into the box, shutting the door behind me. The space wasn't very big and felt very constricting and I had absolutely no idea how this was even going to work as I had never seen such a trick before.

"Posical!" I heard a tap on the side of the box, "Gration!" Another tap, "Loheckle!"

And a loud bang hit the side of the box and suddenly a screen came flying across blocking my exit and I couldn't see anything,

"And here! You will find the Princess has been transported away."

A loud gasp fell through the air and although the sound was muffled, I heard the shock and the claps as they rang through.

"Now, don't worry everyone, I will bring her back in just a few short seconds." A little click as the door shut and then the taps began again, "Loheckle! Gration! Posical!"

But this time the screen did not disappear, it stayed firmly in place and then a shout and a scream could be heard. I was feeling disorientated and didn't like not being able to see fully. I wanted to know what was happening.

"Where is she!?" I could hear Xandious' voice burst through the noise and I felt my heart begin to beat faster. "Lord Matthew's, you bring her back at once!"

Even without me looking I already knew he had flown from his seat and was marching closer to Quiver, perhaps even holding him up by the shirt trying to show he was the overprotective father he claimed to be. Again, three taps went onto the box and the shouting of the same three words and still nothing changed. I was growing anxious and wondering where this was going to go.

"Perhaps her Highness is simply hiding? Let us all look for her shall we." A voice, the same Lord from dinner that one day rang in my ears.

Suddenly out of nowhere the box began to move and I had to brace myself on the sides, wondering if I was going to fall out and for a few minutes I was being pushed backwards and a sick feeling entered my stomach. And finally, after coming to a sudden stop, the wall behind me vanished and I fell out almost instantly into the arms of Quiver's companion and stood next to him was the Lord from dinner, the one who gave me the note.

They helped lift me up and then I had a cloak thrown across my shoulders, Judith handed me a satchel with goddess knows what inside and before I had a chance to ask her, I was being pushed and almost dragged out of the corridor we ended up in and then the Lord moved a tapestry from the wall and behind it was a dark descending staircase, I had never seen this staircase before and was hesitant to move.

"Your Highness, you must go, quickly!" The urgency in his voice made me worry, "Please, we will see each other again."

"But what about Quiver?" I asked, looking at his companion.

"Don't worry about him my lady, he has his ways, and we will meet him outside."

Shouting began and loud thundering noises of feet sounded through the air and without even another thought, the Lord almost pushed me through the doorway and Quiver's companion helped study me and down we went, walking as fast as our feet would take us. Light appeared at the end of the staircase and there at the bottom stood my guard. He quickly ushered us to follow him down a corridor, through another hidden door and then we came to a small metal gate.

"There's a boat you can use to get out of the city, once you are past the canal fork, go left and you will find your horses there waiting for you." My guard looked at me with sincere eyes and I wondered if I had judged him poorly.

"Your Highness, here." He handed me the sword I had taken from him days ago, it was wrapped in its own scabbard and etched on the leather was my family crest. The doe, the crescent moon and the feather, all symbols of the new hope I wanted to bring to Nimra.

"Until we meet again."

I said as he then opened the metal gate and Quiver's companion was the first to step out, checking to see if the coast was clear and then I followed. Hopping into the boat, he rowed the boat quickly and almost at lightning speed.

This must have been a smuggler's way into the castle, that was the only explanation I could think of as to why I didn't know it existed. As we exited outside, the cold air hit me suddenly and I wrapped my cloak around me tightly, grateful for the fact it wasn't snowing.

It was around ten minutes or so when an alarm sounded throughout the city. The only available lights were that of the gas lamps hanging off buildings and on the city streets. I kept my head down and prayed to the Goddess Guinevere no one would stop us and soon enough we came to the fork in the canal.

One way was towards another part of the city while the other looked to be more of the outskirts. I just hoped Quiver had been able to get away when the panic started, and I hoped Xandious didn't lay a hand on him otherwise that would be one more thing to add to my lists of reasons to kill him.

We came to a narrow waterway and the gate appeared to already open, no doubt already sorted for us when we got here. Ducking down under the stonework and out the other side, I looked up and saw the high walls of Minwed, no guard posted at this exit and I wondered if that too had been sorted for our escape.

Perhaps there were many within the castle walls who had been involved with all this all along. We rowed for another fifteen minutes as the castle flew into the distance and then finally, we came to a slow pace.

"As you helped rescue me, I should know your name please."

"Alary your Highness. Captain Alary, I am Lord Quiver's second in command."

"Well thank you Captain Alary. I owe you a great debt of gratitude."

"You owe me nothing, your Highness. I am duty bound to follow my Lord and he ordered we save you and so we did."

"And what a show you both put on, you even had me fooled."

I tried to lighten the situation although I was still filled with dread and hoped I would be able to see my friend again and express my dear thanks. Nearing the edge of a snow-covered grass plain, many of the plants were already dead but there standing tied next to a tree were three horses and a figure of a person awaiting our arrival.

As Alary pulled us towards the shore and then got out smoothly, he held his hand out towards me to help lift me out. He lifted me through the air as if I weighed nothing and then placed me down on the ground. My feet were already freezing, and I longed for my boots to protect me against the cold.

"Took you long enough."

Quiver. Delight fell through my body as I raced over to him and wrapped my arms around him, embracing him in a hug and this time he hugged me back with a small squeeze. He was back to his usual appearance, his beautiful Emerald eyes sparkled in the moonlight as did his golden-brown skin.

Releasing him, he smiled at me and then turned to look at Alary who was no longer in his disguise either. He too had the same golden-brown skin of Quiver, his hair was short and charcoal while his eyes grey, giving off a beautiful contrast of colours.

"We cannot stay here; they will be out searching the wilderness. We must head back to Lake Gloverose before sunup."

Quiver lifted me up onto a horse without a word and then onto his, Alary untiring the reins and then mounting his. I didn't know how long we had until sun rise as I had become so disorientated since the hidden box trick, I just followed Quiver in front and Alary stuck to the back and we rode fast throughout the night, and only briefly stopping to slow down and to check our surroundings, until finally we reached Lake Gloverose and the sun was starting to rise.

Dismounting my horse, I patted her on the side of her neck and gently ran my hands down her neck, she gave a huff and Alary came and took her reins off me. Looking at Quiver he gave me a nod and then looked past my shoulder, following his eyeline I turned and saw someone standing at the lake shores.

They were turned away and watching the sunrise, clearly lost in their own thoughts. I took a step towards them, partly in disbelief as to what I was seeing, was I truly seeing someone? Or had I just become delirious from the adrenalin and the rush from the whole entire night?

I could feel my breath slow down as I took a few more steps. The sky turned into beautiful shades of pinks and oranges, small wisps of clouds flowed through the sky, and you wouldn't have believed it was a winter morning. The snow crunched against my feet and although the sting was still there, I continued. And as if the person finally heard me, they turned their head just as the sun rose into my eyeline.

Covering my eyes a little with my hand to block it out, I watched the person turn fully towards me and it was as if everything felt whole again, the feeling welling me up deep inside, filling me with warmth and joy. The sun moved higher up and there I could see fully.

It was him.

Was I dreaming again? Was this real?

Or a figment of my imagination again?

Was it really him?

Shadow.

My Shadow.

"Shadow!"

I cried out, running towards him and as I almost collided with his body, half expecting to fly through it as I had done previously and fall deep into the lake. But this time, warm strong arms wrapped around me and lifted me up off the ground. My arms wrapped around his neck as I rested my forehead against his, closing my eyes and feeling the tears fall freely. We almost did a spin on the spot as he brought me down to the ground and without a single word or thought, I brought my lips to his and kissed him passionately and deeply. I was filled with longing and the loneliness I had felt the past couple of weeks slipped away into nothingness.

I was home.

I was where I belonged.

16

SHADOW

S he was in my arms, finally, where she belonged. Her warm body was pressed against mine and her lips were where they belonged, on mine.

Wrapping my arms around her tightly I brought her up off the floor and wanted nothing more than to ever let her go again. It felt like an eternity I wasn't at her side, protecting her with every breathe and watching her being taken away in that carriage was heart-breaking. I never wanted to stop kissing her, but I could feel eyes upon us and as I pulled away and placed her gently back down on the ground, Quiver appeared.

"Sorry to cut your reunion short but we must get going before the King sends out his men to follow us."

"He's right, it's not safe for you Giselle while we stay still. Where do you suggest we go, Quiv?" I asked as Giselle turned to face him and I wrapped my arm around her waist, keeping her next to me.

"We are to head to The Withered Mountains, to my home. The King will be unable to find us there."

"We are to meet the Queen?" Giselle asked with a hint of a smile.

"Yes, I fear I have a lot of explaining to do. You see Princess, I went against orders to come and rescue you after myself and Mabon brought Lord Shadow back from reaching the Neverworld."

She turned to look at me quickly with sorrow in her eyes and studied me closely, looking almost at every inch of my body as she examined me.

"I'm fine Princess," Taking her hand, I kissed it gently and then linked it in mine, "Mabon knew what he was doing."

"Good, I will thank him when I see him. How long will it take us to ride to the mountains?" She directed her question at Quiver as Alary came to join us.

"With you on horseback with Lord Shadow, we might be a little slower than we'd like, but we can be there by night-fall if we leave now."

"Then let's move."

She stood firm in her order, and I felt my heart pitch a little with pride, the King had not succeeded in breaking her, which I knew he would have tried. Mounting our horses, I lifted Giselle up first and then sat behind her, my arms now enclosing her and keeping her safe against me. I meant when I said I would never leave her side again, unless death did take me.

With a kick of my heel, we were off following Quiver and Alary at our rear, the sun was starting to rise high in the sky by the time we made it a quarter of the way and I could feel Giselle slump a little in front of me as she rested her head against me and her breathing slowed, she was asleep.

I wondered how she managed to sleep in that castle, surrounded by people who she could no longer trust. Was she tortured? Treated poorly? I had so many questions but at the same time I didn't want to ask to many in-case it upset her. Her feelings were important to me and deep down I knew she'd tell me everything eventually, especially when she felt we were safe once again.

Trekking through the woods that neared the mountains was a mind field on its own and if it wasn't for our two Elven guides we would have been lost instantly. Our horses weren't as fast as before and I was slightly grateful for it, it meant I could learn more of the layout and how you would come and go from the hidden world.

"Are we almost there?"

Giselle's voice startled me, I hadn't realised she had woken up as she was still pressed against me, a hand resting against my thigh, and I don't think she realised how close she was to me.

"Not long now Princess, an hour or two." Shouted Alary.

She shifted a little to make herself more comfortable and her buttocks rubbed against me as she moved, and I felt a twinge in my trousers. Taking a deep breath, I had to calm myself as this was not the time nor the place. She laughed a little under her breath as she leaned against me once again.

"Sorry, am I too close?" She asked, turning her head up towards my neck, her warm breath lashing at my skin.

"I don't think you could get any closer." I joked back, keeping my eyes ahead.

"Oh, I could think of a way we could be much, much closer." Her hand moved up a little more and again I had to calm myself.

"Giselle," I uttered as I closed my eyes for a second and then opened them again to look down at her, "I am trying to steer this horse, behave please."

She laughed again and then moved her hand completely and the cold appeared where her hand was.

"As you wish."

"Damn Princess, you will be the death of me."

Once I calmed my heart rate, I found myself just enjoying being in her company again. Enjoying the simple moments and although we were silent, it was comfortable.

"Did he hurt you?" I finally asked as the question was burning me up.

"No, well not as much as you would have thought. Right at the start he did but I was ok."

"I will kill him for even laying a finger on you."

"I know, but I'm ok. We are ok." She placed a hand against my cheek and smiled up at me before leaning up and kissing me lightly on the cheek.

"Giselle, I wanted to come to you as soon as I woke up, but Quiver and the others suggested I stay behind and I hated waiting at that lake, praying you'd return but also thinking of the worse."

"Seeing you standing there I thought I was starting to lose my mind again."

"Again?"

"Yes, I saw you once back at the castle on my old balcony. I had been drugged that night so it might have just been that, but you were there and so close to touch. It almost broke me thinking I'd never see you again," She paused and looked away from me, wiping a tear from her eye, "After I was captured, I thought you were dead, and the pain was unbearable."

I held the reins in one hand and wrapped my arm around her tighter, pulling her closer into me and her scent caught under my nose. Roses, she always smelt of roses and fresh rain.

"Well, I'm here now and I am never letting you go."

Looking up to face me again, I brought my lips down to meet hers and kissed her gently, I was never letting her go again.

"We are almost there you love birds." Alary shouted as he came up beside us, winking at me as Giselle began to blush a little.

As we passed a clearing of tall oak tree's which surrounded us, concealing us from the world. And then finally we came to the large weeping willow tree with its long droopy branches dipping themselves into a small stream.

Quiver dismounted from his horse and instructed us to do the same, guiding his horse under the branches and as we followed. Moving a branch or two out of the way for Giselle, she went in first and I heard her breath catch as she saw the sight before her.

"What is this magic?" She asked as her feet walked above the water.

"This is Elven magic your Highness," Spoke Alary who came behind me. "The entrance to our world is hidden and only few know of this way in."

"I will keep your secret don't worry. I have never seen magic like this before."

She was in awe as I watched her take careful steps, unsure of where to put her feet. Taking her by my free hand, I linked my fingers with hers and squeezed a little, for reassurance and she smiled back at me. I was going to get use to this feeling of being able to hold her hand and not have to walk on eggshells around her.

"Will Queen Leena be expecting us?" I asked as we came through the other side.

"Eh, I think she knows." Giselle's voice broke as we

came out from the other side of the tree, surrounding us were Elven soldiers and the didn't look very impressed or happy with us.

"Prince Alex, the Queen summons you and your guests to her court."

"Prince?"

Giselle's eyes darted to Quiver as he just shrugged and began to follow the soldiers. Our horses now taken from us, we walked at a rather quick pace, and it was a little difficult to keep up, but we managed it. Giselle appeared to be very overwhelmed, and I could see the wheels turning in her mind as she looked around the place, the city hidden under the mountain and unknowing to her that Quiver was of royalty.

Once we arrived at Queen Leena's home, a few soldiers continued to escort us while the rest stayed outside. I still had hold of Giselle's hand and as much as I wanted to explain everything to her, it would have to wait.

Queen Leena rose from her seat as we walked through the door and into a large dining hall. You wouldn't believe this room existed as her home appeared to be much smaller on the outside. Magic, I presumed.

"You deliberately disobeyed me after I ordered you to stay out of this."

The room shook a little as Queen Leena shouted towards Quiver and then looked at us, her dark green eyes appearing to be blazing with rage until she spotted Giselle standing there.

"My apologises your Highness," She directed her voice to Giselle, "I am happy you are safe, but my brother should not have got involved in your affairs."

"If it wasn't for your brother, I would most certainly still be locked in that castle, being tormented and potentially on my death bed," Giselle let go of my hand and stood in front of the three of us, standing her ground.

"I understand your rule is absolute but what your brother did was brave, and he almost died saving me, I owe him a great debt and will not be stopped from paying that. Now, I know we are guests in your household, but I will be treated the same as any royal as will my companions, that includes your brother whom I had no idea was a prince until moments ago. I was always taught that Elves were kind, welcoming folk but after been escorted here by your guards I am starting to question that knowledge."

Queen Leena appeared to be shocked by how she was being spoken to and it made me laugh a little under my breathe. Giselle appeared to be a lot more grown up since before the village attack and I was happy to see her speaking her mind.

"My apologies again your Highness." Queen Leena sat back down as she spoke in a softer voice. "We are a welcoming community and I understand how frightening it must have been for you to be trapped in that prison, but it still remains the same, my brother disobeyed my orders and will answer to them."

"You will not be punishing him, he is now under my protection and as it stands, I believe my claim is far greater than your own as Elves no longer exist."

It was going to be a power play and Queen Leena's eyes began to blaze again and the room started to shake a little, her anger clearly building. I looked at Quiver who looked surprised by Giselle's words and I feared he had no idea how to defuse this situation.

"Your royal Highnesses, please do not argue," Alary was the one who stepped forward, trying to break the tensions, "It has been a long few days and I feel emotions might be a little high as we are all tired and weary from our journey and you yourself Queen Leena, you must have been sick with worry for your brother."

Queen Leena tutted and turned her head away from us and Giselle herself sighed and rolled her eyes, clearly not happy with how the conversation was going.

"Perhaps after some food and rest, we can discuss the events of the last few days, as I fear this may turn into an argument when there need not be one. We are all on the same side."

Alary spoke great sense and it made me realise why Quiver kept him as his right-hand man, he was a great diplomate and within seconds it appeared the room had stopped shaking and the tension soothed.

"Yes, you are quite right," Giselle was the first to speak, "My apologies Queen Leena, it has been a long journey and I appreciate and am thankful for you opening your doors to me."

Giselle curtsied and although Queen Leena didn't look at us again, I was glad the argument didn't happen and thankful I didn't have to step in.

"Marcus," Queen Leena beckoned to an elf stood at her right, "Get some rooms sorted for our guests, they will be with us for as long as they need."

"Yes, your Majesty." Marcus bowed and quickly left the room.

"Alex, you are banned from leaving the mountain until I say so. Your Highness, my home is your home until you no longer have need of it. Alary, please educate the Princess of our customs. I will be hosting a gathering in due course to celebrate our guest's arrival and I hope we may be able to get to know each other a little more by then."

Queen Leena bowed a little towards Giselle as she left

the room, walking between us four and slamming the door behind her. I heard the sigh of relief as Quiver almost ran over to Giselle and took her by the hands and then getting down on his knees.

"Thank you, Princess."

"Do get up you idiot. Your sister is quite a fisty one, isn't she?" Giselle laughed as we all did, "Now where can we get some food, I'm starving!"

"Right this way, we can raid the kitchen while we wait for your rooms to be ready."

My stomach growled in protest as I realised, we hadn't eaten since the day before and I knew I could quite happily eat anything I got my hands on, Giselle included. Heading to the kitchens, we were greeted happily and passed trayfuls of whatever was available.

17
QUIVER

"Perhaps I was a little reckless in my pursuit to rescue Giselle?"

"A little is an understatement."

Alary handed me a glass of whiskey as we had retired to my study once Giselle and Shadow were shown to their rooms. I doubted very much they would spend time alone however as judging by their reunion I didn't think Shadow would ever let her go again.

"Leena did seem pretty pissed didn't she." Taking a sip of my drink, Alary sat opposite me in one of the plush armchairs that overlooked the Elven city.

"I think you are going to have a lot of making up to do if I'm honest Alex. She isn't one to forgive so easily as well."

"I know, I know but I felt it my duty to rescue Giselle. We need allies on our side once we come out of hiding."

"If we ever come out of hiding, it won't be in Giselle's lifetime. Unless the Queen decides otherwise."

Rubbing my temples, I felt a headache begin to brew and although Elves could function fine with little sleep, I knew it was coming up to that time where I would need a good night's rest and to recharge.

The magic I used during the ball drained me and I was still surprised to be standing up straight at all. Sensing my change, Alary finished up his drink and excused himself soon after and although I would have happily stayed talking for the rest of the night, my bed was calling me and I was grateful once my head hit the pillow and I was out like a light, welcoming sleep.

～

WAKING up the following afternoon as a welcomed change to the early mornings and I hadn't realised I slept for so long until one of Leena's maids came to find me, explaining that Leena had requested my presence. I wasn't going to rush however as I desperately needed a wash and luckily, we had showers here, which meant a bath wasn't required and it also meant I could wash quickly.

Once clean and dressed in proper attire, no longer my 'ranger' clothes as Giselle had called them, wearing a soft cotton white shirt and black trousers with canvas black shoes, I felt a little bit better, especially after my long sleep.

"You rang?"

Entering Leena's chambers, she stood looking out her balcony doors with her back leaning against the door frame holding a hot cup of herbal tea.

"You disobeyed me and almost died in the process."

"Ah, hello brother, it's so lovely for you to be home. Oh, how I've missed you."

"This isn't a joke, Alex. My advisors have all said you should be punished for your disobedience but as you're my brother and heir to the throne, I won't be doing anything like that, even though I should penalise you." She turned to look at me as I joined her near the doorframe. "You risked exposing us by going to Giselle's aid and that's not ok and something I don't think I will be able to forgive."

"Leena, the King didn't see past my spells. We were perfectly safe, Mabon had given myself and Alary a powerful potion, even Giselle herself didn't know it was me."

"How did she know it was you then?"

"She recognised my eyes. Honestly, sister, you can trust her."

"I don't know, she is still her father's daughter."

"But she is also her mothers."

Taking Leena's free hand in mine, I held it tightly, looking at her with tender and loving eyes. She was starting to look like our mother more and more with each passing day and it worried me that she would face the same fate she did. She removed her hand shortly after, walked over to a small table in her room and placed her cup down and then turned to face me once more.

"You are to always keep an eye on Giselle. I will have guard's watching also, I know you say I can trust her, but I am still sceptical. I will always protect our people and if I feel she is a danger, I will have her escorted out with her memories erased. Do you understand?"

"Yes of course, I understand."

Leena waved her hand as to shoo me away and although I was waiting for more of a scolding, I was pleasantly surprised when she didn't kick my ass or worse. Leaving her to her thoughts, I headed down towards the main hall to perhaps find Giselle or Shadow and alas they weren't there. Perhaps they were still resting, Giselle most likely needed to sleep away the terrors of the castle and her father, recharge just as I did.

As I wandered the halls of my home, well more Leena's than mine, I came to the realisation I was most likely on house arrest now and when Giselle and Shadow took their leave, I would be staying here and that didn't sit right with me.

"There you are!"

Alary shouted as he came around a corner and quickly grabbed me by the shoulders, looking panicked and unsure.

"There's something you need to see."

Almost pulling my arm out of my socket and dragging me down a few corridors and towards the stables, I could barely keep up as he was a little faster than usual. What on earth had got into him? I had never seen him this panicked, even when we went into hiding, he was normally very cool, calm and collected.

"What in Goddess name has gotten into you?!"

I shouted as he almost pushed me through the stable doors and there standing in the middle of the stable was Lady Alison. At first, I felt happiness fill my lungs and then suddenly confusion and great anger. How did she get here?

"Alison, what are you doing here?"

"I – eh, well, I followed you."

"Wait, what? How?"

Turning towards Alary who stood there just as confused as me and then back at Alison, I couldn't even come up with a reasonable excuse or idea as to how she managed to follow us.

"Mabon, he eh, he gave me a spell after you left that helped me follow your steps."

"I found her wandering our border this morning, she's

lucky the guards didn't find her as she would have been killed on sight."

"And they would have been killed for such an act." I took a few steps closer towards Alison and then took her hands in mine, she was shaking a little, nerves most likely.

"Alison, it's incredibly dangerous for you to have followed us. You could have been seen or worse. I'm happy you are here and it's lovely to see you but once Queen Leena learns of this, she won't be pleased."

"And she's already pissed off as it is." Said Alary as he rolled his eyes and turned to leave, "My Lord, we will have to be extra careful with Lady Alison being here."

"You're right, as usual Alary. Alison, I am glad you're here, but Mabon should never have given you such a spell, you could have been followed."

"Or your life might have been in danger, and no one would have known." Alary leaned against the stable door-way, his arms crossed with an annoyed look on his face.

"The Queen won't be impressed, perhaps Lady Alison should stay with me? It might be best, but I'm sure the Princess will be happy to see her first."

"Giselle?! She's here? She's safe?" Alison's eyes lit up with joy at the mention of her friend and she let go of my hands to clap almost. "Oh, I must see her, please, it's been so long, and I have missed her."

"I don't know if that will be a good idea, Alison." I replied crossing my arms.

"Please Alex, last time I saw her was when she was going off to battle."

With a deep sigh, I knew this was going to bring us more trouble, especially with Leena as outsiders weren't welcome and she would be deeply hurt by Mabon's somewhat betrayal by giving away our hiding place. I just hoped no one else followed Alison when she entered here.

"Alright, but you will have some explaining to do to Leena should she see you."

"And no doubt, she has already got wind that someone new has arrived."

Alary left us then as he headed back to his post, whereas my nerves were started to grow as panic started to ensue. I was glad Alison had somehow snuck in, after our final good-bye, I now had another chance to fix things.

"How would she now?"

Alison asked taking my hand in hers as I lead her out the stables and back towards the house.

"Trust me, nothing gets past Leena."

18

GISELLE

F eeling the silk fabrics against my clean legs and the feather blanket over me made me smile with such glee as I slowly opened my eyes.

Shadow lay next to me softly breathing away as we had fallen asleep talking about what had happened that day at the village and how Mabon and Quiver had managed to bring him back. It stung my heart to think he was so close to Aithne's gate, and I hated how I was taken from him so suddenly.

He tried to ask me questions about Xandious and my time at the castle but didn't appear to pry too much. I knew however, I had to tell him about Lady Adela, after all they were friends. But the fear in me of him running back towards the castle to save her was overwhelming. I couldn't lose him again.

Looking up at the ceiling and then around each side of the canopy bed we slept in, concealed by sheer fabrics of pinks, whites and pale greens. The sunlight shone through the room and as it hit the curtain's they sparkled a little in the light, magic.

Shadow stirred next to me, rolling on his side to face me and took a deep breathe in, still sound asleep. Not wanting to wake him, I began to shift out of the bed and sat on the edge.

"And where do you think you're going?"

His voice groggy and still sounding asleep, looking over my shoulder I saw he still had his eyes closed but his face had a beautiful smile placed on it.

"Sometimes us ladies have things to do, such as use the lavatory. I will be back in just a moment, don't you worry."

Leaving him there to sleep as I went to freshen up and really take in the view of the bedroom quarters I had been graciously given, I felt a sense of joy and peace for a moment or two. I wasn't in a damp, cold and dark space anymore. This place was filled with beautiful sunlight, the greenery of fresh plants and it felt as if each little decoration had a purpose. The room was decorated in sage greens, pastel shades of pinks and blues and just felt very soothing and calming as you entered.

Washing up at a basin hidden behind a screen as I finished cleaning myself up, the cotton camisole clinging to my body in all the right places. I was very surprised and slightly glad when Shadow kept his hands to himself and only brought his arm around me once we started to feel drowsy and fall asleep. He had suggested going to his own room, but I commanded him not to leave. I didn't want to be alone.

"Oh, I beg your pardon, your Highness."

A maid surprised me as she wandered in, and I appeared from behind the screen. I must not have heard her knock. She came in holding a tray with a teapot on, two cups and what appeared to be some sort of biscuits. Setting them down on one of the side tables in the middle of the room, she smiled sweetly at me and curtsied.

"Thank you,"

"I'm sorry if I woke you, your Highness but Queen Leena insisted you get something to start your day. She did exclaim you were not to be disturbed and she will be ready to receive you once you are well rested."

Curtsying again, the maid turned to leave and before I could even respond, she was out the door as quickly as she arrived. Grateful for the hot drink I poured myself a cup and decided to take it out onto the balcony, to view the Elven city from above and to allow Shadow some more rest.

The landscape was breath-taking, although many had crossed the Withered Mountains before you would never have believed this magical world existed right under your nose. Small dancing lights appeared across the sky as smoke from chimneys rose into the sky, the clouds wispy and white. No snow in sight, only beautiful sunlight and the warmth of a spring day.

Again, magic no doubt and it brought my such delight, snow and I were no longer friends as it only held sad memories. Warm arms appeared around me, and I relaxed my body into him as his bare chest raised with each easing breath. I could get used to this and would never leave.

"You said you'd only be gone a few minutes and I now find you out here basking in the sunlight."

"Can you really blame me? It's beautiful here."

Taking a sip of my tea and feeling the warm liquid fill my insides, it relaxed me down to my core and I couldn't quite understand as to why it did.

"I overheard that lady say you are not to be disturbed and to be well rested. Is that what you want? To be left alone to rest."

Placing my cup on the balcony edge, I turned my body around in his arms and looked up at him as he looked down at me with his soft icy blue eyes as a strand of hair fell across his face, his beard appearing to have grown back since the ball.

"I would like to explore. I think it's a rare sight to be in a city filled with Elves, don't you think?"

"You are the only rare sight I need to see."

A blush appeared across my cheeks as he lifted my chin up and our lips met. It was just a quick, simple kiss and almost felt as if we had done it so many times before. Everything felt different now, I didn't feel that same feeling of pushing Shadow away, the fear of falling deep and inevitably in love with him. And quite frankly I wasn't sure why.

Perhaps it was the circumstances we had come to, the near-death experiences and the losing of one another. Perhaps it was something more and I could sense he too was thinking the same.

Pulling away from me and taking a step back, he looked out into the distance of the city and chuckled lightly.

"What's so funny?"

"You know, they don't think I'm real right? I'm just a legend, a folk tale."

"Why would they think that?"

Shadow was just a Lord as far as I was aware, but Lady Adela did say he was not fully human and it was playing at the back of my mind, maybe now was the best time to ask him? What he truly was.

"Shadow,"

Looking at him as he stood there with his back towards me, his back covered in the scars of war and the pale redness of wounds healed. He was such a beautiful man with his broad shoulders, I could have stared at him all day and once he turned around, my breath caught, the sunlight hitting his beautiful silver hair perfectly it almost shined like starlight itself.

"While I was at the castle, I tried to escape and it didn't end as well as planned," I paused and he looked concerned but listened, "I was attacked and I managed to kill my attackers but was mortally wounded, and once found I was thankfully healed but was taken to the dungeons. There, I found my cell mate," I stopped again, wondering if I should continue, "Lady Adela was there."

His face went from shock, to angry and then to stoic. He wasn't given anything away and he kept quiet, waiting for me to finish.

"She confessed to me about what she was, and she also mentioned to me that it's much harder to kill you as you are not – fully human. Is this true?"

"Damn that woman," He uttered before turning away from me completely. "I don't know what I am fully Giselle. My father was an elf from dragon's peek and my mother is,"

He stopped and, in that moment, I rushed to him and wrapped my arms around him, my chest to his back and he placed a hand on top of mine.

"My mother is the Deity, Goddess Guinevere."

I waited a few seconds allowing his confession to sink in and I felt his body tense as the silence grew. Awaiting my response and I truly felt no shock, it felt as if the puzzle had finally clicked into place and the realisation of something I had already known deep within woke up.

"So, does that make you a God?"

Letting go of him, I came to his side, and he kept his eyes on the horizon, clearly not wishing to look at me for fear of judgement.

"That would explain a lot, the ears for one and the fact you could see past my cloaking spell and why Seniya was so eager for me to stick by your side. Hmmm, do you have the same powers as Guinevere? Or as an elf? What happened to your father?"

I paused for a moment so he could take in all my questions and that's when it hit me in the chest.

"How old are you then?"

He looked stunned as he caught my eye line, confusion hitting me as I tried to put the pieces together even more.

"I'm a little older than you, not by hundreds of years don't worry but I will age slowly now. It's a gift but also a curse. As for magic, I can do some spells but not many and especially not as grand as the Goddess."

"Did she leave you here? How did you get to Countess Elizabeth?"

"I fear you're going to have many questions, so how about we go inside, get you another hot drink and you may ask me as many things as you like and I will try my best to answer them but Giselle, please,"

He took my hands in his and looked at me with sincere eyes, "I don't know all the answers myself. Guinevere left me shortly after I was born so I only know what Fenella and the Countess told me."

"Goddess Fenella? Have you met her?"

"I have met all three, aside from Aithne thankfully."

Shocked and wanting to know more, I also jumped with a little joy as Shadow took my hands and led me back into the bedroom. Sitting me down in one of the armchairs either side of the table, he poured me a fresh cup of tea and handed me a biscuit or two as he took the seat opposite, pouring himself a cup and we sat in silence for a second or two before I couldn't hold it anymore.

"I need to know everything. I already know some things,

but I feel this is a whole other side of you I didn't even know existed."

"Giselle, there's not much you don't already know. I was born in the middle of Bathmod Ruins. I know that much, and Fenella took me soon after Guinevere gave me life. My father, I have no idea who he was or where he is today, even if he is still alive. Elizabeth once told me Guinevere fell in love with him shortly after she found him wounded in her woods and she healed him. Or so the story goes."

I was on the edge of my seat, excited to hear more. I felt almost like a child who was listening to a new bedtime story for the first time, and I was learning a whole new side of Shadow and falling more for him every second.

"Elizabeth would spend many years paying tribute to the Goddesses, begging for a child and well, Fenella answered by giving me to her. She gave Elizabeth a letter detailing my origin, my name and who my parents were but that was all she knew. I found a lot of it myself. Once I was around ten years old, Fenella appeared to me in a dream and told me more of my history and to call on her should I ever need her."

He paused, taking a sip of his drink and then almost shoved an entire biscuit into his mouth.

"I learnt that my father was from Dragon Peak mountains, and this was before the time where Elves went into hiding and the Goddess still walked the world. I'm not too sure when I was conceived but it was shortly after Bathmod was destroyed and Elves hid themselves away. As far as I am concerned however, my mother is Countess Elizabeth, she raised me and taught me how to be a proper gentleman and if it wasn't for her, your mother and her would never have paired us together."

"I am in awe of you, Shadow. This is truly amazing!

Think of all the things you can do, the things you didn't even know about. Mabon might be able to teach you how to hone your magic? Oh, think of all the possibilities."

"I admire your enthusiasm Princess, but perhaps this isn't the right time. We do have a pending war now that you're no longer under the King's grasp."

My face dropped as the moment of joy and happiness was destroyed by the mention of Xandious. I knew Shadow meant no harm in mentioning him and perhaps I was still feeling the sorrow and darkness I felt during my capture. I just wanted to stay in this nice, happy, light bubble and not talk about wars and fights for as long as possible.

"You're right but I don't want to talk about it just yet. Let us just enjoy our peace and quiet together, we haven't had this in a long time."

"Not since the night after Mason's party."

"No, and I don't want anything to ruin it."

A pout almost appeared on my lips as I felt a bit stubborn. I didn't want the bubble to burst and would hold onto it as tightly as I could until I was no longer able to and that wasn't going to be anytime soon.

He laughed his beautiful husky laugh as he finished his drink and then stood up, crossing the small space between us and took the cup out of my hands before lifting me up into his arms.

"Well, if that's the case, what would my Princess like to do?"

Swinging me a little in a dancing motion, I laughed and felt that happiness appeared once again. This bubble was not bursting on my watch, and I would refuse anyone entry into this room if they tried to do such a thing. Cupping his cheek with one hand, I leaned in and gave him a kiss lightly on the lips and felt his smile appear between our lips.

"I say we get dressed and go for that walk."

"As you wish my Lady."

Dipping me a little and then going in for another kiss, my stomach filled with butterflies as my heart fluttered. This moment was perfect, it was all so perfect, and I started to wonder then what was going to destroy it, when was the other shoe going to drop and I waited for a second or two, but it didn't drop and as Shadow put me down on the ground, he wrapped me into a tight hug, and I felt his body relax.

"I will give you a few moments to dress and then we shall go on our walk together."

Letting go of me, he kissed my hand lightly and then turned swiftly on his feet leaving the room and I almost fell over with glee. He was perfect.

19

SHADOW

I t must have been the air, the way the food tasted or the fact I slept a full night's sleep in weeks that was making me happy, more relaxed. Or maybe it was the fact I woke up to Giselle and things seemed more at peace with us. Heading to the room Queen Leena had given me was just a few doors down from Giselle and I was glad I wasn't that far as I was still able to protect her.

The room was a lot larger than what I was used to and was almost fitting for a King. Knowing I had to be a little bit quicker in preparing and the fact I didn't want to be away from Giselle for too long, I decide a quick wash would suffice for now and later I would see about perhaps having a bath.

After washing, I threw on a cotton button down shirt, dark green trousers and a pair of cotton shoes. All of which were in the well-stocked wardrobe and oddly enough all the correct size. As if it had been prepared for my arrival or at least had been done while I stayed with Giselle.

Normally I would have strapped Winterthorn to my side, but I felt this place was safe, we were safe. And I didn't think it appropriate during our stay, I doubted anything would go wrong or the need for violence would appear anyhow.

Heading back to her room, I could already feel my heart start to thump louder in my chest. What had come over me since the lake? I had denied my feelings for the Princess for so long, had they been buried deep within me until now?

Perhaps Mason was right all those months ago, did I love Giselle and had just been denying it? Standing there in the hallway looking very sheepish, I waited for a few seconds to catch my breath, to slow my heart rate and calm myself.

Knocking on the door before entering, Giselle caught me by surprise in a beautiful chiffon pale pink dress. The colour brought out her glow even more, it was as if the dress was made for her. She looked beautiful.

"Are you ready?" She said while running a brush through her blonde locks.

"Ready when you are."

"You are looking very casual, I like it."

She smiled at me before turning away to place the brush down and gave herself a wipe over, checking to see if there was anything else she needed to do and then slipped on a pair of shoes.

"I thought it would be inappropriate for me to bring my sword and for today, I am just Shadow."

"Oh, so no Lord today?"

"Well, unless someone addresses me as that which I highly doubt anyone will be paying attention to me when you're dressed like that."

"You're sweet. So, shall we go?"

Leaving the comfort of her room behind, I hooked Giselle's arm into mine and we took a casual stroll down the many hallways until we came to the room we arrived in yesterday. Guards greeted us as we walked by and after asking them where we could leave to, one was gracious enough to escort us down to the city square.

Leaving us there, many of the folk stopped to stare and watch as we walked by. Giselle didn't appear to notice as much as I did, she was too busy looking at all the beautiful flowers and buildings, pointing out the flag of the city. A large tree with a gold star to the right of it, on a pale blue fabric. The emblem of The Withered Mountains city.

Giselle suddenly left my side as she rushed over to a market stall decorated with sparkling jewels and gems. Picking up a necklace or two before she stopped in her tracks and in a basket near the back of the stall was a pile of gemstones.

Coming to her side, I watched as she lifted a large Emerald, bigger than anyone I had seen before and she held it up towards the sunlight, watching as it glittered and danced with rainbows.

"Lovely, isn't it?"

The lady at the stall caught my attention as she wandered over to us. She appeared to be a lot older than most elves, wrinkles sat at the corners of her eyes and mouth and her hair was a wiry grey. She walked with a slow limp but still had the elegance of an elf about her.

"It's gorgeous. How much is it?"

Giselle asked without taking her eyes off the gem and I realised then we had come on this walk without any gold coins. In fact, I didn't have any since my near death in the village.

"For you Princess, nothing. Take it as a gift."

Startled by her announcement, Giselle dropped the gem and luckily, I caught it before it hit the ground and smashed into a million pieces. I don't think she expected anyone to know who she was.

"I'm sorry if I frightened you, it's just everyone knows who you are, from the moment you arrived. It has long been foretold you'd arrive through our gates, and you will bring us peace and freedom once again."

"Peace and freedom? I'm sure Queen Leena has been able to do such things." I replied while Giselle still gathered her voice.

"Well yes and no, those of us who remember the days of old long to return to our homeland. Before we were driven into hiding and Princess Giselle is our saviour and will be able to do that."

"I think you might have confused me someone else. The last time I even attempted to save anyone, I was attacked and captured."

"Trust the process Princess. You are the maiden of the sun and are here to save us from the darkness."

Shock ran through my core, as did I'm sure it did for Giselle. The riddle Seniya gave Quiver back at Mason's home rang through my mind.

"Beware the maiden with eyes of the moon for when the maiden of the sun and the maiden of the moon collide, chaos will ensnare." Giselle uttered almost as if she had the same brain wave as me.

"Who is the maiden of the moon, if I am the sun?"

"I'm sorry your Highness but we are only told of when to expect you and to aid you in your quest. Please take the gem as it will help guide you to the truth."

"But, I have so many questions."

Almost grabbing the elderly elf by the arm as she started to walk away, she turned back to look at Giselle with kind eyes and then took a hold of Giselle's hands.

"Your Highness, all the answers you seek are right here in the city. Please, visit our temple of Guinevere, she will be able to help answer your questions and perhaps shed more light on the prophecy."

She left us stood there in the market stall while she went off to help other customers who had just arrived and while my brain ran a million miles an hour, working out what we had just been told, I felt Giselle grab my hand and yank me out of there and back into the city square.

The colour from her face had drained and she looked visibly shaken. We had come on our walk for some peace and quiet, a change of scene and already the past was bringing itself back up into the forefront of our minds.

"I have to visit the temple; I need to know if there is any more information about this prophecy."

"Perhaps we should head back to Queen Leena's. She may know more, might have access to achieves, scrolls that will tell us more."

"But she said the temple will be able to help."

"Giselle, I know my mother doesn't answer preys or the words of humans – or any creatures for that matter. Please, let's just head back and we can see what the others have."

"No, go back and find the others if you must. Read through their scroll's and see what you can find. I am on the other hand going to the temple."

"I'm not going to leave you here alone."

"You are, what if your mother answers me? Then what? You're going to just make it about you and her. I'd rather you leave me to do this alone."

She crossed her arms and was clearly set already in her plan and there was no way of me swaying her to decide otherwise. I didn't want to leave her on her own, but I didn't get any impression she wouldn't be safe here. Everyone kept a watchful eye on her and I and there were many guards' walking around the square also watching us.

"Giselle, you know I'm not going to leave you here by yourself."

"Yes, you bloody well are. Now go. Before we start to argue with one another, and this ends up ruining the rest of our day."

She knew how to vex me as I was already getting a little annoyed that she didn't want me at her side, while she was going through this next part of our journey. No, I didn't want Guinevere to answer her calls and then I will have to deal with speaking to her. I also didn't want to see Giselle's disappointment when she went unanswered. I was now in a rock and a hard place.

"I will give you one hour, if you're not back at Queen Leena's, Quiver and I will come searching along with armed guards."

She huffed and rolled her eyes, taking my hands and then leaned up on her toes and kissed me lightly on the cheek.

"You're such a worrier, I will be fine."

"One hour Giselle, no more than that."

She nodded and then turned on her heel, stopping to ask a guard the way to the temple I presumed and off she went down a pathway and then she was gone. My heart hurt as soon as she left my side and I felt such anxiety with not knowing where she was going, but I knew not to question her or argue. She was still my Princess, and I was still under a sapphire oath, bound by orders and blood.

Even still, if she didn't return in the allotted hour, I would burn this city to the ground if I had to, in order to find her.

160

20

GISELLE

Clutching the Emerald in my hands, I walked up the large, stoned steps towards the great temple of Guinevere. This was not how I had pictured our walk, I was hoping for romance, a picnic by the water, going to the market stalls to browse and see if there was anything that caught my eye. The last thing I wanted to do was call upon a Goddess, especially the eldest one who was renowned for vengeance and being unhappy with any creature if she did appear to them.

Pushing open the heavy wooden doors the smell of fresh flowers and trees greeted me firstly and then the smells of burning wood, flames from candles lit along the aisle lit the room. Effigies of the Goddess decorated each marble piler and stained-glass windows of patterns lined the building, each glass telling a different story of the Goddess.

The creation of our world, one of all four sisters coming together, the banishment of Aithne as well as many others. But there near the end of the left side was one of her passing a baby over to one of the sisters, Fenella. It was Shadow and then the next window showed Guinevere turned away with her head in her hands as Fenella left with the baby.

"Wonderful, aren't they?"

A voice startled me, turning around I saw a young female elf standing there. She was sparkling, her skin a gorgeous shade of brown and wore a beautiful white cloak and white dress with gold detail; her hair was hidden but I could just about see a few strands of red hair poking out from under her hood.

"They are. I'm sorry for disturbing you."

"It's quite alright, our temple is always open to those who seek guidance from the Goddess. My name is Anwen, and you must be Princess Giselle."

"Word travels fast around here, doesn't it?"

"Well, when nothing happens for a long time, we take great delight in visits and as you were foretold many centuries ago so we may have been expecting you. Do you seek out the Goddess?"

"I was told this was the best place for me to get answers, about this foretold story."

"In that case, I shall leave you to your prayers. I will be just at the back preparing for our next service. You should come, it can be quite enlightening and perhaps your companion can join you."

Bowing a little, she turned away from me and started walking up the aisle, disappearing through a doorway and now I was alone. The silence was deafening but also peaceful, comforting even.

Walking to the altar, an incredibly large stature of Guinevere stood there, made of marble and gold. She was holding her staff with deer horns and laying at her feet with many other animals, creatures of the woods, including the wolf she was believed to travel with across the plains.

"I have never been to one of your temples, I'm afraid. I have never even asked for your guidance, I guess I'm not a very good subject for worship." I paused looking around me to double check I was still alone.

Holding the Emerald tightly in my hands, I lifted it up to examine it more, holding it up in front of me and looking through it I could just about make out the stature.

"You'd think, as a Princess of this land, I would be accustomed to speaking to you and your sisters. Paying some forms of tributes to help bring me luck, prosperity and more to the throne. Maybe I should have done that in the past, perhaps that's why I lost the throne to start with. I didn't pray or honour you enough."

Taking a seat down on the floor, I rested my legs under me and then dropped my head, looking at the floor, wondering where I was going with any of this.

"Goddess Guinevere, I crave your guidance. I know I may not deserve it and you may not even answer me, but I don't know what to do next, where to go from here. I have no idea who this maiden of the moon could be, I thought the talks of prophecies and chosen ones were just stories my mother told me when I was young. I still don't fully believe them to have any truth to them, but Seniya received that message, and it must have been from you or maybe your sisters. I don't know," I paused, looking back up at the stature and feeling no sense of change or anything. "This is useless, you don't have the time to come answering questions of some human. You probably don't answer anyone really."

Getting up and dusting myself off, I looked at the statue again, admiring it as the craftsmanship was outstanding and I wondered if my mother had ever seen it. Perhaps she knew of this land but kept it hidden from the rest of us, from the world.

Looking to my right, there was a table of remembrance with some lit candles on and I decided it would be best to light one for my mother. Even if she never knew about this place, it would be disrespectful not to honour her soul in one way and Guinevere would be able to protect her in the after-life, or at least that's what I hoped.

"Did you find your answers?"

Anwen had joined me again sitting down in one of the wooden service seats as I lit the white candle for my mother and then another for all the soldiers that lost their lives for our cause.

"The Goddess doesn't answer people like me, she has many other important things to do."

"People like you? What do you mean?"

"Well, I have had many lives lost because of me. I have even taken life when there may have been another way."

"The Goddess doesn't punish those who are only trying to protect themselves and the ones they love. May I ask what it is you asked for guidance with?"

Sitting down next to Anwen, I sunk a little into myself, disappointment starting to rage through my body. Sighing deeply, I crossed my arms and felt my chest tighten a little as I looked back at the stature.

"I asked for help on where to go next, about the prophecy, who the other maiden may be and where do I go from here – it all sounds rather silly."

"It's not silly, the Goddess has many ways to communi-cate with her subjects and perhaps she did hear you but isn't able to answer you or maybe, you are not ready for the answers yet."

"Hmmm, maybe but I could really do with the help now."

"She will come to you when you are ready. As for what to do next, I would go back to your companion, enjoy the rest of your day and you never know, a sign might appear, and everything will become more clearer."

"You might be right; I did say I'd only be an hour and I don't wish to worry anyone," Looking at Anwen, she smiled a soothing smile and made me relax a little more. "Thank you, Anwen, when is your next service? I like to attend if you will have me."

"You are always welcome here your Highness, it is tomorrow night and I'm sure many of the attendees will be happy for you to join us."

Standing up and ready to take my leave, I still felt very lost and unsure of things but took Anwen's words into consideration, perhaps a sign would appear to me and help guide me on my journey. And although I had not heard from the Goddess herself, her priestess appeared to be just as helpful.

"Anwen, before I leave may I ask a question?"

"By all means."

"That window by there, is that the story of Lord Shadow-bane's birth?"

"Yes, it is, he is our white knight in the darkness. His birth was foretold around the same time yours was. Many of us are eager to meet him but we understand he needs to come to us when he is ready."

"Your white knight?"

"Indeed, he will help rid Nimra of the darkness and you both will bring the light back."

"Ah, so no pressure then."

She chuckled a little as I looked back at the windows, wondering how on earth I was going to explain this all to Shadow and if he already in fact knew of his name and role in this entire thing? He once laughed at me for mentioning anything about being a chosen one and now here we were, being told once again that I was one and by all accounts so was he.

Saying goodbye to Anwen and heading back to Queen Leena's almost on the dot, I was glad when he hadn't sent out a search party for me and was kindly escorted back to the house by a guard. Shadow and Alary meeting me at the front door, both looking a little alarmed and concerned.

"What's wrong now?"

I asked as we walked through the front door and then seconds later, I was collided against by another body as arms wrapped around me. Unsure of who it was, I pulled the person off and to my surprise it was Lady Alison standing there.

"Alison? What in Goddess name are you doing here? How?"

Looking at Alary, Shadow and then Quiver as we all stood in the foyer, confused and having absolutely no idea how she was even here, I felt a little happy, selfishly as it felt good to see Alison again.

"It's a long story, Princess, one of which I'm sure Queen Leena is going to be super impressed with."

"Oh, I am all ears."

Alison turned around abruptly as standing at the top of the foyer staircase was Queen Leena looking more radiant and annoyed as she did the day before.

ENTERING Queen Leena's study holding Alison's hand tightly, I could feel her nerves as she shook a little. Leena, although Quiver had mentioned she was a kind woman, right now she appeared to be on a warpath and I believed it was my fault for arriving here with the others, it really threw her off balance.

Shadow stood closely behind me, while Alary idled in the doorway and Quiver stood with his arms crossed, appearing to be angry but I could sense he was still nervous over having this conversation.

"So, who would like to go first?"

Leena sat down at the head of the table, and I rolled my eyes at her, this wasn't some telling off from a parent and already I didn't like her tone.

"Leena, the Princess and Shadow have no idea what has transpired today so I don't see why you have requested they also come here," Quiver was the first one to speak and he sounded mad, "As for Lady Alison's arrival, it would appear Mabon gave her a spell that helped her track us after we rescued her Highness. She is my guest and is to be treated as one."

"It seems dear brother, you have quite a few guests already all of which, weren't invited personally."

"We will be leaving your home by the end of the day, and I will be having my guests stay at my own home soon enough. I'd rather us not deal with your attitude and the walking on eggshells with you."

"I suggest you speak to me with better manners Alex, or you and your lady friend will be locked away as punishment."

"And then you will have a very big problem on your hands."

I stepped in, letting go of Alison and as soon as I moved,

Shadow placed his hand on my shoulder to pull me back. Leena stood up suddenly banging her hands onto the table and the room started to shake as spouts of ivy appeared through her fingers and started to run up her arms.

"You might be a Princess out there but in here I am Queen, and you will speak to me with respect."

"I will give you respect when you earn it. So far you have treated your brother without even an ounce of care or love. You threaten my friend without even a second thought and that isn't ok with me. You hold no regard to anyone else other than yourself and I am quite frankly done with the pretences of pretending to be polite and care about your opinion. I have done enough of that my entire life," I then turned to face Quiver who looked stunned at my outburst.

"How long will you need us to be ready to retire to your home? I'd rather us stay somewhere that is far more welcoming."

"Eh, a half hour?"

"Good, then we shall meet in the main foyer in a half-hour. Alison, you can come with me and as for you, Queen Leena, thank you for your somewhat hospitality but we won't be needing it any longer."

Turning on my heels, I took hold of Alison's hand again and headed to the door as Queen Leena started to shout and the room began to shake once again.

"I will not have you speak to me in this manner. I am still a Queen."

Smiling, I had clearly hit a nerve, I couldn't help myself and turned back staring Leena down.

"And I am the Queen of Nimra, as far as I am concerned you are Queen to a world that has hidden away in the shadows, leaving behind a world out there that could possibly had needed your help and guidance. Especially while

168

Xandious ran through villages, raping and killing poor defenceless people, women, and children but no, instead you hide under a mountain. At least your brother has bigger balls than you to help do what's right."

I could see the red in her face begin to appear as her ivy vines grew beneath her feet and start to run across the floor and up the walls behind her. Magic didn't scare me, and her outburst wasn't going to shake me either.

Alary stepped out of the way as I came to the doorway, still holding Alison's hand with Shadow behind me. Quiver hadn't moved yet and I wondered for a moment if he would leave with us and when he didn't, I took it as a sign for us to go and he would stay to talk to his sister.

Queen Leena appeared to calm herself for a moment or two as the room stopped shaking and we headed back up the staircase towards our bedrooms. Shadow was silent behind me, and I knew he wanted desperately to ask me what had happened in the temple but as we weren't alone, I knew it would have to wait. Alison still appeared visibly shaken beside me and I wished she hadn't seen any of that.

"I'm afraid my arrival may have put you and the Queen at odds. I am sorry your Highness."

"Giselle, please and don't worry about the Queen's feelings, I get the feeling she likes to pull rank of everyone, including her own brother."

"Yes, I heard her mention that, does that mean Alexandra is a Prince?"

"You know, I forget his name was Alex. Thank you for reminding me, I am so used to calling him Quiver. Yes, he is the heir to the Elven throne it seems, I'm not sure if that means to all the thrones in the Elf world or just this one. You would have to ask him."

Opening the door to my bedroom, I let Alison go in first

to take it all in and then turned to Shadow who was still silent. I still had the Emerald in my other hand and not wanting to lose it, I held it out to him.

"Can you keep this safe until later please? I will get ready with Alison and once we are done, I will meet you here."

"You're very lucky Giselle, Leena didn't put you in a cell for what you said down there," He paused clearly thinking of his next words carefully, "Not that I would have allowed her, but you need to be more careful, we are guests in her realm."

"I won't have her threatening my friends and as far as I am concerned, we are Quiver's guests, not hers as she didn't even want us here to start with. Perhaps I will apologise to her once she shows me some kindness to us all."

"Ok, but please just be careful, the last thing I want to do is start a war with the Elves."

He took hold of the Emerald and then placed it into his trouser pocket before leaning down and lightly kissing me on the cheek. Turning towards his bedroom down the corridor I went into my room, shutting the door and started to prepare to leave.

21

QUIVER

><del>~~~~~~~~~~~~~~~~</del>

"You are seriously trying me aren't you brother?" Leena sat down with her head in her hands, shaking it and I already knew we had overstepped the mark.

"You ask me to treat your friends kindly and yet one of them continues to undermine by position, tell me is she rude for the sake of it or was she born this way?"

"Leena, you keep threatening myself and her friends. Giselle is a very kind, trusting and loyal person to have on your side but you are not helping the situation by losing your temper so quickly."

I pulled up a chair next to her as she kept her head low and in her hands. I didn't like falling out with my sister and most certainly didn't want to see her upset over people who I had brought here. Leaving to stay at my own home was the best choice to make and quite frankly, I should have made that decision right from the start.

"I don't appreciate being spoken to that way Alex. It's not ok for you to just stand there and allow it either."

"No, you are right, and I will speak to her about it myself once we leave. I apologise on behalf of her for her behaviour but please take on board what I have said. Will the ball still be going ahead? I understand if you wish to cancel."

"The invitations have already been sent. You still need to attend and as I invited Princess Giselle to be my guest as well as Lord Shadowbane, I'd like them both to still attend," She paused for a second, taking her head out her hands and whipping away some tears that had appeared, most likely from anger, before standing up and straightening out her dress and then crown.

"Please apologise to the Princess from me and I will then apologise formally at the ball once she and I are alone perhaps. I will take on board what you have said."

She nodded and waved her hand at me to dismiss me as she walked out the side door of the study, leaving me standing there with my thoughts.

Alary had already left and I guessed was at the house getting the footman and maids ready for the arrival of Giselle and everyone else. I didn't enjoy the feeling of telling my sister what to do as she was still above me in rank and age, but I was starting to get a little tired of tiptoeing around her when this was my home too.

Entering the foyer, I found Shadow, Giselle and Alison all stood there silent and waiting patiently, I hadn't realised it had been half hour all ready and was grateful they were ready to go.

"It's just a few minutes' walk from here, will you all be ok to walk, or shall I fetch a carriage?"

"Quiver, I'm pretty sure we can do with some fresh air." Shadow said helping clear the tension in the air.

"Yes, quite right, this way."

Shadow carried the ladies' bags and we left out the front door and back onto the stone steps of the city under the mountain. The sun was now setting, and the sky gave off a magical glow of oranges, purples and yellows. My home was anything but beautiful.

Alison hooked her arm into mine as Shadow and Giselle walked behind us and I felt Alison ease a little from her nerves, clearly glad we were no longer in that house.

"Are you alright?" I asked looking down at her.

"I'm fine thank you, are you okay? I didn't know what I'd do if her Highness had argued in front of me with my family."

"When you are in the room with two very head strong women, you learn to just be quiet and let them sort it out themselves. I have no doubt her Highness and the Queen will sort through their differences and become good friends."

"How many times do I have to tell you, call me Giselle please. That goes for both of you, we are friends."

Alison laughed a little as she turned her head slightly to look at Giselle who smiled back, it seemed tensions had been loosened.

"It's rather odd to call a Princess, a Queen, even by her first name. I have been raised as a lady so it will take some getting used to."

Giselle suddenly appeared next to Alison and linked her arm with hers, taking her forward and out of my own arms. Shadow joined at my side as the two ladies walked in front of us, chatting and laughing amongst themselves.

"So, what are you going to do now that Alison is here? And will be staying with us?" Shadow jabbed his elbow into my side as he winked at me, and I rolled my eyes at him.

"I will be a gentleman of course; Lady Alison deserves the upmost respect and that's what I shall be giving her."

"Well, yes, of course she does but I don't think her plan to arrive here was to be treated as a respectable lady."

"Is that what you think of for her Highness."

"Oh, I respect Giselle, in every way possible but if she were to ask me to her bed and not just to sleep, quite frankly I don't think I could contain myself anymore."

"Must be awful – being in love with someone and not being able to do more than share a few kisses and stare into each other's eyes."

"Ah, you seem to forget, Giselle and I are still betrothed, and she has not said otherwise."

"Does she think you are or is that just your excuse?"

Shadow fell silent then as I watched his brain turn with an answer and when he didn't reply, I laughed a little under my breath and as we turned a corner we arrived at a large set of black gates. My home. Alary was already standing there waiting for our arrival and as he pushed open the gates to allow us through, the ladies went first and then we three men followed.

My home wasn't as grand as any castle and most certainly didn't have the touch of a women, it was mainly decorated in earth tones, but it was my sanctuary, my place to escape to and it felt as if I hadn't been here for many months. In fact, the last time I was here was before I was sent off to investigate Giselle.

"Welcome home your Highness."

Mr Beaver, my head of staff and keeper of the keys bowed and greeted us as we stepped through the door. He then turned towards Giselle and bowed low to her, greeting her with the same respect as myself and then welcomed the others.

"I set up dinner in the dining room for you Sir and your guests. Also, your guests' rooms are just being finished momentarily. I will inform you when they are ready. Please follow me into the dining room and leave any bags here, one of the footmen will take them to their required rooms."

"Very fancy Alex." Alison winked at me as she went on ahead with Giselle into the dining room.

"I apologise it's not as grand as the homes you are used to."

"Don't be silly Quiver, its lovely. Thank you for allowing us to stay here."

Giselle was the first to pick from one of the trays of food and started piling on a plate full of fresh meat and fruit. Clearly hungry from the day as was I. Settling down, we each had a seat and full glasses of wine, the atmosphere felt happier, lighter now we were altogether and away from Leena's.

"Will Alary be joining us?" Asked Alison as she sipped from her drink.

"Perhaps, he may have gone home to see his wife."

"Oh, he's married?"

"For quite some time now, his wife is a priestess at the temple. She nursed Alary back to health many years ago when he was gravely poisoned by a plant somewhere in your realm."

"Would that be Anwen? If it is, I met her earlier today."

"You did? Yes, that would be her. She's a kind, gentle women. She's very brave to be one of the Goddesses priestesses."

"May I ask Alex, is the rules of a Queen the same as it is in Nimra? Where Queen's rule and King's may not?" Asked Alison.

"No, actually it goes by the first born and as Leena is a few minutes older than I, she therefore inherited the throne and I am the spare, next in line unless she were to have children."

"And she does not?" Shadow pipped up as he cut into a bit of meat.

"No, I'm afraid after our parents' death, Leena never wanted to have children for fear they would lose her the same way we lost our parents. I told her it's a silly notion, but I fear it will rest on my shoulders to produce an heir once I am King and that won't be for at least another three, four hundred years. Leena is still very young and new in her role."

"How old are you then?"

"Only about three hundred or so years."

"And that's young?" Alison looked stunned as she appeared to try and work something out in her mind.

"Young for an Elf, yes."

"Wow, so you would have seen my grandmother's mother come to the throne, as well as her mother."

"And before that yes. Many Elves of course had been in hiding for longer than I have been around, but I was able to hide amongst humans and watched as history unfolded itself. You guys fight over the smallest things, don't you?"

"Yes, I'm afraid we do."

Sensing the tone had changed in conversation, I left it there and carried on eating some food, while our drinks continued to be topped up and eventually, I was starting to feel a little intoxicated, as were the other's as we laughed and joked about silly notions, things that had happened in our childhood and I got to know Shadow and Giselle a lot more than I had previously.

"I will say one thing though Quiv, your sister doesn't half make a room shake when she's angry." Said Giselle as she helped herself to another glass.

"Ah yeah, that's a gift from the Goddess herself. My mother was so pleased once Leena's powers started to manifest. I on the other hand hated it, she would drop rocks onto me when we were younger when she was having a tantrum."

"Do you have any powers, Alex?" Alison was drinking her drink slowly, clearly keeping her wits about her.

"I do but not as great as Leena's. Mine are more manifesting, growing something from the soil, healing, communicating with some wildlife and as Shadow might tell you, I'm quick on my feet."

"Must be lovely being connected to the Goddess in that way."

"It has its downsides but yes, it can be lovely when you need it."

"Well, I am just about ready to turn in for the night." Giselle had already downed her last glass of wine and was pushing herself out of her chair before she appeared to stumble a little and Shadow caught her by her elbows. She smiled up at him with a kind smile and he rolled his eyes back at her. I wondered if he continued to think on our conversation earlier and if he talks to her about the whole betrothed business.

"I will help her Highness to bed, thank you for a lovely evening."

"Mr Butcher!" I shouted for him, and he appeared almost out of thin air.

"Yes, your Highness."

"Can you please show Lord Shadow where her Highness will be staying."

"Of course, right this way my Lord."

Once Shadow and Giselle had gone, it was just Alison and I and I wondered if I should bring up our last meeting, our last goodbye and if we were past it. Taking a sip of my drink, I felt my nerves well up inside me as she sat silent, before getting up and wandering over to one of the windows.

"Thank you for allowing us to stay here your Highness."

Alison cut the tension but alas appeared to be formal and unlike her usual friendly, relaxed self.

"Please, Alex, we are friends, and your Highness is far too formal for me. You should know that."

"Yes, sorry, I do apologise. It's just a such a shock to me, I didn't expect to hear that you're a prince."

"I don't like telling people my title, it makes them shrink away and not be themselves around me, you most certainly would have been different."

And she would have, even if she tried not to be, Alison was a born and bred lady, bred to wed into royalty or nobility. It was part of her genetics that made her formal when around someone who had a higher birth than her.

"I am still Quiver, that is who I truly am."

"Alright, Quiver or Alex, whichever you wish to be called. I will not call you your Highness ever again. Unless you request it of course."

She smiled at me then, her sweet ever charming smile and I had to look away, keeping my thoughts to myself, she did fill my dreams and although I would have loved to have felt her lips against mine again, it wouldn't have been right.

"I do need to apologise for me showing up here unexpectedly. Mabon thought it would be best I came to join you and Giselle. Not sure why though, I'm not really that important."

"You are important to the Princess, and we are all happy you are here. It was a surprise but a nice one."

She then placed her now empty glass on the table as a blush appeared across her cheeks. Brushing a hand through her fiery hair as her eyes fluttered a little, she looked at me with a passion deeply hidden behind those lashes.

"If it's alright with you, I'd like to retire now."

"Of course, I can show you to your room."

"I fear if you did, I'd ask you to come in."

"Well in that case," I stood up and escorted her to the staircase stopping at the bottom, I took one of her hands in mine and kissed it lightly.

"Sweet dreams my lady."

Smiling up at her, she turned and wandered up the staircase, whilst I stared at her wondering.

22

GISELLE

———❦———

For the next two days we spent at Quiver's home, I felt a lot more relaxed and more at ease then I have done in a very long time. Alison and I spent our mornings walking the grounds of the beautiful manor, Quiver took great pride in his gardens, and although it was winter, it appeared to be spring here.

The flowers were still in bloom and the tree's covered in green foliage. I asked if the disturbing of the season's caused any issues with any of the wildlife and he simply said that they didn't get normal wildlife like we do outside of this realm.

Shadow and I had taken to having lunch together on one of the benches in the gardens that afternoon and it was enjoyable to just sit, talk and be at peace with one another. Alison was eagerly awaiting the ball Queen Leena had decided to host in my honour and part of me felt guilty for speaking to her the way I had previously.

"We need to get you ladies new dresses I think." Spoke Quiver as he bit into his apple.

He was sitting down on the grass in front of us, while

Alison sat next to him reading a book on Elven history. I leaned into Shadow, resting my head on his shoulder and closed my eyes, feeling the sun's rays warm against my skin,

"New dresses sound wonderful, when shall we go?" Replied Alison as she set her book down.

"We can go this afternoon perhaps; do you men also need dress clothes?"

"Shadow and I can go with you both and head to the tailors, while you ladies run off and do lady things."

"Do you hear that Giselle, to do lady things, I wonder what that would include."

"You know what I mean Ally, we would just get in your way if we joined you."

Quiver and Alison had become rather close the past two days and it was wonderful to see how much they had come out of their own individual shells and open to one another more. I could still sense a distance between them both and after asking Alison one evening why that could be, she simply explained that he was a gentleman and didn't want to do anything that may ruin her honour.

"I think a trip to the market sounds like a lovely idea." Shadow said as I lifted my head off his shoulder and stretched out my arms.

"Come along then, we will meet you both at the front doors in ten minutes."

Alison soon stood up and then gracefully took my hand as we walked together back towards the house and to our adjoining rooms. I wanted nothing more than to stay in this world we had started to create, this peace and although part of me felt guilty for wishing to leave the world of Nimra behind and all its troubles, I knew deep down I couldn't leave the innocent people to deal with Xandious and his evil schemes and plans.

Once we were dressed properly, we headed back down-stairs and met both men who were stood there patiently waiting for us. It seemed like such a minor thing, but I was enjoying this courtship in a way of Shadow and I. Linking my arm into his, we left the manor and headed towards the town square.

We hadn't talked much about what happened at the temple yet, I only mentioned that I found nothing and was still waiting for some sort of sign to help guide me on this next part of my, our journey. Passing by many market stalls, ones which were selling jewellery, magic potions, fresh produce, and small other trinkets, we finally came to a dress-maker's shop and with a rather large bag of gold coins, we left the men to do their own thing and wondered it.

The shop smelt of fresh lemons and pine, rails upon rails of dresses lined the walls and it appeared to be a little busy, must have been the news of the ball hitting the streets. Quiver had mentioned everyone had been invited and it did make me wonder how everyone was going to fit in Leena's home and the only explanation I had was trust the process, whatever that meant.

"Oh, your Highness, welcome. How may I be of service to you today?"

A young Elf, with gorgeous long blonde hair appeared out of nowhere wearing a deep low cut, red suit dress. She curtsied and smiled at us both. I didn't know if I enjoyed being recognised while here as I almost wanted to just be Giselle but nevertheless, it was a polite greeting.

"We are here to find some gowns for the upcoming ball, if you happen to have any available."

"Oh, there are many available, it just depends on what type of style dress you are looking for. We have ones that are modest and concealing, we have ones that are revealing and will capture the eye of any man and we also have ones that are sparkling, daring and slightly sheer."

"Alison, is there anything you'd like to wear in particular?" I asked as I looked around the shop at the many styles the dressmaker mentioned.

"Well, there's only the eyes of one man I'd like to capture so maybe we can start by looking for something that might help with that."

Her cheeks flushed as she admitted that to herself, a man she wanted to capture and clearly to her, she had no idea she had already captured the one I believed she was talking about. As another dressmaker wandered over, she smiled at us both and then took Alison away to discuss what I imagined her likes and dislikes in order to find the perfect gown to fit her required needs.

"And for you, your Highness, what is it you were looking for?"

"I'd like something that doesn't scream Princess or Royalty please. I have been brought up to wear large elaborate dresses all my life and so this time, I'd like to wear something that feels a little more me."

"Hmmm, is there any particular colour you'd like to wear?"

"Not really, if I can see some dresses, maybe I can see what works and what doesn't."

"Of course, your Highness."

Wandering around the shop for several minutes, the dressmaker pulled out different styles of dresses and each one didn't give me that spark, that feeling I was hoping to find. I wanted something that not only would make me feel like my true self but also one that would make Shadow go weak at his knees and unable to think straight. I knew what I was looking for and I hoped I could find it.

"Perhaps this one?"

Pulling out a beautiful red dress with a sweetheart neckline and mermaid style bottom did make me think for a second and wonder if that was the one but sadly, shaking my head she put the dress back and looked a lot more puzzled.

"I might have something in the back, it just came in last week and I hadn't put it out yet. I won't be a moment."

Standing there, I looked at the accessory cabinet that was filled with tiaras, earrings and detailed jewelled belts while I waited. I could hear Alison chatting and laughing from the other side of the shop and wandered over to have a little peek at the dress she was trying on.

It was a beautiful maroon dress with a deep V cutting down the neckline and hugged her tightly at the waist and then fell to the floor, it was stunning and as she twirled around a little in the mirror smiling from eye to eye, she caught me looking

"What do you think?"

"He won't know where to put his eyes. You look amazing."

"You should wear your hair up my lady, exposing your neck and delicate features."

"Oh, there you are your Highness, I have pulled the dress out for you. If you like to follow me, maybe you can try it on and see how you feel."

I left Alison to continue twirling around and looking at herself and followed the dressmaker to one of the larger changing rooms in the store. Pulling off my white blouse and black trousers and slip-on shoes, she unzipped a dress bag and pulled out the most beautiful dress I had ever seen.

It was a midnight blue shade, almost black in certain lights and with each movement it glittered. Sliding it onto my body, my arms went through the sheer sleeves that were decorated with what looked like little silver stars. The dress was a figure hugging and low cut and sat just below my shoulders.

Zipping the back up, I could see the dress in its glory while I stared at myself in the mirror. It fitted in all the right places, was long enough to still have that beautiful dance movement but also gave that enchanting magical feel to it.

"It appears this dress was made for you."

"It's gorgeous."

I stared at myself some more as I took in all the little details, from the distance the dress may look plain and ordinary but as you looked at it closely, it glimmered with every moment, every step. It was stitched perfectly and hugged me in all the correct places.

"May I have this then, please."

"Of course, your Highness. I wouldn't be able to sell this to anyone else now, this dress was yours the moment you put it on."

I didn't want to take it off and was reluctant to do so, giving the dress back to the dressmaker she zipped it back up in its safe bag and then took it to the back of the store, explaining it will be delivered to me the day of the ball.

Once Alison and I were waiting to pay, the dressmaker seemed more pleased by the bill and the fact we didn't take more than a second to pay, a hefty price but worth every penny.

Leaving the shop, we decided to head towards the bakers while we waited for the men to join us, both of us hungry. While I waited outside Alison went in and ordered us a few pasties and a couple of cream chocolate cakes. Sitting down at a fountain which was in the middle of the square we sat quietly, enjoying the pasties and then cake, which were delicious.

"I have to ask your Highness,"

"Giselle please."

"Sorry, Giselle. But are you and Lord Shadow now courting? Or are you still betrothed? I only ask because I overhead Alex and him discussing it the other day when we were walking to Alex's home."

"Oh, you know I haven't really thought about it. I believe we are just courting as the betrothal would have ended after my mother's death. But then it's a very old custom, we should be allowed to pick and choose who we fall in love with and marry."

"And are you? – in love with Lord Shadow?"

I paused for a second as I looked around the marketplace, the sun was slowly setting in the sky, and I was starting to wonder where Shadow and Quiver had gone to while we waited for them.

"You know, sometimes I think I do and then other times I want to run my sword through him as he can be incredibly frustrating. I don't have a very good example to pair love to you see, Xandious said he loved my mother, and I knew she loved him, but I don't believe he truly returned her feelings. You don't kill someone you are deeply, madly in love with."

"My mother loved my father, but it was more of a duty thing, rather than a shared feeling. The Governor and her however I believe were made for each other. I'd like a love like that. Perhaps one day."

"Perhaps Quiver might be that love."

"Don't be silly, he doesn't see me anymore than a friend does. We have shared a kiss but that was all it was, a kiss."

She lowered her eyes as she started to play with the ruffles of her dress, taking her hands in mine to somewhat comfort her, she smiled at me softly.

"He'd be a fool to not fall head over heels, madly in love with you. Especially since you came all this way."

"Hmm, unless his heart is already taken."

"Oh, I highly doubt that."

I smiled back at her having a feeling that she was just being coy and knew just how Quiver felt. I had seen the way he watched her do the simplest things as always appeared to be lost in her.

Looking up and around us, the square was still busy with people, and it made me wonder when this magical city did go to sleep, Shadow and Quiver were still not back and I could feel my anxiety start to peek up a little inside my chest and I had to shove the feeling down, they would be fine in a place like this. We were safe.

23

SHADOW

We had left Giselle and Alison for a few hours, and it was no fault of their own but ours, once we had finished getting our formal wear sorted, Quiver and I had decided to get a few pints of ale and a couple of games of cards in at one of the smaller taverns within the city.

I knew Giselle would be safe with Alison and within the city walls, there was nothing here that felt dangerous, and it was good to bond with Quiver. I still had a few questions about the night he rescued Giselle and why I wasn't included in the plan, but I was also grateful he had brought her back to me, as promised.

"Do you think they will be annoyed we haven't gone back to meet them yet?" Quiver asked slurring a little as he took a sip of his ale.

"Possibly, but I'm sure Giselle will understand, it's been a trying few weeks and we all deserve some form of a break. She and Alison might even come find us; Giselle is a great hunter so it wouldn't surprise me if they appeared."

Placing two jacks and an ace of spades down on the table, Quiver looked at me with glaring eyes as he threw his cards down, showing a ten of hearts and a queen. A coy smiled appeared across my lips as I pulled his winning chips towards me, and he huffed a sigh of annoyance.

"I swear you're cheating."

"Nope, you just suck at cards. One more round and shall we go find the girls?"

"One more, but this time I'm winning all my money back."

"By all means Prince, you are welcome to try."

Shuffling the cards and dealing them out again, I sniggered as I saw the distain in Quivers face as he glanced at his cards. As much as he was a great fighter and more, he couldn't bluff to save his life and therefore would always give himself away. He threw in five gold coins and then slid off a ruby encrusted gold ring off his middle finger and then placed it down on the pile.

"Oh, we are playing this way, are we?" I asked grinning.

"Scared, are you?"

"Ha! Never and you know it."

I lifted my cards but kept my face cool and collected, I had a terrible hand and would have to rely purely on luck and hopefully Quiver was just trying to get a rise out of me. He flipped his cards over and showed a full flush, he had two hearts in his hand and there were three hearts on the table. Leaving my pathetic two spades' cards to lose everything.

"HA HA!! Yes!!"

"You bloody river-rat! How in Goddess name did you even manage that?" I asked as Quiver leaned over the table to pull all his winnings, including my own towards him.

"Ah see my friend, you were getting too big for your boots and thought you had me didn't you," Quiver chuckled under his breath as I downed the remainder of my drink,

"Don't worry, I will get us the next drinks seen as though you're a bit short now."

He continued to laugh and clearly was enjoying himself, especially after losing around six of the seven games previously. Rolling my eyes, I waved over towards the barkeep who sent over his waitress to fill up our mugs as Quiver began to count his winnings.

Leaning across, I lifted the ruby ring and began to examine it, rubies were incredibly rare within Nimra, and I hadn't seen many for years, aside from the one Countess Elizabeth gave me as a wedding ring for Giselle.

"It's the ring of royalty if you want to know. It's passed to the next in line to the throne, Leena has the crown with rubies and Emeralds in."

"Emeralds?"

"Yes, they and rubies are believed to be powerful gems, they help us connect to the Goddesses and hold great power. There are many larger more sacred ones hidden within the city and the temple, they are what help keep us shadowed from the outside world."

Handing it back to Quiver and watching him place the ring back on his finger, pocketing his winnings and placing some of the coins into his purse before heading over to the barkeep and handing him over the bag and then coming back to the table.

"What did you do that for?"

"I do not need all that money, no one should have that much, and the cities people can share it out. Now finish up, we must go fetch our ladies who I have no doubt will be a little annoyed at us."

"I think Giselle will only be annoyed she wasn't invited to drink and gamble."

Finishing off our drinks, we headed out.

24

GISELLE

"Giselle?"

Alison and I had decided to leave sitting at the fountain and hunt for the men ourselves. I hated waiting around and I knew I'd be able to find Shadow eventually by tracking him down. Alison had linked her arm into mine as we wandered the cobbled streets being careful to step over any tree roots or flowers that were spouting out between the cracks.

"Yes?"

"Umm, well you might deem this a little strange, but you know, I have never held a sword before, and I wanted to know what it feels like."

It came to no surprise to me that Alison, a lady, had not held a sword before and most likely never even a smaller dagger. She was a born and bred lady, her mother had taught her the ways of royalty, how to dress, how to walk, talk, act and the simplest of tasks.

"Would you like me to teach you?" I asked, looking at her with a smile as she lowered her eyes quickly and a blush appeared. "I don't mind Alison; it might do you some good to know how to fight as we will most likely face battles in the near future, and I'd hate to think you weren't able to look after yourself."

"Only if you have time of course, your Highness."

"I always have time for my friends."

Giving her a little squeeze with my hand, we continued onwards passing multiples of stores, all of which were a different kind. Dress stores, food stores, weapons, a blacksmith and even some sort of pet and magical potion store. There were so many different adventures to be held in the city hidden in the mountains, I knew before I left, I wanted to explore them all.

"Do you have any clue as to where the men could have gone?"

"Most likely a tavern, Shadow is prone to having a few drinks or two when he's in a good mood. I'm not so sure about Quiver, however, don't worry though, we will find them."

"Or we will find you."

Of course, his voice would appear behind us out of nowhere. Shadow was very good at hiding in the shadows. Quiver stood next to him looking unusually smug and Alison left my arms rather quickly when he appeared. Smiling at Shadow and feeling my cheeks rush into a blush, I was enjoying welcoming this feeling of happiness and being in his company.

"Shall we retire home?" Quiver asked bowing a little to both us girls.

"Surely the night is still young." I winked at Shadow, and he returned me a cheeky smile.

"What do you have in mind dear Princess?" He asked out stretching his hand to take mine.

"Well, I see you guys have already started the evening

without us so perhaps take a walk and maybe find a tavern with some good food and music."

"That sounds like a lovely idea!" Gleamed Alison, "And maybe some dancing." She looked hopeful as she looked at Quiver.

"Hmmm, I believe tonight is a frost moon and us woodland Elves like to have gatherings around a fire to celebrate the changing of the seasons, even if we ourselves can't see them past our wards and spells. Would that be something you'd be interested in ladies?"

"That sounds perfect, lead the way."

I smiled as Alison linked arms with Quiver who took to walking in front of us, while Shadow and I slowed our pace behind, enjoying the sights and that of each other's company. He seemed lighter as he walked, almost as if the weight from his shoulders had been lifted and happy. His hair shone beautifully in the moonlight as his ice blue eyes caught the stars, he was beyond a doubt the most beautiful man I had ever laid eyes on and now I was seeing him in a different light.

"Is there something on my face or are you just going to continue to stare at me?" He winked as he looked down at me.

"I can stare all I want thank you very much, I want to remember all the pieces of your face."

"Ah, and all the wrinkles I imagine."

Rolling my eyes, I jabbed him in the side a little as we both laughed. We had come a long way together in such a short space of time but, I was still reserved in many aspects of our courtship, I knew it wouldn't be too long before we succumbed to our emotions and attraction to each other.

"Your face has many stories to tell, that's all and I wish to know them all."

"We will be here for a long time then."

Turning a corner and walking up a few steps, I could hear the faint sound of music coming from afar and saw a red glow in the skyline. The sound of clapping and cheering was pleasant and only wished me to quicken our pace to get there as soon as possible. A festival of some sorts was just what we needed and perfect just before the ball.

"Do you think those two will ever admit their feelings for one another?" I asked as I watched Alison lean a little more into Quiver as they walked.

"Perhaps after a few more drinks Quiver might but we can't push them both as much as you'd like to."

"I just see the way he looks at her and she looks at him."

"Giselle, remember how long it's taken for you to admit any ounce of feelings for me? I think it might take them both just as long."

He was right and I hated when he was, I couldn't push or meddle with Alison's feelings towards Quiver, and I most certainly wasn't able to ask him about his feelings no matter how much I would have loved to see them admit to one another.

"Almost there."

Quiver shouted as we took down an alleyway and then stepped onto a woodland path that opened at the end into an open clearing. Already many Elves were there celebrating, dancing, drinking, and enjoying themselves around the fire. It was beautiful and so wonderful to see.

"Now guys, enjoy yourselves please but be careful. Many of my people will have had much to drink I'm sure and don't agree to any bargains or promises. Shadow knows what I'm talking about, and everything will be fine."

"Promises? What do you mean?" Alison asked while even my own mind was intrigued.

"When an Elf agrees to a promise or an oath, they may

call upon it even in many years to come. It was simply our way of controlling another person, that person may not ask us for the promise or an oath, but we can require one from another creature, Elf, human or otherwise."

"But how do you end up in one of those deals?" I asked, still a little confused as it was something I had never heard about.

"Sometimes it can be something as simple as spilling your drink on an Elves jacket and offering to replace it or clean it. Other times they could have saved your life and therefore you owe them a life debt."

"Does that mean I owe you a life debt then?"

"Your Highness, I pledged my life to you the moment I disobeyed my sister and came to your aid. You will never owe me anything."

Quiver held my hands in his as he looked down at me with sincere and kind eyes, we were friends, and I was grateful for his companionship, ear, and duty to keep me safe whenever it was needed.

"Now, enough talk, let's go and enjoy the celebration and if we do happen to lose one another, go by the bonfire and we will be able to find each other."

Once Quiver and Alison had disappeared into the crowd, I watched as many of the Elves bowed to him as he was their heir and Prince and as Shadow and I walked around to see as much as we could, many bowed to us both as well as looked in awe at Shadow as many hadn't seen him.

"And I thought I was the popular one." Shadow joked.

"You are a legend, remember, almost a folk tale. The priestess at the temple Arwen told me you come from a prophecy foretold so it isn't a surprise to me how everyone is looking at you."

"Interesting, well you will have to tell me this story when we get to bed."

"Hmm, perhaps but then I quite like that you don't in fact know everything."

The music played louder around us as many drums began to ring throughout the woodland, charms of bells, flutes and even a couple of violins played. The sound was spellbinding and unlike anything I have ever heard before, it was cheerful, loud and many of the crowd danced around the fire with their partners, laughing and cheering as they went around.

"Will your Highness care to join us in a dance?"

A young Elf came out from the crowd, he looked no older than thirteen and held out his hand to me bowing. I looked at Shadow who smiled and shrugged his shoulders before giving my hand to him. The Elf appeared happy as my hand slipped into his and he pulled me into a dance of spinning, claps, and cheers as we went around the fire. It felt very uplifting and almost as if we were performing a spell of some kind, perhaps to welcome the frost moon into the winter light.

He danced so smoothly for one who appeared to be so young, and I could feel myself getting lost in the music. I could only catch a glimpse of Shadow as I continued to dance around in the circle, another arm looping around my waist and then another and soon I was being danced with multiple different people, male and female. It was amazing and felt so otherworldly.

Feeling an arm wrap suddenly around my waist, I knew instantly who it was as my body fell into his. As if we were two puzzle pieces filling up the remaining spaces. Swaying into each other, the heat rose in my chest as I rested my head against his chest and heard his heartbeat slowly.

Looking up, I expected to get lost again in his gorgeous

blue eyes but instead I was greeted with red eyes, surrounded by black and my heart sank suddenly, and he wrapped his arm tighter around me, unable to allow me to escape.

"You forget dear sweet Giselle; I will always find you. You are made of my blood and no number of spells or wards can protect you from me. Sooner or later, I will get you back."

My heart continued to pound loudly in my chest, causing my ears to start ringing as the ground underneath my feet felt as if it would swallow me whole. What spell was this? He couldn't really be here, this place was safe, away from his spies and prying eyes.

No, this wasn't real, this couldn't be real. I attempted to push him away and felt his grip loosen as a piercing laugh rang throughout the clearing and everyone around me appeared to stop dead in their tracks, could they possibly see him too?

"Giselle!"

I had no idea whose voice it was as my eyes grew fuzzy and a wave of something fell over me and I felt the ground hit me and then a warm embrace wrapped me up quickly, protecting me from the hideous laugh and whatever was going to come next.

"Giselle, your Highness, are you okay?"

Quiver, he was the one who had quickly enveloped me up into a shielding grasp as the rings of steel came through the air, the laugh growing louder and louder as the musicians stopped.

"No one will be harmed if you release the Princess back to my care," His voice, much darker than before and filled with rage, it was everywhere. "You have till the dawn in two days' time and if she is not at the border, my men will attack your city under the mountain."

And then, there was stillness and the grim feeling had dispensed, there was peace once again. Quiver let go of me as I felt my skin begin to warm again, my heart slowing down. What was a wonderful day was now being overshadowed by dread.

Shadow and Alison appeared suddenly at either side of me and helped me back up onto my feet. But wasn't it Shadow I was just with? Wasn't he the one I was pulled into during the dance?

"Can you walk?" Asked Alison as Quiver kept his watchful eye on me, Shadow was silent.

"I – I think I'm ok. Did that really happen?"

"I'm afraid so," Quiver's voice was stern and angry, "You two, get her back to the manor."

"Where are you going?" Asked Alison worried.

"I need to speak with my sister, this can't be good."

And with that, he disappeared off into the crowd quicker than lightning, followed by Alary who must have been celebrating with his wife. All eyes remained on me as we went through the crowd of people and out of the clearing. I overheard what may have been a guard disbanding everyone and sending them home as we made our way back to the manor.

I felt helpless and a little lost, I hadn't expected reality to show its ugly face so soon as I was looking forward to the ball and sharing a dance with Shadow but alas judging by Quivers urgency need to get away, the ball would most likely be cancelled now and I would be made to leave by Queen Leena as after all, she had to keep her subjects safe.

25

SHADOW

I couldn't speak, it was as if my body was no longer my own as I felt the darkness creep it's way inside of my mind. Almost as if a fever had come over me, I felt myself unable to breathe, to move or to do anything that was of my own body.

I was only stood at the side-lines of the dance as the music blared, people cheered and I watched Giselle spin around, smiling and laughing and then suddenly, she was in my arms and then the world went black. Minutes later I felt my mind clear, and Giselle was being caught by Quiver and I just stood there dazed and confused.

Giselle looked at me just as confused and lost as I, Alison had placed her arm around Giselle's waist to help her stand and without thinking I lifted Giselle up off the ground and began to carry her back to the manor as instructed by Quiver, still silent as my mind raced with what just happened.

Entering Quiver's home as per his request, I set Giselle down in one of the sitting rooms as Alison fretted around her and I took to the glass cabinet that had a few crystal glasses and a filled decanter at the ready, pouring myself a drink and then another one straight after. My mind still fuzzy as dizzy spells came and went suddenly.

His voice began almost as a whisper and then it was as if he was standing next to me and the shock of it made me drop my glass, shattering it across the marble floors and Alison screamed a little as the noise made her jump a mile. Giselle didn't seem fazed; it was as if she too was in the same state as me.

"My Lord Shadow, are you alright?"

Alary appeared at my side as he placed a hand on my shoulder. But searing pain ran through my entire body and the ringing in my ears grew louder as the voice started to shout. I dropped to my knees and held my head tightly as tears streamed down my face, what was happening?

"Shadow!" Her voice, of course it was her voice, came rushing towards me and it was as if light filled the space, "Don't let him win! You can't let him in!"

His voice, his darkness, it was still inside me burrowing its way against the walls of my mind, demanding I give up control and allow him to take over, to get his hands on Giselle and I couldn't allow that to happen. I could feel her warmth against my face as I looked at up her, her image going dark and blurred, it was just the shape of her outline I could see as I battled inside myself to stay, to keep her safe.

"My Shadow, you promised me."

I felt a pull as I felt her body crash into mine as she wrapped herself around my neck and pulled me in tightly, not letting me go.

"I will not let you take him!" She shouted as I could feel my heart begin to beat slower and feel her face become wet with tears. "He's not yours and you will never have him!"

The stretching of my mind was enough to make me cry

out once again as the pain began to become too much. I wanted it to stop, I would have done anything to make it stop, to give me rest. I could feel her body shake against mine, her light becoming dimmer as the darkness seeped its way through the smallest gaps in my mind, slowly trying to break free and take over completely.

"You are not allowed to leave me."

She shuddered as I felt her shift and then her lips were upon mine and as our mouths connected, the light started to grow brighter and brighter. The pain started to ease and deep within myself, I felt it, it was only faint but the softest of magic that had been laid to rest, something was igniting inside me.

Giselle's kiss grew deeper, and my arms wrapped around her waist, bringing her in tighter, closer to me, as close as I could possibly get her to be and the light almost became blinding, filling the spaces of my mind up and easing any of the darkness and I felt the snap, the scream and shouting as he was pushed from my mind and out finally. The pain disappearing almost instantly and the ringing a faded memory.

"I will face the world with you," I whispered as I broke the kiss, "I promised you."

She sobbed as she pulled me into her, forgetting her own strength as she wrapped her arms even tighter around my neck, enveloping me in our emotions.

Kissing me then on my cheeks, my nose and lightly on my lips through her tears, I couldn't make sense of anything, there was only her and then she fell silent, her sobs becoming whispers and little shakes, I kept her in my arms until she broke the hug and left me a few inches, the cold-ness of the room appearing between us as she wiped away whatever tears left in her eyes.

"What in Goddess name just happened?!"

Looking up towards the doorway, Queen Leena stood there with Quiver, both in shock and awe at the scene. I looked around and saw the room completely turned upside down, the glass cabinet smashed, the chairs on their side as was the coffee table and Alison was stood behind Quiver peering over his shoulder, as was Alary. The room was trashed.

"You guys, you did something and suddenly, some form of spell erupted from you both. I have never seen such magic."

Quiver said puzzling as I helped Giselle up on her feet, she appeared to be as right as rein again, as was I, as if nothing had happened.

"I think we best send for your friend Mr Mabon dear brother; he might be the only one who can explain what we just witnessed." Leena crossed her arms as she stepped into the room, crushing broken glass with her shoes.

"I believe we had a visitor this evening and I think it's time we discuss our options and plans, don't you think your Highness?"

She turned to address Giselle and her shock was the same as mine. I think Giselle was half expecting her to remove her from the city and throw her to the wolves, so this was already a nice change, Quiver must have finally won her over.

26

XANDIOUS

A s I flew across the throne room and landed straight into one of the marble pillars, I felt my body fill with rage. Many of my footmen came rushing to help me up but filled with adrenaline, the green sparks on my fingertips lit as quickly as the darkness inside me, flaring outwards and throwing the footmen across the room in several directions.

"BRING ME CORVIN!" I shouted getting to my feet.

Corvin, one of the many mages I kept close to me, not for protection but mainly for control. The spell he gave me wasn't strong enough and now I was back in my own body while Shadow and Giselle walked free unharmed, and this would not do. Sitting down on my throne as one of the footmen got to his feet and rushed out the door to fetch my mage, I clicked my fingers and a goblet of wine appeared seconds later.

"If you spill any of that, it will be your blood decorating my floor next." I told my servant as I took a hold of the goblet, the servant however continued to shake.

"You wished to see me, your Majesty."

Covin arrived within seconds and seemed unfazed by my mood, that would soon change.

"That spell you gave me wasn't good enough Corvin and for that I will have your head."

"Your excellence," He fell to his knees as he rushed to beg in front of me, "Please sire, that spell was the most powerful myself and the rest of the mages were able to create. Something must have happened to break the connection but please, it was not our spell."

"Are you to blame me for this failure?!" I shouted rising to my feet as Corvin lowered his body completely to the floor.

"No sire, of course not. Perhaps something was more powerful."

"Don't be so ridiculous, nothing is more powerful than I."

I narrowed my eyes at him as I sat back down, taking a gulp of my drink and lost myself in thought for a few seconds. No, Giselle couldn't have gained that much strength in such a small space of time and Shadow, certainly not.

I was able to invade Shadow's mind without his or her notice and it was only once Giselle got involved and shouted at me to leave, I was pushed fully out from Shadow's mind.

"My daughter is not powerful enough to break a spell. Lord Shadow isn't either." I spoke aloud.

"It is possible, your Majesty, that together they may be able to join strengths to break a spell. Even one as powerful as that one."

"If that were so, why didn't you give me a better spell! Something that would work and control them."

"I'm sorry my King but we did not know this would happen. We have lost our seer and aren't able to predict the future. We can however go to our scrolls and return with something stronger."

Corvin raised himself slowly off the floor but kept his eyes low to the ground, unable to meet my gaze. I wasn't impressed with his attitude, and it dawned on me how the spell being broken meant I was showing some form of weakness. This would not do. I was done speaking to him and wished for him to leave my sight as he wasn't any help. Waving my hand, he slivered backwards until one of my footmen showed him out.

Tapping my fingers lightly on the arm rests of my throne, I held the goblet to my lips, pondering my next move and wondering if I should try again with entering Shadow's mind but would that be too soon, and would I fail again?

"My King?"

Ayla, her voice drew my eyes up as she appeared through the throne room doors and lowered into a curtsy. Waving her to enter she slowly walked towards me before curtsying again at the foot of the throne steps.

"Will you not come to bed this evening?" She asked me with her eyes low to the floor.

She had started to grow bolder in the days since Giselle escaped and appeared to have changed. Perhaps it was the potions I had slipping into her tea each morning to make her obedient or it was the fact my darkness was now latching onto her own mind whenever she slept, allowing for her own light to dim out as my will took over.

"Is the hour late?" I asked, appearing to care.

"The moon rose many hours ago, sire, I know you have been busy with your work, but we all do need rest."

"I will retire in due course. Head up to my chambers and wait for me."

I had no interest in the girl, there was barely any attraction even if she were pretty, she was plain and nothing like my Enelya.

No one was ever going to compare to Enelya and if it weren't for the need for power and blood, she would have been at my side during all of this. Her light however needed to be extinguished and her soul used for a much greater purpose, my purpose.

"As you wish my King."

Ayla curtsied again and I rolled my eyes looking away as she left the room. Leaving my mind to wander to Enelya. Killing her broke my heart in two and some part of me still ached for the pain I caused her but as soon as the thought came to mind, the darkness ripped it away burying it deeper within myself.

Drinking the rest of my wine and holding my hand out for more, the glass was again filled to the brim as I continued to wonder. Dream.

"Giselle, I will have you, no matter how many times you think you may hide, escape, or beat me… I will always win."

If I were to succeed in the next part of my plan, I needed something Giselle had. And I would need it soon.

27

GISELLE

W e all sat patiently in one of the living quarters for Mabon to arrive after being sent for by Quiver. I stayed firmly put beside Shadow who's hand rested on my knee. Alison sat on the other side of me sketching something in her sketchbook and she kept glancing up at Quiver and then back at her book.

"What are you drawing?" I asked, intrigued.

"Just something from this evening."

She showed me the page and it was a scene from the festival of the Frost moon. Bodies danced around a fire in the middle while the moon shined brightly down, Quiver was to the right of the page and Alison was heavily detailing his eyes.

"You have a talent for art, its beautiful." Shadow spoke as he glanced at the page to.

"Thank you."

"Where is Mabon!?" Leena shouted as she joined us again, this was the fourth time in the last hour, clearly frustrated.

"I did send for him your Majesty, perhaps he is held up." Butcher, the butler looked defeated and scared when Leena turned abruptly towards him, her face filled with anger.

"Well send for him again." She ordered before leaving the room once more.

It must have been a tiring job being Queen and it got me thinking about when I become Queen and what it will be like. Leena is Queen to a small portion of this world, whereas my Queendom will be the entirety of Nimra including all the outskirts and beyond.

Perhaps I would need to make peace with Leena, to ask for advice and some form of guidance as I no longer had my mother to help aid me in the new job I will hopefully have sooner or later. Shadow squeezed my leg a little then to draw my attention to him as we finally heard the door go and Butcher walked in accompanied by Mabon.

"Apologies for the delay your Highness, I got held up healing someone. You sent for me?"

Mabon bowed towards Shadow and I before turning to do the same to Quiver and Leena as she followed behind him. Her face still filled with annoyance, and I just had to roll my eyes at her, she clearly was blowing the whole thing out of proportion.

"Her Highness was able to bring forth a powerful spell this evening, light magic I believe and the last time that form of magic was used was centuries ago." Leena kept her arms crossed as she walked into the room and took the seat at the fireplace, Quivers chair.

"I expect Princess Giselle has inherited magic from her bloodline, many royals of the Minwed household were blessed with a mixture of powers, each given to them by the Goddesses themselves," Mabon paused, turning to look at

208

me with a kind smile. "If you were able to use light magic then I believe, that has come from your mother and grand-mother. The late Queen processed great power of light and earth, perhaps you have the same."

"Maybe, but that doesn't explain how I was able to push my father out from Shadow's mind."

"I beg your pardon? What happened?" Mabon's eyes widened as he looked at Shadow and then to Leena. "What was the King able to do?"

"Xandious," Shadow corrected him, "He was able to enter my mind this evening and I believe if it wasn't for Giselle, he would have taken over me completely. I have never known that to happen, and I didn't know anyone was capable of that kind of magic."

Mabon sat down suddenly as his face turned blank, as if he were searching for something in his mind and for a few seconds was silent, the entire room waiting for him to speak.

"The magic Xandious uses is very dark, it comes from Aithne herself, when he split his soul after killing Enelya he allowed himself to be come darkened with demons. Shadow, when you were at Aithne's gate before Quiver, Alary and I brought you back, your mind was fractured a little. He may have used those cracks to his advantage."

"So will Xandious be able to do it again?" Quiver charmed in, all asking what we were all thinking.

"Her Highness might have fixed those cracks when she pulled him from Shadow's mind. He would have to grow in strength massively if he were to attempt again and for him to do that, he would need great power."

"So, he may try again." I asked looking worried at Shadow and hoping that didn't happen again.

"I don't think he will, to become more powerful, he

would have to do unspeakable things. As for now, he knows you have magic and may attempt to use that to his advantage so please beware Princess."

Mabon stood then and turned to Leena who had suddenly become quiet, the first time since she arrived this evening. He waited a second or two for her to address him and she just looked at him with a concerned expression, possibly they were already talking to one another?

Quiver had mentioned to us during our stay here Alary and him were able to communicate through the mind, as were he and Leena. Maybe Mabon and Leena were doing that.

"I will take my leave now your Majesties, the healers need me to help some more patients. Princess," He turned his attention back to me then, bowing. "Please be mindful of your gifts, they are untrained and unchecked, I would offer to help you but I'm afraid we are now on a deadline. Remember to keep calm and use that to your advantage, should you need to."

With a flick of his hand, Mabon faded away, disappearing right before all our eyes and Alison almost jumped out of her skin when she watched in amazement. He was a mage after all and a powerful one, so he had to always exit in a rememberable way.

"Well, if that is everything everyone, shall we retire for the night?"

Without anyone replying, I stood up almost instantly and left the room without a word to the others. I needed to clear my head as my mind had started to think about the so-called powers that I had inherited from my mother and beyond. I was unaware we even had magic in our blood. I wished for my mother more than anything as I entered my room.

WALKING towards the window of my bedroom and I knew straight away what was about to happen next. What was coming and I couldn't shake the feeling of discomfort or disdain. I had almost just lost Shadow again and my heart tightened in worry at how close we had come to danger.

I had to leave them all downstairs to get some breathing space, to contemplate. Shadow most likely wanted to rush after me, but he knew to leave me, at least for a little bit. My fears were starting to rise again, and I didn't know if I was going to overcome them. I only narrowly escaped from my father's grasp, and it was only because Quiver and Alary had come to my aid, how many more of my friends were going to end up in danger or worse because of me?

"Giselle."

Alison's voice broke my thoughts as she opened the bedroom door and peered her head inside. She looked as worried as I felt. It was foolish of me to think my father wouldn't be able to reach me here, he had some of the most powerful mages in all the land under his command and I had no real idea of how much strength he processed.

"Are you okay? – Silly question actually, of course you're not. Quiver sent me up here to see if you are ready to join us back downstairs. The cook has brought out some food and wine to help ease all our nerves."

She sat down on the edge of the bed, running her fingers through her hair in nerves as I came to join her. Leaning against the vanity table just across from her, clutching the glass of wine I had been nursing for the last half hour.

"The Queen understands you are worried, but she has assured all of us, well, mainly Shadow, that she's not about to send you out of here to potentially any harm and I'm pretty sure if she did order that, Quiver would have something to say or would leave with you and we both know, she doesn't want that."

"I'm worried Alison, he has threatened you all tonight and if I don't go, he will come here and cause more death and destruction, more than what he already has, and the people of this city don't deserve that. They don't deserve to be punished for hiding me," I took a sip of my drink as I felt the headache begin to form, "You are all so important to me and I almost just lost Shadow again, I don't know if I will be able to face what comes next."

She stood from the bed and came over to me, taking the glass out of my hands, setting it down and then taking my hands in hers before wrapping me in a sisterly hug.

"You are our Princess, our Queen. We will go to the ends of the world for you," She let go of me and smiled that kind, sweet smile I was coming to know so well, "And besides, Shadow will never leave your side and wouldn't dare allow you to face any of this alone. He cares for you deeply and I already know he would set the world ablaze to keep you safe."

I knew she was right, in so many ways I knew deep down in my gut that whatever I did now would involve them all, even if it meant leaving in the dead of night which part of me wanted to do. Desperate to keep them safe.

Sighing, I gave myself a little shake as Alison walked back to the bedroom door, clearly expecting me to follow. Diplomatic talks were going to happen next, and my mother had always taught me to put personal feelings aside to get the job done and that's what I was going to have to do from now on.

"You know, if you do have some great magic, you should

use it to your advantage and its obviously strong enough to beat Xandious in some ways."

She smiled again, holding out her hand for me to take. Taking it, we headed back down to the dining hall where everyone had moved to. Shadow stood up as soon as I entered and came rushing over to my side, embracing me into a tight hug and then kissing me lightly on my forehead.

He held my hand securely as he led me to sit down at the other end of the table, opposite was Queen Leena at the head and Quiver and Alary at either side of her. Alison took the seat to my left and Shadow took my right.

"I expected this to happen," Leena was the first to speak appearing to be annoyed and rolling her eyes at me, "I knew as soon as my brother brought you to us, we would have trouble."

"Leena, I don't think her Highness expected the King to find us, let alone use a clearly well-crafted spell to invade the mind of someone he thought dead."

Quiver replied before I could even utter a single word. The Queen huffed in response, and it took every ounce of strength to not call her out on her disregard and disrespect of her own brother. I had no idea why she had a stick up her butt and any other time, I may have tried to get to know her to find out what bothered her deeply but each meeting we had so far, she wasn't making me feel as if she were even a nice person. She reminded me a lot of my grandmother.

"That's a thought, how did he know Shadow was alive?" Alary spoke up and it shook me a little, how did Xandious know Shadow wasn't dead?

"Perhaps our spy that is hiding within Governor Mason's ranks sent word." Quiver replied crossing his arms and leaning back into his chair.

"Either way, we must be careful with what we say in this household as we never know who might be listening."

Leena spoke coldly and downed then her glass of wine, before clicking her fingers and food was brought forward, serving her first and then me. She looked at me with daggers in her eyes and I could sense she was about ready to explode in a rage.

"Queen Leena, I will be the first one to apologise for what has happened on my account," I was sincere in my words but also didn't wish to offend her any more than she already was.

"I did not expect my father to be able to find me, let alone reach me here. I truly believed he wouldn't have been able to cross the barriers and spells that surround your home. However, we all need to stop underestimating him and his powers. Shadow and I will take our leave in the morning, Alison you are to stay here if permitted with Prince Alex and I will face my father head on."

I was sure my words were going to shock Shadow, but he appeared as if he expected it, as if he knew this was going to be my choice and wasn't going to argue with me on it either.

"Now, now, don't be so hasty. Your presence here has deeply vexed me, and I won't deny that my people are now in even greater danger than they were before. But, as my brother and Alary have pointed out already several times this evening, your arrival was also foretold. Arwen, I believe whom you have already met read in some ancient scrolls many years ago that a maiden with the eyes of the sun will appear and I am told that is you," She paused, waiting in bated breath to see my reaction but I kept my face unreadable.

"If this is to be true, then I believe we owe you an army

of the very best soldiers this world has ever seen, and we are to go to war alongside each other."

This was not something I saw coming, although Alison had said Leena wouldn't wish me ill, I did not see her agreeing to help in combating against Xandious and his armies. This was both shocking and somewhat relaxing. I had only heard of how talented Elves were at fighting, and swordsmanship and now she was offering her greatest fighters to me.

"My brother will help with the arrangements and see to it that the men are prepared. If that tyrant wishes to have you by sun up in two days' time, then he will be greeted with swords and bows at the ready. Mabon will also be preparing provisions for spells and potions I believe. You are still a guest of my Kingdom, and my guests will not be threatened or treated poorly."

She stood from the table as did the rest of us in respect, I was still surprised by her sudden empathy and emotion towards me, perhaps she wasn't as bad as I had come to believe.

"Your Highness, as Lady Alison pointed out, you are the rightful heir to your own throne and your father needs to be removed and if that needs to happen by force, my people are fully behind you. Alex, please send letters to the other tribes and notify them their Queen is calling for their aid."

The other tribes? Was there may be more Elves hiding away somewhere that we had no idea about? I had so many questions run through my mind as Quiver bowed and left the room quickly followed by Alison as she offered to help him any way she could.

"I will take my leave and prepare myself. I suggest you get some rest; it sounds as if you both used a large portion of your magic this evening battling the King – Sorry Xandious from your mind." She paused and headed to the doorway before turning and looking at me once again.

"He is not a King and never was, so we shall no longer address him as one." She nodded as if giving an order to everyone in earshot, including myself.

He wasn't a King; he stole a crown that did not belong to him as well as a throne. She was right and I needed to be reminded of that. Her footmen closed the doors behind her, and she left the manor quite quickly after that, leaving both Shadow and I alone in the dining hall, the buffet of food left untouched and unspoiled, but I was still too nervous and feeling lightheaded to eat.

"I think, after today we need a drink, and you need some food. We will then head to bed when you are ready."

Shadow took my hand and gave it a reassuring squeeze before beginning to fill up a plate full of pastries, fruit, and meat, ordering me to sit down as he placed the food in front of me and handed me over a rather large glass of red wine.

"I am surprised at Queen Leena; I was ready for her to throw me out of this place at the first sight of me."

"Well, she was thinking it, but Quiver and Alison managed to calm her down and even if she did attempt to throw you out, she would have had many of us to deal with in repercussions."

"Shadow, I am worried that this may not end well for any of us. I have a horrible feeling in the pit of my stomach that I can't seem to shake."

He took my hand in his once again and looked at me with such deep love and kindness in his eyes.

"I know my love, but we sadly knew this was coming. We couldn't hope to hide in the shadows forever and the Queen is right, you are the rightful heir and Queen to your own Queendom and deserve to be seated on your throne, not being hidden away like some common thief," He raised my hand and brushed his lips against it, smiling a little, "And besides, as much as I love seeing you in armour, you will look even more radiant in your crown."

Kissing my hand, he then leaned towards me and kissed me lightly on the cheek. His warm breath brushed against my skin as I felt the butterflies in my stomach start to dance a little.

"You are not going to seduce me now Shadow, we have too many things to think about."

"Ah, if I were to seduce you, my Princess, you wouldn't be able to say no." He winked at me before moving back and placing a few grapes in his mouth and then finishing his glass of wine.

"Unless of course, you ask me first."

He growled and I could see the fire and wanting in his eyes as he looked back at me, making me blush and let my mind wander if I were to ask him and allow him to do as he pleased. I took a large gulp of my drink and had to look away from him and turned my attention to the windowed doors overlooking the manor gardens, the sky was filled with beautiful midnight blues, shades of purple and sparkling with stars.

I tried to calm myself as I could feel my own heat rise from both nerves and excitement, this man had no idea what he was able to do to me, even without doing anything.

Getting up from the table, I wandered over to the doors and pushed them open, allowing the fresh night air to fill the room and it took my breath away. The air was slightly chilly, and a small shake ran through my body as I felt the chill in my bones. Something had changed.

"Intend to leave me now do you?" Shadow asked as he appeared beside me, following my eyeline.

The large green tree we had been sitting under just this morning was fading to yellows and browns, losing its lushness of summer and the leaves were falling so suddenly, as if the magic that kept this realm fertile and filled with rich colours was disappearing.

"I never intend on leaving you."

I replied as he then came up behind me and wrapped his arms around my waist, burying his head into my neck.

"Good, because I think we would have problems if you did." He said softly before kissing me lightly on my neck, sending shivers down my spine.

"You can't kiss me like that my Lord."

"And why in Goddess name not?" He kissed me again, this time more teasingly.

"Because wooing me won't get you anywhere." I joked as I pulled away, but he pulled me back by my hand and crushed me against his lips.

"You will be the death of me woman."

I smiled between our lips, laughing lightly. He kissed me again, and again, and again and I would swear he tried pulling me closer but there was no space between us left. I wrapped my arms around his neck and pulled myself up slightly on my toes and ran a hand through the back of his head, my fingers getting slightly tangled in his hair.

I could feel the hand he'd placed on my lower back move down as he cupped my bum and then his hand began to wander, pulling at my chiffon dress, lifting it slightly to expose my thigh as our kiss deepened with a sense of urgency.

The wind outside continued to pour into the room and the curtains blew forcefully, one covered us, and I could hear his breath change as a small laugh erupted from his mouth. Pulling away then looking at me tenderly and cupping my cheek with his one hand, letting go of my dress and bringing his hand back up to my back.

"Yes, you will definitely be the death of me."

A coy smile appeared across his face as he kissed me gently, quick on the lips before turning away to head back to the table. Leaving me feeling very flushed and almost dishevelled, I was grateful for the cold wind which helped calm me down slightly and yet I was ravished and wanting more.

"You can't just kiss me like that and then walk away." I said with a little temper behind my voice.

"Well, you my love said I can't kiss you at all, so I was lucky you even allowed me to do any of that." He took a mouthful of his drink and laughed a little more.

If he honestly thought he was going to get away with this kind of cheek, he had another thing coming. Brushing my hair back into place a little and tidying up my dress, I took a deep breath and marched over to him almost with the intent to tell him off but before I knew it, I was back in his arms, and we were deep in a passionate kiss.

Unable to keep our hands from wandering, my hands were back in his hair, and he was pressing himself against me as my back leaned into the table and then came him wrapping an arm around me and lifted me up onto the table and my legs were either side of his body. I didn't really know where to put my hands or to even control them as I wanted to desperately explore every inch I could find.

Pulling at the shoulders of Shadow's jacket and he started to pull it off himself while not breaking from our kiss, my hands rested on his chest then as I waited. Hearing the soft thump as the fabric hit the floor and his hands ran up my back, one pulling at the ribbon in my hair which was tied up in a loose ponytail.

He pulled at it until it came undone and then entangled his fingers into my hair. A rough groan came from his throat as he pushed aside some of the plates behind me, some landing on the floor and smashing into pieces.

He then started to lean forward, pushing me further back until I was lying down on the table, my legs still dangling over the edge. As his lips left mine to kiss down my jaw, neckline and then to my collarbone.

I gave out a satisfying sound of pleasure which only seemed to get him more railed up as he started to lift my dress up and then he was back on my lips, devouring me in his wake. I had to catch my breath in between the motions, our tongues creating a long-awaited dance together.

And I didn't want it to stop there until we heard a soft knock on the dining room door caught our attention.

"Your Highness, are you alright?"

Butcher. He must have heard the noise of the plates falling and thus came to investigate it. Which in turn made us sit up suddenly as Shadow straightened out his shirt and I began to pull my dress down straight and fix my hair once again before rushing to the door, trying to cover my blush and not give away how flustered I was.

"Oh yes, sorry about that, I tripped a little on the table-cloth and well, took out some of the plates. I would be happy to clean it up."

"Are you well your Highness? I will send some of the housemaids in to clean up. Shall I have someone send up the remaining food to your room?"

"That's quite alright, myself and Lord Shadow were just finishing up our conversations and were going to turn in for the night. Thank you for the concern but I am fine."

He bowed and stepped out of the way so I could leave the room, closely followed by Shadow who was clearly trying to keep silent and calm himself down. We had both become so lost in our passion, we forgot that the house would not have gone to sleep until we left the dining room, I felt slightly angry with myself as the hour was late and it was unfair for them to be kept working and waiting for us.

Heading up the staircase, Shadow was quick on my heel and as we reached the top, he gave me that same coy smile and winked at me before he lifted me up and threw me over his shoulders and I erupted into laughter, clearly, he had other ideas of turning in for the night meant and I would gladly welcome them.

He almost broke the bedroom door as he pushed it open and sat me down on the bed, before turning around to shut the door and turning the key, locking us both in. And I heard my breath catch again in my chest, I knew at some point this moment would come but I didn't really expect it to be now, tonight.

And yet, it felt as if it were the perfect time, if in two days we were to face a battle like no other and after the last time, we were heading off to fight Xandious, we were surrounded by other soldiers, whereas now, it was just the two of us.

He looked at me with ravenous eyes and started to unbutton his shirt, clearly saving me from doing it later and flung it onto the vanity table stool, exposing his beautiful muscular chest. He still had those same faded scars from battles previously and then some still pink ones from being stuck in that dungeon of Lord Terrell's.

I hadn't laid with a man before, during my year of escape I had come close to being with one or two men, but this time I knew it would be different. This was Shadow, my Shadow and there was this sense of needing, wanting of each other unlike anything I had ever experienced before.

He came to stand in front of me with his dazzling smile on show and then brushed some strands of hair out of my eye and off my shoulder exposing the skin there. I closed my eyes in response as his fingertips brushed there ever so gently and I could feel that dancing began again in the pit of my stomach and the heat rose within me.

"You look so beautiful right now," His voice was husky, attractive and low and it almost broke me there and then.

"What do you want me to do my Princess?"

I opened my eyes as a blush filled my cheeks, what did I want? I wanted him, all of him but I knew he was asking for my permission, for me to consent just as he has done many times before.

"Depends, what are you willing to give me?" I asked with a cheeky smile.

"Anything you ask of me," He laughed a little as he brushed a thumb across my bottom lip. "All you have to say is the magic words."

"Shadow…" I paused, looking up at him, "Would you still be mine even without the oath?"

"I will be yours even when this world is long gone, when the fires of the Netherworld are extinguished, and we are just stories on a page."

He knelt in front of me and brought both his arms either side of me, now completely eye level with me. He licked his lips and I so desperately wanted to fill the space between us now more than ever.

"I have always been yours."

"Then I want you to," I paused, biting my bottom lip, as nerves flew threw my veins and he watched me closely,

222

clearly waiting for me to finish but also trying hard not to move towards me, waiting.

"I need you, to take me, cover me with your body and fill me up. I want every inch of you, and you will have every inch of me."

I barely got another breath in before he was pulling me into him, our mouths crashing together as I moved my hands all over his chest and it almost felt as if he didn't know where to put his hands as he moved to explore. Pulling at the strings that kept my dress done up at the back and as he loosened them, my dress started to fall off my shoulders, exposing my breasts but he didn't break his kiss.

His hands traced the edges of my hips, and I gasped a little as one of his hands reached one of my breasts. I wasn't expecting his hands to be so warm and large enough to almost cover me completely. As he lightly pinched my nipple, his other hand was running up the inside of my thigh pulling at the fabric of my dress, almost ripping it in his desire.

I broke the kiss, pushing him off me a little as I stood up, allowing the dress to fall and I ran my fingers through his hair as he looked up at me, his ice blue eyes looked even more gorgeous than I had ever seen before. I stood there naked and filled with such desire and demand for him.

He stood up then and swept me up into his arms and then took to carrying me to the side of the bed, laying me down and then began to undo the ties of his trousers and I watched in awe as I felt my craving grow for him between my legs.

The only light that was illuminating him and the room was the fading fire and although the temperature in the air had fallen, I was hot to the touch as was he. He stepped out of his trousers and my eyes went up to see him in all his glory and glory it was. I felt my mouth water and I pulled him down towards me without a second thought, bringing him to lie over me.

He was careful not to put all his weight down and he hovered for a moment or two, studying me, looking at me and a smile crossed his lips.

"I will stop whenever you wish for me to stop. You must only have to say," He paused, licking his lips, "But I will also mention, I have wanted you for so long you may have to smack me to get my attention."

No matter what was happening he appeared to always still be concerned about what I wanted, what was happening and the need to keep me safe. He was more wonderful than he truly knew, and I was falling madly, truly, deeply in love with him.

"I will tell you to stop, but only if we need to."

I pulled him down closer to me, so I could feel his skin against mine and he kissed me, passionately, lovingly, and only a few seconds later did I feel him begin to take me.

First painfully slowly, gently, and clearly waiting to see my reaction. I gave out a moan of pleasure and protest, he was bigger than I had expected but the pain was minimal and eased within a few more thrusts until finally I could feel his full weight deep within my core.

He broke our kiss and turned his attention to my jaw, my neck and collarbone again, clearly knowing that was a spot I could come undone on as he began to pick up his speed.

The feeling was overwhelming, and I could hardly concentrate, my moans growing louder and louder by the second and for a moment, I was glad my room was one of the furthest down the hall.

He growled in pleasure as I ran my nails down his back and he thrusted harder, bringing me close to ecstasy and to the point where I could no longer control myself as my release came and then seconds later another one arrived.

He took a hold of the base of my back, wrapping his arm around there as he lifted me a little off the bed, my legs wrapping tightly around his legs and then he collided with my mouth as I let out another moan and as I did, he smiled against my lips before coming to the same pleasure as I just had.

28

SHADOW

A lthough I had a feeling, we would end up somewhat in a touching situation, I had not expected Giselle to allow me to get her upstairs and into bed, let alone naked and yet here we were, embraced in each other's arms while she drew imaginary swirl patterns on my chest, tracing the lines of my new and old scars while resting her head there, breathing softly.

"We should really get some sleep; the Queen and the others will be expecting us in a few hours."

"They can wait, I refuse for this moment to end." She was a little forceful in her tone, but I knew it was due to her now wanting to burst our 'bubble of happiness' as she called it earlier. I didn't have to remind her of the responsibilities she had, and truth be told, I didn't want this moment to end either.

Feeling the warmth of her skin against mine made my heart sing just a little, she was the most beautiful creature I had ever laid eyes on, and it only made me want her more.

"I don't want the sun to rise, I want this moment to last forever."

She was beginning to sound tired as she looked at me, her green eyes glittering in the candlelight.

"We can stay here for as long as you want. I am not ready to move either."

She smiled before resting her head back to where it was and I brought both my arms around her, wrapping her in tightly. The bedsheet just resting on top of our hips and for a few seconds I thought about trying for another round, the urge beckoning me deep within my stomach and as she lifted one of her legs to wrap around my own, the temptation was just a little bit too much and I began to feel myself grow with lust once again.

"I couldn't possibly go another round."

She said suddenly and it drew me to look down at her as I felt her hand move slowly and under the bed sheet, resting just on my hip bone, teasingly placed there but stopped before she got any lower.

"You already seem to have other ideas."

I smiled as I closed my eyes, waiting patiently and I was thankful I didn't have to wait long. She moved her hand lower and began to run her fingers up and down my length, lightly stroking and again teasing me perfectly.

Had she done this before? The thought angered me a little as I knew she was a virgin. Even if she wasn't and had laid with a man before, it still made me angry. The idea of another man touching her body made me feel a little primal.

She wrapped her fingers around me then, snapping me out of my thoughts and I let out a small, surprised moan as she moved up and down, creating a rhythm that was just perfect. I wasn't expecting this as I had started to think she was falling asleep, but I was glad she clearly wasn't that tired.

My eyes rolled into the back of my head almost as she

picked up the pace in motion and just as I was about to moan again, she let go and moved herself on top of me, guiding me to slide in deep and as I did, she moaned that sweet sensational noise she gave me earlier and it almost took me over the edge. As I went to move my hands up to her hips, she threw them off her and then placed both my wrists above my head.

"No, it's my turn." She winked at me.

"Do with me as you wish, my Queen."

And so, she did, and she knew just what she wanted. Creating a speed that was perfect for her and I watched as she threw her head back moaning, enjoying every wave of pleasure that took over her body, again and again and as she slowed, allowing the emotions to take over her body, she let go of my wrists and fell a little forward.

Sitting up, I left her to rest for a second before taking over. I wrapped my arms around the back of her, lifting her up and down gently, embraced in each others arms until we were both moaning in desire and coming to the finishing line.

"You're amazing."

I whispered breathlessly as we stopped, I was still holding her tightly and she brought her lips down to mine. Catching our breath, I felt her leave me and I groaned in protest as I had to let go of her and she laid down beside me while I cleaned up.

"I could get used to this." She uttered as she rolled on to her side, watching me closely, "But I'm afraid you might be right, we do need to try and get some sleep before they arrive."

Joining her back in bed, she turned around and cuddled into me, while I relaxed next to her, keeping her back warm with my body as she pulled up the blanket to cover us both.

Kissing her on the cheek, the neck and then top of her shoulder, I could feel my eyes growing heavier and I listened closely to her as her breathing slowed and she fell into a deep sleep, closely followed by me. I felt peace just by lying next to her.

∼

WAKING up to find Giselle still in my arms as dawn flowed throughout the room, the suns golden rays reaching the end of the bed and almost dancing up towards us made me feel blessed for the day. She didn't stir when I moved to leave and head to the small wash basin on the other side of the room to splash some cold water on my face, I would need a shower before this morning's meetings began but hated the idea of leaving her so soon.

Catching a glimpse of myself in the mirror, I could see how messy my hair was and I smelt more of sex than anything else. Yes, indeed a shower was required. Taking a towel from the small shelf beside the basin and wrapping it around my hips, I left the room quietly to head to the bathing room down the hall.

Sure enough, the house was still silent, most still asleep, or perhaps Quiver and Alison hadn't returned home after they left together. Turning the shower on to be greeted with luke-warm water, although cold at first and gave me a little shock, I was glad of the change in temperature. Giselle was like a hot fire all night and I needed to cool down, desperately.

Once showered and feeling fresher than before, I headed back to her, our, bedroom and found her still sound asleep. She looked as if the entire world could shake and she would not wake, I would have enjoyed climbing back into bed with her, into her arms but as the sun had risen in the sky, bringing in the new day, I knew I'd have to wake her shortly as she would most likely want to wash and prepare for the long day ahead. The day where she would need to be fitted for armour, to again fight for her survival and I hated every second of it.

This time however, we would not be betrayed, we were amongst friends, and we were going to be surrounded by the strongest fighters known to man. Ayla appeared in my mind as I pulled on some trousers and a shirt and the anger deep inside be bellowed and wanted to escape, once I got my hands on that girl, I would make her pay for what she put Giselle through.

"You're awake," Her sweet voice filled me with joy as I turned to look at her, leaning up exposing her beautiful rose kissed skin. "I half expected to find you still lying next to me."

"I'm sorry my love, I needed to wash after our own adventure last night."

"But the sun has only just risen, you should be lying here next to me."

"And I will for as long as you want me to, but for now I think it's best if you go and bath and I go and ask the household staff to bring up some breakfast for us. I'm sure you're hungry."

"Staving but not for food." She winked at me, and I rolled my eyes, trying to cover my smile.

"Greedy little thing aren't you."

She stood from the bed and came up to me, wrapping her arms around me and I brought my arms to hug her back, kissing her on the top of her head as she buried herself.

"You know I would do anything to stay here with you, but we do have a very important day ahead of us."

She sighed, looking up at me and I could see the small glimmer of pain that crossed her eyes and then disappeared seconds later. She straightened up and then took my towel that I had placed down on the armchair behind me.

"Fine, I will go and have a much-needed bath, to sooth my aching muscles and you may send for some breakfast. But if we aren't sent for in the next hour or so, we aren't leaving this bedroom until we are both deeply satisfied."

"Ha ha, yes my love, that sounds like a very good plan to me."

I brought my hand up to her chin, lifting her lips to mine and lightly kissed her before watching her throw on a robe and head to the bathing room. Leaving me to do as I was ordered to and wait for her return.

29

GISELLE

I felt the warm water rush over my body as I stood under the shower, still in a sense of happiness and shock at yesterday's events. First with Xandious appearing as Shadow, then trying to take over his mind and beating him until finally taking that next needed step with Shadow.

Lost in my own world, my heart started to race slightly as I began to feel as if Shadow's hands were still placed firmly around my body. The same feeling you sometimes got after wearing a helmet or hat too long and once you remove it, you still have that sense of feeling as if it's still there. He was now a part of me, and I felt whole.

I felt my love for him throughout my entire body and more, it was a feeling of relief when I came to realise these feelings and allow them to appear.

Thinking back while I was held captive and left to my old room, my mind would always drift back to Shadow. We didn't have enough time together during the first few weeks, while preparing with Governor Mason and although we did have a few moments together alone, nothing could compare to the days we have had together here.

Turning off the water and wrapping myself up into a towel, I headed back down to my room, still hoping to find a half-naked Shadow waiting for me and to my dismay, he was sitting down on the balcony with a hot cup of something and the small table in the living quarters of my room was filled with trays of breakfast goodies.

I was secretly hoping no one had answered his request as it was early and we could head back to bed for some more satisfying fun, now that we had started it, I didn't want it to ever end.

Throwing on a cotton ankle length red dress and then wrapping a shawl over my shoulders, I made myself a cup of tea and joined Shadow outside. The brisk cool air hitting my skin and wet hair, sending a slight chill down the back of my spine.

Placing my cup down on the small table between the balcony chairs, I then wrapped my arms around Shadow's shoulders, and he placed a hand on top of mine, giving it a lovingly squeeze.

"You were gone for a long time." He said letting go of me as I took the seat next to him.

"Well, one did have to wash all the sin off me." I said jokingly, he chuckled under his breath and continued to drink his drink.

"I see how breakfast arrived, have you heard any of the others yet?"

"Not yet my love, they might still be sleeping, or they may not have even returned. We were a little busy last night to hear if anyone even walked past the door."

"Yes, that's very true. Once we've had breakfast, we may have to go seek them out."

"Or we could stick to your original plan and wait to be sent for and satisfy our own needs."

233

He placed a hand on my knee and looked at me with a coy and cheeky smile, rolling my eyes. I leaned in and gave him a light kiss on the lips. As much as I loved the idea and would lock us both in this bedroom until we did in fact need to come up for air, it wouldn't have been our best idea especially when we had people waiting for me.

"I would love that also but as you have stated many, many times I do have responsibilities and I should answer them."

"Well then, we best prepare ourselves for todays adventure."

Taking my hand, he lifted me up from my seat and took me into the bedroom and sat me down in one of the armchairs before placing some fruit and pastries onto a plate and handed it to me, he then left me to get our cups and brought them over to the table, placing each down before setting himself up a plate and sitting opposite me.

It was such a simple act, but I could feel those butterflies stirring again, seeing him at such an ease and relaxed nature was wonderful. I was so use to him being on high alert all the time, it was nice we had this moment together. It would most likely be our last peaceful moment for a long time as I didn't know what was next to come.

Enjoying our breakfast together and then both getting ourselves dressed properly for the day, I changed into my black cotton trousers, white cotton shirt and lace up corset and then Shadow was kind enough to lace up my black boots for me, Quiver had ordered a new wardrobe for me once we had arrived at his home. I would forever be grateful to that elf.

"I hope they are awake, otherwise I am dressing you for no reason when I should be undressing you." Shadow uttered as he tied the knot on my boot then came up to join me.

"I don't think I will ever get used to you being this way." I replied.

"In what way?"

"This carefree, happy way. I have become so used to you being broody and the end of the world, it's nice to see this side of you."

"Well, I should hope you see this side of me from now on. Unless you prefer my broody end of the world nature."

Trailing my fingers up the side of his arm, I smiled as I thought about my answer for a second.

"I'd like both please, this happy carefree when we are alone and then my loyal soldier and broody protector outside."

"And what about when we are in bed together?" He smiled.

"Well then, I wish for you to be your greedy and loving self."

He wrapped his arm around my waist then and pulled me into a deep and passionate kiss, my arms wrapping around his neck as I pulled him down a little towards me while standing on my toes. And he growled under his breath, running his fingers into the back of my hair, and pulling a little.

If it wasn't for the fact, we had things to do outside of this room, I would have let him take me there and then and do as he so desired.

Breathless, I pulled away a little and then kissed him softly again, leaving the space between us and I could feel his gaze on me as I turned to sort my hair out in the mirror. Clearly, I still had bed hair, and this would not do.

"I would love to continue that kiss but I'm afraid I am going to send you downstairs to see if Quiver and Lady

Alison are back. If they're not, then we may lock the door and stay here."

"You truly are such a tease."

He came up behind me, brushing the hair away from my neck and leaving a small kiss there, catching me off guard and almost making me turn around to resume where we had just left off. But he was gone before I could allow that thought to become real and out the door he went, leaving me to my own thoughts and urges.

30
AYLA

O nce I left Xandious and headed up to the royal suite to wait for him, I began to feel disorientated and realised I hadn't taken my medicine for the day. Carlton, the royal mage had started given me something to help my fertility as it was required of me now as Queen and wife of the King, I would eventually need to produce an heir.

"He only wants you as a breeding machine, he doesn't love you."

Ignoring the voice as best as I could was the only way I could get through my days, the voice growing louder since Giselle's escape. Reminding me that it was my fault she was in this mess to start with and why she ran away.

Xandious meant her no harm, not really, he was just hurt over the death of his ex-wife and hated how his daughter had blamed him for it.

"She was right, you're a stupid idiot. You know what really happened."

Looking at myself in the mirror, the shadow draped itself over my shoulders, giving me a hug and although I had resisted it at first, the power the shadow gave me was too hard to ignore.

"She did murder her mother. The King was willing to forgive her and pardon her for her misdeeds, she ran away ready to start a war, she's a traitor."

I spoke to the room, to the voice inside my head as my reflection stared back at me, rolling its eyes, and looking as if it were fed up with the sight of me. I had become a little too comfortable talking to myself, answering back to the voice whenever it said something I couldn't ignore. It continued to try and control me, the voice of my old self, someone who was weak and needed to be put down.

I was tired of dealing with the guilt of my past self, of the things I was condemned to do, the lives lost at my own hand. Xandious had told me to use those deaths as strengths, things to push myself forward with, their deaths held a purpose and aided in Xandious's plan. To make Nimra great once again.

"My apologies my Queen,"

He entered the room suddenly then and I had been so lost in thought, I hadn't heard his announcement. Quickly dropping into a curtesy, he waved his hand at me as he began unbuttoning the top buttons of his shirt. One of his servants tried to help him and he shot them the look we all knew too well, the get the hell away from me or die look.

Pouring him a drink then, he took it gracefully and downed it in one gulp before handing me the glass again and I refilled it as usual. This was our nightly routine, the routine of husband and wife.

I watched him closely as he pulled his shirt off then, exposing his muscular strong arms and chiselled chest, his skin almost flawless, just a few small scars from battles once forth.

His short black hair unkept and he appeared to be in a mood, more so than usual and I didn't know how I was to approach him. He may treat me tenderly sometimes but most of my treatment was that of a servant and he reminded me daily that I was replaceable if I didn't do as I were told.

"You should run, escape, Giselle will forgive you. Protect you from him. Go, as soon as he's asleep."

Shaking my head of the silly thoughts as I poured myself a drink and took a few sips, trying to calm my nerves. This was the part of the evening I hated the most, having to wait, wait to be summoned to bed when he was ready and deal with that.

"Your ladies informed me you didn't drink your potion today."

I gulped, not knowing where this conversation was going. Forgetting he orders my ladies to inform him about everything I do.

"They told me they couldn't find any and would bring me some this evening."

"It is the evening now so where is it?"

"I'm not sure your Majesty, I will send for someone now."

Looking over to Xandious's servant who stood silent at the door, he looked petrified. Making eye contact with me he quickly dropped his head, he had been the brant of many magic trials with me at the command of Xandious and as such, had become scared of me.

"Fetch one of my ladies' maids and my potion, please."

He bowed, escaping quickly out the door and I knew deep down he was grateful to run away for a little bit. Just being near Xandious when he was in a mood was terrifying enough as his darkness filled the room, sucking out any warmth or happiness along with it.

"Well, you won't be able to do your duty this evening as the potion doesn't work as fast as you believe it to."

"I'm sorry your Majesty, I did not know that."

"Of course, you didn't, you're just a stupid girl."

Lowering my eyes from him, he started to undo his belt then and I hoped, prayed even he put it away and didn't plan on using it tonight. I had come to learn he enjoyed either using it as a restraint on me or as a weapon, both of which I disliked but as he was the King, I had to do as I was told and do the duty of a wife.

"My King, shall I get you another glass of wine?"

"No, I will not be requiring you this evening. Leave. I will have your lady instead; she does what she's told unlike you."

I could leave. For the first time in a month, I didn't have to deal with his body pressed up against mine, I could almost feel the joy that bounced in my stomach as I curtsied again and took my leave, trying to keep the smile from my face.

"Ayla, don't ever forget your potion again otherwise you will face dire consequences."

"Yes, my King."

Opening the door, I bumped into my lady maid who was about ready to knock, and her eyes looked shocked as well as worried. I knew she wanted to plead for me to not leave but I had no care for her or her feelings. I was grateful that it was going to be her and not me.

"Take care of my husband, Lady Clare."

Smiling then as she nodded and went into the room as I came out, shutting the door behind her. I walked down the corridor, and her screams could be heard throughout as the King took what he needed.

"You should be ashamed; you should have saved her. She's going to die."

"Then there goes another one, I'm sure her replacement will arrive in the morning."

∼

KNOCKING me flying across the training arena, I landed with a thud and the air was knocked out of my chest. Kara stood across the room with a smug look on her face as she swung her spear over her shoulder.

"Again!" Shouted Xandious from the side-lines.

Lifting myself up then, I pulled the air back into my lungs, ignoring the pain that now ran through my body. Kara wasn't the best partner to practice with but at least I could try and take some of my anger out on her, pay her back for the torture she put me through all those months ago.

Calming myself, I lifted my hand up and aimed for her, allowing the blue magic to fly out from my palm and towards Kara and I successfully managed to throw her across the room and into one of the exercise benches. Pleased with myself that I was able to finally do something to her, this being the first time since we began our training weeks ago.

"Good Ayla. Again!"

Kara stood then and began a running charge at me, throwing her spear towards me. Dropping into a roll and getting out of the way as it landed in the space I was seconds again. I shot another beam out but sadly missed her as she dodged out of the way.

Pulling the daggers from her belt, she began throwing them towards me, narrowing missing me as I darted out of the way, again and again. She was a killing machine, and I knew if Xandious ordered it, I'd be dead in moments.

Again, sending my magic to her I caught her on her leg, but it didn't do anything, and I started to feel drained. This magic I processed was only small in comparsion to some, I could only do small spells and I was only able to stun my opponent, not kill them.

"Do better Ayla!"

Kara shouted at me then, as she grabbed her spear and then knocked me off my feet, taking me down. Standing over me then, she held the spear towards my throat and applied some pressure, trying to scare me into submission.

"You're getting distracted!"

"I am not!"

"Yes, you are. If you were paying attention, I wouldn't have gotten this close to you."

"I was not distracted!"

I shouted as magic flew out of my entire body and propelled Kara up in the air and completely off me. I wasn't going to show any weakness towards her, even if she did still scare me sometimes.

"Better," Xandious said with a dark smile. "We shall call it for the day, tomorrow we will try again and this time, Kara won't attempt to kill you."

He left the arena then, leaving Kara to lick her wounds as I laid on the floor staring up at the ceiling, wondering if this was going to be my life now or until he was done with me.

31
GISELLE

S itting downstairs in the living room patiently waiting for Quiver to arrive as he and Shadow had been called up to Queen Leena's, I fiddled with my belt a little while Alison sat reading a book by the window. She didn't seem to really be reading as her eyes kept darting up to the window and then back down to her book, clearly waiting for Quiver to get back.

"What did you guys get up to after Quiver and you left? Did you manage to get any sleep?" I asked.

"Oh, eh, I slept an hour or so on the chair in the Queen's study. She did offer me a room, but I wanted to stay with Alex. I'm sorry we were gone so long."

"It's perfectly alright. Perhaps you can go rest now while we wait."

"No, no, I'm fine thank you. I will go later," She paused, closing her book, and then coming over to sit by me, "What did you guys get up to after we left? Shadow seems to be in very good spirits."

She gave me a look as if she already knew the answer but was clearly hoping I would tell her and part of me wanted to spill my guts out there and then, sharing every little detail I possibly could and then the other part of me, the one that was brought up not to share such things was shouting at me to stay quiet.

"We chatted, ate dinner, and then headed up to bed."

"Is that all you guys did?" She smiled at me still pressing and I rolled my eyes laughing a little in return.

"Why? Did you hear something?" I winked while feeling my face blush a little, "We went to bed, honestly."

"Was that after he was done tearing your clothes off or before?"

"Alison!" I laughed, pretending to be shocked. "I can't believe what I'm hearing from such a respectable lady."

She bellowed out a large laugh and I couldn't help but join her, we had become such great friends after she arrived, I was grateful for her company.

Part of me realised she was a different kind of friend to that of Ayla. My heart pinched a little at the reminder of her name and part of me wished to know if she was safe and well, but I quickly threw that thought out of my mind.

"Respectable or not your Highness, a girl has to get the information somehow and I can tell by the way you are this morning, something clearly happened, so spill."

"He was a perfect gentleman as usual and then more some, it was wonderful, and I'd happily do that for the rest of my life, no matter how long that is."

She smiled her sweet kind smile and took a hold of my hands that were still playing with my belt.

"You will have a long and happy life together; I can already see it. Lord Shadow loves you dearly and I can see how much you love him, its beautiful to watch and I only wish I will one day receive such love."

I placed a hand on top of hers and squeezed a little, to give her some reassurance.

"You will have that, I believe you may already have it, you just don't know or see it yet."

"You mean with Alex? – Oh no, I highly doubt that." She leaned back into her chair, looking back out the window for a second and I watched her face drop a little, her smile disappearing.

"We are friends, but I think he only sees me as that, he's a Prince, an Elf one for that matter and I have read many books that say they do not crossbreed with humans or other creatures, only their own kind."

"You don't know if that to be true or not, don't forget a lot of what we know of the Elves are from rumours, folk tales and now, you can ask a real-life Elf what the custom is. Alex doesn't strike me as one to follow the rules, so I bet you'd be surprised by the answer."

It was true, even I didn't know the way an Elf conducted themselves in the matter of love or marriage, perhaps it was like what humans did. Marriage to strengthen bonds if you were raised higher in the ranks and you were lucky to marry for love unless you were lower.

Many families I came across in the cities during my year of hiding, married for love and for the ability to create a family, whereas while growing up as the Princess, many marriages were of connivence. Sighing a little, I could feel the soreness of my muscles shouting at me for respite, perhaps we overdid it a little last night.

"Quiver does have feelings for you, he cares for you a great deal and I have no doubt he will want to explore those feelings, when the time is right."

"And that time is clearly not now."

She lowered her head a little and then went back to

looking at the window, waiting patiently for the men to return and thankfully it was only about an hour later did they return, and I had nodded off a little in my chair.

"My love, the Queen is arriving."

Shadow woke me up with a little shake and gave me a few moments to gather myself as Butcher opened the doors and the Queen and her guard's walked in through the foyer and headed straight to the dining room. Taking Shadow's hand, he guided me into the dining room where everyone was waiting.

"I have decided," The Queen began to speak as we all took our seats, "The ball will continue as planned tonight, most of the guards will be stationed around the borders of the city and some will be at the gathering. Quiver and Lord Shadow will also be on guard to protect you, your Highness. Mabon and the other mages here have carried out spells during the early hours this morning to help protect us from a breech."

"Thank you, Queen Leena, and thank you for not cancelling the ball, I believe your people will be happy with that decision as I'm sure everyone could use a little pick me up right now."

"You can thank you friend Alison here, she reminded me that during times of prevail, we cannot let darkness prevail and destroy our happiness," She looked over at Alison and smiled a little, it was such a small movement, you wouldn't have noticed it if you weren't watching her closely.

"You have a great advisor there with you, two in fact. Don't waste them or I will make sure they stay in this court."

"I am very grateful for them both."

"Now, my brother has assured me that all letters have been sent out this morning and we should hopefully receive a response or two in the next couple of hours. Once we do, I will send a messenger to inform you, as for now, I suggest you all rest as much as you can, we might be in for a couple of long nights, I won't be surprised if the enemy tries to snuff us out, but he has no idea how resilient we Elves can be."

Leena sounded confident, and it gave me some strength and reminded me of what my mother was like. Powerful, knew her strength and didn't take any prisoners. Leena showed a great fighting spirit, and it made me relax, even for just a few seconds that I had come to the right place for aid.

"I will see you all this evening, dress your best but prepare yourselves. Anything can happen."

She stood then, as did we all and watched as she left the room with her guards. Quiver gave Alary a glance of worry for a split second but then replaced it with harsh lines. Catching my eyes on him he smiled and headed out the room behind Leena and then seconds later came back in.

"I apologise for leaving you all night your Highness, but the staff assured me you were kept occupied and well looked after." Quiver said as he took his seat back down.

"Oh, she was very well looked after." Alison joked under her breath, and I shot her a look of shut up.

"Alary, will you be joining us for lunch?" I asked, quickly changing the subject.

"That's very kind of you to offer your Highness, but alas I fear my Arwen has been up waiting for me and I don't like to keep her waiting or worrying but I shall be sure to see you all at the ball."

Alary bowed towards me and quickly left the room moments later, it was now just the four of us and for a second I sighed. The three of them had each become something special to me and it pained me dearly to think they would be put in harm's way just to protect me.

Lunch arrived once we had sat back down, Quiver filling up our glasses with whiskey and took some time to talk to Alison while Shadow and I sat quietly, enjoying each other's companions but as the afternoon went on, I could feel my eyelids become to grow heavy and I longed for some more sleep. Judging by Alison, she appeared to feel the same way as I and I took my chance.

"Alison, would you like to retire for a little bit, I could do with some rest and I'm sure you could also."

"Yes, that sounds lovely. Do you mind Alex?"

"Of course, I don't mind. You both need to get some sleep before this evening's events as we have no telling what will happen. I'm sure Shadow and I will be doing the same shortly."

Placing a hand on Shadows cheek, I leaned down and gave him a little peak and then took a hold of Alison's hand, leading her up the stairs and wishing her well as she went into her room. Leaving me to my own and as I entered the room felt empty, cold. I had become used to walking with Shadow behind me or already here awaiting my arrival.

We had shared this space from the moment we arrived, and I didn't wish to share it with anyone else. Nevertheless, sleep was calling and sitting on the edge of the bed, I undid my boots reluctantly as well as my corset and then my head hit the pillow, welcoming sleep as it quickly took me over.

32
QUIVER

———◆◆◇◆◇◆◇◆◇◆◆———

O nce the ladies had left the room, Shadow and I retired to the living room where we were left to our own thoughts in silence. I could tell by the lines on his forehead he was deep in thought, but I knew not to pry, not until he came to some sort of conclusion and started up a conversation.

Taking a sip of my drink, I slumped a little in my chair as my mind went elsewhere. It would be many years, if not since the time of my parents, that the Elven clans would join forces and unite against a common foe.

The last time was before Leena, and I were born, and we had only read about it during our history lessons. And that was against the acts of men, now we would be joining forces with them. Unbeknown to Leena I had also sent word to Governor Mason and Lord Reid, calling for their aid and I hoped the letter would reach them in time.

"You seem deep in thought my friend." Shadow looked at me with sorrow deep within his eyes.

"As do you. Care to share your troubles?"

"You know my troubles only lie with that of Giselle. I

worry I may lose her again." He lowered his eyes and finished his drink.

"I worry about that also, but the Princess is strong, stronger than all of us I believe. She survived the torment Xandious put her through while being captured and I don't see her allowing that to happen again."

"Do you think Leena will keep her word? I know she is your sister, but she too has people she needs to protect."

"My sister might be a pain and overbearing at times, but she has always kept her word. I do not believe for one second, she would forsake us. She sees herself in Giselle quite a bit, especially when she was younger. And before our parents left us."

Getting up and filling his glass, Shadow looked out the window of the living room and again continued to appear deep in thought. All this sombre talk grew heavy on my chest, and I knew deep down many would not live to see the next sunrise or the freedom of their people once this was all over.

"I had a thought," I said as almost a light went off in my mind, "I know you love the Princess dearly and I know deep down you would do anything for her. Have you thought perhaps about marrying her? Before this war begins?"

He turned suddenly to face me and the shock on his face made me laugh a little under my breath. It wasn't the worst idea I had, and it simply made sense, they clearly wanted to be together, and it would be a grand celebration to have, should they agree to it. He came and sat back down opposite me, his fingers tapping lightly on his glass as the wheels of his brain turned.

"I won't deny I haven't thought about asking her, properly this time as before we were simply told that was what was happening," He paused, smiling a little, "Goddess, that was a long time ago. I know Giselle however and she would just laugh at me and tell me to wait, we have more pressing matters to attend to. I love her with every part of me and it wasn't until she was taken from me did, I fully realised the extent of that love. Perhaps, when this is all over, we may have that wedding but for now, we should keep this between ourselves."

I simply nodded in response, already having a feeling that would be his answer and it made me wonder if Giselle would give the same reasoning.

"We best also head up and rest for a bit before tonight's events begin. I can tell you most certainly need it."

Shadow chuckled and rolled his eyes at me before downing the remainder of his drink and left the room, to perhaps head to the room he was given or back to Giselle's chambers, where he had spent mostly every night. I, on the other hand, had business to attend to in the city and that would take some time to get right and to prepare.

~

"Did you really think you could sneak out without me?"

As I pulled my jacket on, her voice broke the silence in the hallway. Alison. Turning around, she stood at the top of the staircase in an outfit I knew Giselle had some influence in wearing, her red curls let loose to roam across her shoulders, exposing her cream untouched skin.

One of the sleeves of her blouse had fallen off her shoulders and I felt a twinge in my stomach and could only imagine kissing that part of her. Shaking my head, I rolled up my eyes as she slowly descended the stairs, noticing a dagger in its halt sitting on her right hip bone.

"And what pray tell you going to use that for?" I asked

her as I started to do the buttons up of my coat. "And if you are to join me, you will be wearing something warmer, the temperature has begun to drop."

"Yes boss," She winked at me as Butcher brought out her coat. "And the dagger is just a precaution, but I'm sure I am safe with you."

"You are always safe with me." I replied as she linked her arm into mine.

"So where are we off?"

"I have some business to attend to in the city, nothing special but I feel it's best to sort it now, before tonight's events."

"Can you give me a clue of what that might be?"

"And spoil the surprise? Sorry my dear, you will just have to wait and see."

Alison chuckled lightly as we left the manor and headed into my carriage. I wasn't in the slightest annoyed that she wanted to tag alone, she may have felt as uneasy as I did about this whole situation with the King, and I suspected she wanted to leave Giselle to rest or perhaps Shadow and the Princess were taken over by lust once again and Alison needed to get out of the house. Either way, I was grateful for the company, especially that it was hers.

The ride to the city didn't take long and we were already arriving at the first destination. A small shop tucked away down a side street off the main market, filled with trinkets, magical potions, and special weapons.

Helping Alison out, she stuck close to my side as I opened the door, the unusual smell of herbs, spells and more hitting my nostrils and dulling my senses a little. Alison quickly left my side as she spotted a cabinet filled with spell books and crystal type options while I went looking for the shop owner.

252

"What is this place?" I heard her ask as I headed to the front desk.

"It's a shop of wonders." A voice came from behind me.

Out from the stacks of shelves popped the owner. She was a tall, and a mysterious woman and a powerful mage and seer. Dana, she had the longest blonde hair of all the elves, it trailed behind her like a cape as she walked over to Alison and took her hands tenderly on her own.

"You have a great destiny about you, I can see it in your eyes and the brightest aura I have ever seen," She spoke softly as Alison's eyes perked up in wonder, "Tell me, have you ever had your cards read."

"My cards?"

"Dana, I need to speak to you."

"In a moment my Prince. The Goddesses wish for me to show this lady her life path before anything else."

"Oh, I don't have a life path, I am just here to help my friends."

"My dear, if you truly believe that then you are mistaken, you mean more to them than you realise. Please, come, sit at my table."

She pulled Alison towards the front desk and then took her through the curtain at the back and I followed in tow, not so much as a believer of the cards but I did always enjoy when Dana read someone, to see what she could see.

The room in the back was dusty and smelt like an old library, stacks of books were dotted around the tables and floor, even the bookshelves looked as if they'd topple from the weight of the many parchments, scrolls and novels left to gather dust. Candles littered the room, many of which were still lit and stuck in their places by dried wax.

Dana sat Alison down in the chair opposite her and then threw a load of papers and books onto the floor, exposing another seat and almost shoving me into it, before she took her seat across the table and pulled out a stack of cards from nowhere.

"Please, if you will, shuffle these."

She slid them across the table and Alison took a few seconds before gathering some courage to pick them up and start shuffling them as best as she could and then handed them back to Dana.

Dana parted them into three uneven piles then, lifting one card from the top of each pile and then turned them upwards in front of her and then took the bottom card from each pile and placed them next to the other ones, keeping them covered.

"Page of cups, this is your past. You have a creative spirit about you however, you can never keep your mind at rest, always chasing another outlet but your heart lies deep within the colours of paints, drawn to the scenes around you and yet, you have not fully picked up a pencil since you arrived here, apart from one simple drawing, a drawing of ones heart" She paused looking at Alison who tried to keep her face from giving anything away.

"This is your present," Dana turned the card over and went quiet for a second or two before continuing. "The Tower, reversed. I expected as much, you are stuck on where you should head next. You are resisting of change, the life you once led and now the world is pushing you to step onto this new path and yet you are fighting it. There is crisis looming over you and you fear the foundations of your world will crumble but you must let them."

Alison's eyes appeared glassy as if she were holding back tears and as she caught my gaze, she quickly looked away trying not to make eye contact with me or Dana, staring only at the cards.

"Lady Alison,"

Dana took a hold of Alison's hand and Alison's eyes rushed up to meet Dana's as shocked appeared on her face, she nor I had given her name, but it was no surprise Dana already knew who she was, she was the seer and would even give Mabon a run for his money.

"Change does not come easy to anyone, but we must not resist it or push it away. We must learn to accept it as either way, change will happen whether we like it or not." She paused, smiling at Alison before letting go of her hand. "Let us see what your future has in store for you."

Turning over the third card, Dana smiled a half smile as the card revealed The Lover's and even, I couldn't help but smile a little.

"Oh, I suspect this is about something you have been deep in thought about," Dana looked at me with sly eyes and then back to the card.

"You have a great balance of love in front of you, staring at you right in the face screaming for you to pay attention. You feel secure, happy and at peace here. But don't be fooled, the lover's card doesn't always mean a love between two people, it can also show the love of two friends, companions, and that of family. You are being set on this path once you accept your life has changed and it will be for the greater good."

The last card seemed to ease any anxiety Alison appeared to have and she took a hold of the last card, looking intensively at it before handing it back to Dana.

"Now for the final three cards I pulled for you, these are your messages from spirit, your guide, our Goddesses."

Dana turned the final three cards over and suddenly flew back from the table, the candles all going out unexpectedly and looking at both Alison and I as the room grew cold.

Alison stood up quickly as I joined her at her side, placing a protective arm around her waist as Dana appeared to calm herself down.

"What do you see?" I asked.

"A great darkness, a shadow across these lands. She," Dana paused catching her breath. "Beware the Maiden with eyes of the moon for when the Maiden of the sun and the Maiden of the moon collide. Chaos will ensnare"

The same words Seniya had spoken to me many months ago. The prophecy. Giselle and I hadn't discussed the riddle really, other than it being mentioned a few times, more so about Giselle's appearance being foretold. Foretold by Dana.

"Beware, who? What? I have no idea what you are talking about, I will not bring any darkness to this world. I don't understand."

"No – no, not you my dear. Your friend."

"Giselle?"

Alison looked at me with tears already in her eyes as I kept my eyes on Dana, she waved her hands and relit her candles, bringing some life back to the room and sat back down at the table. Alison and I hadn't spoken about the prophecy, and I half expected Giselle had mentioned it to her, but judging by her reaction, she was unaware of any of it.

"Please, sit back down. I'm sorry for my sudden outburst, the energy took me by surprise, I wasn't expecting such a message to come through."

Alison was hesitant to sit back down but after a few seconds she did, whereas I stood behind her, ever watchful with my hand on the hilt on my sword just in case something was to happen again.

"Seniya told me that riddle many months ago. Is that who sent you the message?" I asked intrigued.

"Possibly, I don't always see spirits face. The energy was great though."

Dana composed herself and took a deep breath in, Alison still sat there with tears still in her eyes and I placed a hand on her shoulder.

"You see, these cards might look innocent to you both but to me, they tell a whole different story. This card is in the upright position," She gestured to a card named The Hanged Man, it showed a man hanging upside down from a tree, his left leg bound while his other hung freely, with his arms behind his back and he appeared to be calm and content in his position.

"This card is an indication of sacrifice, but taking your time to do it, not running headfirst and planning your attack."

"Surely, that can be a good thing?" Alison asked as I placed my hand on her shoulder.

"Yes, but this card has been coupled with these other two cards. The emperor reversed, which I am certain you both know who this card might mean. There is a lot of reckless-ness that is about to come, a tyrant who is out for bloodshed and ruin," She paused, pushing the card forward and then pushed the third card next to it.

"The Magician reversed. He is a trickster, someone here to pull you off the path and lure you into his world of selfish-ness and disbelief. There is someone among you who is pretending to have your best interests in mind, they are not to be trusted."

Shock and dismay flew through my body at her last words, no one stuck in my mind while I pondered her sentence, and I could tell by Alison she too was stuck thinking.

"Thank you, Dana, for the reading, but I think it is best

we are heading home. We must prepare for the ball. I am sure you will also be needing to prepare as I suspect the Queen hopes to see you in attendance."

"But Alex, wasn't there something you came here for?" Alison asked as she stood from her chair and my mind went blank.

"Yes, there was, but it's alright. I will return another time. Let us head back to the manor, I'm sure her Highness and his Lordship will be wondering where we ran off to by now."

I didn't really give Alison much time to think before I guided her out from the room and out of the shop, leaving Dana to her cards and we climbed into the carriage.

My mind spinning as I replied to Dana's words again and again, her reading of Alison appeared to be accurate and very close to who she was but the last reading read as if Dana was doing one for Giselle. Was she perhaps the one we needed to be careful with? No, of course not, she had proven herself time and time again she was willing to give up her life for others.

"Alex, I am very confused. What did Dana mean?" Alison began to fidget with the hem of her blouse as she looked at me with lost eyes. I sat next to her and placed my hand on my knee, unsure of what I could say to comfort her.

"When I met her Highness, the witch of the forest Seniya gave me a message to pass to her and that message was the one of the maidens. I had really thought much about it until the prophecy was brought up and well, I too am a little confused and worried.

I have no idea who she might be talking about, someone who is a trickster, and I don't wish to think it could be either of our companions, or even you for that matter," I paused sensing the tension oozing from her body. "I trust you, please don't worry about that but I am worried, perhaps we have been too closed minded and relaxed, when we should have been preparing."

The carriage came to a stop and the door opened quickly, almost being pulled off its hinges as Shadow poked his head in quickly looking at us both with frantic eyes.

"Where is she?" He shouted. "She's not here!"

He looked angry and panicked, his eyes turning from the ice blue to a midnight blue, almost black.

"Where is who?" Alison asked but I already knew the answer.

"Giselle! I can't find her anywhere. Queen Leena has sent Alary and some guards to go find her, but she took her weapons. I'm worried she's gone to the border."

"Then we best head there quickly."

Shadow nodded, shouting to the coachman to get there quickly, and jumped in. He looked restless and flushed, his mind clearly running a million miles an hour while thinking of the worse.

"She wouldn't just abandon us, would she?" Alison teary eyed once again.

"She wouldn't want us to fight or kill for her either, I have no doubt she left to try and save us."

Shadow stayed quiet as he looked out the carriage window, waiting and ever watching as we raced through the city towards the border. He held tightly to his sword almost ready and waiting to rip it out and take out anyone who got in his way.

"I'm sure she is fine, and we will reach her in time." I tried to comfort him, but he looked almost as if he'd gone mad and I felt that more had happened than he wanted us to know.

33

GISELLE

HOUR'S BEFORE

Lying next to Shadow as he snored away the afternoon sky, I laid there pretending to be asleep when he snuck in ever so gently, trying desperately not to wake me as he kissed my forehead and settled into bed.

My mind was racing in circles, wondering back to my conversations the past few days about Shadow always being at my side, many will fight for my cause and protect me at all costs but what if I just left now, handed myself over to Xandious and took him out from the inside?

I had more to fight for now, Shadow was alive, Alison was here as was Quiver, I had found a family that I never knew I could have. I was stronger than I was back the first time stuck behind those walls and now I knew I could do something. Maybe.

I contemplated getting up as soon as I knew Shadow had fallen into a deep sleep, but I felt my body ache with the idea of leaving him so soon, we had only just got each other back and it took a lot for Quiver and Alary to rescue me when they did.

I didn't want to disappoint anyone, but I also didn't potentially want to watch my friends lose their lives over the case of keeping me safe. I needed to face this, I had pushed the event of my mother's death and the things leading up to right this moment so deep inside me, I was almost pushing away the responsibilities I had set in front of me as a future Queen.

Getting up slowly out of bed, it felt as if the weight of the world was resting squarely on my shoulders, refusing to budge and the tension in my body was becoming too much as tears formed in my eyes. Shadow shifted a little and rolled over to his side facing away from me and I could hear him sigh, almost a blissful sigh of relief and the guilt filled up inside me.

Could I do this? Could I really leave him when I had been so desperate to get back to him? Rubbing my face with my hands and giving myself a little shake, I pushed off the bed and began to dress. Trousers, blouse, corset, fur lined coat and weapons placed in their holders, I had to keep this courage up, push away the guilt and get moving.

"I'm not stupid you know."

His voice made me jump out of my skin as he came up behind me, holding his hand over the dagger he had given me so long ago, the oath he had promised.

"I know what you're like. You think by leaving us, this will save us from ruin and distraction, but it will only make matters worse."

"Shadow, please, I have to do this." I started to choke back tears as I pulled away from him.

"You think you have to do this, but we are all here to

support you, to be at your side and you know as well as I do, we will all be with you right up until the very end."

"That's what I'm afraid of, I don't want there to be an end for any of you on my account."

"My love. We all die in the end and if it means dying for what we believe is right, for fighting for our loved ones and defeating evil, then we will do that. You have no control or say over what others choose to do with their lives."

He was right, of course he was right, but I had to do what I believed to be right, to leave and help protect them all the best way I knew how. If I handed myself over, I could bargain for their lives, to do as Xandious wanted in exchange for leaving them alone and keeping them safe.

"I know you may think you are doing the right thing but you're not," He turned to look at me as I moved closer to the door.

"Xandious will try and kill us even if you are his captive or not, he doesn't want anyone in his way or to start rebellion after rebellion in your name or any other person's name. And if you think going to him now will help us, you're wrong."

"Shadow, you said yourself I have no control or say over what other's do, which also means you have no say over what I do."

He stepped forward, closing the space between us and brought his hands upon my shoulders, almost pulling me towards him, away from the door but I stepped back, breaking his grip.

"You, I do have some degree of control over what you do. I am as you've said many times, important to you so I believe my opinion and feelings have more say than others."

"You have no control over me." I spat back, angry a little

at the sudden idea that he has any ounce of power over me, no one did. "I will incharge my own life, to save you all. I am going, you cannot stop me."

"Like Goddess you are… you are mine."

He growled, grabbing me then around the waist, tightly and forcefully bringing me closer to him and a snarl almost escaped his lips as his eyes flashed a red tint, something I had never seen before.

He squeezed more as he slammed his lips against mine, almost with desperation and need and I tried to push him away, but my strength was of no use. Sliding the dagger out from its holder, I drew it quickly and managed to slice his cheek a little and he pulled away suddenly.

"Don't you dare ever do that again," He took a step forward looking at me with darkness in his eyes, "Come any closer and I will kill you."

Holding the dagger up between us both, my eyes filled again with tears as my rage and heart ached, was Shadow being controlled again?

"Please, let me go – don't make me hurt you." I pleaded, the last thing I wanted was us to fight.

It was almost as if a light went off in his mind and he stepped back, his hand touching his cheek and looking at the blood that appeared on his hand and then looked at me hurt and confused.

"Giselle, I'm sorry, I – I don't know what happened."

He stepped forward holding his hands out to me, but I returned with a step back, scared.

"Stay away from me."

Turning quickly, I swung the bedroom door open and left, running down the stairs and towards the front door. As I heard Shadow's voice echo throughout the manor.

"Giselle! Come back!"

Feeling my body tense with the sudden cold as I stepped over a fallen branch, hoping to remember the way to the border, the entrance in the mountain we had come through weeks ago.

The change in weather stopped me in my tracks for a second, how had it suddenly started to become cold? When did all the leaves start to fall from the trees? Something didn't seem right, the magic that kept the seasons bright, beautiful, and warm wasn't working.

My thoughts started to linger back and forth to the events in the bedroom, that wasn't Shadow. He would never force himself upon me and his eyes had never changed colour like that before, maybe it was something left over from when Xandious tried to take over his mind, leftover magic neither of us had been able to fully rid his mind of or perhaps Xandious was trying to break through the cracks again? And made Shadow lose himself a little.

The weather became colder as I reached a stream, unsure of where I was but guessing I was close as the magic didn't seem as strong the closer, I got to the edge of the mountain range. I would reach Xandious and his army surely by night-fall at this pace.

The thundering of horses was the first thing I heard and then the shouting came unexpectedly, my name ringing over the wind. No surprise Shadow had caught up to me, but I wasn't expecting the other voices.

"Giselle... Stop!"

Turning around, I watched as Shadow jumped out of the carriage before it came to a halt, closely followed by Quiver and then Alison, all looking rather frantic and worried. I stood my ground and continued onwards as Shadow ran over to me, turning me around and feeling my sword greet him in his chest, just as it had done before outside that Tavern.

"Please Giselle." Came the pleas of Alison who appeared to start to cry.

"Your Highness, I understand the position you are in." Spoke Quiver next as he stepped around Shadow and raised his hand to try and lower my sword.

"I am a Prince, I know the responsibilities you have laid out in front of you, to protect your people, to keep them safe and to keep those closest to you safe. But this isn't the way, you cannot sacrifice yourself thinking it will help."

"It won't, my love. Xandious has set this trap and just wants all of us to leave after you, exposing this land and the people in it."

"Giselle, please. Your father will murder hundreds if he manages to get past the barriers."

I felt my heart tighten in my chest as I thought about the people who had taken me in, to hide me. Queen Leena and her people didn't deserve to fall at the hands of my father and by leaving, I was protecting all those lives. If I stayed, they would most likely all die and that was the last thing I wanted.

I felt stuck, a foot in each world, unsure of what path to take. Leave my friends, my found family behind to protect them or stay and hope Xandious and his army don't break through the spells surrounding this place and wait until the rest of the Elven clans arrive to help aid us in any way they can.

"I don't know what to do." My thoughts spoke out loudly as I tried not to break down.

My body felt tired and overwhelmed, the adrenaline

disappearing as I lowered my sword and felt myself begin to sob as Shadow wrapped his arms around me, carrying my weight as I fell to my knees, a small part of me breaking away as Alison came racing over to hug me from behind.

"We got you," Shadow whispered in my ear as I couldn't control my tears, "I have always got you." He kissed the top of my head as his arms tightened around me.

"We need to get back to the city, we are too close to the border." Spoke Quiver with a slight hint of panic in his voice.

Shadow tried to lift me to my feet, but my legs had given way, I hadn't cried like this since the day Kara threw me into the back of that carriage as they dragged me away from Shadow's body.

Had I been withholding all these emotions? Pushing them aside and pretending that everything was ok now that he was alive, and I was no longer a captive? Perhaps. Mother always did say I had a way of hiding how I truly felt.

Shadow lifted me into his arms and Alison picked up my sword, holding it close to her chest as we headed back to the carriage, Quiver following behind but looking more alert than ever.

"What is it?"

Shadow asked as he placed me into the carriage, finally noticing Quiver's expression. He wound his hand tightly onto the hilt of his sword as he too began to listen to our surroundings.

"It's quiet, a little too quiet for this part of the woods, not even a songbird can be heard." Quiver pulled his bow around him and placed an arrow, ready to fire as he closed his eyes listening closely.

Alison sat opposite me and tried to keep quiet, handing me a handkerchief from her pocket. My tears only started to come in small bursts now as I attempted to catch my breath, to calm myself. For both men to sense something, I knew I had to calm myself down, just in case.

"Is there anything out there?" Alison broke the silence as an arrow flew, landing on the roof of the carriage, and then another into the carriage driver, taking us all by surprise.

"Shit!"

Quiver shouted as he then shot an arrow back and a sudden thud came as a body from a nearby tree fell from its hiding place. I pulled myself up and back out of the carriage as I watched him run over to the body, turning it over and his eyes widened before he was racing back to us and instructing us to get back into the carriage quickly.

"What is it?" I asked as he shoved me inside and ran to the front with Shadow, one of them took the horse reins and turned us around quickly, heading back into the city.

Alison fell forward from her seat, and I narrowly caught her as she almost whacked her head onto the seat opposite. We were now racing, feeling every bump and hole in the road, we must have been nearing the city gates as a horn ran out through the air. "Quiver's war alarm." Alison uttered as she poked her head out of the carriage window and then back in, looking paler than usual.

"I think we may have a problem."

What felt like a few seconds later, we were stopping abruptly, and the carriage door was almost ripped from its hinges as Shadow pulled both Alison and I out. We stopped outside Queen Leena's and already Quiver was running up the stairs, quicker than I ever thought possible, as we all followed him as best as we could.

"Alex, what's the matter?"

Leena appeared in the hallway then, even though we

hadn't been announced, she must have heard our arrival, after all Elves had amazing hearing.

"We have been infiltrated, betrayed."

Queen Leena's eyes widened as she looked at us four standing there, all very much confused as to what had just happened. My heart pounded in my ears as Alison clung an arm into mine, she appeared to be shaking a little and Shadow was standing more protectively next to me that he had done before.

"How do you know?" Leena asked.

"We were at the border,"

"Why were you at the border!?" She shouted.

"That's beside the point, Leena, we were shot at by a Dark Elf, he was hiding in one of the trees."

"And how did a Dark Elf get past our borders without going unnoticed?"

"I'm sorry but a Dark Elf?" Alison asked, "I thought there were only the five Elven clans to match the elements, fire, earth, ice, water and air?"

"Dark Elves are abominations; they belong to a mixture group of Elves that were bonded by fire and ice. They spit on what makes us Elves and should have been sent to Aithne's gate a long time ago."

Leena appeared to be angrier than usual while talking about this kind of Elf. Alison was right as we had only learnt about the five other clans, the ones who Quiver had called to for help and to aid us against Xandious.

"Please sister, do not give your prejudice over to our guests. I killed the one that shot at us, but I have no doubt there are more hiding in the city, I will send word to Alary to gather a group of guards to fish them out."

"I wouldn't be surprised if they are here on the orders of

Xandious, it sounds like something he would do." Shadow said and Quiver nodded in agreement.

"Shadow, take the girls back to the manor and I will join you shortly," Quiver ordered, "Sister, I will go with Alary to help but I feel the party might cause a problem if there are Dark Elves running around, it will just put a target on yours and her Highnesses back."

"No, we will continue as planned, Lord Shadow you will stay here with her Highness and Lady Alison. I will send someone to fetch your things, its better if we all stick together during this time, for safety."

As much as I hated to admit it to myself, Leena was right, it was better if we all stayed under one roof, protected and united.

"Everyone from the city has been invited to the party, we have already doubled the guards and the other clans have yet to arrive. The Dark Elves will show themselves soon enough, but we will be on the lookout nonetheless."

She stood more regal and demanding than ever, reminding me of the power my mother processed and showed during times of need and worry. I was starting to admire Leena, even if she did slightly annoy me. She had a job to do and was unswayed by any of her emotions. She wanted to keep her people safe, and it would appear I had become one of those people, otherwise she would have sent me away a long time ago.

"Gloria," She shouted, and a lady appeared out of nowhere from the room Leena had been in when we arrived, "Go and prepare a room for her Highness and Lady Alison, they are to prepare for the party."

"Yes, my Queen." She curtsied and rushed up the set of stairs somewhere.

"Lord Shadow, if you would be so kind as to go with my

269

brother to help him in any way. Ladies, please follow me, there is much we need to discuss I think."

Without even a beat, Alison followed Leena and Shadow just squeezed my hand as he left the hallway with Quiver and it took me a few seconds to get my feet moving to follow Leena and Alison, the shock still not settling in just yet.

34

SHADOW

I hated leaving Giselle at that moment when we clearly had other things we needed to discuss, especially what came over me at manor and why she had even thought that leaving was the best idea. She could have been hurt, wounded or worse if we hadn't shown up, that Elf could have decided to take her straight to Xandious if we weren't there to stop him.

Walking as fast as I could behind Quiver as he passed multiple people in the street as he either whistled or called over guards to follow, it was amazing to see how much command and control he held. The streets were filled with festivities, the hustle and bustle as everyone prepared for the party, the sky a glow of reds, oranges and yellows as the sun began to set.

We came to a sudden stop at a house and with a rather large urgent knock, a lady appeared, and Quiver didn't really say much other than push past her and head into the hallway of the house. The house appeared to be large on the outside but as you stepped over, it was cosy, warm, and inviting.

Alary and a woman, whom I assumed was his wife

Anwen, sat at a table eating and talking but as soon as they saw Quiver enter the room they stopped instantly and stood up in respect, which he waved them to sit down and took a seat next to Alary and then pulled out an arrow from his quill and placed it on the table.

"What on earth?" Arwen broke the silence as I stood in the doorway leaning, waiting.

"A Dark Elf. He and maybe more have crossed our borders and are in the city. I apologise for disturbing your evening but Alary,"

"I am needed, of course your Highness. I will get the men prepared to hunt for more."

"We must keep this between us all, we cannot start a panic within the city."

Anwen placed her hand on Alary as he shook his head looking at her, her eyes filled with worry and teary. There was more to these Dark Elves then what Leena had let on and I didn't like the tone in the room.

"If I may," I jumped in, and Anwen suddenly looked at me as if she only just now noticed me standing there. "I feel I am at a loss; I understand that these guys are well, the bad guys and anyone who tries to harm Giselle I am the first one to throw the punches, but I think you aren't telling me the whole story so if I may, Lady Anwen," I turned my attention to her and her faced changed from worried to shocked as my addressing her.

"Giselle mentioned you and her have met previously and I feel you might be the only one to give me some form of truth here. Why are these guys, such bad guys? You all appear to be more anxious than you did when Xandious took hold of me at the moon gathering."

Anwen looked at both Alary and Quiver as if to seek permission and Quiver just nodded while Alary placed his

272

hand on Anwen's shoulder. She then stood and went over to a bookshelf, hunting for something specific and then pulled out a rather large, dusty book and it huffed as she dropped it back onto the table.

"In the beginning, as I'm sure you know my Lord Shadow very much of, there were the five Elven clans. Many believe they were the first human-like creatures the Goddesses created, and each clan was blessed with certain powers from each Goddess. We are a part of the Earth, blessed by Genevieve herself."

She paused, opening a page in the beginning of the book, and running her finger down the text, as if to look for something.

"I won't list all the other clans as I'm sure you have heard the stories of where they came from before but the Dark Elves, well they are something else entirely. The Goddess Aithne's fire Elves and Fenella's ice, banded together to create a more powerful version of themselves. Dark Elves are basically a mixture of the two, but they are also mixed with the blood of demons. Aithne's demons. They are highly dangerous as their magics are unchecked, untrained and they rely purely on rage, emotions, and instinct. They will kill without question."

"And you guys aren't big on emotions are you." I joked.

"We're not statutes my Lord but no, a lot of us find they cloud our judgement whereas others find when they are trained and can control their emotions, they are able to use them to their advantage. Dark Elves run purely on our primal instinct. This can prove very useful if they are placed in the right circumstances."

"Like if they were being ordered to do the bidding of a mad King." Quiver popped in as he stole Alary's drink.

"Yes, and when there is one, there is more. When you

chop one down, another one will take its place and they will continue to come until they have completed their mission."

"So how do we stop them from coming?" I joined them at the table then as Alary poured himself a new drink and then handed one to me.

"We cut off the head of their leader." Quiver snarled.

"And that would be Xandious?"

"Perhaps. But that would mean we need to either leave the protection we have here or get him to come to us."

"Alary, I don't think my sister will allow either of those things to happen."

"With all due respect, Quiver, she may not have a choice."

Quiver and Alary appeared to be butting heads as the conversation carried on and my mind went to that of Giselle's and wondering how she was feeling with all this mess. She already blamed herself for most of all of this but if only she knew, this would have happened even if she were dead.

Xandious was on a power trip, and something had brought him here, not just Giselle, but I had a weird feeling that there was something else under this mountain he wanted.

35
QUIVER

Preparing to leave Alary's once Anwen came over to the idea that he would be coming with us and sadly not escorting her to the party. Although a Priestess appeared to enjoy the simple things in life, attending a ball was something else.

I had offered her the carriage to take her back to Leena's home so she may get ready with the other two ladies, but she refused and insisted on getting prepared by herself.

"Shadow, you and a few of the guard's take the marketplace, Alary and I will take to the rooftops, we will snuff these bastards out."

Anger bellowed in the pit of my stomach, annoyed at how they managed to break down our barrier and get in but then again, Dark Elves had incredible magic at their disposal and even one small crack in our border, they could easily break it for a few seconds before it came back up, giving them enough time to sneak in. I made a mental note to ask Mabon about it as he should have strengthened the spells shortly after Shadow was mind attacked.

"I have not seen Mabon since Shadow's mind attack,

have you seen him?" I asked Alary as we scaled a wall and climbed onto a roof to get a better viewpoint.

"You know," Alary stung an arrow onto his bow, prepped and ready, "I haven't seen him either, odd. Has he been with Queen Leena perhaps?"

"Maybe, it just seems rather odd as he hasn't even been spotted in the city."

"He may just like the peace and quiet of the forest, I wouldn't think on it too much."

Maybe Alary was right, Mabon was a mage, and it was very rare to find them coped up inside a house or somewhere that had a roof. The woods would be a nice quiet place for him to retire to, but something bothered me about the whole situation, Mabon was normally the first one to be called in times of crisis and well, this was starting to become one.

"Do you hear anything?"

"No Quiv, it is silent, well save the noises coming from the houses as people get ready. I do not spy any bad guys."

"Let's keep looking, they are bound to be hiding somewhere."

Darting and jumping from rooftop to another rooftop, we kept our eyes peeled for anything suspicious or if we could find any clues but alas, nothing.

Maybe it was just one Dark Elf and more would arrive as the party began? It frustrated me as I hated feeling useless and unable to protect the people I cared about and the people I held a responsibility to.

Re-joining Shadow and the men at the fountain in the centre of the square, he too came up empty handed which confirmed my idea that perhaps there was only one and the others hadn't been able to get into the city walls.

I knew this would make Leena happy or at least put her at ease but that feeling was still in the pit of my stomach, something didn't feel right. And I wasn't sure what it could be without looking as if I had gone mad.

"Alary, if you can send word to Mabon somehow and get him to come to the Queen's, ideally I'd like to keep him close to us." I ordered as my second-in-command nodded and left with a few other guardsmen leaving Shadow and I to make our way back.

"You seem nervous." Shadow said in a low voice.

"That's because I am."

"I thought Elves didn't get nervous or worried."

"Those are the stupid ones, this is the time to be nervous," I paused and flicked my hand to send the other guards to walk ahead of us. "I am nervous that a Dark Elf managed to break into our borders and Mabon is nowhere to be seen, I am concerned he may have allowed it to happen."

"Don't be daft, Mabon is on our side, he's on Giselle's side and has been right from the moment we met him."

"Has he though? He has a wife and child in Xandious's hold. If he promised to return them safely, Mabon may have already switched sides with the hope of seeing his family again."

"You just sent Alary to find him though?"

"Yes, and if my suspicions are correct, he will have already left our lands. Come, we will see my friend Dana. She is our seer and may know what's going on."

Heading back to Dana's shop, I pushed open the shop door and it was met with a blockage, something heavy rested against it.

With Shadow's help he managed to push whatever it was out of the way and found it to be a fallen bookcase and as I poked my head round even more a shot of purple fire came at me, only just missing my head as Shadow pulled me out of the way.

277

"Dana! It is me!" I shouted behind the door.

"That's what the other guy said earlier!" She shouted back and I heard another fireball fly, hitting the door once again.

"Please Dana, you know I would not harm you; we have been friends since childhood."

"How can I believe you!"

I looked at Shadow who appeared weary eyed but ready with his sword, posed in case he had to jump in alongside me.

"Eh – Umm - Okay, I will tell you something only I would know,"

I thought for a second trying to bring a memory to mind but as Elves grew older, their younger memories began to fade. Another blast at the door as I heard rustling on the other side.

"You and I use to play in the temple, underneath the statue where the light tree Elmery was before it was destroyed. We were caught by the high priestess as you went to touch one of the sacred leaves. Instead of witnessing you take the punishment of whipping, I took it for you and received twenty lashes rather than the ten."

Silence and for a moment or two, I wondered if she had run off to the back of the shop and left somehow but the door slowly crept open as her purple eyes appeared around the frame. She smiled a little as she opened the door more, allowing us both to enter.

The shop was ransacked and destroyed, most of Dana's books were scattered around the floor or burnt to a crisp. Her crystals and a lot of her glass ornaments were broken, and she appeared haggard and ready to drop.

Shadow shut the door tightly behind us as we stepped over many of the obstacles in our way and headed to the back room which didn't seem to be as bad. A large amethyst crystal was glowing in the middle of the table, and it felt as if it were sending out vibrations.

"What happened here?" Shadow asked as Dana huffed into her seat, sighing deeply.

"The prince, well someone who looked like him came to see me again today. I thought it odd as he had only shortly left with the lady, but I did not question it. He kept asking about a certain item I had hidden away and when we entered, my crystal's all started to glow and alarm me of danger and then the rest was a blur. I was shot back but of course, I managed to give as good as I got and destroy the poor bugger. I blasted him with a true shock, and he changed right in front of my eyes."

She paused and looked at me and I could see how drained she was, it was then I noticed her dress was covered in scorch marks from flames, she must have been getting ready for the party.

"It was a Dark Elf Alex. What on earth is a Dark Elf doing here? How?"

"You said he was looking for something, what was it?"

She started to speak but stopped suddenly, as if her voice no longer wanted to work or if as if she didn't want to share with me the knowledge she knew.

"Dana, truly, it is me, I would never do anything to hurt you. But I can't protect you if it was after something, others may come back and try and finish the job."

She looked at me and then Shadow, studying him and her eyes widened after a few seconds of looking at him. Dana had powerful gifts and could see the aura of a person, to be fooled by someone pretending to be me, they must have been very powerful.

"You can trust Lord Shadow."

"Oh, I know I can. He is after all very important to our story."

It was an odd thing for her to say but nothing as unusual as something I had been used to before and Shadow didn't even seem to question her words, he just stood there with his arms crossed waiting.

"I am the keeper of the true Emerald. The one your Princess carries is but a decoy, a tool to throw off thieves. I have the real one and he was asking about it."

"What do you mean the real one?" Shadow said, looking more interested.

"When Elves went into hiding, our elder Priestess took the Emerald from the witch Seniya to protect it, to keep it safe and hidden within our walls but when it was foretold of the maidens destroying the world, the Emerald was given to the mages of The Withered Mountains, my family and I am its last keeper. I have been preparing it for her Highnesses arrival."

"What can it do?"

"It can close a gate but with great sacrifice. Her Highness was to be gifted it this evening at the ball, however I fear if we are to bring it out from hiding now, it will be the end to us all."

A gate? I had never heard of the story of the Emerald crystal before in all my youth. My mother would tell many stories but never this, did Leena know about this crystal? As surely, she would also need to protect it and keep it away from evil. My mind wandered as I thought more on it, watching Dana slowly start to sink into herself a little.

"Are you alright my friend?" I asked, going over, and bending down to her eye level.

"I fear I may have wounded myself earlier today and after using the last of my magic thinking I was keeping myself safe and away from another version of you, I have taxed myself and I must rest."

"We should take you to see the healers." Shadow commented as he took a step forward.

"No, I must stay here and protect the crystal with my life."

"Is there any way we can take it? To protect it, perhaps Anwen will know where we can hide it in the temple."

"My Prince, the crystal is within the temple but hidden deep underneath. There is a hidden passage there, Arwen has always protected the crystal, she is related to my family, she is my half-sister."

I had no idea they were related, let alone sisters and it shocked me. Did Alary know? Dana wasn't at their wedding so perhaps this entire secret was far more guarded than I first thought.

"Shadow, can you stand guard here while I send for a carriage to take Dana to the healers, please."

"I do not need a healer."

"With all due respect, you have severe burns and I'd like for them to at least get checked. Shadow will stay here; he will make sure no one comes in and out and I will return with him shortly after I have left you. We will not leave this place unguarded; you have my word."

She thought about it for a moment or two before sighing and lifted her hands up to take mine, to allow me to lift her into my arms and then start to carry her out of the shop.

Shadow would be fine on his own and I could trust him with my own life, let alone the lives of others and a magical crystal I knew nothing about.

36

SHADOW

＊━◦◦◇◇◇━◇◇◇◦◦━＊

L ooking around the shop once Quiver had left made me a little nervous as I wasn't too sure of my surroundings. It was obvious Quiver's friend, Dana I think he said her name was, appeared to be very powerful and if she was someone who was guarding this magical crystal Giselle would need soon, then she would be a magical foe to anyone.

Deciding to be a little bit helpful, I lifted one of the bookcases off its side and upright, then stuck some books onto the shelves, no idea if anything had an order but doing so kept my mind from going into overdrive and to think about what had happened this afternoon at the border where Giselle had broken down.

It was only this morning we were blissfully in each other's arms, sharing in each other's bodies and enjoying one another. Had I missed something during our time together? Had I not noticed how much she was struggling with some inner demons or voice about what had happened the last time we went up against Xandious.

Maybe her reasoning behind trying to leave was because

I was 'killed' last time, did she know I was standing at Aithne's door when Quiver and Mabon pulled me back? When her own voice pulled me back.

She had so much power over me that I sometimes felt feral when around her, as if I would happily burn the world around us if it kept her safe. I was brought up to protect your own and she was all I wanted to protect, especially now I knew how special she was becoming and how important she was to our survival.

I hated that all this pressure was placed on her and wished I could help ease some of it but unless she spoke to me of her troubles, I would be still stuck on the side-lines hoping she'd bring down more walls so I could be there for her.

Lifting another bookcase up I could hear the crunch of broken glass under my feet as I saw many crystals, magical or healing, shattered into millions of pieces. One piece stood out from the rest, it was a shard of dark ruby red, it was a ruby almost as beautiful as the one Giselle used to wear around her neck.

Where was that necklace? I had not seen it since before the ball at Governor Mason's, which felt almost a lifetime ago. Did Giselle even have the necklace? Perhaps she lost it.

"Right!"

Quiver's voice startled me as I jumped up, hitting my head on the bookcase and he laughed a little at me while I rubbed the new forming bump.

"Dana is at the healers, let's see if we can tidy this place up a little for her."

"I am already doing that."

I gestured around the room and picked up a few more books, placing them on the shelves. Quiver started doing the same and soon enough after half an hour or so the back room

283

looked a little less like a broken shop and we headed out the front to see what we could do there. Cleaning up as we went along, sweeping up glass and bits of chard paper until finally there was some form of a walkway around the shop.

Quiver used some form of a spell to fix the front door and it settled into place, locking firmly from the inside. He dusted his jacket off with his hands and then turned to me as I took a seat down on a chair, a little exhausted and unsure of what the time was.

"We should head back, the ladies will be waiting for us and as my sister won't listen to reason, the ball is still going ahead."

"I think Leena just wants some sense of normal with her people, Giselle has thrown a lot of spanners into the work and now these so-called Dark Elves are here, they are both most likely on pins."

"You speak as if you understand Leena's feelings."

"Giselle was worried when we went to Governor Mason's ball, this was before she revealed herself. She didn't wish to go in case something happened but once she was there, she danced, enjoyed herself a little and I think she felt as if she could be herself again for that short amount of time. Leena might be feeling the same, I don't know," I paused laughing a little, "A woman's mind is a confusing place to be, and I don't claim to know how it works."

"No, you might be right but nevertheless, we should head back. Dana will be able to open the door with her own magic and I am waiting for Alary to report back on the whereabouts of Mabon."

"Do you think he had something to do with all of the recent events?"

"Perhaps, I won't be sure until Alary comes back."

Opening the front door, Quiver waited for me to exit first

and then he shut the door behind him with a glowing green light. He appeared to be slightly on edge, and I suspected he would be until he was back at Leena's and Alary had arrived.

There was a wave in the air that made you feel uneasy and unsure of what was going to happen next and if it was going to be under your control or not. Quiver's guards had returned along with bringing us two horses and we headed back to Leena's with them following in toe.

The moon had started to rise and there was a slight chill in the air. It was winter now in Nimra and although the Elven magic was strong here, it was beginning to fade and the warm sunshine feeling we had when we arrived was disappearing.

~

I HADN'T EXPECTED to see Giselle as soon as we arrived back at Leena's but there she was, standing at the top of the staircase looking out at the stars in a beautiful dark blue dress, almost black and it curved into her as if it were skin.

She always took my breath away and I would have run to her in that moment if Quiver hadn't asked me to follow him into Leena's study to discuss this afternoon's events and to then prepare to get ready for the ball.

Giselle's image played again and again in my mind as she laughed along with Alison, her blonde hair running down her back, I couldn't wait to get her on the dance space to twirl her around and have my hands upon her.

Once dressed in a white shirt and black dress jacket with black trousers and comfortable shoes I knew I'd be able to waltz in. I placed Winterthorn into her scabbed and attached her to my belt loop. I was hoping deeply I wouldn't have to use it this evening, but things weren't currently going as planned and I knew Quiver would be on edge and I needed to be prepared to protect Giselle at any cost.

I found her sitting next to Leena at the head of a table that had been set up near the top of the hall. Many bodies danced, spun, and breezed across the floor, it seemed most of the city folk had arrived to celebrate the festivities as well as most of the city guards were stationed everywhere I could see. The room was decorated in beautiful whites, pale blues and greens, symbols of the mountain Elves colours.

"It seems everyone arrived this evening." Alison came up behind me and handed me a drink of something. "Isn't it lovely, much more relaxing than the ones my mother would throw, I feel as if I could stay here forever."

"Yes, it does seem as if everyone is relaxed, more so than expected." I took a step of my drink and let my eyes wander more around the room, "You look lovely this evening by the way."

"Thank you, my Lord." Alison curtsied with a cheeky smile running across her lips as she too looked around the room.

"He was speaking with Alary when I came down, I am sure he will be soon to offer you a dance."

"I don't know who you're talking about." She rolled her eyes at me and then took a few last sips of her own drink, "You should go and interrupt the Queen, she's been holding your dear Princess hostage since you both left earlier, I'm afraid she might be blaming Giselle for this entire mess."

With that, I bowed to Alison and headed over to rescue my love. The Queen certainly wouldn't be able to stop me from taking Giselle onto the dance floor and helping ease her woes or any sorrows she had welled up inside her.

"Excuse me your Highnesses," I bowed to them both and

a smile appeared on Giselle's lips as she looked me up and down.

"Lovely for you to join us this evening Lord Shadow, I trust everything is still well in order."

"Yes of course, your Majesty." I stood up straight and gestured my hand out towards Giselle, "May I steal her Highness for a dance if you are done with her?"

"If the Princess wishes to dance then by all means, please go right ahead."

Giselle's eyes lit up under her long eyelashes as she stood up and came around the table, taking my hand tenderly into hers and I squeezed it gently. It felt like an eternity since we last danced together and if it wasn't for that night, everything would still be the same, she would potentially still be hiding, and we would not be standing here together.

We reached the middle of the floor, and she placed one hand on my shoulder and the other still in my hand as I placed my free hand on the base of her back, and we began our waltz. Unspoken words but she kept my gaze throughout each step, each beat and I could see her eyes begin to glass as if tears would appear.

"I almost lost you today." I confessed.

"But you brought me back."

"I will always bring you back my love."

She leaned up and kissed me lightly on the lips as the music slowed to a finish. And I pulled her into my arms, feeling her body pressed against mine as I made the kiss last longer, wanting to savour every taste of her, when a slow clap broke the atmosphere around us.

"I should have known you'd have brought him back from the dead."

Giselle's eyes widened as she heard the female voice, pulling back from me quickly and then turning to face in the direction the voice came from. I could almost taste the tension in the air as my hand reached for my sword and Giselle began to shake a little. I wasn't sure if it were from nerves or anger.

"You were always so predictable; you know that right."

The guests began to part ways as a person came slowly through the middle and at first, I thought it was Kara who had gate crashed the party but instead it was Ayla and shock waves went through my body. Alison and Quiver quickly joined our side as did many of Quiver's men.

"Uninvited guests are to be escorted from the property." Queen Leena's voice rang supreme as Ayla stood a few feet from us.

"Don't worry Queenie, I won't be overstaying my welcome, I'm just here to pass on a message to my dear old friend here. And for that matter, I'm not here figuratively speaking."

She waved her hand through her face, and it went through, as if she were a ghost.

"You have until sunrise the King degrees, he's being kind by allowing you one final night with your pals here but then if you are not handed over when the sun hits the horizon, our warriors will descend on this small city of yours and none will survive. It's your choice if you wish to endanger all your people for the sake of this," She pointed at Giselle and a sinister smile washed over her face, "Murderer."

I felt the shudder go through Giselle's body as she took a step back, pressing against my chest and I had never seen her this afraid, she was ready to kill Ayla after we reunited at the lake but now, she appeared to be broken and just like she was when I found her again. No courage and no willing to fight and I didn't understand it.

"Then you best ready your armies then." Queen Leena

said as she waved her hand and a gust of wind appeared, disbursing Ayla's appearance into nothingness.

There was a commotion as many of the guests mumbled to themselves, whispering words of Giselle and to send her away now, to save themselves and I felt the rage boil within me, wrapping my arm around her waist to protect her as much as I could.

"I won't hear any talk of the Princess being sent away, she is our loyal guest and needs our protection. If you question my judgement, then you may spend a night in the dungeons for your own protection. Now, continue this evening's party, music shall be played, and we will celebrate. Princess Giselle is to become Queen of the realms and she deserves our loyalty and respect."

Queen Leena again surprised me as she had every right to send Giselle packing, but she appeared headstrong and unwilling to allow Xandious's threats to get to her.

I felt Giselle sigh a little in my arms as the music started to play again and once everyone relaxed, they started to dance once more as did Quiver and Alison. Whereas I pulled Giselle off the floor and out one of the side doors to the gardens, so she could breathe and talk to me.

"Giselle, talk to me, you are not yourself."

She paced back and forth for a minute or two, rubbing her hands together as if she were cold and then she sighed deeply sitting by one of the fountains and looked up at the night starlight sky and sat quietly for a few minutes.

"I feel I am no longer myself."

She broke the silence that was almost deafening.

"After the night we bonded with that magic, I felt as if a part of me was ready to explode and my head was filled with all this noise. Questioning everything I do, every thought feeling as if they aren't even mine," She paused, appearing to hold back tears.

"What happens if they aren't my thoughts? What if they're my fathers and he's somehow deep within my mind and I can't get him out."

She held her head in her hands as I heard her begin to sob. The stress and worry she was feeling escaped from her body and almost crushed my own soul with how I had missed this battle she had been having with herself. Rushing over to her, I knelt at her feet and pulled her hands away, her eyes red and puffy and began wiping away her tears.

"You are nothing like your father and I know for certain he is not buried inside your every thought and every motion. You are Giselle, my love, my Princess. I can see in your eyes there is no darkness there, you are perfect. The light that we all need and an inspiration."

She continued to cry, and I rushed up to pull her into a deep, warm, and protective hug.

"You should have told me this is how you've been feeling."

"I feared you may judge me."

"I will never judge you," I kissed the top of her head as she wrapped her arms around me, returning my hug.

"I have felt darkness many times in my life and my love, you most certainly do not have any within you. Please always talk to me, I am here for you and always will be."

I felt the words fall out so easily as my mind, heart, and soul burst and all I could see, and think was her. Despite everything, she had pulled me from my own darkness so many times, even without knowing and if she needed me to help her, bring her back towards the beautiful light she admitted, I would do just that. No matter what the cost to me.

37

GISELLE

hadow knew the words that would ease my heart, every single time, even when I was spinning and feeling as if I were starting to lose my mind. I was getting so sick and tired of feeling uneasy, not strong enough, not brave enough and not ready to become the future Queen.

My mother would be ashamed of me if she could see me now, heck my grandmother would be ready with some form of punishment to shape me into something that she deemed acceptable.

Ayla appearing just confirmed more of my feelings, she had clearly been lost to the darkness that held my father captive and the aura she appeared to have around her even frightened me a little.

My best friend, my sister was gone and all I could do was think about taking her away from that world, perhaps I could use the magic inside me to bring her back to the light, just as I did with Shadow. But if that failed, I would have to destroy her.

"I need some fresh air." I said pulling away from Shadow and feeling his arms loosen lightly.

"Shall I come with you?"

"If it's ok, I'd like to be alone for a moment or two."

"Well, I will be standing here watching, I know you don't like me being overprotective but now is not the time to be annoyed by it."

"I understand that."

Placing my hand on his cheek, he leaned in and kissed the inner side of my palm and then let me leave walk further into the garden. The cold fresh air hit my lungs quickly and it was just what I needed, perhaps to help shake me out of this mood I had put myself in, to wake me up a little.

Rubbing my arms for some sort of warmth, I looked up at the clear night sky, the stars glittered beautifully in the moonlight, and I felt a small sense of ease.

Taking a step down towards the main gardens, I headed towards the large fountain that had become frozen at some point during the evening. The magic appearing to fade slowly in this place, and I wondered how or why. Was it my presence? Xandious influence outside the wall of trees? Or was it something else? Maybe something much more threatening. Sitting down on the side of the fountain, I looked up again at the sky and breathed a sigh.

"The magic has been fading for quite some time now."

Startled, I looked towards Leena as she appeared almost out of thin air, holding out a shawl to me, she wore an almost identical one. Taking the shawl, I was grateful for the sudden warmth across my shoulders, it was only then did she take a seat next to me.

Now I could see her closer than ever before, she had that same magical aura that Quiver had around his body. Her green eyes piercing and almost daring for you to look within them, her skin was golden and shimmered in the moonlight, while her red hair was worn loose around her face and bounced with curls. She was memorising and a true sight to beyond.

"When did it start fading?" I asked, breaking the silence.

"Around the time of your mother's death, we are not sure why, perhaps she was tied to this place somehow or maybe when her light went out, so did the magic that she gave this world," She paused, almost appearing to hold back her words, "Well that was, until I saw you shine like the sun, perhaps she transferred it to you before she died."

"I highly doubt that, my mother wasn't magical, I think this source of magic comes from Xandious."

"You're wrong, Enelya had great power and to this day it surprises me how Xandious was able to overpower her."

"I think – I believe, it was because of me."

I stopped for a second thinking of my words and what I was going to potentially admit out loud. I hadn't even admitted this to Shadow but for some reason, I felt Leena would understand the pain I held deep within myself, hidden away from all eyes to see.

"If she hadn't been so distracted by me being in that room, she might have been more prepared. I knew my parents fought, they would argue a lot, especially as I hit maturity and was due to be married. Xandious would often make sly comments towards my mother, and she would just roll her eyes and ignore them, which only angered him more. It has only been as I have replayed back so many memories of the three of us, have I come to realise he has always been cruel."

"It's funny that isn't it - when we remind ourselves of times past and we notice things differently. It must be because of our growth, we are no longer looking at things from a childlike mind, but that of an adult."

Leena bowed her head as she began to fiddle with what

293

looked like a gold ring on her middle finger, in the middle held a beautiful ruby and it reminded me of my necklace.

"You're right, as we grow, we see things with fresher eyes. What looked good before, might not look the same as now."

"Am I going to regret helping you Giselle?" She was forthcoming with her words, and I felt deep down she was regretting her decision to help me.

"I hope not, and I will do everything I can to make sure you don't regret it. As you said before, Xandious must be stopped and by helping me, you are helping make that happen and I won't forget it."

"You will forget, if you're dead."

She stood then, taking me by surprise at her words. I decided then I would never know where I stood with the Queen of the Earth Elves and part of me wanted to scream out of frustration but the other part of me understood, she was a Queen, she had people to protect and serve. One day, that might be me.

"I will be heading back inside now, I think you should do the same, the air is getting colder, and I am sure Lord Shadow is getting anxious waiting for you."

She didn't give me a chance to respond before she headed back inside and for a minute of two, I stayed put, enjoying the small space of calm and quiet I had created for myself out here, knowing full well this would be my last chance of peace.

I felt the nerves and fear well up inside me as I was almost rushed back to that day we left the camp, to the day we went to that small little village, where Ayla had betrayed us, betrayed me and I nearly lost Shadow there and then. Losing so many lives that day all because of me made me feel queasy, would that happen again? Would tomorrow be like it was before? Would we lose?

I held my head in my hands and rubbed at my temples, the shawl falling off my shoulders and landing in the icy cold waters of the fountain. Annoyed at my stupidity, I turned a little to pull it out of the water quickly, knowing it would be of no use now, but I couldn't just leave it there when the water began to swirl and twist and twinkle, it was almost as if I were looking in the looking orb back in the cottage.

The cottage, a place I hadn't thought about in so long and a twinge in my heart appeared as some of the memories came flooding back before a white light shot from the water and into the sky. The force of the blast threw me backwards and I heard Shadow shout my name as he must have come running as he was behind me in seconds, lifting me up from my feet. As the light started to fade, a tall dark figure emerged from the light and within seconds there were many Elven guards surrounding us, with Quiver now standing slightly in front of me, his bow poised and ready to fire.

As the shape began to emerge into something more, I watched as long purple hair of the being wrapped around its body and the creature held a large wooden staff whereas her body was draped in a beautiful midnight blue gown. I knew who it was the moment the light cleared from her eyes.

"Seniya!" I almost shouted as she stepped off the fountain and all the guard's raised their weapons. "Lower your weapons, please." I commanded but they didn't move.

"Quiver, please, you know Seniya, she is a close friend of mine and I'm sure even yours."

He didn't move for a second or two, waiting and assessing the situation and Seniya just waited patiently, looking at me with worry in her forest green eyes as her hair dragged across the floor. She took a step forward and Quiver tightened his fingers around his arrow, ready to fire. Perhaps he was being overly cautious due to the Dark Elves. It made no sense why he would need to worry about Seniya.

Breaking out of Shadows hold, I put myself in front of Quiver's bow and blocked him from aiming at Seniya. I knew she would not have left the woods without reason as she had a job to do there and for her to arrive in this fashion, I knew it meant something.

"Please Alex, she truly means no harm."

"Pardon my intrusion," Seniya's voice oozed calmness as her magic ran across the garden. "I am here to speak to her Highness and his Lordship; it is of grave importance I do."

"How did you get in here? Past our spells?" Quiver asked as he finally lowered his weapon.

"Your highness, no spell can keep me out. I am Seniya, the witch of the woods, keeper of the sacred items and daughter of the four Goddesses. No spell has ever blocked me for I am the creator of many spells you yourself use."

My eyes widened at her sudden reveal of secrets, I had no idea she created such spells and I had always believed Seniya was created by the Goddesses, not that she was the daughter of them, that would mean she was at least a half sister to Shadow. My eyes widened at the realisation as I looked at Shadow and he lowered his eyes and then I turned quickly to look at Seniya and she just nodded, almost confirming my realisation. They were related in some way.

"If you are here to discuss anything with her Highness, then I am to stay."

"As will I!" A voice shouted from the back and Alison was quick on her heels, pushing through the guards to stand beside Quiver.

"How do I know it's truly you?" Quiver asked still with his bow raised.

"Little Prince, look at me, you have known me since the moment you were born." She placed a hand on my shoulder and moved me gently aside, looking deeply at Quiver then.

"I am here to help."

He looked at her more closely then and I could see the wheels of his mind turning, spinning, and trying to decide if his mind was playing tricks on him, until finally he lowered his weapon.

"Good, now release your men please. I require somewhere private to discuss some matters."

Quiver did as he was asked and he ushered us to follow him inside, through the ballroom as many of the guests and people of the city stared in awe and wonder at Seniya, even Leena stood up to join us, but Quiver quickly told her to stay put, most likely speaking through their minds again as she sat back down, looking both frustrated and angry.

We headed into Leena's office and as Quiver shut the door behind us, Seniya banged her staff on the floor and a small rumble went through the floor and the sudden sound of locks and a light wrapped around the room, securing us inside.

"A spell to keep the spies out. It will hold until we are done here."

"Seniya, it's wonderful to see you." I said as I went to wrap my arms around her, but she stepped back.

"I am sorry your Highness I was not able to save you from your father. I am glad however the images I sent you to remind you to keep going helped."

Suddenly, the image of Shadow on the balcony brought back memories, I was in a dark place during those days and honestly thought I was losing my mind, it made me relax a little to realise I wasn't.

"That was you? I thought I was going crazy seeing things."

"Images?" Shadow asked as he squeezed my hand coming up behind me.

"I sent her Highness images of you, Shadow, to give her hope in the darkness as it was the only way I could get messages to her. I had hoped she would escape but I know now it was his Highness who managed the daring rescue. Which I am very grateful for."

I was the first to sit down at the desk as my head began to spin a little, all the sudden information was throwing me off and I was lost for words, unable to feel even my own footing and I just about made it to the seat before I fell.

Alison came and sat next to me, taking her hand into mine and holding it tightly, while Shadow stood behind the chair and placed a hand on the back of it, supporting it and Quiver just leaned up against the doorframe, all of us waiting for Seniya to speak the news she so urgently needed to tell me.

38

SHADOW

I felt a sudden unrest as soon as Giselle left my side to go get some fresh air, but it soon eased once I spotted Leena had joined her. I hoped deep down they would become friends of some sort, Giselle needed someone to talk to about the responsibilities of looking after a Kingdom, Queendom and Leena was clearly very good at her job.

I kept watching from the door but once the light filled the sky, I felt my heart sink in my boots, and I was ready to destroy the world if Xandious had somehow managed to get into the city walls and tried to hurt Giselle again. I was thankful it wasn't the case and now we were all in a room, sealed by magic by the witch of the woods, Seniya.

The realisation on Giselle's face when she heard Seniya's linage and looked at me for almost confirmation, I was lost for words, but I knew she would bring up the subject at some point.

Truth be told however, I didn't know much of my family tree, I imagined it was rather large and I was most likely related to all sorts of creatures and things alike. Half the time

I didn't wish to know any of it, as far as I was concerned Countess Elizabeth raised me and I was happy with that knowledge as she was a wonderful mother and friend.

"I sensed before my arrival a dark magic had been awoken. Do you know anything about this?" Seniya directed her questions to Quiver first before looking at Giselle, "I also sensed you, your Highness. I can still feel you even now."

"What dark magic? And how has Giselle suddenly got magic?" I asked, the question had been burning at the back of my mind since she used it.

"Her mother, but I do believe she has always possessed some form of light magic. Your mother must have passed on her abilities to you before she died, it is a custom of the royal line to do so on their death bed's."

"How come I was never told of this?"

"It isn't something that is spoken about until the very end and well, your circumstances were different as your mother never had time to discuss it with you."

Placing my hand on Giselle's shoulder, I could feel her body tense up as Seniya continued to speak. She must have become awfully stressed and uncomfortable at all this sudden news.

I had no idea even Enelya had powers but then again it didn't surprise me, the royal line were descendants from a long list of powerful beings, many believed even children from the Goddesses but only they would know the truth of that.

"The dark magic I sensed, I am not fully sure what it was or where it's come from. All I know it's bad and it's brewing."

"Well, that's not entirely helpful now is it." Quiver spoke with more sarcasm in his voice that I heard before. "You

300

going to tell us what this big message is about then Seniya or we going to wait here all day?"

"Giselle, do you remember the message his Highness gave you?"

"Course. Beware the Maiden with eyes of the moon for when the Maiden of the sun and the Maiden of the moon collide. Chaos will ensnare. – I still don't fully understand what you mean. I keep being told I am the maiden of the sun, but I don't really believe it."

Giselle had only told me a handful of times about the warning message she had been given, a lifetime ago and I had forgotten about it for a moment or two, especially after none of us could work out what it meant.

"The maiden of the sun," Alison uttered under her breath, and I watched as the wheels in her brain began to turn. "That would make sense Giselle."

We all turned to look at her, a little confused as to how she came up with that assumption. We already had many messages from the Goddesses given to us these past few weeks. Nefret warning me that Giselle would be my undoing as well as the message about the Emerald that was deeply hidden away under the city.

"Oh gosh, not you to." Giselle sighed and rubbed her temples, "What makes you think I am the maiden of the sun?"

"Well, think about it, you have light magic as Seniya says. What if the light magic is a part of the sun? I mean, I've saw how bright you glowed that night when you pulled Shadow out of the hands of Xandious."

"Not just a pretty face, are you." I overheard Quiver say under his breath as he went to the drinks cabinet in the room and poured himself a glass of whiskey.

"Lady Alison is correct." Seniya said.

"If that's the case, who is the maiden of the moon?" Giselle asked looking more confused than before.

"Surely that should be an easy one now that you think about it?" Quiver tossed his drink back and then poured himself another one. "It's Ayla, isn't it? She oozes dark magics and since she has been with Xandious, I'd imagine she's only become more powerful."

It felt as if a switch went off in my mind, of course it was going to be Ayla. This all was going to end up with her and Giselle ending up on the battlefield together. Perhaps she had known about this entire plan all along? Maybe she even faked being kidnapped and tortured?

It made me hate the woman even more than I already did. I had seen her use magic once before, back in that Tavern before we were all captured and she seemed powerful then but then again, she fainted shortly afterwards, was she faking that? Did she truly faint?

Giselle tensed more under my hand, and I just wanted to scoop her up into my arms and help release some of her tension in some shape or form, be that training, allowing her to shout, cry or even take her to bed.

I could feel the fire inside me rise as I continued to think about Ayla and what she had already put Giselle through and now we were figuring out who she really was.

"Did you know what she was when you sent her to me?" Giselle broke the silence, and I could hear the sadness and anger under her voice.

"At the time, no, I didn't think you were in any danger with Ayla, and I believe the only reason you are having any problems with her now is due to your fathers influence."

"Oh, give me a fucking break Seniya. She knows who she is and I'm sure she's always known. She took great delight in threatening me this evening."

302

"I don't believe that was the Ayla you knew, that is someone else, her soul is trapped in the darkness of your father's magic. The only way to release her is, I'm afraid death."

"That's fine, I already planned on killing her myself after what she did. I will be happy to release her from his spells. Overjoyed even."

Giselle stood then from her seat, taking me by surprise as she headed towards the door to leave, but stopped realising the containment spell was still there.

"Are we done now?" She asked with a hint of anger in her voice.

"I'm afraid there's more – your Highness," Seniya directed her voice to Quiver who was now halfway through the decanter of whiskey.

"Your mage, Mabon. Your suspensions of him are correct, I believe Xandious has offered him his family back for his corporation and in the next few hours, the barrier around the city will fall and Xandious soldiers will descend on the city. I can, however, take as many as I can to safety using my magic if you wish."

Suddenly we all appeared even more anxious that before, we knew that Xandious and his men were outside the city borders waiting for us to send out Giselle but if they were just going to come into the city before we had a chance to plan or prepare, they were coming here for blood.

Giselle looked at me and it was as if we shared the same thought, we needed to get everyone ready and find somewhere to send the city folk, the elderly, and the children to a safe place.

"I will go warn the Queen. Alison, can you go and find Alary and tell him to find me at once please. Seniya, please save as many as you can from the healers and any, if not all the children and let us out of this room so we may prepare."

With a bang of her staff, the light dimmed from around the door and both Quiver and Alison were the first ones to leave in a hurry, leaving Giselle and I with Seniya who looked more awkward than ever before.

"Seniya, how do you know all of what is to happen?" Giselle took a step towards her, almost frightened to know the answer.

"I am connected with the Goddesses; I sometimes hear what they are discussing, and I am often shown images of what may come to pass."

"Do you know if we will win this battle then?"

"There are many outcomes my Princess, I am not able to just see one. Many things can change how something happens, you might decide to go left when I saw you go right, there is no set-in stone matter when it comes to the future."

"So does that mean that Ayla and I may not end up battling it out?"

"I am sorry my dear, but that has been foretold for centuries. That will have to come to past to give birth to what is yet to come. Now, if you excuse me, I will tend to those his Prince has asked."

Seniya left the room in another beam of light and from where she stood in between Giselle and I, I felt every urge in my body to rush over and wrap my arms around her, enclose her into a safe space but she didn't seem to want anyone near her. After taking a step forward, she took a step back and I could feel that gap growing in-between us just as it did once before.

"Giselle, please." I held my hand out to her and she hesitated for a second or two before finally taking it.

"I am nervous and so mad; I'm confused at what all these feelings are."

"I understand, but I am here, never forgetting that. I will always be at your side."

Kissing her hand then, she smiled a little before letting go and leaving the room, and leaving me to prepare myself.

39
QUIVER

———※◇◇◇◇◇◇◇◇※———

I was growing angry with every passing minute, annoyed
at myself, and wondering if I should have listened to my
sister all those weeks ago when she forbade me to go and
help Giselle. Would we have Xandious at our door if I had
done as I was told? Would the Dark Elves have been able to
enter the city?

So many questions came and went in my mind, but it
was no use, what was done was done. I reminded myself to
not regret my decision, if I hadn't done what I did, Lord
Shadow would not be alive, and I wouldn't have seen Lady
Alison again.

She was slowly becoming of great importance to me, and
I was enjoying finding out more about her every time we
spoke. I longed deeply for her but as we had many more
important matters to attend to, I had not been able to act out
any desires. Perhaps if we survived this whole ordeal, I
would finally do something about my feelings.

Heading back into the ballroom, there festivities were
still going ahead while music played quietly in the back-
ground and food was being served out to the guests. Leena

was sitting on her large golden chair at the top of the room with a stern hard look on her face and as she spotted me, I felt the daggers and sudden shockwaves as her powers entered my body. She was angry.

"I hope you are here to tell me our uninvited guest has left." She spoke through our mind channel as I came to stand beside her.

"Seniya, that's who our guest is, and she isn't to be trifled with Leena, she is one of the most powerful beings in this world."

"And she's here because?"

"She's here to warn us, we have a few hours to prepare and then Mabon will be lowering our barriers and Xandious soldiers will attack the city."

More power flew lightly through my body as I watched small vines grow from underneath Leena's hands and I leant down quickly to hold one in my hands, kneeling beside her, I drew her attention to my face, trying to calm her. I knew she wouldn't want to have an outburst in front of everyone and it was our responsibility to keep everyone calm and unaware of what was going to happen.

"Leena, we need to get our people to safety. Lady Alison is gone to fetch Alary from one of the posts and I believe Seniya will transport people to a safe location once we decide where that is."

"I'm sorry to impose your majesty's,"

Anwen and Dana appeared out of nowhere suddenly and both looked just as shaken up as I'm sure Leena was feeling.

"Perhaps we can hide the people in the vaults." Anwen suggested.

"The vaults? You mean the ones you've only now told us about, us being me." I replied as Leena dropped my hand and looked at me with a flash of anger appearing in her eyes.

"More secrets?!" She shouted and the room fell silent quickly.

"No, your majesty not a secret at all. Your late parents knew of the vaults, Goddess rest their souls. We hadn't informed you of them yet as it wasn't time, but now is the time and as your people need a safe place, the vaults are the safest in the city."

Dana was still quiet at this point, and I wondered what was rolling around in her head, she still seemed shaken up by her attack earlier that day and it pained me to see my friend wounded and worried.

"How do we know Mabon won't be able to break into them?" I asked.

"He won't your Highness, the magic is as old as the world itself. I believe the creature who created the spells surrounding the place is here this evening. Seniya will protect the seals if Xandious does manage to get near them."

"Well, we don't have much time do we. Alex, round up the guards and get my people to safety, Anwen and you, Dana, prepare these vaults with as much food and water as you can, my personal guards will escort you."

It was almost all hands-on deck as both ladies bowed and Leena's guards followed them out. I knew I would need to sit down with Leena once this was all over and we survived to talk to her about everything, tell her all that I knew. I never meant to keep her in the dark with the news and knowledge I had found out, especially the news about Mabon's betrayal, it would explain why he had disappeared suddenly but as we were used to his comings and goings, it was expected for him to not always be around.

"Alex, I think you and I will need a chat once all this is over." Leena stood from her seat and looked me dead in the eyes, her power oozing from every pore.

"My dear sweet people, I am saddened to tell you this, but our time is near, and we will soon be under attack. If you could all please follow our Prince and our guards out of here, they will be taking you to a place which will keep you safe and secure. If you have younglings, please head home to get them and any personal belongings you wish to save and return here to the main doors where a team of guards will be waiting, you have thirty minutes."

And with that, the music stopped and everyone without even an ounce of panic began rounding up and leaving with the guards. One of the many traits Elves processed was the act of calmness, we weren't the type of creatures to panic when things became scary or overwhelming, even the younglings were just as calm as their guardians.

"What are you going to do now Leena?"

"Fight of course, what a stupid question. Alex, go and do your duty to keep the people safe and I will do mine. Where is her Highness by the way? I have her armour ready for her in my chambers, please inform her to meet me there as soon as she can."

"Of course, we will survive this."

She locked her hand onto my forearm, and I did the same with her, a vine appearing from her hand and wrapped itself around mine as my own magic melted into her magic, creating an unbreakable bond.

"We will always survive."

40

GISELLE

tanding in the doorway as Quiver, Alison and Seniya went around me, I felt my heart sink into my shoes as the sudden feeling of overwhelming dread took over. Wrapping my arms around myself, mostly to keep myself from panicking, I felt Shadows arms come around me from behind and wrapped me into a tight hug, holding my back close to his chest heaves of breath came in and out quickly and he didn't loosen his grip until they slowed down.

"I am here, what do you need?" He asked gently and kissed the top of my head.

"Just stay here for a minute."

He wrapped his arms a little tighter then as I held onto his forearm, breathing in and out ever so slowly until finally I felt my heart settle. I was beginning to wonder if I would ever get over these sudden bursts of panic or if I was going to live with them for the rest of my life. I hoped not.

We stood still in that position for a couple more minutes before I started to pull loose and as I did Shadow turned me on my heel and cupped my face in both his hands, looking at me with his deep ice pool eyes and then kissed me ever so lightly on my lips. A peak almost, a quick goodbye kiss but also one that filled with love. As he pulled away, I wrapped my arms around him again, hugging him tightly and feeling his large arms return the hug.

"We had such a wonderful morning; I wish we had never got out of bed." I confessed, burying my head into his chest. "I wish we had just locked the door and kept ourselves away."

"And then we would never have been able to help all these people." He admitted as I pulled away.

"Shadow, I am not going to lie to you here, this feels the same as it did that night in Bathmod, where I felt, I was going to lose you and, in the end, I did. What if that happens again?"

Again, cupping my face, he smiled down at me tenderly.

"We are together now, and I don't believe it will happen again. However, if we lose one another somehow, I will always find you. I will always come when you call. Not even death can keep me away. You are a part of me, I can feel you in the depths of my soul, through every breath, every beat of my own heart. It beats for you. I was made for you."

He made my heart skip a beat as he confessed his feelings, and it made me think about how lucky I had become in these short few weeks. Here was a man who was willing to not only die for me but take the world along with him if it meant keeping me safe.

I knew it was wrong to be happy in knowing that but the amount of love stories I had read where the hero, the guy was happy to sacrifice his love for the world rather than keep his love safe. Whereas here Shadow was quite happy to protect me, even if that meant destroying everything, some would think of him as a villain, but he was a hero in my story.

"I think – No, I know I was made for you to."

Leaning up onto my toes, I kissed him deeply this time, wrapping my arms around his neck as his hands touched the base of my back and dipped me a little.

"Eh em." A cough in the doorway, "Can you for one minute keep your hands off each other," Quiver joked smiling at us both, "You know, you can carry on after we have finished saving the world, Leena wishes to see you, Giselle and Shadow, if you can, I could use your help and battle skills."

We pulled away but Shadow kept one of his hands linked in with mine, our fingers intertwined and tangled up with each other and as much as I didn't ever want to let go, the clock was ticking, and we had to get prepped and ready for what was going to come next.

"The people are being taken down to the underground vaults for safety. Shadow, if you can assist that would be great."

"Of course, not a problem."

Shadow started to walk away but I squeezed his hand in protest and he brought mine up to his lips, running his lips across my knuckles and then kissing them lightly.

"I will be right back, don't you worry."

Seconds later, he was gone along with Quiver, while I stood in that office still in my beautiful dress, I had been so excited to try on and seduce Shadow in taking it off. How the evening had changed so quickly, I did wish deep down we had been able to lock ourselves away in our room, away from all the worries, the fighting, Xandious and everything else that came along with it but alas my duties and life came knocking.

312

KNOCKING on the door of what I believed to be Leena's room, a small, rounded Elf opened the door and escorted me inside. Firstly, into a large sitting area where there was a dining table large enough to host a party of twenty, a fireplace that had a small fire lit and a smaller seating area.

Then through a set of double doors, I followed the Elf down a short corridor and in through a set of cream double doors with gold edging and stepped into what appeared to be Leena's bedroom and dressing room. She stood there in front of great full-length mirror while many other Elves dressed her in armour, and one pinned her hair up out of the way. She looked just as a warrior Queen should, elegantly posed but deadly.

"I had my blacksmiths create you the finest armour the other day when I suspected we would end up on this path. It's over there." She didn't look up at me as she continued to be pampered. "Jada and Rei will help dress you as this type of armour requires some help."

"Thank you, your Majesty, that is very kind of you."

"I believe your sword has also been polished and sharpened, as has your dagger. Lord Shadow requested you have both ready for you."

One of Leena's ladies took me by the hand and pulled me gently over to one of the smaller dress stools in the middle of the room and as one started to undo my hair, the other began unzipping my dress and as it fell to the floor, my hopes of how I would have liked the night to end fell to. It was now battle time and I needed to get my game face on.

Slipping off my heels and even to the point my underwear was changed to something more comfortable pulled me back into reality. Light cotton trousers first and then a brassiere followed by Elven chainmail, something I had already worn before, but this felt even lighter. It was tied at the back of my neck, the middle of my back and then base and it almost felt as if I was wearing nothing, there was no weight to it at all.

A black cotton shirt was chucked over the top and then came the rest of the amour, all a shade of black dragon steel with intercut designs of Elven protection spells and then finally as the shoulder pieces were placed on, my mother's crest was pride and place. A doe, a feather, and a crescent moon, it made me smile a little as I felt her close to me when spotting it.

Then finally, Lightbringer was placed in her scabbard and tied to my waist, along with the dagger Shadow gifted me after his oath. How they found my weapons, I didn't ask. I had thought Xandious would have taken them when he captured me, but they were here in my hands, and I felt a little more relaxed.

"We will both ride out in front of the soldiers shortly, they need to see the one they are fighting for, the Queen of this new world."

"They will be fighting for you." I replied stepping down from the stool and allowing one of the ladies put my hair into a loose plait.

"Believe it or not, they are fighting for you as well as to protect their home. They're our people."

Looking at myself now in the mirror, I felt more than a Princess, I was becoming a warrior and I needed to get rid of these feelings of fear and anxiety once and for all. I couldn't fight if I didn't believe in what I was fighting for and that was to free the people of Nimra from the darkness, the cruel world my father had created and to fight for what my mother had always believed in.

It was my job to do this now and as much as I knew Leena and the others were going to be there helping fight alongside me, this would all end up on my shoulders and end with me.

"Thank you, Leena, I know this wouldn't have been easy for you, offering a stranger not only shelter but your army and protection."

"My brother see's something in you and if he has faith in you, then I must have faith in him."

She always seemed to be forward and never sugar-coated her words towards me, perhaps it was just in her nature or maybe she didn't like helping me at all but as she said, was doing it for her brother. I owed Quiver so much already and my debt was mounting up. I hoped at the end of all of this, we could talk just as normal friends and not friends who constantly have to fight for the other's survival.

"Your Majesty – your Highness. Excuse my interruption but the Prince requires her Highness downstairs."

Alary arrived just in time before I had to continue the conversation with Leena and I had no idea how, other than to apologise again for my arrival.

I was grateful for the summing's and as Leena waved me away without a word, I followed Alary downstairs to see Quiver, Shadow and Alison all dressed, ready and waiting in their armour and they all looked as if they had come to share another secret with me.

"We have an idea." Shadow was the first to speak as I took the last step. "Well, it was Alison's. In the vaults there's something we've been told you need but to get it, we need to get past Anwen, Dana, and possibly Seniya but we believe it might help us win the battle."

"And what could this mystery weapon be?"

"Well, it's not a weapon, at least we don't think but Quiver and I were told, it's something you were meant to have a long time ago. It's an Emerald."

"I already have an Emerald."

"One that actually works and isn't a fake," Quiver pipped up in his cheeky voice, "The one you were given isn't real but the one in the vaults sure is."

"Ok, so how are we meant to get it?"

"Well, we need Anwen and the other ladies to allow us in to get it. So, eh – not sure how we are to do that, yet." Alison said with a sigh and a smile.

41
AYLA

X andious, my king had suddenly trusted me with the job of collecting Giselle along with Kara as she commanded his armies outside the border of the Elves hidden world. I was still in awe that they had stayed concealed away for hundreds of years and when I was projected into the ballroom, I was taken aback by just how many there were, most likely more.

"Do you think they're stupid enough to not send Giselle out? Even with the thousands of us waiting." I asked as I took my seat across the table in Kara's tent.

"Of course, they are, Giselle will have made them believe they have a chance of beating us."

Kara had become much to overconfident these past few weeks as Xandious gave her more power and responsibilities. I was just his bride, his Queen and needed to take great care of myself, especially if I was to carry the next heir to the throne.

"Idiot. He doesn't care about you."

The small inner voice began to creep up on me again and I was annoyed as I thought with Xandious's help and magic I had been able to keep it silent. Shaking my head and counting to three, breathing slowly, I felt it quieten down until finally the fuzzy feeling in the back of my head disappeared.

"Did you hear what I said?"

Now Kara stood inches from my face and her bi-eyes staring at me with intensity and I felt a cold rush through my body, the fear of her torment and torture still riddled through me.

"Apologies, what did you say?"

"I said, if you actually bothered to listen,"

She stood up straight quickly then, tutting and walking back over to the table that was littered with battle papers, a large map of Nimra and objects that symbolised the armies and Giselle's small group.

"Did you see how many fighters then had?"

"No, I didn't get a chance."

"For fuck's sake, what use are you then? You weren't just sent over there to intimidate Giselle but to see how many men she had. I will have to send more Dark Elves to do your job."

With a huff and then a ringing of a bell, in came a foot solider and he looked as scared as I felt at the sight of Kara. No matter how small she was or how gentle her face appeared, she was one of the scariest people I had ever come across, possibly more than Xandious as at least you knew he was dark, whereas Kara was a trained assassin and knew how to hide in plain sight.

"You, send two of those disgusting Elves across the border and get them to see how many of Giselle's men are there, I want exact numbers in the next hour." She ordered and he nodded before heading back out as quickly as he arrived.

"The King sent a messenger for you while you were gone doing Goddess knows what. He's in your tent." She told me as she went back to looking at the map and completely ignoring my existence.

My tent was next to Kara's and a lot smaller than hers Although I thought as Xandious's wife, I would be given more privileges yet, I was still required to be kept under constant guard and watch, in case I was planning on running away.

"You should die for what you did."

Studying myself as I entered my tent the voice shocking me deeply, it must have been only awake due to me seeing Giselle. That had to be the reason why it was acting up now as it had been quiet since the night she escaped.

"My Lady, apologies for the late encounter but his King wishes for you to have these ready for the battle in the morning."

The messenger was stood in the middle of my tent waiting patiently when I entered. He looked as if he were a peasant from Minwed and would have travelling far and for a few days to arrive here. He must have been sent a day after we left ourselves, he looked like he needed a good meal and a nice bath. Handing me over a paper wrapped gift, I could tell what it was by the shape in which it was wrapped.

"Thank you, was there anything else?"

"Only that he wishes his Queen well and good luck for the coming days."

"Right, thank you."

Giving him a few coins from the purse I had tucked away beside my bed; he flinched a little as I handed him the coins and although my face appeared to be soft and welcoming, the magic that now ran through my body thanks to Xandious took delight in his fear. I smiled a little as to show him I wasn't as scary as the other's had made me out to be.

"Please, take these and head to one of the tents where you can wash and have something to eat before heading back."

He didn't move for a second and the smell of fear ran through my tent. I took a step forward and he stayed still, frozen in fear. Taking his hand in mine, I placed the coins in his.

"I'm not as scary as they make me out to be."

"No, you're worse."

He chuckled nervously and quickly took his hand away as I stepped back ignoring the voice.

"Thank you, my Lady, that is very kind of you."

Bowing quickly, he was gone in a flash then as I placed the gift on my small cot bed and wrapped my shoulders in a warm fur shawl. The weather had changed, and snow was deeply falling across the plains now, which would make fighting a bit more difficult than expected but nevertheless, we would still head out by daybreak if Giselle hadn't arrived.

Sitting down on the bed, I unwrapped the gift and found it to be a beautiful, crafted sword and small identical dagger. Both had dark Obsidian crystals on the hilts and the handles were wrapped in black leather, they were beautiful and a wonderful gift.

"A fitting gift for a murderer and traitor."

"Shut up! I am not a murderer or traitor. I did what I needed to do to keep Giselle safe."

Getting off my bed quickly, I headed towards the small mirror on a vanity I had in the tent, which also housed an empty basin and the toilet bucket we had been condemned to use while here.

Looking at myself in the mirror, I could see how my body and face had changed and watched as a dark shadow leaked itself out from my body, enfolding itself tightly across my shoulders and the sinking feeling at the pit of my stomach begin again.

"You are nothing. You are worthless. Your death will come as a blessing, a gift to this world."

"No, I am none of these things!"

My reflection looked back at me with sly sinister eyes, and the darkness grip become more intensive around my body. Small blue sparks appeared at the tips of my fingers as I felt my magic slice through my body like razor blades.

I no longer whimpered or screamed out in pain, having become use to it and every reminder of the pain gave me flashbacks of my lessons with Xandious as he would punish me for getting something wrong.

"She's going to kill you, especially when she finds out what else you've done, all the wrongs you've committed."

My reflection was now something else, it wasn't my true reflection but something that was now talking to me, moving freely and her expression never changed.

"She will find out about Tessa and why you hid away and why it was so easy for you to betray her. She will find out just how disgusting and evil you truly are."

"She will not! She will never know!!"

I shouted back as I felt my body filling up all my senses with magic, but all my reflection did was smile back at me, happily and enjoying every moment of my angst.

It wasn't real, this was my imagination, my mind playing tricks on me and as I heard the reflection laugh uncontrollably, the power escaped from my body, knocking me flying across my tent and into my bed, winding me and causing the room to fade.

SWEET PEAS, so many sweet peas had blossomed in one of the small meadows in Blackwell Forest, the sun was low in the sky and casting out beautiful shades of orange, pinks, and yellows.

If I could capture the memory in my mind forever, it would be imprinted there, and I'd visit every chance I could get.

"Do you think we will ever see this place again?

Her voice took me by surprise and made me spin on my heels to find her resting against a tree, holding one of the sweet peas stems in her hand as she held it up against the golden light. Her blonde hair loose across her shoulders and she appeared to be wearing some part of armour, her eyes were closed as she took in the last of the sun's rays.

"Where are we?"

"I'm not too sure, I woke up here a little while ago but it's nice, isn't it? Peaceful," Opening her eyes she smiled at me, and I couldn't help but smile back. "I like your dress."

Looking down at myself I hadn't even noticed what I was wearing, a form fitted long dark green dress with ribbons that tied around the waist, bust, and then ended at my wrists with sheer black sleeves. It was beautiful and something I would love to own one day.

"Come, sit with me for a moment."

She held her arms out to me as if for a hug and I almost ran towards her but kept my cool and walked over slowly, sitting down beside her as she wrapped her arms around me.

"I've missed you."

She said, kissing the top of my forehead, I returned her hug and wrapped my arms around her waist, holding back my tears as I felt all my emotions flood. I missed my friend, my sister, the person I had fallen madly in love with and had hoped she understood everything I did, I did for her.

"I have deeply missed you to." I said choking back the tears forming in my eyes. "I am so sorry for the pain I caused you."

"It's ok, we don't need to talk about that, I know you were only trying to protect me."

"Yes, yes, I was! I only ever wanted to keep you safe."

She brushed the back of my head then and began to play with my hair and I could feel my eyes start to grow heavier as we sat there while the sun continued to set. It was beautiful.

"But you didn't keep me safe, did you? You failed and I lost everything because of you." She eventually said minutes later.

I felt my heart sink at her words and I quickly sat up, looking at her as her eyes began to change from the beautiful green to a dark shade of blue, the air around her changing as the sun set completely and a darkness overtook the meadow.

"You murdered the love of my life, and you honestly think I will forgive you for that."

"What? I didn't do anything."

"Oh no, of course you didn't." She stood up then suddenly, pushing me backwards as she did.

"Poor little Ayla never did anything wrong, you're just the victim here aren't you? Maybe you didn't even get kidnapped and tortured, perhaps that was all part of your plan from the beginning."

"Plan? What plan? You aren't making any sense Elle."

The shadow behind her was growing larger and larger, eclipsing any ounce of light now that appeared from the moon and I could feel my heart begin to beat faster and faster in my chest, the fear almost consuming me.

"Giselle, please, I honestly never meant to hurt you. You mean everything to me."

"Well, you mean nothing to me, you never did. You are just a stain on this world that deserves to die."

"Why are you saying these horrid things? This isn't really you; you aren't this cruel."

A loud cackle escaped from her lips then as she took a step forward towards me, pulling me up to my feet by my shoulders and looked me dead in the face with a calm but a terrifying look in her eyes.

"Just wait, tomorrow, when I get my hands on you, you will wish you were never born."

Breaking her grip of me, I managed to push her off and took to running scared for my life as her laugh rang through the meadow, the grass beneath my feet almost disappearing with each step as the world around me began to shake.

No, this wasn't real, none of this was happening, it was all in my mind. The darkness testing me, testing my faith in Xandious and if I would give away any of our secrets while unaware. He'd done something like this before, but he had never used Giselle as my tormenter, it had usually been Kara or Lord Terrell.

Stopping dead in my tracks then as I realised it wasn't real, none of this was happening in real life and I felt the blue sparks in my body flare up again and flung my right hand out, sending a beam of magic towards Giselle and knocking her backwards into the tree we had been resting on and again she just laughed as she hunched over herself.

"You are not real. You aren't here and even if you were, you'd never say these things to me."

"You're still an idiot then I see, stupid women who truly believes she's worth something, worth saving, worth – loving."

I shot another beam towards her and again it didn't do much of anything, other than make her laugh even more as the darkness around her grew taller, as if it were feeding itself using my powers and the emotions I was clearly exploding with.

"You think you will be able to stop all of this, everything that is happening." Giselle shouted at me, almost clearing the meadow, and standing a few centimetres away from me then.

"Once the sun rises tomorrow, we will face each other in battle, and you will lose."

"We will only lose if you have the Emerald, which I know you don't, yours isn't even the real one."

"The Emerald?"

My hands shot up to my lips, covering my shock as I realised, I had given away information I didn't mean to, she had got me so rallied up I was telling her secrets I didn't mean to. Xandious would kill me if he found out, which I imagined he already knew by now as he had sent this image as a test.

"Forget I said that!" I shouted back quickly as tears began to form in my eyes, I was done for.

"Thank you, I appreciate you sharing this information with me."

And with that, Giselle vanished in the darkness, and I felt my eyes open. I was still lying half on the floor and half on the cot bed from the blast of magic earlier that evening and as soon as I realised where I was, the fear of death came rushing in.

Xandious was going to murder me once he arrived, I should never have given away any of our secrets but again I let my emotions get the best of me as they usually do and now, I was going to pay the price.

42

GISELLE

W aking up suddenly, my body jolted out from the chair in the study we had been in an hour or so before, I had no idea I had even fallen asleep and was slightly annoyed at myself as my eyes opened suddenly to a room filled with a few people.

Shadow sat next to me with his hand resting on my knee looking at me with worried eyes and Alison was on the opposite side while ringing out water from a cloth and appeared to be ready to put it on my head.

"What happened?"

Confused, I didn't even remember falling asleep or even coming into the study. The last thing I remembered was leaving Leena's bedroom and now she was standing in the doorway looking at me with anger in her eyes.

"You fainted at the bottom of the staircase; Shadow brought you in here as soon as he caught you."

"I fainted? – I don't understand."

"One minute I was standing talking to you about if I should come with you to the battlefield and the next you were hitting the ground hard." Alison patted the cloth on my head, and I almost battered her away forcefully before realising how hot and clammy I had become.

"Are you ok?" Shadow asked, bringing his hand up to my face.

"Ayla." I uttered almost a whisper and his eyes looked at me with a slight hint of red as anger flashed through him.

"What about her?"

"She – Actually I'm not sure, I think I was in her mind somehow. But I was saying such awful things."

"Thing's she probably deserved." Alison said as she wet the cloth again.

"What were you saying? What happened?" Quiver now stepped in the room, almost pushing past Leena as she still stood there silently watching us.

I thought for a moment or two, wondering if I should continue as the whole thing felt very much like a dream, a fever dream, as I had no control over anything I was saying or what I was doing. It was unlike any other dream I previously had but it felt just as real as the one I had of my mother back in Lord Terrell's cells.

"Ayla is the key," I whispered as the thought came back to my mind, that's what my mother had said. "Is the Emerald I have a fake?"

Shadow and Quiver lowered their eyes quickly then and it confirmed my question. That's why when I tried using the crystal in the temple of Guinevere and it never worked, I never received an answer from the Goddess as I was praying to her with a fake stone one that held no power and no respect for the Goddess herself.

"What are you not telling me?"

"Oh, they keep secrets from you to, good, I'm glad I'm

not the only one." Leena spoke sarcastically but clearly with a bitter taste in her mouth.

"Shadow, Quiv, what are you keeping from me? Is the Emerald not real?"

"No, I'm afraid it's not." Alison answered and both men looked at her shocked, "You men don't keep secrets very well and besides Dana told me after she had a few to many drinks this evening while panicking over what has happened to her home."

Quiver huffed and rolled his eyes as he appeared to hide his anger and then relaxed almost instantly, putting his hands in his pockets.

"The Emerald you are meant to have, the real one is hidden deep under the city. Dana and Anwen are the only ones who have access to that part of the vaults, and I believe if it wasn't for the last few 'events' we've had, they were planning on giving you the crystal tonight."

"It's meant to be yours Giselle, but due to Dana being attacked earlier today, they are being extra careful with the stone. We believe she was attacked because Xandious also wants the stone for himself, we have no idea why as we haven't found time to find out."

"So, why am I sat here? We need to go get it before he does."

"Eh – Well, we have no idea how or where it is, and Anwen and Dana are helping secure the city folk safely."

Frustration and confusion were clearly my emotions for this evening, so many things had been confessed this evening alone and I was beginning to feel very much as if I were walking on eggshells with everything and everyone.

Standing up and almost brushing off the feeling and whatever left over emotions I had from that very weird dream of Ayla, I tightened my hand a little on the hilt of my sword, almost for it to fill my body up with strength.

"Well, we are going to go find Anwen and this Dana and I will get them to show me the entrance or whatever I must do to get this stone. If Xandious does want it, we must get it before he does, and we need to do it fast. Leena, if we are to do this and the city does come under attack, will you be able to stall or keep his soldiers at bay until we are able to help."

Leena didn't seem at all shocked by my addressing her so informally, if anything it defused some tension between us both.

"Yes, now that some of the Elven clans have arrived, we have plenty of men here to help protect the city and my people. But I suggest you don't take forever as we need all hands-on deck."

Nodding at her and holding out my hand to Alison, she took it as Shadow stood the same time. My two people standing behind me giving me the strength I needed to put one foot in front of the other while Quiver just looked at me with wonder and appreciation in his eyes.

"Alex, are you coming with us, or shall you be staying here?"

"I need to command the army; I will be staying here and will send Alary if there are any changes and you need to get out of the city quick."

Things were beginning to move faster than I had expected, I didn't expect Xandious to come to our front door and I most certainly didn't expect to be sucked into Ayla's mind somehow but now was not the time to think about such things, we had to get to the vault as quickly as possible.

"Where can I find the entrance of the vaults?" I asked as I exited the study.

"There's an entrance in the temple, behind the stature of Guinevere. I'd imagine Anwen will be there directing people to safety." Alary followed us out as the other's went towards the main hall which I guessed was where the other clan members had congregated.

"Thank you Alary for your help."

"I will come if I am required but please your Highness, all of you, be careful."

∾

ARRIVING at the temple I felt this sudden urge of discomfort and worry, whatever was going to happen next, I had to accept and prepare myself for the endless possibilities of potential threats, trials, or anything else I had to do to get the crystal.

Anwen and Dana were prepping some provision bags on the steps at the foot of the Guinevere stature and weren't at all surprised when Shadow, Alison and I arrived, in fact they appeared to have expected it.

"I am here to claim the real crystal, please."

"We know, but neither of us are able to be your guides as we are getting ready for what comes next."

This was the first time I met Dana and she seemed very unhinged and spoke with an unwelcoming tone, as if she had enough of the day and didn't want to see or speak to anyone. Anwen however, her demeanour was kind and inviting.

"I will take them, it is our duty to guide her Highness, we have waited for this day for hundreds of years and now the time is here."

The anticipation was killing me as I knew we were running out of time and sooner or later Xandious would be able to get in the city once Mabon dropped the barriers.

I hoped Seniya would help keep the barriers up, but I knew she wouldn't impose on what was meant to happen, she tried to stay very much out of the affairs of men and if she helped keep Xandious out, then that would mean she would be involved, and I knew the Goddesses would punish her for it. She was just the messenger if anything and protector of the magics and the natural order of things.

"If you three will follow me."

Anwen broke my train of thought as she walked behind the stature and pushed open a secret door. It was almost moulded to the marble and stonework of the temple and unless you knew of its hiding place, you would have walked past it as it just looked as if it were a part of the walls.

Taking a torch from the wall, she gestured for us to continue down a set of stone stairs and as we descended further down into the darkness the air grew colder and damp and you could hear the slightest faint trickle of water, as if we were near a waterfall.

"These vaults were built hundreds of years ago just after the battle of the great Kings & Queens."

"Why were they built?" Alison asked from behind me as we carried on our way down into the depts of the mountain.

"They were built to hold the greatest and most powerful prisoners as well as used to mine for Dragon steel. It is believed this mountain and that of Dragons Peek are filled with thousands of the stuff but during the digging, a creature was disturbed, and it was only defeated when the Goddesses aided the men to put it into a deep slumber."

"Great, let me guess if I have any challenges to get this crystal it will be to not wake the beast." I rolled my eyes at how predictable it all seemed, as if I were reading a story book.

"Funnily enough, no, I believe that was going to be a

test, but it would be far too easy, and the Goddess Guinevere wanted the true owner of the crystal to go through a lot more difficult challenges, but we will get to them once we arrived."

"What happened to the digging once the creature was put to sleep? Did men carry on mining the steel?" Alison, the ever interested in our history.

"No, they never returned here and soon the vaults were forgotten about, it was my great, great grandmother who decided to keep the crystal down here and she invoked the Goddess to help protect it. It is also said that this is where the Goddess Aithne was imprisoned, but that is just a folk tale."

Finally arriving at a long corridor, Anwen leant up towards another torch on the wall and lit it with the fire of her own and as she did, every single one along the walls either side lit up in sync one after the other, revealing the beautiful artwork that decorated the walls.

There were many paintings of our history. The Goddesses arrival and our creation, the battle of the Kings & Queen's, Shadows birth, Aithne's capture, a portrait of Seniya kneeling in front of Guinevere, the crowning of Enelya, the birth of I believed to be me, the death of Enelya under my wedding alter, and then a painting of what looked to be myself and Xandious fighting our blades clashing together on a battlefield.

"These paintings, do they -"

"Tell the past and what is yet to come, yes – Well, kinda. The one's for the future change, depending on the choices we make as beings. Nothing of the future is set in stone, it is ever changing and bending to fit the new narrative that may occur."

At the end of the corridor was a blocked end but of

course, more magic, and hidden doors awaited us. Anwen placed her hand on a part of the wall and a rumble ran through the floor and I almost stumbled into Shadow as it took me by surprise and as it did, a space appeared in the wall and as a door slowly opened dust and staleness filled the air, it had clearly not been open for a long time.

"Now, when you enter this room not everything will appear as it seems. Giselle, your mind, body, and soul will be tried and tested. The two of you, you are to act as her helpers, support her but Princess, please be aware this is part of the trials and tests you must undertake to pass through and gain the trust of the Goddess and to be gifted the crystal."

"Do you know how long it will take?" Shadow asked as he pushed past me a little keen to go inside.

"I am afraid not, no one has ever past these tests."

"What happened to those who didn't past?" Alison asked nervously.

"They became prisoners themselves."

"Oh, so no pressure to not mess up." I said sarcastically.

"Are you sure you want to do this Giselle? It's ok if you want to turn back." Shadow placed a reassuring hand on my elbow, his blue eyes appearing worried.

"It's what we need to do, we can't turn back now and Xandious can't get his hands on this crystal either. As you said, it's part of my duty and clearly, I am meant to be here."

"Alright, if this is what you want then I will go to the end with you."

"As will I your Highness. We are family."

Alison touched my other elbow and gave me a soft smile. I felt fear in the bottom of my stomach but pushed it down further, I didn't have time to be nervous or scared, now I needed to be the bravest I had ever been before.

Mustering all my courage and keeping my cool was

essential. I had no idea what was going to happen once we stepped through the door, but I knew I needed to be successful, no matter what.

"I wish you luck, your Highness."

"Thank you, I may need it."

43
SHADOW

Crossing the threshold of the doorway my body shuddered at the sudden cold burst of air and into the darkness I stepped, unsure of where to even put my footing afraid I would take a step and suddenly wind up on the floor or down a hole or worse. I felt someone tug at my hand behind and guessed it to be Alison as I could still feel Giselle's warm presence beside me. I needed to keep her close, to protect her.

"Where do we go?" I heard Alison break the silence that had surrounded us.

"I have no idea, I guess we just keep going until we come across something." I replied.

The distant sound of water from earlier was appearing to become louder and louder with each step we took until finally a small trickle of light appeared at the end of the corridor, it felt as if we had been walking for hours but most likely only a few minutes.

Walking towards the light until finally we got to a small opening, it was a large archway cut into the middle of the stone wall and for a second or two we took it all in, looking at the craftsmanship and design.

There were swirls carved into the stone as well as runes, protection spells no doubt and I thought for a moment then we would not be able to cross over but Giselle reached out with her hand and although, I expected her to meet some form of forcefield, her hand passed through the archway without any issues.

"Wait Giselle, let me go through first."

I almost pushed Giselle aside as I took a step forward and as I did, I was blasted backwards into one of the side walls by a large force. Anwen said I we might be tested and perhaps that meant Giselle would have to do this alone or she would have to at least go first.

"I'm guessing the Goddess doesn't want you in here." Alison said sarcastically as she offered Shadow a hand up.

"I guess not – It would seem Giselle, love, you'd have to go in there first."

"Yes, I think so."

Turning back towards the archway, she took a deep breath and a step through the doorway, again without any issues or being hurt by the magical forcefield. Alison although nervous and clearly worried about something happening to them, stepped through then and finally, I went through with ease this time.

"Okay, note to us, if there's a doorway I go first."

The room suddenly lit up as we entered and exposed four rather large and beautiful statues of each Goddess. Guinevere in all her glory along with her wolf companion both carved out of white stone, Nefret in her birdlike creature state carved from slate.

Fenella surrounded by splashes of water carved from dragon steel and then Aithne, she was stood in a firm pose with her arms crossed in a dress that I was unsure where it began or ended, and her stature was carved out from obsidian stone. Each statue had an engraving carved into the bottom of it, written was each name of the Goddess and what their Domaine was.

"You know Shadow, when you're this close up to your mother, you do look a bit like her."

I appeared at Giselle's side while Alison was looking at the other statues around the room, while Giselle stood in front of Guinevere's, I wondered if she was picturing what part of my appearance was that of Guinevere's, I hoped none of them were.

"She might be my mother by blood, but not of life."

"I know, the Countess was more of a mother than anyone else."

"Giselle, you've met Fenella, haven't you?" Alison asked, standing in front of that statue.

"Yes, when I was lost in the forest, she was the one who helped me find Lanwe, he was a fawn and helper of Seniya's."

"Shadow, have you met any of them?" She now turned her attention to me while I continued to look at Guinevere's stature.

"I have met all but Aithne. My mother, my biological mother, is Guinevere. But she gave me up and I was raised by the Countess Elizabeth."

"Wow. Well, that makes sense then especially with how all the younglings talked about you." She paused for a moment, unbothered by the sudden news, "Was that the Countess of Zerfina? My mother met her once, before she passed, I'm sorry for your loss."

"She was a wonderful woman, but I am grateful she is no longer here to see what Xandious has done to this world."

Stepping away from the statues, Giselle left us then, clearing wondering and thinking of what to do next. I thought about the first 'test' and how it was going to begin, maybe we had to trigger something? Perhaps there was some sort of lever or step stone we had to use for the room to know we were here unless it already knew and was stalling.

The only thing that appeared in the room were the statues so they must be a part of the test, perhaps, or maybe they hid an entrance somewhere. As I began to examine the statue of Nefret, running my hands down the cold slate hoping I'd come across something, I had no such luck.

"Look at the statues and see if you can find something different, I think there might be an entrance somewhere."

We each took turns to look at each statue, trying to spot if there was anything sticking out, out of place or just appeared to be different. Until finally, Alison started squealing and pointing at something on the stature of Nefret.

"Here! There's an inscription, it's old mind and rubbed off slightly but maybe this is something." She shouted with excitement as we came up beside her.

"It's in a language I have never read or heard of before."

Giselle ran her fingers across the words, if none of us could read the inscription, we would be stuck here.

"Quaerenti potestatem, prius oportet animum ad inscia accessurum." I read the script as if it were nothing, a second language to me, which it was.

"What in Goddess name does that mean?" Asked Alison baffled.

"It means - To the one who seeks the power, you must first sacrifice your mind to gain access to the unknowing."

"Great ok, so how am I meant to sacrifice my mind? Does it want me to cut my head off or something?"

Giselle sat down on the floor holding her head in her

hands, looking very confused already. Anwen hadn't really given us any clues as to what we'd expect other than guided us down the set of never ending stairs. Sacrifice her mind made absolutely no sense to me as it wasn't something I thought possible.

"Perhaps it means you must let your mind go, relax, allow it to open?" Alison sat next to me as she too clearly started thinking. "Or, maybe you need to say you sacrifice your mind to the Goddess?"

"Well, I guess it's worth a try."

Standing up, Giselle again took a deep breath and seemed deep in thought for a second. Perhaps she thought it silly to stand in front of an inanimate object proclaiming some form of herself to it, but alas it was for the greater good, even if she did think it stupid.

"To the Goddess Nefret, I sacrifice my mind to you."

For a moment or two we all waited in suspense, wondering if something were to suddenly happen and yet the room was still as silent as it was before.

"Perhaps, you need to say it in the language written?" I spoke up as I leant against the wall behind Giselle.

"And how do you suppose I do that? When I can't even say it myself."

"Just repeat after me."

Walking up

Standing behind Giselle then, I lowered my head to meet her ear and my breath tickled her skin, and it made even my heart flutter as anytime I came near her, I was reminded of her touch and longed for her.

"Deae Nefret,"

"Deae Nefret," I repeated.

"Sacrificamus tibi,"

"Sacrificamus tibi,"

"Animum meum."

"Animum meum."

As Giselle said the words, a rumble filled the space and the floor began to shake, making her stumble backwards a little into me and unexpectedly Nefret's stature started to turn around, exposing a door that had been hidden at the back of her stature.

"Well, ok, guess you were both right."

"This is why you needed us, this is why Anwen said we would be your guides, your helpers." Alison filled the room with glee as she stood back up to join Giselle's side.

It was now or never, and I wondered how long the door would stay open. We didn't want to leave it to chance and have it close on us before we managed to do this challenge.

Giselle took the first brave step in and as we went to join, of course, the door slammed behind Giselle leaving her stand in the darkness while I shouted and pounded on the door, demanding it open for Alison and me but nothing. Giselle was meant to do this by herself.

44

GISELLE

"*No surprises then, I must do this on my own.*"
I thought, waiting for the next thing to happen and take me by surprise. More darkness, more unknowing of where I stood or where I was.

Holding tightly to Lightbringer's handle I sighed and stepped forward and as I did, my eyes appeared to become blurry, as if I could no longer see and I felt myself begin to panic and had to try and remind myself this was all part of the test, it must have been.

A light broke through my vision and the sound of clacketing dishes, people moving around me, and the sudden sound of music took me by surprise. Bumping into someone, I brought my sword out in response to whoever or whatever it was that bumped into me as my vision began to clear up again.

"Oh, I'm sorry your Highness, I didn't mean to, please forgive me."

A voice startled me as I now saw a lady on her knees begging me to forgive her as she quickly began picking up flowers she had appeared to have dropped.

"It's quite alright." I said putting Lightbringer back in her scabbard.

"Oh, thank you, thank you for your mercy your Highness."

"My mercy?" I asked confused, before bending down and helping her pick up the flowers.

"Giselle! We do not help the help."

Shouted a voice from other side of the room, a voice that shook me to my core. Xandious, only this wasn't the Xandious I knew now, this was the one from before.

"I will do no such thing," I shouted back, handing the flowers to the lady, and helping her up, "Pay no attention to him." I whispered as she looked scared before she quickly scurried off frightened.

"You will do as you are told, remember you are a Princess of Nimra, and you must never forget your station."

"Oh Xandious, you know our daughter will always help those in need."

Mother. She came up behind me placing an arm around my shoulder and I tried not to suddenly turn around and embrace her in a tight hug. This wasn't real, none of it was.

I had played this scene once before, when I was around the age of fourteen, when Xandious was hell bent on reminding me of who I was and meant to be, continuingly telling me how I was going to fail him as a daughter if I didn't do better at my swordsmanship or my lessons. Idiot man, he would meet the end of my sword soon enough and then know how good I was at using a blade.

"You need to stop encouraging her Enelya, if she is to become Queen one day, she must learn the peaking order."

Mother rolled her eyes at him, laughing as she fanned herself before taking my hand and pulling me out of the doorway of the dining hall as our staff continued to prepare for another party. During this time we would have weekly balls, inviting all types of eligible men to dance with 'the Princess'.

Had I known then what I knew now, I would have avoided mostly all of them, well unless Lord Shadowbane was attending, and he only ever attended one or two as he had reached maturity by this point.

"Giselle, my sweet girl, you are all skin and bones. Let us sit down, eat, and discuss this evening's event."

Mother almost pulled me into a seat next to her as our staff piled food in front of me, enough to feed many families for weeks. It was ridiculous how much food we had access to and how much we wasted, I made a note deep down that once I become Queen, I will do more and help more families in need.

"Lord Michaels is coming tonight; I have already told him you'd give him a dance or two."

"I'd rather not, he's very handsy and a lot older than me, it's disgusting."

"Do as your mother say's Giselle. You will dance with whomever we set you up with."

Xandious came and sat at the head of the table, pouring himself a glass of wine but refusing food as he usually did. Looking at him now, I could see the darkness appear behind his eyes and disappear moments later. Pompous asshole.

"I will still avoid him like a plague, even if you begged me to dance with him. No thank you, the man is a pervert and is only after me for my crown."

Xandious rolled his eyes and continued to drink his wine, looking away from both mother and I, while she just carried on eating her food without a care in the world.

"You will find Giselle, all men are after your crown." My mother spoke in-between mouthfuls of food.

343

I began to wonder what this test was going to be, was this even a test? Or was it a reminder of the day's past? Mother seemed to be happier here, Xandious was clearly good at hiding his evil in plain sight and neither of us were none the wiser.

If I could run my sword through him right now, I would but it wouldn't change the present time sadly, as much as I would have liked to see his face as I killed him before he killed mother.

"Do you know if Lord Shadowbane is coming this evening?" I said without even realising what I was saying.

"Taken a fancy to our close friend's son, have you?" Mother replied with a wink as she took a sip of her drink.

"Well, we are friends after all, and it would be lovely to see him."

"He might attend, I did invite his mother, the Countess, but she informed me he was off hunting or something. But you never know, I know he's quite fond of you."

"He's fond of her title, nothing else."

"Don't be silly, men would go to war for this beautiful face."

Mother cupped my face then and smiled tenderly at me. I missed that smile. I missed being beside her and longed for her presence more so than ever before.

She still looked as beautiful as she always did, her auburn hair set-in loose curls around her delicate face with her gorgeous hazel eyes staring at me with so much love hidden behind them, it made my heart ache.

"You know Giselle, your mother and I have already discussed it that on your wedding day, your mother will die."

Xandious's words took me by surprise and the shock on my face said it all. My mother however appeared unchanged and continued drinking her drink and laughing.

"Yes, it's going to be wonderful, a wonderful day for you my sweet girl."

"She's going to bleed right under the alter, she will paint the floor red with her blood and it will be a beautiful sight to see."

"Are you serious right now?" I stood up from my seat and as I went to walk towards him mother grabbed my hand and pulled me back.

"Don't worry your little head about it, we all die at some point, and I just happen to die that day but then again you don't help either. You watch it happen and don't even stop your father."

"What?"

Looking at my mother then and then back at Xandious, a flash of memory filled the space quickly. My mother lying under the alter in my arms bleeding from her wounds as Xandious stood over us both laughing and savouring the moment.

"You know, you did see him raise his sword and made no attempt to save me – To save your own mother."

"No, that's not what happened."

"Isn't it Giselle? You saw me pull my sword and you had the power to stop me, but you just stood there as I went to stab your mother, clearly taking great delight in it, enjoying it."

Another flash of memory, this time it made me stagger and fall slightly into the table, taking me off balance as my head began to sting with immense amount of pain. This time the memory was of me stood in the aisle as mother stood between Xandious and I with her hands up slightly in surrender as he pulled his sword out.

"You could have stopped it, but you were to much of a coward then, just as much as you are now."

345

Mother was now stood in front of me, her appearance changing to that of an elder woman, her skin sagging and her eyes appearing to be sucked inwards into the sockets, her cheeks doing the same. Her hair thinning and my stomach turned at the sudden change in smell, she was rotting. Her beautiful face no longer there but a corpse standing in front of me.

"You killed me, and you know it, deep down you are the true murderer."

"No, no that's not me – I never."

"Never saved her and now look at her, now she is worms' food."

Xandious stood behind my mother and placed a hand on her shoulder, his darkness growing behind him and filling the empty space. I could feel my eyes begin to tear up suddenly as all the feelings I had buried deep within me were rising to the surface. I did see Xandious draw his sword, but I was frozen to the spot, unable to move or to step in front of my mother to protect her, to take his blade. I watched her die, and I did nothing.

"You killed me."

"No!" I shouted.

Pushing them both aside I took to the door I'd came in to find it gone as the pain in my head grew larger, disorientating me and throwing me off balance as I fell to my knees, hugging my head and screaming out in agony as the pain ran down the back of my neck and through my spine.

"You have to accept what you did, you killed me, and you know it, deep down you know."

Mother knelt beside me whispering in my ear, her breathe overtaking any smell in the air and I heaved in response. I had always blamed myself for my mother's death, I shouldn't have gone in that room when I did, I should have stayed in mine, waited for her.

She would not have been in the hall, she would have come to my room and finished helping me get ready, I would have been married to Shadow and none of this would have happened.

"Wait. This would have happened even if I did try and stop Xandious." I said out loud realising something. "You needed to die for the ritual to begin."

"What?" Mother stood up quickly as I looked at her with a tear-stained face.

"You were always meant to die, Xandious planned it from the moment he met you, I have no doubt. His one great, true love, that was you."

I stood then and she took a step back.

"He had to kill you to destroy his soul, to bring the powers out of him. Your death had nothing to do with me, it was all him."

Mabon had said a person would break their soul and darkness would fill that space if they killed their one true love, allowing that person to become a great and powerful mage of some sorts, the person would process a type of magic that was unlike of the Goddesses. It was born via the death of their great love on a certain moon, the moon that was there the night I was due to get married.

"You died because of him. Not because of me."

"No – you did this to me - it was you."

"It was Xandious who killed you, not me mother. I would never have harmed a single hair on your head, the murderer was your husband. Someone who was always meant to protect you, he failed you."

I felt more sadness as the words escaped from my lips, the pain easing in my head as the realisation came. I had blamed myself for almost two years that I had been the cause of my mother's death, when it was my fathers.

He had planned it for so long and used me as his scape goat and I fell for it. I fell for his lies to the world and hid away, when I should have been there in the open fighting for my mother's life, fighting for my role as Queen and I would have had the proof he was evil within a matter of days after her death as the whole of Nimra had seen it now.

"I'm sorry mother you were not protected or loved enough. But it wasn't because of me."

As the words left my mouth, I heard a clap from behind me and as I turned, Nefret stood there in a form unknown to myself or anyone for that matter.

She had beautiful pink hair that sat on her shoulders and wore a gorgeous white dress, she looked so plain but also so beautiful, words could not truly describe how she looked. She appeared gentle and warm.

"Well-done Princess. I thought you would become his undoing, but it would seem you are becoming smarter." She stood in front of me and placed both her hands on my shoulders, her birdlike claws still there.

"You have passed the first test, the test of the mind. The doorway is open for you once again."

"Do you know who the next test is with?"

"I cannot answer that, but you will find out the answer soon enough."

"I always thought you were a bird and spoke in some sort of riddle."

"Oh, I can be that to, but this is my truest form and only those who past this test may be blessed to see it. And I guess," She smiled, "You're the only human who has ever seen it now, congratulations."

She clapped again then and the doorway behind me

opened and I could see Shadow and Alison still stood there, waiting eagerly for me to come back, Shadow more anxious than Alison. As I went to say thank you to Nefret she had gone, as had the entire seen around me and I was back in the darkness.

45
QUIVER

The air no longer smelt sweet or filled with honey as usually did. Now standing at the border where we found Giselle almost giving herself up and now, I stood at the head of rows upon rows of Elven warriors. Leena beside me on her horse, wearing our mothers armour and there was silence.

Xandious's army was just behind the veil, waiting for it to fall and I made a note to take Mabon out as soon as I saw him, even if he was only trying to get his family back, he had betrayed the Elven clans, my people and he would pay for it.

Taking a deep breath as the sun started to rise behind Xandious's soldiers, I spotted two women at the helm. Both of which I had met at the masked ball many weeks ago. Lady Ayla and Kara, both in their armour with swords at the ready, they clearly meant business and I would happily hand it to them. They would not pass me or my fighters, they were staying in this place no matter the cost.

"Are you ready brother?"

"Always."

Looking up at Leena as the solider beside her handed her

our mother's helmet made of dragon's steel. All our weapons and gear were made of the compound, and I hoped, prayed to the Goddess they would hold and keep our people safe.

The sound of drums began in the distance as our Ice Elven brothers prepared for battle, a battle we all never wished would arrive, but it was written that one day this would come to pass.

"We need to buy Giselle and the other's enough time to get through the trials," I turned to Alary who was ready for anything, "Alary, if we should fall, you must head to the temple to warn them."

"You will not fail my friend, or at least not alone."

He turned and took my forearm in his hand, and I did the same in return, although we showed no emotions, I knew this might be our final goodbye if we did fall.

"May the Goddess protect you."

"And may she always bring light to our hearts."

It was almost as if a clock was ticking down the minutes as we all stood there waiting, Leena's horse eager to get going and run until finally, the barrier went down in a flash that if we couldn't balance unlike that of men, we would have fallen with the sudden blast of wind and light that headed our way.

Leena raised her sword into the air and the few hundreds of soldiers behind us shifted their weight, the sound of metal clicking in sync as swords were drawn and bows were tightened. The enemy would not cross this line, not today, not ever.

"For our families! For our people!"

Shouted Leena as she clicked her boots into her horse and off into a sprint she went. I didn't expect her to make the first move but then again, she was always filled with surprises. The enemy on the other side took this as a signal and they too began running towards us in great numbers. Perhaps even greater than our own.

Looking at Alary I nodded, and we too shouted at the top of our lungs and began our run, followed by my men who had always willingly offered to die in a battle for my family, for theirs, for our people.

Leena's magic began sprouting everywhere, tree roots attacking and attaching themselves to the men who wished to kill us, where I aimed for as many of the enemy soldiers I could. Blades clashed and arrows flew in the air, my archers holding the line behind us while the few hundreds at the front battled to keep Xandious's men away from us, they would not be allowed to cross.

Spotting Alary as he took a slash to the leg and then he quickly swiped up with his sword cutting his attacker in two, I knew I didn't need to worry as he would be able to take care of himself.

However, Leena hadn't been in battle for many years and barely trained so her skills weren't up to the same level as my own and I needed to protect her and should she fall, I needed to get her back to the safety of our lines before she was mortally wounded or worse.

Sending a bolt of green light out from my hand, I blasted away a few lines of soldiers and made my way to Leena as her horse flew back onto its hind legs and knocked her off as she became surrounded by men.

Her magic again revealing itself to our opponents as tree's grew out from beneath one or two of them, wrapping their roots around them and entering their mouths, noses, and ears. It was a disgusting and painful sight to watch as they screamed in pain and then out of nowhere, a dagger came flying forward and landed in Leena's right shoulder.

Leena shouted out in pain, I let loose another arrow or

two almost a few meters away from reaching her as I watched another dagger fly and land in one of her thighs.

"Where is he?!" I shouted, looking around for her attacker, spotting Alary in the process.

"The Queen!"

I shouted towards him, and he took to a run, cutting down anyone in his path to get to her just as I was coming up to the right side of her. They were aiming for her, she was our leader and once you cut the leader's head off, the army would fail or so that was what our rivals believed, unbeknown to them I was also here.

Alary finally reached her and as he did, he swung his sword round and knocked a dagger out of thin air that was seconds away from hitting Leena again, this time a lot higher and clearly aimed for her face. I reached them a second later and Alary quickly threw Leena into his arms and started to run back towards our lines, back to protection.

Looking around, I could see many of my men already perished as flashes of magic flew, Ayla and Mabon were stood next to each other using their spells in tandem and the anger inside me grew.

They were killing my people, the people Mabon had been welcomed by with opened arms, I would cut him down from where he stood without question, without failure, without mercy.

Pulling an arrow out from my pack and hooking it to my bow, I aimed and once Mabon was in my sight, I fired and as expected, the arrow hit the shield that was placed up in front of them both. Cowards. I knew I had to get closer, and I would be able to distract him long enough to bring that shield down and bring him down. He needed to die.

46

SHADOW

Once that door shut behind her and she descended into darkness, my heart sank, and my rage took over. I was ready to break down the entire statue to get her out when what felt like hours, but a few minutes later she reappeared.

Her eyes were red and face a little blotchy from crying and without even stopping for a breath, I took her in my arms and hugged her tightly.

"What happened? Are you okay?" Alison came beside me and placed a hand on Giselle's back as she pulled away from me.

"I'm alright," She paused looking between us both, "I had to face my truth and that in fact I didn't kill my mother."

"Well, we already knew that." Alison interrupted her and Giselle rolled her eyes in response.

"I know, well, I know that now. A part of me always blamed myself, thinking if I hadn't entered that room when I did, they wouldn't have fought, and she'd still be here but the test made me realise that it would have happened anyways. Xandious needed to kill Enelya to awaken his powers, to destroy his own soul and allow the darkness to freely flow in."

She turned away and looked back at the stature of Nefret and appeared happier, lighter in fact and I felt my shoulders ease from the tension that had been building there for months. The shadow around her easing slowly, perhaps these tests were going to help.

"I never killed my mother and with that knowledge, I am grateful more so to Nefret than ever before – Thank you Goddess."

"That's great! I guess, so umm, the next test, any ideas on how we get you to it?"

Alison took the words right out of my mouth, and I was happy she had come down here with us, she offered some sort of light heartedness to this situation. I just knew though; I didn't just have Giselle to protect but also Alison as I was almost certain she had no idea how to even throw a punch and so would be useless in a fight.

She could easily become a liability to Giselle and I and if it came down to which girl to save, I'd pick Giselle in a heartbeat. Heck, I would happily destroy everyone if it meant protecting Giselle.

"I am guessing the statues are the entrances to each test so maybe we should just pick one."

Giselle took to examining Fenella's stature then, I stood back and waited for her to either say she had found something or not. I didn't think it would be as simple as an inscription again as that would be too easy and if we knew the Goddesses by now, they were never going to offer up something so easy.

"There's something Fenella's pointing to if you look." She said and pointed in the same direction.

Sure enough, Fenella was pointing towards a small

trickle of water that was dripping from one of the walls and a puddle underneath was forming where the water landed. How none of us noticed before now was beyond me, perhaps it only appeared after you completed the first challenge but then how did the Goddesses know that Nefret would be the first challenge a person did?

"There's water here, Fenella is the Goddess of water and ice, isn't she? Perhaps this is the door to her test."

Giselle didn't take even a moment before she reached out and touched the water, her hand appearing to disappear into the wall it was running down, an illusion of some sort.

Looking back at Alison and I, she smiled and then she pushed her arm through the water and then the rest of her body. Disappearing into the wall and again my heart sank as I felt her vanish, her soul no longer apart of this world but elsewhere.

I hadn't realised up until that moment why I felt the anger well up inside me, it was because the other part of me was no longer around, not here standing beside me or near me.

After Giselle had done that spell in the dining room using her light, I felt her with each breath, every movement, and every emotion. We were now joined as one and it surprised me but also excited me, this would make fighting at her side easier and perhaps in the future we could learn to use these new abilities to our own advantage. Perhaps, this is what it felt like to be truly bonded to someone, to find ones true everlasting love.

"I wonder what this test will be." Alison slumped down on the stone floor and fiddled with her blouse hem.

"Hopefully nothing too challenging but nothing our girl can't beat, I'm sure."

"Aren't you worried even a little?"

"Worried about what?"

"She might come back different, if her mind, body and soul is changed after all of this, she might not be the same Giselle we all know and love."

"She will be fine. She always is."

Alison left me with food for thought as I hadn't thought about these tests and what effect they may have on Giselle and deep down I hoped they didn't.

"How long have you known Giselle anyhow? She never talks about her past and I don't blame her, it sounds traumatic."

"It never was, until her mother's death but then again, I wasn't around much once I came of age. We grew up together for the most part, spending summer and winters at the palace. The Queen and my mother, the Countess, were great friends, it was my mother's suggestion that I should wed Giselle. But I didn't know that until the very last minute."

"How come you didn't know?"

"It's customary in the royal family to only meet your betrothed the day of the wedding. It's very weird and I've never understood it but then again Countess Elizabeth was never one for the rules so perhaps she suggested Giselle because I already knew her."

"Maybe, it's strange how both of your lives have so intertwined with each other's. She told me about that night in the meadow and how she didn't recognise you, but you knew straight away who she was."

"Ah ha" I laughed a little recalling that memory and how annoyed I was at Giselle. "I sadly was there to do the duty I had been ordered to do by Xandious. I had to return Giselle to him but after she escaped and I left to travel unknowing what I was going to do, the Goddess Guinevere visited me

357

and told me not in so many words but to change my path and not always trust everyone. I'm glad she did though, as otherwise I wouldn't be standing here at Giselle's side."

"Did you ever suspect she had killed the Queen though?"

"Deep down, I think – no, I knew she would never have hurt her mother. She's to kind and it wasn't really that hard for me to forget Xandious's orders and follow Giselle." I paused thinking back to that moment I realised she wasn't the threat, "Heck, I'd go to the ends of the world for her if she asked me."

Guinevere had changed my mind that day one way or another, I had a feeling, a voice in the back of my head telling me Giselle was innocent, but I had become so hellbent on my orders, I didn't want to fail. I am glad I did change my mind and realised that Giselle was worth protecting and saving. Although I did fail at Elder Grove Village and I almost lost her, I know now I needed to give her everything to keep to my sapphire oath, to keep her safe, to love and to protect her heart.

"She's important to you, isn't she?"

I nodded, smiling a coy smile.

"She is my everything."

47

GISELLE

alling. Ever falling as if I were falling through the world itself and once, I landed, I landed harder than I ever expected. Landing into a large pool of water as cold as ice and the air was sucked from my lungs as I gasped and swam to the surface in a panic.

My armour thankfully did not weigh me down, Elven armour was always surprising me and right now, I was grateful for that it wasn't as heavy as the ones man made.

Taking in my surroundings, I was in what looked to be a cavern of some kind, the entrance I had fallen through so high up it would take wings to get back up there. But I finally found the waterfall I had been hearing since we arrived.

The entire place was beautiful, bushes of beautiful blue flowers sat on the edge of the pool with large evergreen trees behind them, rising high up into the sky. The water was cloudy but had a glittering shine to it, as if the moon light was reflecting off it.

"Okay, now what."

I asked myself, waiting for the next chain of events to

happen as the last one just happened suddenly and without me even realising. This might take a while, or I may already be a part of the test and had to figure it out for myself.

As I started to swim towards the edge of the pool, it seemed as if to move further and further away from me, no matter how much I tried and pushed myself, the edge wasn't in my reach and my body was already starting to ache from the landing I made and from the cold that was filling up inside me.

With each stroke, the edge moved away and no matter which side I aimed for, it was an impossible task to get to. Unexpectedly a splash came from the far-right side of the pool and then another on the left and behind me.

"Here we go."

It really felt as if I had read all this in a book before, the tests, the way things worked, how much I was already expecting to happen was happening but then there was silence. As if whatever had joined me in the pool could hear my thoughts and stopped dead in its tracks, either to change tactics or to surprise me.

Looking around for anything, I managed to place my hand into the water and reach down to my dagger in its holder and drew it, holding it a little outwards towards me but at the ready should I need to strike anything.

"Well, that's not very nice."

A voice startled me and as I swung round to swing at whatever the voice came from; the creature or person had disappeared.

"I know, I thought she wanted to become friends."

Again, I swung back round to where I was to start with and the other voice had gone, this was getting frustrating.

"Don't be silly sister, we can't be friends with humans. She would need to be like us."

"Like you? What are you?" I was now frantically turning around to find where the voices were coming from but came up empty handed.

"We are what the Goddess calls her daughters."

"Creatures from long ago."

"Hidden deep in the waters. Ever waiting for a new sister to join us."

"So, you're mermaids."

"Oh! You're a smart one. Sisters, this one has brains."

"Maybe we should eat them, so we can become clever too."

"I dare you to try but you will be the ones at the end of my blade."

I was still unable to see where the creatures were. Mermaids were only ever told in folk tales, they didn't appear in our world anymore and many believed them to just be a myth, a tale to keep children from playing in open waters and in the oceans. They were known cannibals and would happily eat anything they got their fins on. Sailors feared them and hoped they would never cross one.

"That was rude."

Finally, three pairs of eyes appeared above the surface of the water in front of me, none of the mermaids had any hair on their heads, just protruding fins, sharp fins by the look of it.

"We just wanted to be friends." The one with bright yellow eyes said in an almost childlike voice.

"I have enough friends thank you."

"You entered here, therefore you must want something." The one with red eyes sounded stern, demanding, as if she were the leader or at least the one in charge.

"I actually fell in here and have no idea how to get out."

"We can help you, if you like." The last one with dark purple eyes rose from the surface more.

Naked, all three of them were on their top half and their tales matched their eyes. They were enchanting and it made sense why sailors would go to their deaths if they ever saw one, there was something about them that drew you in closer.

They weren't like sirens who I believed were almost close cousins to them, no sirens were able to walk on land whereas mermaids were bound to the water and yet both were deadly and able to lure humans to their deaths by their enchanting look and songs.

"How then?" I asked still with my dagger drawn.

"You must beat us, before we get you."

"Beat you? A game? Or in a fight?"

"A fight of course, to the death."

The red eyed mermaid flew towards me, exposing her razor-like teeth as the others stayed back and as she came towards me, she managed to startle me, throwing me off and I almost dropped my dagger as I slashed towards her, catching her by the upper arm.

She snarled and roared in protest as she swam behind me and under the gloomy water. The purple eyed one then came next and as she did, I felt something grab my leg and pull me under the water.

"Shit, shit! Shit!!" I thought.

The cold water wrapping itself tightly around my body and as I felt the mermaid let me go, I aimed to get back to the surface, but the purple eyed mermaid came up behind me and bit down hard on my shoulder.

As I screamed out in pain, water began to fill my lungs. I had to think fast, still waiting on the third one to appear. Quickly, I pulled my dagger up behind me and managed to catch the mermaid in the side of her neck, leaving a deep cut and as she released me from her grip, I swam upwards as fast as my legs would take me.

Nothing followed me for those few seconds and as my face breached the surface, I took a deep breath of air in and then felt myself being pulled back down.

The red eyed mermaid swam around me in circles, circling her prey and as she came towards me, I grabbed my sword from her holder, still holding my dagger and weaponised both my hands, ready to strike.

I wasn't about to let another mermaid take a chunk out of me and I most certainly wasn't going to drown in these muddy waters. I had a job to do.

Waiting for as long as my lungs would allow, for her to attack again and only a second or two later did she swim at me at top speed. I missed my attack, my sword narrowing cutting her tail as she hit me full force with it, winding me. I needed air. I could feel my head going dizzy as my vision blurred and my lungs screamed out in pain from the burning sensation.

She came at me again but this time I didn't miss and managed to stab her directly in the stomach, almost barbecuing her to my sword as I held her upwards.

Pulling it out in one quick motion and letting her lifeless body fall to the bottom of the pool, I swam up and as I reached the fresh air I so desperately needed, I felt glee and happiness as it filled my lungs.

Looking around, I noticed the yellow eyed mermaid had disappeared and I was unsure of where she had gone, worried for a moment as the bite on my neck continued to bleed.

"My sisters, so impatient."

Her childlike voice came from the edge of the pool as

she sat on a rock carelessly playing with her tail fins in the water.

"We have always won when someone like yourself arrives, I don't think they expected you to fight back. Such a shame, I guess I will be here alone from now on. With no one to talk to."

"I'm sorry." I responded as I attempted yet again to make it to the edge, this time it wasn't moving in front of me, and I was able to reach it.

"It's alright, they are fools and always have been. Not me though see, I knew you'd win. I saw it in your eyes."

"Can you tell me how to get out of here now?"

"Only if you say please."

Biting back my teeth as the pain in my neck continued and I wondered how I was going to stop the bleeding; we didn't have any supplies with us to stop something like this and I would most likely end up eventually bleeding out if untreated as I could feel the wound was deep.

"Please, can you tell me how I can leave?"

"That's a nasty bite my sister gave you. You may use one of the blue flowers to help the pain but I'm afraid a mermaid's bite is poisonous if untreated."

"Oh great, thank you for telling me."

Swimming over to the edge where the blue flower bushes were, I pulled off a few flower petals and then lifted myself up out of the pool and sat on the edge, placing one or two down onto the cut and instantly feeling relief.

"The exit is that way. You have passed this test Princess Giselle."

The yellow eyed mermaid changed appearance and, in her place, sat Fenella. Her long pale blue hair flowed freely down into the pool as a white dress that looked like sea foam wrapped around her, the tips of her fingers were bright blue, almost as if ice and water were infused in them.

"You are one step closer to gaining the crystal but be warned, someone else is near and they will stop at nothing to get it."

"Xandious, I know he is on his way."

"He's a lot closer than you think. Be careful and look after my nephew."

She didn't seem fazed by me, or it made me relax a little as we had already met but this time she was, like Nefret in her truest form and it was beautiful. Looking towards the doorway she had pointed at, showing me the exit, I took off in a jog, wanting to get out of here and back to Shadow and Alison as quickly as I could.

Stepping through, I fell face first onto the stone floor with a thud, not expecting to feel dizzy or tired. That test took a lot of my strength, and I wasn't looking forward to the next one as much now.

48

SHADOW

S he appeared back to us as if almost out of thin air and with a rather large bang as her body hit the floor. Taking myself and Alison both by surprise, I rushed over to lift Giselle off the floor and not only were her clothes soaking wet and ice cold. She was also covered in blood.

"Goddess, what the fuck happened?"

Throwing off my jacket and quickly wrapping it over Giselle's shoulders, I rubbed her arms up and down to create some form of heat as her teeth chattered together and her body shivered.

"Mermaids."

"Mermaids?" Exclaimed Alison wide eyed.

"Yep, mermaids and they are a bunch of nasty basterds if I do say so myself. One managed to take a chunk out of my shoulder and another tried to drown me, honestly it wasn't that fun."

"But did you complete the test?" I asked and she scowled at me as if it was the wrong time to ask.

"Yes Shadow, I completed whatever the bloody test was. Now I need to rest for a moment before I do the next one."

She took to sitting down on the floor, resting her head against a wall as she pulled my jacket closer to her body. Looking around, I tried to find something that may allow us to start a fire for warmth or maybe there were some old rags left behind by another one of the previous people who had tried these tests but no such luck. It was just the three of us in this open, cold, and damp room.

"Can I look at your wound?"

Alison sat down next to Giselle as she pulled back my jacket and then whatever was left of Giselle's clothing on her shoulder, Giselle winced at the motion and turned away quickly so as not to see the damage.

The creature had managed to completely break through her shoulder armour, and it even gave me a shock, their teeth must have been incredibly strong to do that as dragon steel was almost impenetrable.

"The bleeding appears to have slowed down, not stopped. Slow is good though, but it doesn't look very pretty. Once we can, we will get a healer to check it out."

"I have a suggestion…" An idea popped suddenly into my head, and I wondered if it would work or if Giselle would be interested in doing it.

"I'm all ears." She said through gritted teeth, she was obviously in pain.

"If you can, why don't you use your magic? We aren't sure if it has any healing properties but maybe you should try it? At least the light might help clot the wound?"

"Sure why not, today has been full of surprises as it is so it's worth a try, I guess."

Putting a hand over her wound then, she moaned lightly out of pain and then seemed to take a deep breath and closed her eyes, wishing for her magic to appear.

None of us had even attempted to get some form of

training done for her as Mabon had, of course, disappeared so it was unknown to all just how powerful Giselle could be. Nothing happened at first and the frustration in Giselle's face was enough to say she was already getting annoyed as her brow pinched together.

"Calm your emotions. Magic only comes when you are fully aware of what you intend to do. Wish for your light to heal, feel it fill you up from the base of your feet to the top of your head."

I was only ever able to do simple spells and the odd conjuring, but I knew from lessons that you needed to keep your cool.

Xandious's magic was different and was purely run-on emotion and instinct whereas the magic we were blessed with was a little different. You needed to feel the magic, visualise it coursing through your veins and wish for it to come.

She took another deep breath and relaxed her body and as she did small golden sparks emerged from her fingertips and then it ran through up her arm and then through her entire body. She lit up so brilliantly and beautifully, it was as if the sun was in the room with us. Her golden hair rose above her head and a slight wind flew through the room and just like that, within seconds it stopped, and she opened her eyes.

"Did it work?" Alison asked excitingly and then looked back at the wound. "It did! And your clothes, you're dry! Wow, now that is a useful gift."

"A useful one indeed, now that that's done with, shall we see about getting through the last test and getting the hell out of here?"

She was already up on her feet completely fine and heading towards Guinevere's statue, as if she knew that was

368

where the last test would be and as before looking around, expecting in and seeing what might be different or stood out.

"How are you so sure it's that statue? Perhaps it's Aithne's?"

I asked looking at Aithne's, out of the four sisters she could be presumed the most beautiful and the deadliest. There was just something about the aura around her that spoke power and beauty but with that also came deception and dread.

"I just know. It's this one and the sooner we find out the entrance, the sooner we can get back up top and help the others."

"Alright but any ideas on how we are going to do that?"

"Alison, you know a lot about the Goddess lore, don't you? Anything that stands out for Guinevere?"

Alison as a lady would have studied all tales about Nimra, real or not, she was filled with a lot of knowledge and had already helped Giselle many times down here, it was only fitting she asked her for help.

I was no use as I didn't know much about Guinevere other than what I had been told growing up as after I found out she was my birth mother, I refused to know anything else.

49

QUIVER

My body slammed hard onto the now bloodstained greenery as bodies littered it, my own men and that of my foes. Kara was whipping off blood from her newly opened wound on her lips as she held her sword tightly looking at me with vengefulness in her eyes.

I wasn't going to let her beat me, Mabon had already run away after he saw me gunning for him and now, I had to deal with this 'girl' who believed she was the greatest fighter in all of Nimra. Oh, how wrong she was.

I had lost sight of Ayla after she was taken over by several of my men and once Kara and I began clashing blades, she was all I saw. I intended to take her out first after spotting her throwing more daggers towards my sister as Alary carried her away wounded.

"You stupid Elf, I will have your head!"

She spat harsh words at me, and I tried to hold back my laughter, rolling my eyes at her as she clearly thought very highly of herself but was no match for me. Years of training had made me skilled in the art form of all fighting styles and

I wasn't about to let her get past me if it meant she would head towards my sister or Giselle.

Flipping myself upwards and landing on my feet gracefully, I held my sword in one hand and close to my body, I knew she'd strike again and again and therefore I waited until she began to tire and within a few minutes she was already starting to pant and becoming out of breath, now was my chance.

Striking first, raising my sword up as hers came up to meet mine, I was quick on my feet. And for a couple of seconds or two, she caught every action, I wanted to tire her out some more until finally there was my opening. I knew of her dreadful deeds to all living creatures, and I wasn't going to allow her to live or to recover from any wounds. Thrusting my sword forward quickly, my blade went through her stomach and out the other side, there was no chance of survival. Pulling my sword back out, she hunched over, looking stunned and held her stomach dropping her weapons. I moved my sword upwards then and with another swing came down onto Kara's neck and her head came clean off.

I took no pleasure in killing and would ask forgiveness from the Goddess when all this was over but for now, it was necessary, and I would do anything to keep my people safe. Kara didn't deserve to live.

As her body hit the ground, I looked up to see a large dark cloud coming towards us, covering the plains in darkness. Xandious. He was finally here, and I was happy for his arrival, eager even as it meant I could finally get my blade or bow in him for all the hurt he had caused upon this world.

And yet, the cloud kept coming, not only covering the plains of the battlefield but the city of the forest to. He wasn't stopping and I had this feeling of unease wash over my body he wasn't aiming for us. No, he was aiming for a part of the city where Giselle and the others were. Looking around, Ayla was nowhere to be seen and neither was Mabon.

"Shit."

An idiot I was, I was so caught up in fighting Kara I had allowed Ayla to give me the slip and without Alary aiding me as he had taken Leena, my other set of eyes had disappeared. I needed to get to the temple quickly if I were to warn the others.

Alison.

The thought of her entered my mind and left just as quickly, she was undefended and unprotected, Shadow and Giselle would do their best to keep her safe, but they also would want to keep each other safe and were hellbent on their own revenge, she would be caught in the crossfire, and I couldn't risk losing her.

She meant more to me than I wanted to admit, and I knew I had to be the one to keep her away from harm or die trying.

Running through the battlefield, taking down as many enemy soldiers as I could while defending myself, I crossed the line of my own and many without even an order followed me, running behind me until I reached Alary and Leena who was getting patched up quickly.

"Xandious, he's arrived."

"Where?" Leena stood up quickly looking towards the fighting, her eyes darting between everyone.

"He used magic and got through our lines. He's headed for the temple."

"Then go! We will keep the line holding here."

"Alary keep my sister safe, send word to get our people out to safety, you are in charge now."

Alary nodded as I gave the order and we both went opposite directions, Leena following him with her sword and many more soldiers as I took my small group back into the city and raced to the temple as quickly as my feet would take me.

Reaching it many minutes later, I was greeted with Dark Elves who had taken to guarding the main door which told me exactly what I needed to know, Xandious was already inside.

My soldiers all ran up the stairs before I even said anything and began fighting, leaving me the opening to get inside which I was grateful for, grateful for their sacrifice. Heading through the doors I saw the massacre inside, many of the soldiers who had gone with Anwen and Dana to help were dead, some split into two and the blood desecrated the temple. Xandious was nowhere to be seen and lying at the foot of Guinevere's sacred statue was the body of Dana, my friend.

Rushing over to her, I fell to my knees, dropping my sword and lifted her body up a little onto my lap and she opened her eyes a little, slowly before coughing up blood. Looking down towards her stomach, I could see her holding herself there as blood poured from her many wounds.

"It's not too bad my Prince."

"I'm sorry I couldn't protect you."

"It's alright, I put up a bit of a fight, you'd be proud."

"Where is he?"

"He took Anwen, they went through the door, please," She coughed once again and her eyes closed for a second before opening once more, "Please save her."

"I will, of course I will!"

Using what energy, she had left, she lifted her hand up and a small glimmer of light shot out and revealed a hidden door, the door Xandious and the other's must have used. I didn't want to leave Dana here alone but as I looked down at her, I watched her eyes close one last time and her chest failed to rise. She was gone.

"May the Goddess protect you as you cross over."

Slowly lowering her back down, I picked up my sword and headed through the door. He would only be a few minutes ahead of me, but it was long enough for him to do any sort of damage.

50

GISELLE

I knew the Goddess would want us to truly look for the entrance to her test, but I didn't think she would make it near damn impossible to find out where it was or even how we gained access. It was becoming incredibly frustrating as I started to feel as if I were failing, as if this were all for nothing.

"Do you really think it's here? Honestly, we would have found something by now." Alison's voice sounded just as I felt, annoyed, and almost finished.

"I hope it's here. It must be, she wouldn't leave this last test to Aithne, if this crystal is as powerful as it's meant to be, there's no way it would be left in the hands of the Goddess who hates mankind."

"No, I guess you're right, but Goddess only knows how we're meant to start this thing."

"Shadow," I turned to look at him as he sat down on the floor almost looking bored, "What is the name of Guinevere's wolf?"

"Ehh Titas, why?"

"It might be nothing, but I swear he was in a different position when we arrived."

Sure enough, the wolf was standing on all fours when I first observed the statue and now, he was sitting back, resting on his hind legs with one front paw raised a little off the floor while the other sat in front of him.

"And I swear he's following me around the room."

Every step I took, I could see his eyes move and follow me, perhaps it was just my imagination or the poison from the mermaid's bite sinking in, but something was different. Maybe this was the entrance to the next test, something not as simple as a door.

"Titas, are you here watching? Waiting?"

Nothing. Or did he twitch? I was clearly starting to lose my mind being here. I grumbled a sigh and sat in front of the statue still lost at what to do next. Looking at Alison as she just stared at the statue clearing thinking of what to do when Shadow stood up and he too looked a little wide eyed.

It was then I could feel the warm breath of something down my neck and a small sliver of something wet ran down my face. I didn't want to turn around as fear rooted me to the spot, but I had a feeling perhaps whatever I did had worked.

"Did he wake up then?" I asked looking up at Alison who just nodded in reply, clearly just as scared as I was.

"Hello Titas."

I slowly raised my hands up in surrender and turned around with the speed of a snail, part of me believing he was going to rip my head off if I moved too quickly and the other part of me dying to see what he looked like. Many tales said he was the first to attack anyone who came near Guinevere and if she didn't want you around, she'd send him after you.

He was large, almost giant like, pitch black with striking silver eyes that caught the little light we had in the room so perfectly. He looked at me as if almost to bare into my soul and I kept my eyes locked with his, afraid to move even an inch, waiting for what was going to come next, showing him I was no threat.

He moved an inch closer towards my face and then slowly placed his wet, cold nose upon my own and as he did, I closed my eyes feeling an intense feeling of calm and tranquillity. It was euphoric and electrifying, something I had never felt before and I felt myself wishing to chase this feeling forever.

Opening my eyes, I found I was no longer in the room with the others but in my meadow. The meadow in which I re-met Shadow, the meadow my mother visited me and told me about Ayla being a key of some sorts. Titas was still in front of me but this time he was lying down, appearing to enjoy the softness of the grass and the sun rays as it hit us both.

"He must see something in you dear Princess for you to be allowed here."

She was beyond words; I couldn't even bring any to mind as she appeared. Guinevere. Her silver hair sparkled in the sunlight, it appeared almost as if the sun had created it itself, flowers and small plant life grew where she stood as her skin changed from pink to tan with every glimmer of light. She was our creator and she held that title proudly, her dress was made of the earth, I neither knew where it began or ended. She had a small daisy in her hand as she played with the petals, blowing them into the wind.

"I have been here before." I spoke softly, not wanting to anger her in any way.

"Yes, because I have allowed it. Once to meet my son and once again on the wish and almost demand of your mother. And now," She paused and let the flower go completely, "My sweet Titas has invited you."

"I am grateful for any guidance you may wish to bestow on me."

"What is it you wish to know?"

I thought for a second or two then, wondering what it was I wanted to ask her that day in the temple, for guidance but as I have gone through the previous tests, I didn't feel I needed to ask her anymore as I was coming to my own conclusions and choosing a path myself.

"The Emerald."

"Ah, the Emerald. What about it?"

"What is it? And why is it so important? Why has it been protected for so long and now I have been tasked to get it."

She stepped towards me and then came to sit beside Titas, who in turn placed his head upon her lap and closed his eyes. She rubbed his ears a little and then sighed, as if she were already bored, holding her hand out towards me. Taking it, she pulled me down a little to sit in front of her and the calm feeling Titas had given me intensified.

"When my sisters and I put Aithne in her prison, the Emerald was created when we joined our powers to shut the gateway, giving a piece of us each away. It's a powerful tool and if it fell into the wrong hands, it could be used to create a great weapon."

"So surely it would be best if it were kept hidden away, safe."

"It can only be used when it is with the other objects, however I am afraid you already processed those two objects and therefore the Emerald has now been called and demands to be free."

My eyes widened as I repeated what she said again and

378

again in my mind, other objects? I processed nothing and owned nothing.

"What are these objects?"

"Dear Princess, you carry one with you right now."

She pointed then at my dagger and shockwaves fell through my body, the dagger was part of some sort of spell.

"So, all these items when together will they open Aithne's prison? How many are there in total?"

"Not quite, the Emerald can close the gate should it ever be opened but it would take great power and sacrifice to close it, there are four objects in total. However, there is something else that can open her prison."

Confusion and worry came to mind, this dagger belonged to Shadow, who had it gifted to him by Xandious.

"The stone the blade carries is part of the great weapon. The Sapphire, the same dagger my son bestowed his oath to you. Quite symbolic isn't it when you think about it."

"And what is the other object I had then?"

"You no longer have that object; it was stolen from you. Your ruby."

"The necklace!"

My hand ran to my neck then as I realised, I hadn't had my necklace since we left Governor Mason's manor to start on this entire journey. Foolish of me to leave it behind but I believed I no longer needed it, I wished I had it that day when Ayla was found, it would have flashed its ruby shade and told me she was not to be trusted and I was in danger.

"That stone was topaz though?"

"Topaz yes but hidden inside was the ruby. It's why it would change colour when you were in danger, a part of Fenella's magic is sensing danger."

"And what is the forth item?"

"That is something you can only find on The Unclaimed

379

lands. A rose that isn't quite a rose, it's very well protected and extremely difficult to get."

I needed a second to let this information sink in, these three objects together would create a weapon and be able to close the door to Aithne's prison and according to Anwen, folk tale said we were standing near it by being in the vaults and thinking about it, we were deathly close to the Kingdom of Solum which was a known entrance to the Netherworld.

It felt as if all the pieces were starting to fall together then, as if we had been all put on this path for a reason and the reason was either to keep the gateway closed or to keep the objects hidden safe, away from evil.

"Okay, apart from the ruby and this rose that's not a rose. How do I get the Emerald?"

"You must answer just one question."

"One question? That doesn't seem too difficult."

"It is a question that will determine if your soul is pure or not and if it is not, I'm afraid you will be trapped in this prison like so many of the other's before you."

"No pressure then."

"Would you kill to save a life? A life of someone whom you truly love, or would you kill them to save millions of others? Would you watch the world burn instead of taking that one life?"

I was taken aback by the question; I had expected something else. Well, anything but a question of my love and if I could kill it. Kill Shadow. Could I really kill him if the fate of the world was at stake? The easy answer as a Queen would be yes, because taking one life to save millions would be the correct answer but the girl inside me, the one who was madly and indescribably in love would happily light the match if it meant keeping him safe.

I could already feel the tears in my eyes forming as I

thought about it, I had already lost Shadow once and I hated that feeling having him back was everything I wanted and more. So, would I be able to live without him if it meant saving so many others?

"I – eh, I would," I stopped.

"I understand it is difficult to answer, I too faced this same dilemma many, many years ago. I fell in love with a mortal man, he was my everything or at least that's what I thought. He helped me in many ways, including bringing my son into the world and yet, when a great battle almost ruined my creation, I had to choose between him and my world."

"You chose this world instead of being with him? That's awfully sad."

"A leader must put aside her feelings for the safety and feelings of her people."

"I would," Again I paused as I tried to bring myself to say the next set of words, unsure of what they might even be.

"Shadow, I love him with my whole heart, my entire being and it took me a long time to realise that but," I stopped again, choking back tears, "I am a Queen, a leader and therefore must put my people first. If killing Shadow meant saving everyone, then I would put aside my feelings and choose them."

Guinevere smiled then but her smile soon changed to sadness as a small tear escaped from her eye.

"I see a lot of myself in you Princess and I understand why you would choose your people over love. It's a shame what leaders must do as we should be allowed both but sadly, the world I created doesn't work like that."

She stood then and tapped the side of her thigh as Titas stood in response and she turned to walk away from me. I feared then I had failed her test and would be stuck here forever, leaving behind everyone to Xandious and his evil.

"What about the Emerald? Did I fail?" She didn't answer me, just continued walking away. "Did I fail!" I shouted and she stopped, turning slightly towards me.

"Not today but you may fail if you don't hurry back now. Your friends are in grave danger, and I believe you will be needing this to help save them."

She threw something in the air towards me and as I caught it, a large beautiful oval shaped crystal landed in my hands, the Emerald, and this time the real one.

"It doesn't just close gateways, I'm sure you will find out soon enough what else it does."

Suddenly a puff of smoke came from her right hand and a large staff appeared with a deer skull on top of it and as she tapped the ground hard, a sound rang through the meadow and my eyes closed and then reopened and I was back in the room with Alison and Shadow still holding the Emerald tightly in my hands.

"Hello Giselle…"

51

SHADOW

A s we all turned around at the sudden voice, his voice my blood instantly turned red hot from the rage building up inside me. Anwen's body was held up in front of him, he had a hand holding her up a little off the floor by the back of her neck and she wasn't moving.

Throwing her to the floor as if discarding trash, the thud as her head hit the stone floor confirmed she was most likely already dead.

Giselle stood up and drew her sword within seconds of his arrival and I could feel her body tense from emotions while she pushed Alison behind her, guarding her. Drawing Winterthorn from its scabbard, I held it in front of me, taking a step forward to cover both girls.

"Now, now, none of that. We are all friends here."

"Ha! Friends isn't the word I would use." Giselle spat back. "You are nothing but a murderer."

"Well, there is no need for name calling. I was coming here to make a deal with you."

A deal with death, there was no chance under any circumstances Giselle would make a deal with him and most certainly she wouldn't let him get out of this room alive. His fingers sparked green as he smiled sinisterly at us and Alison put her hand around one of my arms, feeling her shake behind me.

"Who's the beauty standing behind you both? I'm sure this deal would be worth something if it meant her survival."

"Touch her and I will rip your heart out." Giselle raised her sword a little more as gold light started to pour out from her fingertips.

"You should really watch your tone with me, I am still your father," His smile grew larger as he looked down, spotting her magic, "Oh, what's this? Has my daughter been blessed by the Goddesses herself?" His eyes disappeared into black then, no more showing an iris as he looked at Giselle as if she were a meal.

I wanted at that moment to run towards him and bring my blade down, but I knew if I did, it would put us in a position we didn't want but he was now fully blocking our exit and although the room was large, there were no other ways out.

Would the Goddesses arrive to help us? Doubtful. Maybe Seniya? Brushing those thoughts away, I wanted nothing more than to keep Giselle safe, but she clearly had other ideas as she took yet another step away from us both, creating a small distance between us.

"First of all, you lost your right to call me your daughter a long time ago," Another step which made me grow anxious, "And secondly, the Goddesses blessed me with these powers so I may destroy you and protect this world."

Thankfully, she stopped moving closer towards Xandious, but her body was beginning to glow brighter as her emotions started to take over. I wanted to remind her to remain calm, her powers were still unchecked and none of us had any idea of how capable or powerful she was.

"I want to go home." Alison whispered and Xandious erupted into a disturbing laughter.

"I can send you there if you like but it would be home to your soul. Aithne I'm sure would appreciate my gift."

Aithne? My mind started to run wild at all the possibilities as to why she would even be concerned what Xandious did, or anyone he sent her. She was the collector of souls, yes, but she lay dormant in her prison unable to escape and would never be able to walk these plains again. That was her punishment.

"Alison, stand behind me and stay there." I uttered back and placed a hand on top of hers, trying to reassure her.

"You'd swear she was the chosen one, the one you both are trying to keep her safe."

Ayla. Ayla had arrived and I could feel my body fill with the slightest ounce of glee. She would be my target one way or another and as such, she would regret ever stepping foot down here and judging from Giselle's reaction, she was feeling the same way as me. This was perfect.

52

GISELLE

There she was, there he was, both my targets right in front of me and not on a battlefield, they had come to me and although I was slightly wounded and tired from the tests, I processed the Emerald, and it was now safely hidden on my person. If he was here to take it, he would have to pry it out of my cold dead hands and even then, I would come back to fight him some more.

He was not going to get the Emerald no matter what, if it were to help become a great weapon and for that matter, I had to always keep the dagger with me. I couldn't let either of these items fell into his hands and I had no idea if he already had the so called Rose item and I couldn't risk it, just in case. I now held the key to what closed Aithne's prison doors.

"The key."

I whispered as my mind started to put two and two together, protect Ayla, keep her away from your father. My mother's words to me in the meadow, did she already know this was going to happen? Ayla, why was she so important? What was she? Was she the key to all of this?

"Ayla's the key."

"She's what?" Shadow asked me.

Suddenly, I realised then that's why Xandious wanted Ayla so badly, why he tortured her, made her into his puppet. She was the key to open the gate, to open Aithne's prison. I had to keep this realisation to myself, not let Xandious know I had caught on what his plan was and had been for months now. He was going to use Ayla somehow to open Aithne's gate and he wanted the Emerald to stop it from being closed.

I had half expected more of his army, Kara at least to be standing with him as she was his right hand and no doubt would have enjoyed being here, she must have been up top commanding his soldiers.

Although I felt sadness for what he had done to Anwen and part of me wanted to rush over to her and aid her anyway I was capable of but as she laid there unmoving, I feared the worse.

"Yes, please tell us who this beautiful redhead friend is?" Xandious asked then.

"The names Alison and I will cut you where you stand."

Suddenly Alison pulled a dagger from Shadow's holder and stood out from behind him and appeared to take a run at Xandious, but I quickly grabbed her by the arm pulling her back, my eyes widened by her sudden bravery.

"She's feisty, isn't she?"

Ayla draped herself against Xandious and I almost heaved at the sight of it all. She was clearly still under his spell, that or she was always this disgusting person.

He placed a hand upon hers and then lightly kissed her on the forehead but never breaking eye contact with me. I was glad my mother wasn't here to witness this revolting act, it just continued to fuel me with more anger to light the fire within me.

387

I no longer wanted to stand here and banter back and forth, it was becoming boring and uninteresting. Xandious came here for a purpose but seemed to be stalling somehow, even Ayla didn't seem that interested in moving to the next stage. It made me stop for a second and wonder why, why hadn't they moved? Why were they still standing in the doorway almost?

Mabon.

Seniya had mentioned he was now doing the bidding of Xandious, what if he was doing something for him now? And all this talk was just binding them some more time, time for whatever they had planned next.

Turning around, I looked at Shadow and he stared back at me, the same emotions channelling through our odd and new connection. He had pulled Alison back behind him as she tried to calm herself, even though she seemed shocked at her outburst.

"I believe you have something that belongs to me Giselle, several things in fact."

Xandious's darkness was growing larger and had started to creep up the wall behind him, making him appear taller and more menacing. He, however, was no longer terrifying to me and therefore his tricks no longer worked.

"I highly doubt that." I replied, taking my stance again.

"Ayla, dear do you have the item I told you to fetch before arriving here?"

"Yes, it's here."

Watching her as she fished for something down the front of her armour, she began to pull out something on a silver chain and in that moment, I was ready to lose it all and cut her where she stood. My necklace. She must have stolen it from the camp before we left with the small group of soldiers she had murdered, how had I not noticed?

388

"That does not belong to you."

I was ready to swing my sword at them both and would happily have a good fight. Seniya had given me that necklace and I stupidly left it behind believing I was surrounded by people I could trust, clearly, I wasn't as it would have warned me about her.

"That's where you are wrong daughter, everything belongs to me."

Xandious took the necklace then and tucked it away into his pocket before his fingers started to flash green once again and then seconds later, he shot his hand up and aimed for the three of us.

Without thinking and without even intending to, a wall of bright golden light shot up in front of us as I lifted my hand to block his attack. Magic, my magic had protected us and as he shot the same attack, again and again, the wall held.

Shadow and Alison had moved closer to stand behind me then as another green flash of light came towards us, this time it was more powerful than the last and it took me out, throwing me backwards into the wall in which the water flowed from. Luckily, I missed both Alison and Shadow, but it managed to wind me in the process.

Now I was angry, infuriated even and ready for anything, shots were fired, and I welcomed them with open arms. A smile crept across my face and almost synchronised, Shadow sensed me as he swung round on the ball of his foot and took to a sprint towards Xandious and Ayla. Xandious disappeared into a puff of smoke, but Ayla was taken by surprise.

She flung out her sword from its scabbard and narrowing caught Shadow's blade as it almost cut her down, a few seconds later and it would have.

Alison stood there watching the actions unfold and as I

got to my feet, I ran towards her, pulling her back to me and then gently shoving her to stand in the middle of the four statues, hoping they would be of some protection as I waited for Xandious to reappear. and right on cue he did.

"Behind you!" Alison shouted.

Turning on the ball of my feet, my sword clashed with his and a loud ring flew. And again, our blades joined each other, Shadow had taught me more skills than I ever learnt from my tutors at the palace or Ayla in the forest, my sword and I were now one.

He caught me on the top of my shoulder, the one that was still stained with my blood and although I knew he cut me, the pain was not there, I was running on pure rage and adrenaline.

Quickly, without much of a thought, I shot up my hand and light flashed from it, pushing him back a few feet and then I brought my sword down towards him and caught him nicely on one of his thighs.

Ayla and Shadow were fighting behind me while Alison ducked behind Guinevere's statue cowering and as much as I would have liked to get her out of here and to safety, she wasn't my concern as much as killing Xandious was.

"Shadow! Get Alison out of here!" I shouted over the sounds of swords.

"Eh – I'm a little busy at the moment."

He shouted back as I felt the angst from him flow through me, setting my balance a little off. This would have to take some getting used to whatever this new power was.

"Alison."

His voice felt as if a glimmer of hope entered the room, Quiver and he was here for Alison. She needed to be out of here and at least away to safety wherever that might end up being. She had become my sister and I couldn't have her hurt because of me, even if she had put her life on the line already for me.

Looking towards her, I could see the light of happiness flash over her face as he reached her, taking her by the hand and pulling her out from the statues and towards the door where Shadow and Ayla had moved away from amongst their fighting.

"Not quite."

Coughing as smoke surrounded me and the entire room, I couldn't see and the burning sensation of not being able to breathe filled my lungs. I could hear everyone else cough as I hit the floor on my knees, gasping for air, the pain was unbearable and agonising.

Once the smoke started to clear and the burning in my eyes eased, I saw Shadow on his knees while Ayla had somehow got the better of him and Quiver had his bow and arrow pointed towards Xandious who was holding Alison around her throat, her back towards him as she faced us with tears in her eyes.

"Let her go!" I shouted as I got up and then stumbled back down onto one knee catching my breath. "You quarrel with me. She has nothing to do with this."

"I shall be the judge of that, you seem to care a great deal about this girl, its pitiful."

Quiver tightened his bow, and I knew if I allowed him, he would get the perfect shot to either kill or at least wound Xandious, but he held still, looking at me and then back at Alison waiting for my orders.

"Give me the crystals and I will let her go."

Shadow had Ayla's sword pointed at his throat and his sword pointed at his heart. She smiled at me wickedly enjoying this. It was as if I was watching Guinevere's question play itself out in front of me and yet this time, I knew I would pick differently.

"Well Giselle."

A coy smile appeared across my cheeks as I made my decision. Standing up straight, I took a deep breath and calmed any nerves I had remaining and then seconds later, sent a large bright beam of light towards Ayla catching her and throwing her through the air and hitting a wall as Quiver let go of his bow and the arrow caught Xandious in his shoulder but not before he drew his blade and stabbed Alison in her stomach and again disappeared into smoke.

Quiver ran to Alison as I ran towards Shadow, helping him off the floor. We only had a second or two before Ayla came and Xandious reappeared.

"Quiver, get her out of here, please."

I pleaded as he scooped up Alison in his arms and ran out the door, but not before turning back towards us and giving us a little hopeful smile and then he vanished through the veil. It was just us four now and the fate of our world rested in the balance.

"I'm alright my love, I'm ok. Let's just beat these sons of bitches."

Shadow said as he lifted up Winterthorn and then became back-to-back with me, both of us holding our swords up at the ready, waiting for Xandious to attack.

"You're a coward if you keep hiding in your smoke and mirrors."

I was trying to fish him out as I was growing inpatient, this fight was becoming redundant with the vanishing acts. I never pictured him as one who kept hiding in the shadows, I expected more from him.

"I'm very disappointed, I had hoped for this epic battle."

That did the trick as the room began to shake, sending

rocks falling and landing around us, luckily. Watching Ayla as she slowly arose from her unexpected sleep, she took hold of her sword which lay beside her as she lifted herself up looking at me with deadly eyes, her pupils now gone to a black, just like Xandious. His magic and hers clearly combined.

Screaming at the top of her lungs caught us by surprise as we both covered our ears and then she started at speed running towards us, her sword up high and as she brought it down, I narrowly missed it leaping out of the way. She turned again and aimed at me and as Shadow grabbed her from behind, he was attacked with the same green light Xandious processed which sent him back. I was now her target, and this made me incredibly happy.

Finally, my sword met her, and we kept at the same speed, inharmonious clashing of steel hit each other as Xandious's control took over her even more. I hated seeing her unable to do anything for herself, but this was no longer my friend, this wasn't the person I had come to know and cared for, that Ayla had long gone and this one now took her place.

Xandious caught my eye as I saw him lean up against the statue of Aithne as he watched us fight, fight to the death as Shadow regained consciousness searching for his sword.

Xandious clapped at Ayla and I as we continued to hit each other, as she looked at him, I took a chance and my fist met her face as she turned back towards me and then my boot hit her clean in the stomach and knocked her back a few steps, winding her.

In that moment, it gave Shadow the chance to come up behind her and he took the opportunity I know we had both been looking for. Hearing another scream and then silence, he had stabbed her in the back with his dagger. It was gratifying after what she did to me, symbolically stabbing me in the back and betraying my trust.

Xandious stood there staring at me and then looked at Ayla as she reached out towards him, stumbling towards him and falling into his arms. I thought I saw some form of emotion flash in his eyes as he caught her, but it was gone in a blink of an eye.

"Please, my King, help."

I should have taken that moment he was distracted to arm myself and attack but what he did next even I was surprised. Watching as he lifted Ayla up to stand, he placed a hand on her cheek and she leant into it and then with a flick of his hand, he drew a dagger across her throat and sliced it clean open.

As she began to bleed out, he stepped out of the way for her to fall. She clung to Aithne's statue as she started to slide down it, a pool of blood around her feet and as she face-planted the feet of Aithne, Xandious cleaned his blade off on the back of his jacket and popped the dagger back in its hilt, as if nothing happened.

"No." The word escaped my mouth before I could stop it.

As we stood there both stunned, the room began to shake tremendously and I fell into Shadow as he rocked backwards into one of the walls, breaking our fall as the walls above us seemed to crumble.

"What the fuck is happening?" He shouted over the noise as we looked around.

"Ayla! She – She was the key." I shouted back, "Look!"

We both looked at Aithne's statue which was now shaking on the spot and a black light came up from underneath it, splitting the statue in two, almost ripping it apart and the room continued to shake until finally it stopped.

Xandious didn't seem fazed by what was happening if anything he seemed pleased.

He wanted this, he planned this. Ayla's blood was the key to opening the gate, that's why she was down here, why she fought me, he knew Shadow, or I would eventually kill her.

I held my sword tightly, the cuts across my knuckles stinging as I stared towards Xandious from across the room, he was guarding the statue as if it were some prized possession. I had now made it my mission to stop my father, whatever the cost.

Looking at Shadow then, realising that this might be it, the moment we had been talking about, the moment I had been so frightened of facing. I felt grateful we had reached this point together. We had managed to get this far and now we were finally facing this final step, despite already losing so many of our loved ones.

Xandious's green glow surrounded him as his power oozed out beneath his feet and through his fingertips. I could feel my light welling inside me, begging to explode and take him out but I needed to wait, to keep it boiling and waiting for the right moment. The more I thought about it, the more I realised that if I managed to use the full extent of my powers to take Xandious out, would that also destroy me?

Calming my breathing, I began to run towards Xandious and as I leapt towards him, he drew his sword, and it met mine and a loud ringing ran through the room. A swing on my heel and I turned, catching him on the shoulder, slicing there and he didn't flinch. His eyes were total pits of black, there was no emotion left in him and his face read only that of death.

My sword and his collied every time, as if he anticipated my moves even before I did. He smiled a disturbing smile as he brought his sword up and managed to slice an almost identical cut on my shoulder to the one I had gifted him.

"You are powerless to stop me my dear sweet daughter." He said as I whined back, clutching my arm for a second as blood poured from it. "This has been foretold for centuries and I will bring it to being."

"You're forgetting one thing father," I slashed Lightbringer into the air and he lunged out of the way as my blade came crashing down. "I have been foretold to stop you and I will do everything I can to do so."

He caught me at the back of my leg as he spun round on his feet, and I winced almost falling to my knees, catching myself and pushing through the pain we fought back and forth.

An arrow flew out from nowhere and hit Xandious in his wounded shoulder and he fell to his knees in pain, and I looked to see Quiver had returned and was loading up his bow again, firing at quick succession, aiming for any part of Xandious he could.

"You have lost, when will you see that!"

He shouted between each arrow. Shadow had been stood there watching as we fought, and I finally caught his eye. He took a step forward raising his sword, but I shook my head, reminding him that this was my fight, he was to leave me to fight alone, even if it bothered him.

He turned his attention to helping Quiver then as I watched another arrow fly towards Xandious almost hitting him in the chest, but he managed to catch it before it broke through his skin.

"No daughter, it is you who has lost."

Suddenly I felt a sharp pain run through my veins as he brought his hand up into the air and green sparks came flying towards me as they hit me in my chest, knocking me down.

Moments later, I was lifted then from my feet as he stood up, I began clutching at the invisible hand that was wrapped around my neck, dropping my sword as I gasped for air.

The sound of running footsteps came towards me and a clash of something hitting a barrier, looking with the corner of my eye, I could see as Quiver and Shadow began slashing at the imperceptible force, a force that was keeping them from me.

Xandious began pulling the arrows from his body as if they were nothing, they were nothing to him. Closing my eyes as tears began to steam, I could feel my breathing begin to slow, but I had to try not to pass out, I had to win this battle, the world depended on it.

Xandious took a few more steps closing the gap between us and was now inches away from my face, his grin never changing and with some quick thinking on my part, I pulled the sapphire oath dagger out from its hilt and slashed at Xandious face. He backed away quickly, dropping his hand and holding the side of his face as blood poured from his newly opened wound.

"You bitch!" He shouted as I fell to my knees coughing and trying to fill my lungs back up with air, the dizziness and wooziness clouding my mind and filling my stomach up with bile.

"You – Will – Not," I coughed as I got back up, lifting my sword up in front of me, "Not, Win!"

I shouted as I rushed towards him, my sword slicing across his chest catching him off guard and exposing his skin and as I did darkness flew out from his body, crashing into mine and flinging me backwards again.

I felt the stone wall behind me crash into my back and winding me as I slid down to the ground, I had not expected that. He was at me again suddenly and faster than I predicted, lifting me up off the ground and then I felt it, the sting, the sudden burning sensation, and the taste of metallic in my mouth.

"GISELLE!"

His shout came from afar, my ears ringing and the world feeling as if it were to fade away right in front of me. I looked down towards Xandious' other hand and he had pierced his sword right through my armour and into my stomach.

The movement was so fast I didn't even notice he had pulled his blade up towards me. I looked back up at him as the tears began to form in my eyes and I could see the blackness of his eyes start to fade, only for a second and if you weren't looking, you couldn't have noticed it.

He dropped me then and took a sudden step backwards, his face bloody and unrecognisable. I tried to stand but the pain was too much, I needed to release my light, it was now or never.

Bringing my hand up, I held it out towards Xandious, the sparks only lightly coming forth and he laughed in response to my clear attempt.

I looked towards Shadow as he continually bashing against the barrier, his eyes meeting mine and I could see, feel his desperation to get to me fill the gap between us.

"No, it couldn't end like this, I wouldn't allow it to."

Closing my eyes, I felt for Shadow, for his body and there in the darkness a small slither of light appeared, pulling towards it I felt my body grow little by little in strength, dulling the pain from my wounds as blood still continuously fell.

Lifting my hand up again, I felt my body begin to warm up as that golden magic reached its peak and out shot a light. A most beautiful, clear, calming light and it zoomed into

Xandious, into his oozing black wound and lifted him off his feet.

He clutched at whatever he could, almost as if he were trying to pull the light from deep within him and as I managed to get up, I lifted my other hand and light shot from that one. I thought deep down, if I shot him with enough light, I would be able to defeat him without killing him, bring back the man who had brought me up before evil took hold of his mind and soul.

As more and more light shot out from me, I could feel my essence, my heart began to slow and I knew if I continued, especially with these wounds and the poison from the mermaid's bite, I would surely die. But I couldn't stop, I needed to see this through.

I could feel Shadow tense as the barrier came down and he joined me at my side, dropping to his knees and wrapping his arms around my waist.

"Stop my love, please." He begged, "I've got you."

He pleaded but I couldn't stop now, I was too close.

"Let me help you!"

His arms tense around my body as if to try and break my concentration but the magic had now taken full control of me.

Shooting another larger beam this time, not only from my hands but my entire body, it pushed Shadow away and soared outwards and towards Xandious and expelled the darkness from him and he fell to the floor with a loud thud, as did I.

"No, no, no!"

I felt the energy fade from me as the world faded into nothingness, my wounds bleeding profusely and it was as if I could feel my last breath escape from my chest and then there was nothing.

53

SHADOW

I felt it, her life force draining and disappearing from my own, she was leaving me, and I had no control over it. Rushing towards her body, the room fell silent, I held her body up onto my lap as I cupped her cheek, lowering down to listen to her breathing and there was nothing, not even a gasp.

A cry erupted from my mouth as I began to pull her closer towards me, lifting her arms up and tears stinging my eyes.

"Giselle, please – please – no" I hugged her tightly towards me, "Stay with me, stay – with – me." I pledged again, "Please, Goddess please!" I shouted as if Guinevere would listen. "You promised me."

"My lord Shadow, we need to leave, right now." Quiver's voice rang through the room as he took a step backwards towards me, his bow still aimed towards Xandious, who may have appeared to be passed out, neither of us trusted that.

"No, no! I won't leave her."

"Shadow, please."

"No! I promised never to leave."

As the world began to quake underneath us, I looked towards Xandious body which started to move and stir and something inside me felt as if it had broken, snapped into two pieces and I lifted Giselle's sword up as I lowered her body down, I was going to kill him.

"YOU!"

I shouted as I ran towards him ready to cut him down and then suddenly something burst through the broken statue and the blast of wind was enough to knock everyone off their feet.

Falling, I scrambled to get my bearings and as I looked up, I saw it, something large and black lifted itself up from the cracks and a loud roar bellowed out from the blackness. It's had large wings but that was all I could make out in the shadow as the shaking started again.

Looking towards Quiver who managed to get up on his feet and was rushing towards Giselle's body, he lifted it up and took off towards the door, begging for me to come with but I needed to see, I needed to watch what was growing out from the pit.

It was there I saw her. Her body erupted and wrapped with shadows and fire, she appeared to be naked while her hair fell around her body. Her creature, her dragon appeared to stand behind her, shadowing her with his body as both of their eyes glowed red, like the same blaze she arose from.

She looked towards Xandious and with a flick of her finger, lifted him up onto his feet and brought him towards her, kissing him then lightly on the lips and it was as if his body evaporated into nothing, dust flew where his body was and then he was gone.

I knew then who this was, and I looked at Quiver as he seemed to come to the same conclusion. I needed to get out of here before she spotted me and so I ran for it and to my surprise she let us go without even flicking a glance at us.

As Quiver, and I ran out the door and up the never-ending staircase, we reached the top and ran out of the secret temple door. Only to be greeted by Xandious's soldiers and more Dark Elves.

Quiver's men had been unsuccessful it would seem due to the many Earth Elves bodies littering the temple floor. More shaking started as a loud roar came from beneath the temple and erupting through the middle of the hall, the marble steps flying upwards and landing on some of the soldiers.

The dragons' claws appeared from the hole and as it slowly lifted itself up, its large wings filled the space above it and the horror and screams of soldiers could be heard throughout the temple.

Quiver and I needed to get past the dragon before it fully emerged and as the soldiers watched in amazement and fear we made our escape. Darting around them as well as the debris that continued to fall, we reached the door to leave just in time.

The dragon was now out completely and already making meals out of the men, many of which ran past us to escape themselves.

Aithne then arose, floating and smiling a little at the carnage around her. Quiver ran still holding Giselle's body tightly to his chest, as she turned to look at us, her eyes finding mine and her smile grew larger.

"Hello nephew."

Aithne had returned and we were now powerless to stop her...

NIMRA'S WORLD

TO BE
CONTINUED

BOOK THREE
AUTUMN 2023

Acknowledgments

Wow. This book was incredibly hard to write for so many reasons. One main was the fact halfway through writing book two, I gave birth to my second daughter. It's been a crazy journey thus far and I am forever grateful for this ride.

You, the readers are astounding, the support and love I've received since the release of book one The Sapphire Oath has been astronomical. Thank you so much for believing in me and my characters.

Jack, my husband, my person. You're everything to me. I'd not be doing any of this if it wasn't for your love and support. Thank you.

My girls, Alice & Charlotte. I do this for you. To my bestie Tanya from across the pond, I would have nothing if it wasn't for all your help, love, and support. You've been here since the beginning, and I am forever grateful for everything you've done for me.

My writer girls chat, thank you! Thank you for the brainstorming sessions, for the rants, the random chats and keeping me sane and on this road to writing. You're all incredible and I am so grateful I get to watch your writer journeys.

My mum of course, for always believing in me and supporting everything I put my mind to. I love you.

And finally, to everyone who is here, who read book two and will continue joining me in the world of Nimra.

Remember, you are the light, and you can beat the darkness.

About the Author

Melanie Davies began writing when she was in her early teens, starting off first in vampire role play forums, she began to learn her voice and teach herself how to write creatively.

The world of Nimra started off as a simple adventure story of a girl and a guy. Going back to the original storyline, many aspects have changed but the message is still the same.

During the lockdown of 2020, Melanie picked her book back up after many rewrites, and in November 2021 she joined the National Novel Writing Month with the encouragement of her friends and family and within just a few short weeks, The Nimra World series was reborn into what you see today.

Writing has always been a dream of hers and one she is excited to achieve.

Printed in Great Britain
by Amazon